LOVE & KNIVES

In a city built on smoke and sin, love might be the deadliest risk of all.

WHITNEY WALQUIST

This book was a labour of love bordering on madness.
For anyone who's ever had a dream.
I'm rooting for you.

Cover Design: Books and Moods

ISBN (ebook): 978-1-7642670-9-0

ISBN (print): 978-1-7642670-6-9

First edition 2025

PLAYLIST FROM THE AUTHOR

1. "Wicked Game" — Claire Haeving
2. "No Good" — KALEO
3. "After Dark" — Mr. Kitty
4. "Let Me Touch Your Fire" — ARIZONA
5. "Supernatural" — Barns Courtney
6. "Drugs You Should Try It" — Travis Scott
7. "Atmosphere" — Joy Division
8. "Medicine Man" — Dorothy
9. "Arsonist's Lullaby" — Hozier
10. "Silhouette" — Aquilo
11. "Ghost Town" — Benson Boone
12. "Black Holes (Solid Ground)" — The Blue Stones
13. "Dopamine" — Barns Courtney
14. "Worship" — Amber Run
15. "I Can't Go On Without You" — KALEO
16. "Your Eyes Tell Stories" — Bo Staloch
17. "Without Fear" — Dermot Kennedy

Author's Note

Dear reader, this is a 1920s British/Irish gangster (flat cap era) inspired historical dark romance. If that's enough to explain the mature content in this book, keep reading darling and welcome to the Knives.

Trigger Warnings:
This book contains profanity—a lot. Explicit sexual content, the descriptive mention of suicide, grief, WWI flashbacks, drug abuse, alcohol abuse, violence and blood. This book is not intended for anyone under the age of 18.

Chapter 1

ELISABETH
Year 1922—A Date

A MAN, CLOAKED IN shadow, stood staring at a head-stone in the Warstone Lane cemetery in Birmingham, England. He was handsome, or at least from what I could see from this distance while sitting by my mother's grave with a journal in my lap.

Wait, was he smiling at me?

Men typically didn't pay me any attention during my visits. A woman grieving for her dead mother wasn't an attractive quality. But there was no one else around, so he had to be. But why?

The curve of his smile, mostly hidden under his black flat cap, intrigued me. There was a darkness about him, enveloping him as he stood with his hands tucked into his wool coat. Familiar yet terrible and dangerously alluring. An eerie feeling crept under my skin, sending shivers down my arms as a strong gust of wind blew through the stones. I scribbled a few words in my journal, looking up again, but he was gone.

Like, perhaps he was never there at all.

My heart pounded in my chest, searching for him, but he was nowhere to be found. Being at the cemetery alone didn't feel safe anymore. My journal closed with a thud as I rose from the ground, deciding to head home. The iron gates creaked open, and a fancy silver car turned the corner, glinting in the morning light.

We moved to the city of Birmingham fourteen months ago, leaving our grand estate in the Cotswolds to pursue better health-care for my mother, Victoria. She had been fighting an illness even before the economic distress of the Great War. My father did every-thing he could to prolong her life, taking on massive debts. If there had been a way to save her, he would have found it.

But even after everything, it still wasn't enough.

In the sweltering summer of July 1921, my mother decided to put a bullet in her head, shattering our entire world. Only leaving a note beside her that read:

I could no longer be a burden to you all.

Forgive me,
Victoria Montgomery

But how does one forgive something like that?

The memory of my mother covered in blood with a silver pistol in her fragile hand will haunt me forever. I was the first to walk into the room and find her, eyes open and unblinking. The echo of the gunfire ricocheting off the walls of our new home in Birmingham was a spine-chilling sound that no amount of time could ever erase. Nor could it erase the fear of a weapon that could do such unforgivable things.

We lived in a small two-story residence wedged between many others on a mediocre street. Filled with well-loved purple furniture, floral-patterned rugs, various paintings from the previous owners, and Mother's old room, which we never dared enter.

After returning home, I sat on the velvet bench seat at the piano, letting my fingers glide effortlessly along the black and white keys. Since the age of seven, this piano has been my best friend. We have spent almost every afternoon together playing jazz, classical, and other songs of my own creation. For some reason, Father had let me keep it when we moved, and lately, it has been the only thing in my life holding me together.

My sadness and stress dulled to a small roar inside my troubled mind as the music filled my ears, humming down my spine. Everything felt peaceful and distant as our Corgi, Finton Montgomery, lay on the couch. Fast asleep with a black bow tie around his fluffy neck. The world around me faded, but like every good thing, it never lasted for too long.

"Lizzie, have you seen the keys to the car? I need to go to Cobb's." Margaret, my older sister of twenty-eight, staggered into the drawing room wearing sunglasses. She lifted the well-worn couch cushions and tossed them on the floor.

Drunk as usual.

"You're not going to the shop like this," I shook my head. Cobb's was a small shop that sold beer, wine and spirits. A place we frequented quite often, but Margaret was in no condition to drive the car.

"Like what? I'm fine," she threw down another couch cushion, and Finton jumped off, retreating to the next room.

At least she was fully dressed today and out of her nightgown, wearing a shimmering skull cap over her short brown hair and a blue dress. Almost looking like the Margaret I used to know before the war, and before her husband left her with nothing but a broken heart and a drinking problem. Some days she fought back, but today it seemed she was letting the deep sadness in her heart win.

"What do you need from the shop?" I asked, rising from the piano bench seat.

"We're out of giggle juice."

I stifled a laugh. "That is not a good enough reason to take the car."

Our father, Frank Montgomery, left the car for us most days while working at the factory. But he left it for important things, not last-minute liquor runs, or 'giggle juice' as Margaret liked to call it.

She left the room, so I followed. Only to find her in the hall, looking through the pockets of the wool coats before tossing them on the floor. Making an absolute mess. She rummaged through the dresser drawers by the front door and then slammed them shut.

"Why is everyone always bloody hiding things from me?" She yelled, stepping back with her arms tight against her large chest, which she left exposed for men to see.

With a sigh, I picked up the coats off the floor, hanging them back on the rack. "Come on. Let's go for a walk."

"A walk?" She drawled, turning up her nose.

"Yes, a walk." The front door opened, and warm September air pushed into the hall. "Fresh air will be good for both of us." And maybe it would help clear her head.

She huffed and stepped outside into the afternoon sun, adjusting her long navy silk gloves, muttering under her breath.

"Pearl!" I shouted up the wooden stairs. A frail older woman with short blonde hair appeared in seconds, wearing a black high-collared dress with black stockings. "I'm just going out for a bit with Margaret."

"Good luck, mistress," she gestured to Margaret with a cheeky smile. "I'll have a cup of tea ready for you when you return."

"Thank you, Pearl." I smiled back.

Pearl wasn't just a maid to us. She had been a part of our family for over twenty years. When we asked her to move to Birmingham, she had no hesitation, claiming that we were the only family she had ever known. And for that, we have always been thankful.

Pearl nodded and took off down the hall.

While glancing in the gold antique mirror, I fixed the sleeves on my delicate emerald green chiffon dress, before running my fingers through my long auburn hair, releasing a few knots. Well, that was about as good as it was going to get.

Of course, Margaret was already in a flirtatious conversation with the postman. A grumble escaped my lips as I took her arm in mine, pulling her down the street away from her dark temptations.

It was a twenty-minute walk to the nearest shop, and Margaret complained the whole way there. But at least she agreed to walk with me. Getting Margaret out of the house has been a struggle lately. Hell, getting her out of bed was even harder on some days, and even more difficult with the strange men I sometimes found lying naked next to her. Awkward couldn't even begin to describe how those mornings went.

By the time we reached the shop, the hot afternoon sun left us both with sweaty foreheads and reddened skin. Cobb's: Beer, wine & spirits was painted in white on the red brick wall of the old corner building, just as faded and worn as the other businesses surrounding Cobb's.

"Thank Christ," Margaret wheezed, heading towards the selection of red wines as the doorbell chimed in a shrill hum.

"Good afternoon, Elisabeth," Freddie greeted me with an easy smile, straightening his silk blue tie. He was a young man, likely a few years older than me, who worked at the shop most weeks when I collected gin for Father and wine for Margaret.

"Hi Freddie, how are you?" I asked, waiting by the front counter.

"Doing swell, thank you," his smile grew wider.

"Good," I said mindlessly as Margaret grabbed far too many bottles of wine—bottles we couldn't afford, as she staggered up to the counter in a balancing game she was about to lose. I grabbed a bottle before it smashed to the floor.

"You're looking good—" Freddie cleared his throat, turning a shade of crimson as he reached for the wine. "I mean, lovely today."

"What?" I blinked.

Perhaps I'd misheard him. He was always nice to me, but our conversations were usually about the weather or the shop. They were never; *you look lovely today.*

"You look lovely," he repeated.

"Oh. Thank you."

Margaret placed six bottles of wine on the counter.

"And your hair is... it looks shiny," Freddie continued.

"Thank you, that's very kind." I wasn't sure where this was going, but Freddie's cheeks were burning hotter by the second.

Margaret started to laugh, about what I wasn't sure, but her smile looked as devious as a child in a lollipop store.

"Margaret, we can't afford all of these," I whispered, hoping Freddie wouldn't hear.

"What do you mean?" she asked.

My cheeks tinged red with embarrassment. The shops next door could have heard her response. She knew very well what I meant. Margaret was no stranger to our financial circumstances. But before I could answer, Freddie spoke.

"It's all right. I can cover your tab today," he said, placing the bottles in a paper bag.

"What? No, that's—" I started.

"The boy says he can cover it. Let him do it," Margaret waved a hand unbothered by the whole situation.

"It's no trouble at all," he confirmed with his gentle smile.

My fingers anxiously fidgeted with my green chiffon dress. "I can pay you back on Monday when our father gets paid."

He handed the bag to me. "Don't worry about it. It's my pleasure," he brushed his calloused hand against mine.

Margaret was already gone with one of the bags before I could protest the kind gesture. I thanked him, grabbed the second bag and met Margaret out on the sidewalk.

"Margaret, do we really need all of these?" I struggled to hold the bag in my hands.

"That boy was flirting with you," she grinned beneath her sunglasses. "Did you realise that?"

"He was just being nice." As Freddie always was with me.

She snorted at my response, taking off back into the shop with a wicked gleam in her rich brown eyes. Her curvy, thick frame braced the doorway, balancing the bag in her arm as the welcome bell chimed again. "Freddie, do you want to go on a date with my sister?"

"Margaret!" I nearly dropped the bag of wine. What did she think she was doing?

He stood up straighter. "Yes. I would like that very much."

He would? My eyes shifted to him. A rush of heat filled my pale, freckled cheeks. Margaret's smile grew wider as she fluttered her eyelashes, making a look that said *I told you so.*

"You free tonight?" Margaret continued, tapping her long-painted nails on the door.

What had gotten into her head? My sister was out of control this morning.

"Yes. I am," he answered with his easy smile.

Well, I didn't expect him to say yes.

"Great. Pick us up at seven," Margaret smiled, walking away.

Freddie smiled at me through the glass door as it closed. My mouth opened, feeling like cotton was lodged inside, but nothing came out. Heat burned in my cheeks. This was one of the most awkward moments of my life.

I curtsied, rushing after my sister before she could get too far.

"I don't think Freddie has a car, Margaret." Our old lavish life afforded us one, and luckily, our father didn't want to part with it when we moved. But I was pretty sure that Freddie didn't have one.

"Then we'll take ours," she smiled.

"We? But *you* don't even have a date?" Oh Christ, if she even thought...

"I plan on finding one there, Lizzie," she huffed. "Don't you worry, I'm quite capable of getting myself a date," she winked and continued walking down the street as cars rushed past.

Capable. Confident. Fierce. Words that described Margaret perfectly. Words I'd love to feel about myself, but right now, she was all of the things that made my blood boil.

"Margaret, stop," I scolded, holding my ground. "We can't keep doing this. We can't even afford these."

She stopped, staring at the ground in thought.

"We shouldn't even be going out tonight," I added. Father made decent money from working at the factory, but it was just enough to live comfortably in the middle class.

"I know," her brown eyes burned into mine. Sunlight reflected off her shimmering skull cap. "But I'm not going to keep watching life pass you by, Lizzie. You can't keep hiding away at the piano for the rest of your life."

"As opposed to this?" I gestured to the bag in her hands.

Maybe I had been hiding, but at least I wasn't drinking away my sorrows.

She paused. "It's officially been four years. Today. Since Tom left." Her ex-husband, Tom. They were married at nineteen. He wanted kids, and so did Margaret at one time. But years later, we found out that she couldn't conceive. Still, he stayed. However, when we started losing everything after the war, he left. As selfish men do. He remarried, of course, to some younger, richer woman in the Cotswolds. It nearly broke her.

Her dark mood suddenly made perfect sense. My eyes fell to the ground, unable to hold her gaze.

"I just need today, Lizzie. Maybe tomorrow. Can I please have that?" Tears formed in her eyes.

"Of course," I murmured, feeling a tug in my chest.

I would do anything for my sister, and there was no use in fighting her anyway. It was a fight I would never win. She was a much better fighter.

"Thank you," she wiped the tears from her face, recomposing

herself. "Now, come on. We need to get ready." With that, she took off on her heels. Silent for the rest of the walk home.

I guess I was going on a date with Freddie.

Tonight.

My first date, although I was uncertain if I wanted it to be. Freddie was nice, well-mannered, and kind, but did I find him attractive? Was there a spark between us? Perhaps my sister was right. Some time ago, I'd stopped trying, stopped caring about making a life for myself. Even so, the eerie cemetery seemed like a better option given my anxiety about this date. I should have just taken my chances with the shadow man.

Chapter 2

JAMES

Drugs & Scars

A LARGE FIST MADE a connection to my jaw, making me lose my balance. I spat out blood into the dirt, smiling at my opponent, all gowed up. The crowd yelled and spat words of violence and encouragement, depending on who they were betting for. He went to swing again, but this time I ducked and slammed my fist into his ribs, making a cracking noise as he cried out in pain.

Fuck, I loved that. The raw experience of bare-knuckle fighting was exhilarating. Direct and bloody. Skin against skin.

Nothing felt better.

The fairground was full tonight in Liverpool. Many desperate men wanted to make quick cush to fill their empty pockets, and the bare-knuckle fighting ring was a great place for that. Full of action and opportunity. Life on the streets was rough for many after World War I, and those who did return were not the same. Coming home with fewer limbs and troubled minds. Luck was with me in that regard. I returned from the war in one piece, minus a few scars and night terrors that were cured with cigarettes, whiskey, and opium for the ones I couldn't shake—a survival mechanism that has been working for me for years.

Another strike, and he cried out, allowing me a brief advantage as my bloodied fist slammed into his gut and then his large chin. He collapsed into the dirt, and I laughed with blood in my teeth, wiping the sweat from my dark brows.

A short man in a black bowler hat came up and grabbed my fist, lifting it in the air. "Winner!"

The crowd cheered and yelled in delight.

Normal work didn't suit me, but fighting? It was something I had always been good at. I could make a man's monthly earnings from just one good fight. As a kid, I survived the harsh streets in Birmingham by joining a gang called The Black Knives. I'd fought in many rings back then, too, and learned how to work the streets for money until... well, until everything in my life changed for the worse. And I've been running ever since.

Long ago, I'd learned how to crawl out of the darkness, and fighting in the ring brought me peace. Peace that didn't exist anywhere else. Fighting was the only way I knew how to survive, and the only path I had left to follow.

"Hell of a fight, James MacGuire. Remind me to never get on your bad side." Cameron Hayes, my best friend and business partner of sorts, grinned from ear to ear as he approached me holding my personal things.

Cam had thick brown hair, a tidy side part that he occasionally gelled back, and a trim reddish-brown moustache. He was roughly at the age of twenty-six, the same age as me. We'd been friends since we were fourteen, forming a strong bond of hardship and trauma in the dirty streets of Birmingham. A little over a decade together, and he'd never left, even in my darkest moments.

Somehow, we came back from the war as free men. Still unsure how we fit into the world. A world that never liked lawless men like us anyway.

"You don't have to say my full name," I said, while slipping a white linen shirt over my freckled and bruised body, followed by a black vest, before pulling out a silver Celtic ring and placing it on my middle finger. A ring that was given to me by my mother before she died. She had never made it to England.

"Just making sure everyone knows who to bet on next time," Cameron smiled, nodding his head to a few disgruntled men who cursed in his direction.

We combined our money before each fight, betting it all on me, and we always won. Allowing us to make quite a profit because of my skills in the ring. Enough money to travel from city to city doing pretty much as we pleased, a fairly easy life after everything we'd been through.

After wrapping a black leather wristband around, I slipped on a leather shoulder holster that held a Webley Revolver, with my last name engraved on the side of the silver.

"Come, let's go for the lash. We've got a hell of a lot to celebrate tonight," Cam joyously slapped my back.

A brown-haired lass in the corner of the room then caught my attention with a wave of her hand, followed by a wicked smile on her dark, rouged lips. It had been quite some time since I'd last seen her, and she had gotten prettier somehow, or perhaps I had gotten hit a lot harder than I thought. I smiled back at her, interested in seeing where this went as I pulled on a black flat cap, pulling it down to sit just above my dark brows.

Cam glanced in her direction, noticing my lack of focus and scratched at his short stubble. "In fact, why don't you go enjoy yourself? You've earned yourself some... entertainment," he smiled. "I've got my eye on something, too," he grinned at a woman across the room. "I'll see you in the morning."

Clara ran her tongue along her teeth and approached me as Cam left. Her black dress shimmered with each step in the dark and noisy room.

"I thought that was you in the ring. No one moves like you do," she smirked with her thin lips, trailing her eyes up and down.

"A compliment... here I thought you'd be mad at me."

Considering I left last time without saying goodbye, I expected her to be angrier with me. Not smiling at me with bad intentions.

She smacked my chest, which I hardly felt. "Of course, I am." Then she stepped closer, enveloping me in her perfume. Not my favourite scent, but for now it was working for me. "You have a lot of forgiveness to earn, James."

"Is that so?"

"I've missed that voice," she curved her mouth to the side, pushing a lock of black hair out of my face. "Do you have a room?"

"Across the street at the Inn."

Clara smiled and took my hand.

Muddy trenches surrounded me as I held a gun in my hand. Except it wasn't a military rifle, and my outfit wasn't a standardised uniform. A long wool coat wrapped around me, paired with a suit, a black tie, and a matching flat cap. Like I was back working for The Black Knives.

Thick smoke drifted through the narrow and muddy walls as I stood there in the deafening silence, alone. No gun's firing. No ear-shattering explosions.

No screams.

No pain.

Until I turned around, finding three young men covered in blood, with bullet holes through their foreheads.

"Why'd you murder us, James?" The one in the middle cried.

My hand was suddenly covered in blood, dripping into the dirt. Shaking with regret. "I never wanted to hurt—"

"James," a woman's voice sounded behind me. A haunting voice that I would recognise anywhere.

I shivered.

When I turned around, Madeline Grey was staring back at me, covered in blood. The sight of her and her golden blonde hair nearly made me fall to my knees. "Mads," my voice cracked as I reached for the woman I'd been in love with since I was seventeen. Only to lose her too soon.

"Why didn't you save us?" she cried, cradling her enlarged stomach.

Tears fell from my eyes. "Mads," I cried again.

I wanted to hold her. To stop what I knew was coming, but I couldn't reach her.

I never could.

And then a gunshot sounded, ricocheting into my soul as I shook myself awake, gasping for breath.

"Good morning, James," Clara smiled, leaning over me, wearing nothing but her tanned young skin while she stroked my chest. "I think you were having a nightmare."

A few Irish curses slipped through my lips as I adjusted to the hazy morning light and the sight of her next to me. Why was she still here? After my exertions both in the ring and with her, my memory was fuzzy.

"Did I ask you to stay?" I rubbed my eyes, putting a hand through my hair. My head pounded with a dizzying hangover. Empty bottles of whiskey cluttered the floor.

Fuck, I hoped I didn't ask her to stay with me. Sure, I had sex with plenty of women, but slept with? There was only one woman I had ever done that with.

And now two.

Goddamnit.

"No," she frowned. "But I thought you might like some company. Did you know that you talk in your sleep? You said some interesting things last night..." Her hand trailed down my torso, begging for something I was no longer in the mood for.

I removed her arm from my waist, rose from the bed and began putting on my black trousers. Desperately needing another drink to wash away the nightmares. The pub across the street was my intended destination.

"You're angry with me." She pulled the sheet around her naked body.

"Yes." I was never looking for more than sex, and I thought she knew that. "You should leave." I grabbed my white linen shirt and slipped it on. "This is done."

"You can be such a prick." She rose out of bed, wearing only the thin sheet.

"You know I'm a prick. Yet, here you are," I grinned, tucking in my shirt before pulling up my suspenders. "Did you really expect something different?" If she expected I'd wake up with intimate feelings for her, she was wrong. I wasn't a fan of intimacy, nor was I ever looking for it. That version of myself died a long time ago.

"God help the woman who does finally catch your eye," she muttered. "Or will you push her away too with your cruel heart?"

Many women caught my eye. No one was that special for what she was suggesting.

Soft laughter rose from my throat. "Things will never change for me, Clara. Deep down, you know that." This heart of mine, if it still worked, was black.

Permanently.

She stepped closer as I finished buttoning my shirt, leaving the top few buttons undone. "If you keep doing this, James, you'll end up all alone."

Ending up alone instead of the countless other horrifying deaths waiting for me didn't bother me, but Clara could do better. She needed to hear the truth, no matter how harsh it was.

I grabbed my flat cap off the dresser, placing it on my head. "So will you, Clara, if you keep fucking guys like me."

Her eyes dropped to the floor, gazing back at me with anger. "You're right. This is done. We're done." She grabbed her clothes, making a vulgar gesture as she slammed the door behind her, still only wearing a white sheet.

With a deep exhale, I pulled on my black boots and slung my

leather holster over my shoulders. Spinning the barrel of my gun, enjoying the vibrating sound it made, reminding myself to clean it later before sheathing it at my side. After throwing on a vest and a wool coat with a red satin lining, I left the room, leaving the unwanted mess behind.

The cold air felt refreshing on my face as I exited the Inn, making my way to a pub across the street. A few people were scattered around the dark room, talking in hushed tones while they smoked. This old pub was a bit rough around the edges, but charming, with stained glass windows and wood-panelled walls. Thankfully, it was quiet as I sat at the worn-out bar and ordered a whiskey, losing myself in thought.

"How'd you make out last night?" Cam leaned against the bar. The top three buttons of his blue shirt were still undone.

My eyes caught sight of a giant hickey on his neck. "Not as good as you, it seems." I smiled, gesturing to his neck.

He laughed and ordered himself a whiskey, pulling out a banknote worth ten pounds. "Your cut," he slid it towards me.

"Thanks," I shoved it in my pocket.

"How's Clara?" He grinned after a few moments.

"She's just fine." Pissed off at me, but fine. I rolled my shoulders, releasing the tension in my neck from the morning I'd had.

"That bad?" He laughed, taking a sip from his glass. Clearly, finding this amusing.

The whiskey washed away the bad taste in my mouth. "Where to next?" It was his turn to pick a city, and I was more than ready to leave Liverpool.

"It's a surprise," he smiled, stroking his thin moustache. The rest of his face was freshly shaven, smooth, and clean-cut.

"I don't like surprises." I knew that smile. It was a surprise I wasn't going to like. A nice surprise would've been Cam shaving that damn moustache. Did he realise how fucking ridiculous it looked? Or was it just me?

Cam put on a dark grey flat cap, adjusting the brim to sit just below his brows. "We've got a long drive ahead of us. Let's get going," he slapped my back. "I'm driving."

My mouth opened in protest, but he was already out the door, heading towards our black Rolls-Royce Phantom. I tossed back what was left in my glass and cursed under my breath, leaving a few shillings on the bar.

The sun descended behind the smokestacks as Cameron parked the car on a wealthy street in fucking Birmingham. Chaos brewed in my mind, stirring up bad memories.

"Welcome home," he smiled.

Home? Birmingham hadn't been my home in a long time. "What the fuck are we doing here?" Blood rushed to my heart, screaming in my ears.

He sighed. "I got us a job. It pays well—"

"Drive the car." There wasn't a job good enough that was worth coming back to this place.

"You don't even know what the job is?"

"Drive the fucking car, Cam!" I clenched my shaking fists, biting out my words.

He let out a long breath, but before he could speak, I pulled off my flat cap and jumped out of the car. Unintelligible Irish expletives escaped my mouth as I lit up a cigarette, inhaling it deep into my lungs. He'd already decided we were staying here, for whatever fucking reason I didn't care. I was planning on leaving tomorrow.

With or without him.

Birmingham was my home for most of my life, but I can't say that I'd ever been to this particular street full of ladies' shops and trimmed gardens, with finely dressed people milling about. Probably the nicest part in the whole of the city that wasn't infested with rats or filled with the sounds of metal clanging.

Fuck this place.

An older man with a grey beard hobbled by, smiling at the car. "Good morning," he smiled, tilting his head. "That's a lovely vehicle."

"She sure is," I blew out a thick cloud of smoke.

When his eyes caught mine, they drifted to the tattoo of a black knife covered in thorns on my right forearm. His eyes went wide. Then he scurried away, as smart men usually did. I guess it still meant something to the people here.

I rolled down my sleeves.

Cam got out of the car slowly and shut the door, walking towards me with caution. Good move on his part. I was itching for a fight, and I didn't want to hurt the only person I had left.

He tucked his hands into his wool coat. "Some investors saw your fight in Liverpool and offered us a place in the pit."

The pit.

I hadn't heard that name in many years. It was the biggest fighting arena around, and I was practically raised in it.

"There are a lot of people who are looking forward to seeing you fight again," he continued. "And they are willing to pay quite handsomely for it."

"I'm sure they are," I ground out every syllable with annoyance.

Cam pulled out money from his pocket. "They gave us an advance of thirty pounds and offered us three times as much if you win. Which we both know, you will."

I stared at the money in his hand, blowing out smoke. "We could make money elsewhere—"

"Not like this," he interrupted.

I shook my head. "I'm not fighting in the pit, Cam." No amount of money in the world would convince me otherwise. I couldn't even believe he thought that I would just go back. What the hell was he thinking?

He let out a breath. "I can't keep," he sighed, taking a moment to find his words. "I can't keep running, James. Over the last four years, I've done it your way. I'm tired of sleeping in pubs and living day by day—"

"You haven't been complaining," I flicked ash from my cigarette.

"Well, I am now." He paused. "Aren't you tired of just... surviving?"

"That's what we do, Cam. That's what we've always done."

Surviving together was the foundation of our friendship and the literal nightmares that we both shared.

"Yeah, well, this is our city. Our home," he gestured around us. "With the contract for the fights, we could do very well here. We could do better than just survive." He stepped closer to me. "Do this. For me. Please, just give it a chance," he pleaded.

Seeing Cameron beg was a new sight. He never begged for anything, which meant that he truly wanted this.

Smoke wafted around my face as I considered his words. "For how long?"

He perked up. "Give me three months."

Three months? There's no fucking way I'm staying in this godforsaken city for three fucking months. He was out of his mind.

"Fine. Two," he caved, noticing my distress. "When your birthday rolls around in November, if you still want to leave, we can go wherever you want. Deal?"

I blew out a thick cloud of angry smoke, glaring at him. A part of me owed it to him. To at least try, considering all he'd done for me, but I fucking hated it. "Do I have a fucking choice?"

He smiled widely with a twinkle in his eyes. "Not this time. Now," he straightened his red tie. "I'm going to see if I can find any more investors for your fight tomorrow night."

I laughed under my breath, taking another drag.

"What's funny about that?" he asked.

"I've been wondering why you parked on this ritzy street. Thought maybe you were thinking of buying a dress." I inhaled another drag, feeling the burn deep in my soul, right where I needed it.

He frowned. "Fuck you, too," he shoved my shoulder. "Fight's tomorrow. You'd better be ready." With that, Cam walked off, approaching some well-dressed gentlemen across the street.

He shook their hands, presenting himself like a reputable businessman. They seemed interested, but rage had already buried itself deep into my veins.

I tossed my cigarette on the ground, walking around the busy streets until coming upon an empty alleyway. Withdrawing a small vial of cocaine and snorting it off my finger for a quick hit. Instantly feeling better. More alive and more awake. But as the Birmingham stacks loomed and billowed in the distance, I couldn't help but relive old memories and think of *her*.

The city where she died because of me...

The city that destroyed me.

I was going to need to find stronger drugs.

Chapter 3

ELISABETH

The Gilded Glow

ORANGE LIGHT BOUNCED AROUND my room as the sun descended from the smoke-filled sky. An old brick fireplace was on one side, a bookshelf and a bed on the other, with floral-patterned pillows sitting atop a white quilt. My writing desk was stacked full of romance novels, many of which were my favourites, and there was a small vanity with a few jewels glinting in the evening light, and an antique dresser in the corner.

It was a small and quaint little room, but cosy. Probably the best room in the house, with the best view of the city. Many nights, I would sit on the green velvet window seat and stare at the bright city lights, glimpsing stars through the smoke.

Like I used to back in the Cotswolds.

Would I ever stop missing home? The picturesque rolling hills of the countryside and the fresh air? The city was a different kind of beauty, all architecture and streetlights, but nothing could compare to home. Margaret was missing home too, even though she never spoke about it. Her wine addiction and difficulty getting out of bed in the mornings told me more than her words could.

My long hair cascaded down my back as I craned my neck to

view my delicate pink chiffon dress in the mirror. Finton was on the wooden floor, watching me with judging eyes.

"What do you think, Fin?" I asked him as if he could understand me. His large ears tilted up as if he were trying to.

Freddie and I had a date tonight, but I didn't know his last name or where we were going. Was my outfit appropriate? What do women wear for dates like this? Questions I should know the answer to. But at twenty-two, this was my first date. Pathetic considering how many dates my sister has been on.

Margaret entered the room, bringing with her the smell of hibiscus, wearing a tight black dress and sparkling jewels. I wasn't sure if this date was for me or her at this point, but it was nice to see her excited about something other than the drink.

"Wow," I said as my eyes trailed along her dress.

She smiled and took a turn. "I know. I clean up well. You could use a little more lipstick, especially if you want to be kissed tonight," she pursed her full, bright red lips.

"Margaret, it's only our first date."

Did kissing happen on the first date? Christ. I should know more about these things. But worrying about being kissed was never a priority. Taking care of Margaret, Father, and Finton was a full-time job. Dating just never seemed... necessary. But I couldn't deny that I was somewhat excited to finally go on a date and see what the fuss was all about.

She pulled out lipstick from her purse and began applying it. "Yes, it's your first date, and you've never been kissed. It's about bloody time, don't you think?"

I hated that she knew so much about my personal life. "Does kissing really happen on a first date?" I asked her.

She gave me a sly smile. "On a good one, yes." Once she finished applying the lipstick, she stepped back to view my appearance. "I've never realised how tragic you were, Lizzie. I feel like I failed you somewhere." Her eyes drifted down, catching on my dress. "Is this a church dress?" She grabbed the fabric, scrunching her nose.

"This is a very nice dress," I defended, pulling it away from her. "And I could say the same about you." Mother would be appalled if she knew how far Margaret had fallen in proper society.

She grinned. "There's that fire," she grabbed my chin and pinched it with two fingers. "Keep it and use it. You'll get kissed."

I swatted her hand away, but before I could respond, a knock at the door nearly stopped my heart.

He was here.

I followed Margaret down the stairs, finding Freddie standing by the front door next to Pearl, wearing a tan suit and his usual blue tie with his blonde hair slicked to the side. He looked handsome, more so than I had ever noticed before. Tall and lanky, but handsome.

"You look..." he started when I approached him.

"Lovely?" I filled in his words.

"Yes," he smiled as pink filled his cheeks. A trait of his that I was beginning to find endearing.

"Thank you," Margaret said, accentuating her figure.

Typical. I scoffed.

"Now, let's go. I'm already bored." Margaret pulled us out the door.

Margaret decided to drive us to a bar she'd heard of called The Gilded Glow. It was full of finely dressed people, crystal chandeliers, dimmed feathered lights, and thick velvet curtains. Everything about this place was romantic and whimsical—and very expensive.

I didn't know how any of us were going to afford this ritzy place, but it was too late now, as I was already sitting in a velvet booth across from Freddie while Margaret sat at the bar inlaid with gold filigree.

"I'm so sorry about Margaret," I said. There wasn't an apology big enough to excuse her behaviour.

"It's all right. I have a sibling myself, so I know what it's like," he smiled.

"You do?" He'd never mentioned it before.

"I have a younger brother. He just turned fifteen, and he thinks he knows everything." I laughed, taking a sip of my drink. I couldn't think of a clever response. "I like your laugh," his smile grew bigger.

My cheeks flushed pink, taking another sip. "Thank you." He was always full of compliments, wasn't he?

"I'm very thankful for your sister because otherwise, I never would have had the nerve to ask you myself," he continued, staring at the table as he spoke.

"Just don't tell her that, or it will go to her already inflated head." Thankful for Margaret? No, she could never hear those words. I'd never hear the end of it.

He laughed. "I promise I won't."

Silence passed between us as the dull voices of chatter, laughter, and jazz music filled the luxuriant space. Couples danced joyously under the golden chandeliers, and at the bar, Margaret was laughing wildly, surrounded by men as her black dress shimmered in the dim yellow lights.

"I'm happy she's enjoying herself," I murmured. "It's been too long since I've seen her smile." When was the last time she had laughed? Like, *truly* laughed? Tears began to burn in my eyes.

"Would you—would you like to dance?" Freddie stammered.

I turned back towards him and smiled. "Sure." I took his hand, which was clammy. Or sweaty? I wasn't quite sure. Either way, I could tell he was nervous. Maybe even more nervous than I was.

Freddie led me onto the dancefloor, swaying us slowly from side to side. It took him a while to figure out where to put his hands, but we figured it out, eventually. He held me about an arm's width apart, which didn't seem right, but who was I to know? His eyes were a pretty shade of blue, like the afternoon sky. Something I'd never noticed before. Little wrinkles appeared at the corners of his wide mouth when he smiled, and the red hue in his cheeks never disappeared.

As we danced, I thought that maybe I could see myself with him—that maybe he and I could find some kind of happiness in my dark and lonely life, but as he walked me to my front door after our date and kissed me... I felt nothing.

And I should have. Right?

I mean, I should have felt *something*.

But his lips felt cold, and his hands were too clammy. Yes, decidedly clammy. It wasn't at all like the first kiss I had been imagining since the age of thirteen. There was no rush of heat or weak-in-the-knees feeling. It just felt... awkward. Like kissing a relative.

Just. Gross.

After forcing Margaret to drink a glass of water, I rolled her into her bed, removing her black velvet heels. Finton plopped down on her feet, choosing his bed for the night.

"I had so much fun tonight," she buzzed, half asleep in her blue satin sheets.

"I'm glad."

"Lizzie?" She said as I stood at the door, trying to leave. "Did he kiss you?"

I nodded, not wanting to talk about it.

"Did you like it?" she asked.

"Yes," I lied. I didn't want my information about my awkward kiss to ruin her buzz or make her feel anything but the happiness that was currently radiating from her round but defined face.

"Did he use his tongue?"

Thank Christ he didn't. "Goodnight, Margaret," I said in a way that meant this conversation was over.

She was still smiling when I left her to go check on Father, but he wasn't in his room.

Odd? He was normally home by now.

I roamed the dark halls looking for Pearl to see if she'd seen him come home, when voices downstairs snapped my attention.

The loud sounds of banging and yelling led me to Father's office, where he was having one of his drunken fits. Pearl was trying to reason with him unsuccessfully. Chairs were tipped over, papers were strewn about, and paintings had fallen into disarray on the floor. A complete mess. Father was hunched in the corner, crying, with his arms wrapped tightly around his knees. Still wearing his brown fedora, matching brown wool vest, and his plaid green coat.

He must have come home drunk. Again.

"It's all my fault! She's not supposed to be gone! She's not supposed to be gone," he cried, repeating the words over and over again like it would bring my mother back.

Pearl rushed towards me. "I'm so sorry, Lizzie. I tried to reason with him, but he's very drunk." Dark circles clung to the bags under her eyes.

I placed a gentle hand on her arm. "It's all right, Pearl. You can go to bed. I can handle him." Thankfully, it wasn't one of his bad fits. The 'missing Victoria fit' was easy enough to handle.

Most of the time.

But he didn't seem too far gone yet.

I knelt on the wooden floor, placing my hand in his. "Father?"

He snapped his gaze to mine, and his brown eyes seemed to sparkle for a moment through his tears as he blinked. "Victoria?"

My throat closed up. "No. It's me, Father. It's Lizzie."

He stared at me for a long moment before he smiled under his white whiskers. "You look just like your mother," he sniffed.

"I know." And it nearly broke my heart every time that he said it. "Come on. Let's get you into bed."

I pulled him off the floor and helped him upstairs to his bed.

While he took off his fedora and coat, I adjusted Mother's

picture on his nightstand. One of the only photos we had of her, besides the one sitting above the fireplace in the drawing room— an older photo of her when she was healthy and happy, wearing her favourite green dress. Pictures of Father in uniform from his time in the Boer Wars sat next to it, as well as a few military photos that he kept in his room.

He was particularly fond of his military rifle that hung above the fireplace—a trophy from his younger days of service. But since Mother died, it had disappeared. Which was good because I couldn't stand the sight of a gun in this house after the horror I witnessed.

Something my father knew very well.

He hopped into bed, and I pulled the blankets over him.

"I'm so sorry. I—I want to be better. I want to be there. For you and Margaret." Tears began to stream down his weathered face.

"You are there for us," I ran a hand through his grey hair. "Get some rest."

"Pearl told me you had a date tonight. How did it go?"

"It was fine," I smiled with a shrug.

He let out a small laugh. "Just fine?"

"He was nice. Now, get some rest or you'll be too tired for work in the morning."

The floor creaked as I reached for the door handle.

"I miss her," he sobbed. "I miss her so much."

It took all my strength not to fall to my knees. "I know." I swallowed, holding back my emotions. "Goodnight, Father."

When I returned to my room, I fell to the floor and cried and cried for hours in the darkness alone. Only the light of the moon for comfort. I missed her, too.

Chapter 4

JAMES

Old Friends

MY HEART WAS RACING, beating to the point of pain, as a thin layer of sweat covered my bruised body. I was never nervous about a fight, but the minute my name was said in that pit, everyone would know I was back in town.

Cameron had lost his goddamn mind.

The dim light illuminated the dust floating in the air as I stared into an old, cracked mirror above a small sink, feeling the weight of time pressing around me. Green eyes stared back at me as I observed the small scar on my left eyebrow and a faint one on the side of my chin. The most significant scar on my body was on my left shoulder, which I received from my service in the war. My gaze drifted to the tattoo that sat on my right forearm while the sink dripped a steady stream of grey water, reminding me of the stakes of my presence here at the pit.

Drip.

Drip.

Drip.

I pulled cocaine out of my pants pocket before I went insane, pouring a small amount on the top of my hand between my thumb and pointer finger. Inhaling it quickly, shoving the rest away before Cam entered the room. Not wanting to explain to him that I had it. That I hadn't stopped, and I never wanted to. Without the rush flowing through my veins, fighting didn't feel the same.

He said, "It's time," at the same time I countered with, "This is fucking stupid Cam."

He gestured toward the door. "Have you seen how many people are here tonight? The warehouse is packed full—"

"That's what I'm afraid of." I stepped away from the sink, crossing my arms over my bare chest. "Do you recognise anyone out there?"

He smiled, which did not comfort me. "By my count, it's been eight years. Our bad luck is over."

"We're so fucked," I muttered, heading towards the ring, feeling the rush of the snow in my veins. It was the only thing pushing me forward as my heart beat wildly in my chest.

"That's the spirit," he grinned, following me out into the crowd.

The room was packed as Cam said it would be. Men of all ages, shapes and sizes filled every corner of the old two-story warehouse. Women were scattered about wearing shimmering dresses, shouting for blood just as much as the men. The upper classes were on the second level, while the lower and middle classes were packed into the main floor like sardines in a can. The warehouse used to be an old factory, but it shut down a long time ago, becoming a prime location for entertainment.

They announced my name, and I jumped in the ring.

"Give 'em hell!" Cam shouted as I came face to face with a man who was over-six-and-a-half foot-tall. About three inches taller than me, with a stocky build and veiny arms, grinning at me with a degenerate smile.

An announcer who went by the name of Roy Roberts, wearing a classic pinstripe suit and black leather gloves, shouted into a microphone. He had a musical voice that you'd never forget.

I couldn't believe that he was still here after all these years, still donning that same ridiculous moustache.

"You're not going to believe this, ladies and gents, but I think I've seen a ghost. Is that James MacGuire back from the dead?"

The sound of my full name made me wince.

Hushed tones and whispers filled the room.

"Do you still know how to use these fists?" He jested as I approached him, cracking my knuckles.

"You're about to fucking find out," I muttered.

He grinned so wide, like his jaw disconnected from his face. "Place your bets and let the match begin!"

The bell chimed, and the room roared.

My opponent cracked his neck, smiling at me with missing teeth, circling me like a vulture. I was getting sick of his taunts, so I called him to me with a shit-eating grin on my face. He swung right, and I dodged left, striking his ribs hard with my fist. The man cried out and stepped back, throwing a few punches as I blocked some but not all. His weight was much heavier than mine, causing me to slide back to the ropes. Pinning me into the corner. Not the best place to be, but I planned to use it against him.

When he finally slowed, I threw a few fast punches, confusing him. Then hit him again in that exact spot in the ribs.

Crack.

He cried out and fell to his knees.

I struck him again in the jaw, sending him to the floor as blood stained the ground. The warehouse erupted with applause as the three-minute bell chimed, ending the fight. Money flowed around the room like living water as I took in my next opponent. Cam cheered me on from the sidelines, loud and encouraging.

Four fights and four wins later, I stepped outside in the night air to smoke. With my vest still undone, I rolled up my sleeves as a man walked out of the shadows, taking me by surprise.

"Just like the good old days, hey James?"

That voice.

It seems the ghosts and devils weren't done with me yet.

"Aidan Murphy." I turned, blowing out smoke, to see a man whom I used to know. I hadn't seen him in years since we parted on account of bad blood. He was probably in his thirties now.

Aidan smiled and approached me with a cigarette in the corner of his mouth. "You've looked better," he said, stepping back. Pointing out the bruises on my face and my swollen and bleeding bottom lip. The few hits I allowed my opponents to take tonight just to feel the rush.

Aidan looked the same. Slicked back brown hair, a fine suit, a wool coat and a black flat cap. And the same scar that I left on his right cheekbone. A scar he fucking deserved. Too bad I couldn't see the one I left on his skull. One more hit, and this little thing between us would have ended a long time ago.

I took another drag of my cigarette, holding in my rage. "I should fucking kill you."

"We've been down that road." He whistled, placing his hands in the pockets of his coat as seven men walked out of the shadows, smiling under their flat caps. Four of them I recognised from my younger days in the gang. They stood behind him, revealing their guns in their coats. "I don't think you'd be so inclined to do so now," he finished.

A threat, but I wasn't fucking afraid of Aidan Murphy. "So, you finally got everything you wanted, hey?"

The men were now his. That much was clear.

"There are a lot of people who underestimated me, and now all of those people are dead."

"What happened to McKenzie?" Our old boss and a sort of father figure when we were growing up in the streets.

He had always liked me best.

"I guess you could say he retired. Some years ago," he grinned, but something dark lurked in the corners of his mouth.

I chuckled under my breath. "Right." So, he took his spot at the top by whatever means necessary. Not that I was surprised. It was where Aidan always wanted to be, but McKenzie deserved better.

"So, why have you come to my city?" He tossed his cigarette on the ground, crossing his arms in front of him.

His city? Fuck him.

My revolver was still in the warehouse, a complete mistake on my part, but my knife was still as sharp as the day it was given to me. While checking over my shoulder to make sure this wasn't a trap, I reached into my pocket, wrapping my hand around the grip.

"Relax. I'm not here to kill you," he smiled a devil's smile.

Not today anyway. He forgot to add.

"You should keep that knife right where it is." He pointed at my pocket. "I'd hate to have to shoot you now when we're just getting reacquainted."

I loosened my grip as Cameron appeared out of the darkness. Stopping dead in his tracks as his eyes drifted to Aidan's.

"Cameron," Aidan greeted him.

"Fuck," Cameron muttered. "We're not looking for trouble, Aidan." He raised his hands in surrender, approaching us slowly.

"Good," Aidan replied. "Because that would be a mistake."

I bit my tongue, preventing myself from saying things that would only get us killed as Cameron stood next to me.

Cameron glanced around. "Where's McKenzie?"

"He's gone, Cam." I filled in the blanks with a look. Cameron's eyes went wide, clenching his jaw.

Aidan took another long drag from his cigarette as if he had all the time in the world to intimidate us. "Right. I need to lay down some rules. Seeing as you're new here. I'm happy for you to continue fighting in the pit. As long as you stay away from the racetracks and my operations on the South Side."

I scoffed. "Today. Tomorrow. Why not just do it now?" I couldn't help myself.

"Shut up, James." Cameron hissed.

Aidan stepped closer to me, a fucking dangerous move considering my knife and I were old friends. "Why would I kill you now?" His dark eyes burned into mine. "You don't have anything I want," his mouth curled into a smile.

What would he *want*? He was so fucking close, but if I withdrew my knife, those men watching would fire in two seconds. I couldn't risk anything happening to Cam.

"Besides, I could use a good fighter in the pit. I'm a man of business after all."

Man of business.

"Every fight you win, I want sixty per cent," Aidan continued.

"Sixty per cent?" Cam blurted. "That's fucking robbery!"

Aidan only continued smiling.

"Thirty," I said. I knew the game he was playing, and I would play it better.

"Fifty," Aidan said, looking annoyed.

"Twenty," I countered.

He laughed. "Well, now you've just gone backwards," Aidan smiled.

"Good to see your brain still fucking works after that crack I left in your skull," my lips curved into a smile.

Aidan's eyes burned brighter.

Cameron jumped in between us, pulling my arm back. "Okay. Okay. Fifty. Fifty, alright?"

Aidan shook his head, laughing, and stepped back. "At least he still has some fucking common sense." Then he turned and walked off, followed by his men. "Welcome back to Birmingham," he muttered over his shoulder, disappearing from the darkness he came from, while four of his men stayed behind.

The three I knew glanced over their shoulders with sullen expressions. The last one I recognised approached me—an old friend, Harry Gardiner, wearing his usual grey suit and matching flat cap. His once fully red beard had traces of grey. For a moment,

I glimpsed my old friend, Red Harry, as we used to call him. But that was many, many years ago.

The other men grabbed our arms, bracing them behind our backs.

This was about to get ugly.

"I'm sorry. But if we don't do this, he'll only make it worse," Harry said.

"Just fucking get it over with, Harry," I spat.

Cameron recited the Catholic prayer under his breath.

Harry pulled his flat cap to the brim of his brows. "It's good to see you, Cameron." Then he paused, as some kind of distressed emotion shone through his dark blue eyes as he focused on me. "James."

A wrinkle formed between Harry's dark brows, taking a moment. Just a brief moment before he swung his fist into my jaw, sending me plummeting to the ground. The other men punched us hard in the gut, kicking us as we lay in the dirt.

Welcome back to Birmingham.

An hour later, Cam and I sat in the Rolls-Royce Phantom. Parked on a random street in the city with a bottle of whiskey in each of our hands. The night air felt warm as it drifted in through the open windows while we sat in the darkness, illuminated only by the glow of streetlights.

"Fifty per cent," I muttered under my breath before taking a drink straight from the bottle.

"Better than dead," Cam murmured, rinsing out the taste of his words with whiskey. "I can't believe he cut down McKenzie."

I turned towards him. "Did you like getting roughed up? Or can we fucking go now?"

It could've gone much worse. We only took one hit to the face and then the rest to our bodies. For some reason, Harry had held back. I'd seen him hit men a hell of a lot harder. But I wasn't going to tell Cam this. He'd try to say something insightful.

"Of course, I fucking didn't." He gave me an annoyed glance, his eyes glazing over. Then, he downed another shot of whiskey and hopped out of the car. "Come on," he sighed, tapping the hood.

With the bottle still in my hand, I stepped out of the car and followed him through a small iron gate and then to a door. He pulled out keys from his pocket and opened the door wide, gesturing for me to go inside.

Where the hell did he get the keys to this place?

I entered a dark wooden hall, taking in the vintage green furniture and a roaring fireplace in the spacious drawing room. Dim yellow lights filled the corners, and an antique chandelier hung from the ceiling above thick, patterned rugs. Perhaps he'd stolen the keys from one of those fancy gentlemen he was with earlier.

"Are we robbing this place?" I asked him, setting my bottle of whiskey on the wooden floor, as I slumped onto a green velvet couch in the centre of the room, gliding my fingers along the smooth fabric.

"It's ours."

"What?" I blinked.

He sat down in a matching chair across from me. "I said. It's ours. I finalised it this morning with our savings."

We'd been saving since after the war ended. For what I was never sure, but still, this was a goddamn surprise. "You bought a fucking house? In Birmingham?" Hundreds of other cities, and he had to pick this one.

"I told you. I'm done running." He rose off the couch, grabbed my bottle off the floor, and ambled over to a drink cart on the opposite side of the room, pouring himself a glass of whiskey. "I want to start a life. A real life by whatever means necessary. A house seemed like a good place to start," he sipped from his crystal glass.

Who was he right now?

"If we stay here... this could be the last fucking city we ever see." Aidan had made that pretty clear. He'd use us to make a profit, but if it ever stopped, we'd be useless to him.

"I'd like to try. We can't run forever, James."

Well, I fucking could. I shook my head and rose off the couch, heading for the door. Whatever had come over him, I was done with it. This fantasy was just too much for me.

"Before you make a decision," he sat on the couch, crossing one leg over the other. "You should head upstairs. Your room is on the left." He caressed the fabric of the couch as if he too was shocked by its softness.

My room?

He sipped from his glass, reaching for a book on the side table. Ignoring me as my thoughts raged. But soon, curiosity won over my need to storm out and slam the book in his face, so I sauntered up the stairs instead.

The room was thick with warmth as I crossed the threshold. A brick fireplace roared with orange flames, and two red velvet chairs sat in front of it with a golden candelabra between them. A large bed was in the middle of the room with black bedding, red satin sheets, and black satin pillows. The walls were charcoal patterned with geometric shapes to match the dark-coloured wooden floors, and a golden horse statue sat on a dark wooden dresser. Gothically plush in all the ways that I could have decorated it myself.

He knew me too well.

"What do you think?" Cam leaned in the door frame, taking me by surprise.

I wanted to make a joke, but this meant something to him. I could see it in his eyes—soft, patient, and hopeful, watching me carefully. And then it hit me like a hard punch to the gut. He didn't just do this for himself.

He did this for us.

Stabbing pains filled my chest with all the emotions coming to the surface.

We'd never had this much in our entire lives.

"If you really don't like it. We'll sell it," he added, with a low and contemplative voice.

Tears began to form, so I shook it off, refusing to let the tears fall. I peeled off my coat and shoulder holster, lying down on the softest bed I'd ever felt. My strained muscles relaxed, and my tired and troubled mind drifted off as I closed my eyes. When was the last time I had truly slept?

"I'm going to sleep." I paused and then turned to him. "And tonight, we're going to celebrate," I smiled.

Cam grinned, closing the door as he left the room.

He was always the selfless one, so perhaps it was my turn. But still, two fucking months? If we survived for that long in Birmingham, it would be a goddamn surprise.

November couldn't come fast enough.

Chapter 5

ELISABETH

In the Smoke

IT WAS MID-MORNING when I finished up the chores with Pearl while Margaret was still asleep in her bed. Pearl always insisted that I didn't have to help, but she needed it. Back in the Cotswolds, she had six others to share the work with, and now there was just her. It was a lot to ask of her, but she never complained.

"The work keeps me young," she would say with a pleasant smile.

After hanging out the clean clothes on the line, I sat at the grand piano, staring at the keys. Normally, songs would just come to me, but this morning I felt uninspired and hopeless as the sunlight streamed in through the windows, casting fractured light around the room. Margaret staggered in a few moments later, wearing a light blue silk nightgown and robe with matching silk slippers. She sat on the purple couch and began pouring herself a cup of tea. And to my surprise, she wasn't mixing it with wine.

"You're not playing," she said as she added two teaspoons of sugar to her tea.

"I don't know what to play," I stared at the keys.

She tapped the seat next to her.

I sighed, ambling over to the couch. Finton plopped his head on my lap, comforting me as I ran my fingers through his soft fur.

"So... when is your next date with Freddie?" Steam from her teacup wafted against her full lips. Smells of Chai and honey filled my nose.

"I don't know if there will be a second date." And I didn't want one.

She snorted. "What do you mean? That boy is crazy about you." She sipped her tea, making loud slurping noises.

"We didn't talk about having another date."

"What did you talk about?" She slurped again.

I stroked Finton's fur, scratching that spot between his big ears that he loved. "Nothing."

"Nothing?" she repeated.

"He's not very conversational. We danced and... nothing." Nothing was exactly the problem.

"Maybe you don't need to *talk* with him," she smirked, pursing her lips. "Talking is overrated anyway, considering how much fun you could be having."

"Margaret." My tone and literal flinch sent Finton jumping to the floor. Margaret continued smiling as I poured myself a cup of Chai tea, shaking my head to erase the thoughts that began to consume me.

"Well, I had such a great time," she fluffed up her short brown hair. "I haven't felt that alive in quite a long time," she stared off into the distance towards the bookshelf, lost in thought.

It had been a long time. Our lives had become so dreadfully boring and empty since we moved to Birmingham. I think a part of me forgot how much excitement still existed out there in the world, for I'd never been to a more captivating place, and yet I felt lost. Freddie was a perfectly acceptable man, kind and genuine. Perhaps something was internally wrong with me. Perhaps grief had truly broken me much more than I realised.

She paused, smiling at me with a big grin. "I'd like to go out again. Tonight." I started to protest, but she continued, placing her hand on my knee as if to stop me from interrupting. "I met some gentlemen last night who told me there was going to be a very good band tonight. Apparently, one of the best in town. Perhaps you could invite Freddie," she winked.

"I don't think that's a good idea." Asking Freddie on a date would only confuse the rather thin friendship as it was.

"Alright, then we can go. Just us. Oh, come on, we never do things together anymore," she whined.

"We're together all the time." Margaret was delusional if she thought that was true. We spent every waking hour together.

"Oh, you know what I mean." She slapped my knee and slumped back onto the couch. "We never do fun things anymore, Lizzie."

No, we didn't. But it was a bad idea.

"You might be content with all of this," she gestured around the room. "But I am not. Boring and dreary is not my style. This cannot be our life, Lizzie. I cannot bear it."

But I wasn't content with our life either.

I sat back with a cup of tea in my hand, letting the steam waft in my face as I considered her proposal. As much as it filled me with conflicting feelings, another night out did sound tempting... and I liked seeing Margaret excited for something other than drinking herself into oblivion. But it was a very expensive place. We could not make a habit of it.

"If we go, this must be the last time."

She barely let me finish my words before she jumped off the couch with glee, spilling tea on the wooden floor that Finton was now licking up.

"Oh, this will be so fun! I can't wait. Except this time," she pointed at me with a playful finger. "I'm picking out your outfit. It's time to show off what God gave you." She ran a hand down her curves, leaving the room before I could respond.

That afternoon, I went for a walk to the city gardens, admiring the flowers. It was the closest place to find peace in this loud and busy city that wasn't the cemetery. An idyllic place I would have loved to show my mother before she left us.

Hours passed as I lay in the soft grass, gazing at the sky with the warm sun reflecting off my pale skin.

We shouldn't be going out again tonight.

I couldn't let Margaret think this was a new habit we could afford. But perhaps it would be nice to have an evening out of the house with her instead of watching her cry and drink in the bathtub. An evening with just us. To watch her laugh and enjoy herself once more before reality slapped us back into our melancholic situation.

We parked down the street from the bar, narrowly securing a spot before someone else pulled in. Droves of finely dressed people headed towards the same place, filling the air with laughter and excitement.

I stepped out of the car wearing a tight red silk dress, a dress that Margaret forced me to wear. The front was cut in a V-neck, and the back fell in a long, plunging line towards my rear. My hair was pinned back to one side as luscious auburn curls cascaded down my bare back.

A car horn beeped as I took Margaret's arm and we crossed the street, following a stream of people into the dark alley towards the hidden door of The Gilded Glow.

"I can't believe you got me to wear this." I adjusted my breasts in the tight dress. Hardly any room for the imagination, and I was nervous as hell about wearing it in public. I'd never shown off so much skin.

"It's about time you did," she smiled.

She'd purchased this scandalous dress as a gift for my last

birthday in April, but I'd never had an excuse big enough to wear it, and even now I wasn't so sure if this was a good idea.

"You need to learn to live a little," she continued. "And this exceptional dress is a good place to start."

"If you say so," I sighed.

A man whistled.

Heat flushed my cheeks, and I laughed when Margaret smiled deviantly. She fluffed up her short brown hair, which made me smile even more as I caught someone staring at us from the shadows. Smoke curled around his face, a face I could barely see in the darkness that he blended into so perfectly—like he was the darkness itself.

A tingle rolled down my spine before we passed the threshold into the opulence of The Gilded Glow, descending the stairs into a haze of golden glamour, sparkling gowns, soft jazz music, and the smells of luxurious perfumes.

I swear his shadow followed us in, but perhaps it was only my wild imagination.

Chapter 6

JAMES

The Red Dress

MY NEW BED WAS the most comfortable bed I'd ever had, and yet the nightmares were worse. It's like my body finally realised it could relax, so my mind decided to haunt me. After cleaning my gun and snorting some snow, I threw on something decent for tonight's fun. Shoving down all my trauma and then heading out the door. Intending to find something to distract myself with. And if that failed, hopefully my old opium dealer was still in town.

Blood. Murder. Pain. Regret.

I couldn't take much more of it.

I'd never been to this particular bar, but Cameron wanted to go somewhere 'fancy.' Well, this place was exactly that. Lush and exotic in a city full of trash.

Tonight was supposed to be fun, but my current date would not stop talking about herself. I couldn't even remember her name at this point. Her mouth moved while the band played vibrant music, and I smoked. Losing myself in my thoughts, watching the smoke dissipate in the haze and glamour of the room. Cam sat across from us in the velvet booth, huddled up close to a pretty young blonde.

At least he was having a good time.

My date's muddy brown eyes suddenly connected with mine, and her small mouth stopped moving, which was hilarious because in no way did this hinder her from being the loudest girl in the room.

Fuck, why was I here?

"What?" I muttered at her stare, annoyed that she couldn't just master the art of sitting in silence.

She laughed, a high-pitched, nervous laugh. "I said, would you like to dance?"

Smoke wafted around my face as a laugh escaped my lips. Enduring any more of this torture wasn't worth the sex, and I was done pretending that I was remotely interested in her. "No." I rose from the table. Cam's gaze drifted to mine. "I'm going to smoke."

Cam nodded, turning back to his date.

"But you're already smoking?" My very boring date said.

I left before she finished her sentence.

The cold night air on my skin was relief in itself as I exited the bar to the alley. Chilling the frustration inside of me. Smoke filled the air as my back rested against the brick wall, staring at the night sky. Perhaps I could just stay out here all night, hiding in the shadows. Would Cam even notice? Considering how distracted he was just before, I doubted it.

A car horn sounded, as I reached for another hit of snow, drawing my attention to the street.

The next few moments seemed to happen in slow motion as a girl in a red dress hopped out of a car. Car lights flashed, which brought attention to the shimmer of her silk dress and the lustre of her red hair as it brushed her pale shoulders. My tongue watered as my gaze drifted down to her breasts and then to her curves as she crossed the street towards me with a small smile on her delicate face. Then a man whistled out, which made her blush with the prettiest heat in her cheeks.

Who was this girl?

Her arm was around a thicker woman next to her as she entered the alley where I stood. When she finally caught my stare, she didn't smile, but I wasn't sure if she could see me.

Yet.

Or perhaps I scared her.

Either one was a good enough reason to head back in and introduce myself.

I shoved the cocaine back in my pocket and tossed my cigarette on the ground. Excitement coursed through my veins as I rolled up my white sleeves to my elbows, falling in behind her after running a hand through my hair to smooth it down. My eyes followed her bare back to the golden bar where she ordered drinks, aching to touch her beautiful, smooth skin.

I was about to approach her when another man came up, causing me to retreat a step and lean on the golden bar.

Curious to see his interaction with her, I ordered a whiskey to pass the time. And if he did anything wrong, I would do it right. He seemed to be getting nowhere, or she just wasn't interested. My mouth curved into a smile as I drank from my glass, waiting for my turn.

"—I've just ordered a drink. But my sister, Margaret, is available to dance," she said.

"Alright then," he said, extending his hand for the sister.

Well, he gave up easily, something I wasn't planning on doing. Easy was never worth it anyway, and a challenge was much more thrilling.

Before her sister could take his hand, another man came up who seemed to know this, Margaret. They smiled and laughed, taking to the dance floor. The first guy left muttering under his breath, leaving her alone. Finally.

Time to make my move.

I shot back the rest of my whiskey, stepping closer. "Dance with me," my voice was low and deep, hiding the nervousness I suddenly felt.

She laughed, finishing her sip of an amber-liquid cocktail. "Like I told the last guy, I've just ordered a drink and—" Then she turned to me and blinked three times as if she was adjusting her focus. Her throat bobbed and she licked her full red lips—*damn*.

"I'm James," I smiled and extended my hand for hers, knocking her out of her daze. "And you are?" Her name was unnecessary, a term of endearment that only made things more complicated, but an appropriate part to earn her trust.

Blush crept into her cheeks. "Elisabeth." She nervously placed her hand in mine. Her skin was like silk, smooth and pristine... nothing like I'd ever encountered before. My lips lingered on her hand, wanting to explore more of her.

"Is that a yes?" I smiled.

A breath rolled through her. "Alright."

Soft and slow music began to play as I led her onto the black and gold Art Deco dance floor. One hand cradled hers as the other found her slim waist. I pulled her in close, feeling her breath hitch. Enraptured by the colours of her hazel eyes and the smell of her perfume, like jasmine and oranges. Or was it her natural scent? I wasn't sure, but it was practically hypnotic. It took all of my self-control not to run my hands down her bare back.

"So, James. What brings you here tonight?" she asked.

"I'm celebrating," I smiled.

"Celebrating what?"

"Well, I've just purchased a house." A house I never wanted.

Her hazel eyes peaked with interest. "Really? So, you live here, then?"

"For now." Her gaze drifted down. "What about you?" I asked, pulling her focus and those eyes back to me.

She smiled. "I'm here because my sister wanted to go out," she glanced over at her, laughing and dancing with someone near us.

"And you didn't?"

"Well, I—I don't know."

She either truly didn't know or she was too shy to admit it.

"Hmm. So, this dress… it didn't have any intentions tonight?" My gaze drifted down to her perfect breasts. This dress definitely had intentions, whether she was aware of it or not.

She followed my gaze. "Intentions?" She laughed nervously. "It's just a dress."

"No, it's not," I curved my mouth to the side. "That's like saying rain doesn't make you wet."

"Well, I'm not wearing this to make you wet," she fired back.

I'm not sure if she realised what she just said, but when she caught my grin, her cheeks flushed the brightest shade of red. My new favourite shade of red at the moment, and I had yet to see what her heat looked like when she orgasmed.

"I mean—I'm not. I'm—" she flustered. Her hand started to sweat. "You said that on purpose, didn't you?" She narrowed her pretty eyes at me.

"Maybe." I twirled her around, pulling her closer so she could feel a glimpse of what I was offering. "Or maybe you just like saying dirty things to men you've just met."

Her cheeks blushed again. "I do not—" she shook her head. "You tricked me."

I laughed. "I was simply stating a metaphor. You're the one who decided to take it there."

"Because you wanted me to take it there." Fire burned in her golden eyes. Flaring and narrowing on me as I pushed her out of her comfort zone.

Fucking beautiful.

I laughed again, but this one felt like real laughter. Oh, the places I could take her response, but I'm pretty sure she'd walk away if I told her where I'd like her to take it. Which, now, was a fantasy that would consume me. All of her small and lovely places I would fill with my—

She slapped my shoulder, which I hardly felt. "James. Get your mind out of those dark places."

"While I may have a house now, my first home will always be

the darkness, sweetheart." The darkness. The street. I knew where I belonged. Metaphorically and physically.

She went to say something else, but then stopped herself by biting her tongue. So, we danced. It took her a while to meet my eyes again, but when they did, her chest moved up and down like she was struggling to breathe.

I'd never had quite this much of an effect on someone. I couldn't get enough of this, of *her*—and addiction was always my greatest weakness.

Chapter 7

ELISABETH

Soup

I SHOULDN'T HAVE AGREED to dance with James, but how could I say no to those vivid green eyes? He was tall, dark and possibly the most handsome man I had ever met. With a captivating smile that would take hold of anyone he set his sights on. I didn't even realise I had a type until now, and it was definitely James.

His voice was like thick warm Irish honey, his hair was blacker than a moonless night, slightly tousled but natural, and his eyes—well, of course, they were my favourite colour. And perhaps the most surreal shade of green that seemed to defy the laws of reality. But here he was, holding me close and smiling at me with his perfect dimples in such a way that I could not stop sweating.

"Are you hot?" I said after some time.

"That depends on your point of view," he smirked.

Christ. I couldn't even entertain him. I needed a drink, and fast.

"Come on," he laughed, pulling my hand. The fact that his large hand practically swallowed mine made me shiver.

By some unknown force, he seemed to have read my mind and

walked us towards the golden bar, never letting go of my hand. Except he walked right past the bar and led me out into the frigid night air, where he finally let go, retreating a small step away from me.

I inhaled a deep breath and exhaled water vapour. When did it get so cold?

"Are you alright?" he asked.

"Yes, I just—" A breeze blew through my satin dress, causing me to hold my arms in tight. "I forgot to eat today. I'm just feeling a bit faint." And overwhelmed... by *him*. I should have eaten, but time went by quickly around Margaret, a bright bubble of unwanted distractions this past afternoon.

He paused as a few people exited the bar, smiling and nodding at them as they passed by. "I know a place. It's just down the street," he offered.

Go... alone?

Noise from The Gilded Glow vibrated in the air.

"I shouldn't."—*even though I wanted to*—"My sister. I can't just leave her. I should—" Great. Now I was shivering.

"It won't take long," his mouth curved into a smile, showing off that perfect dimple. "We'll be right back," he insisted. Then he started walking down the street, looking back at me, nodding to follow him.

So, I did.

Yes, Lizzie. Let's follow the handsome man into the darkness alone. What a fantastic idea. I couldn't even blame my actions on drunkenness. I hadn't even finished a drink yet. This was just stupid. He could be taking me somewhere to murder me, yet here I was. Unable to keep my foolish eyes off him.

He approached a shiny black car, a beautiful car that fit him perfectly, and opened the door. My eyes went wide. I hadn't considered kidnapping until now. My mouth moved in protest, but he wrapped a black wool coat around me before words could come out, enveloping me in warmth.

"Oh," I said as my cheeks flushed pink. I'm assuming the coat was his because it smelled divine, like *him*. A scent I didn't know how to describe yet, only that it heightened some primal part of me. The inside of his coat was so silky and warm. A rush of relief washed over me as the shivering ceased.

"It's just up the street," he offered his arm, and I took it.

Again, I probably should have refused, because as my fingers curled around his solid arm in his thin white shirt, my thoughts wandered to desire. Freddie had nowhere near this amount of muscle on his body. If his arm felt this good, what would the rest of James feel like?

Indecent things I should not be thinking about while walking with him down the dark street.

Alone.

Thank goodness this place was close, like he mentioned. My fantasies about his arms or the fact that he lent me his coat enveloped in his alluring scent only lasted for several minutes.

He opened the door, and I walked into a cosy little restaurant with candles on the wooden tables. Pictures of the city were splattered on the walls, and it was filled with people, mostly middle-class. He managed to find us a table in the back corner, dimly lit by a candle and a barely-there light on the wall. I sat, and he left for the bar, returning a minute later as he sat across from me. Lighting up a cigarette in one fluid movement.

I needed to stop finding him attractive while doing basic things but watching the smoke waft around his smooth face was art. Something people paid to frame. I was jealous of the smoke that flowed from his lips and everything it was allowed to touch. I wondered what it would be like to touch him myself...

He laughed. "What?"

My cheeks burned. I didn't realise he knew I was staring at him, or drooling. Christ, was I drooling? How long was I just staring at him?

"Nothing." I tucked a lock of hair behind my ear, forcing myself to stare at the candle flickering on the table.

"Haven't you seen a man smoke before?" he smiled.

Not as intimately as he smoked a cigarette, but I wasn't going to say that.

My gaze drifted down to his wrist, noticing a black leather wristband adorned with gold dots. Fitting for someone like him. And on his other arm was a tattoo. I tilted my head to the side to get a better view. "Does your tattoo mean anything?" His tattoo covered most of his right forearm. A black knife surrounded by thorns, but I didn't see any roses.

He rolled his forearm over to rest on the table, covering it. "It used to," he said before blowing out a cloud of smoke.

Before I could ask another question he obviously didn't want to answer, a bowl of soup was put before me. "Wow," I exclaimed as an explosion of flavour and warmth radiated to my stomach.

"Good?" He asked, but his eyes never left my mouth.

I nodded, unable to respond as I had already shoved down another spoonful. This soup was the best thing I had ever tasted, and I couldn't even describe such a flavour. It tasted of comfort and relief, warming me deep into my bones.

"I'm surprised this place is still around," he glanced around the cosy room. "I used to come here as a boy. I'm glad you like it."

He must have grown up here, but I hadn't met many Irish people. Not that I'd lived in Birmingham long enough to know. I'd have to start trying to meet more of them, although I doubted any of them would compare to him. I took another bite. "What about your family? Do they live in Birmingham?"

Something flickered in his jaw.

I could tell I hit a nerve. One I didn't mean to.

"I don't have a family," he murmured.

I stopped eating and blinked. "Oh. I didn't mean to—"

"It's alright." He blew out smoke, letting a minute pass by as he stared at me. As if he were deciding whether to answer my question. Then he propped an elbow on the table, tapping a silver ring etched with Celtic knots with his forefinger. "My mother gave me this. Just before she died on the ship from Dublin. My father," he laughed darkly. "Was a mutt bastard. I never knew him."

Something in me ached at the thought that we had both watched our mothers die. "So, are you originally from Dublin?"

"Yes," he smiled. "Is that why you asked? You wanted to know if I was Irish?"

I hummed while taking another bite. It was only the question I'd been dying to ask. Where he came from. How he existed. Common questions you would ask a person you just met.

"And you?" he asked, snapping me out of my daze.

Was he just being polite, or did he truly want to know? I decided to answer honestly. "My mother was very sick. When we ran out of money, we moved to Birmingham from the Cotswolds. Then she... died," I swallowed, feeling my throat constrict. "My father and sister are still around, but they like to pretend they're not. It's not a very exciting story."

His eyes dropped to the table. "I'm sorry."

I paused, taking in the seriousness of his face. "Is this the type of conversation you normally have with women?" I didn't know how the subject had gotten so dark, but it seemed we had much more in common than what was on the surface.

He laughed, soft laughter. "No. I don't normally talk much with women."

"Now that's funny," I snorted.

"Why is it funny?" He genuinely seemed confused.

"Because it's such a lie." An obvious lie. He knew how attractive he was. I'm sure girls lined up in the streets just to talk to him.

He smiled and leaned forward, taking his cigarette out of his mouth. My pulse skittered as I watched his lips when he spoke. "It's not a lie. I don't talk much with women because we're not normally... *talking*."

I stared at him blankly. "Then, what are you normally doing?" He made no sense to me.

His eyes drifted to my mouth, and he smiled. "Wouldn't you like to know. I'm almost tempted to tell you. Would you like me to?"

Tell me about the things he did with women... It all clicked, and I nearly dropped my spoon. "Oh. No, please. That's not necessary." Another rush of heat filled my cheeks as I fumbled for a glass of something that wasn't there. I pretty much walked right into that one. "That's umm—so then, why are you talking to me?" I dared to ask, meeting his sultry stare.

He curved his mouth to the side, sinfully putting his cigarette back in his mouth. "We're talking now, but I don't plan on talking later."

My heart skipped a beat, sending my pulse racing. I was not expecting that response. "That's very presumptuous."

"Is it?" His eyes met mine, holding my stare like he was looking for an invitation. His gaze drifted to my mouth again, and my heart thundered in response.

Was it? My insides roared.

I cleared my throat and swallowed, trying to think of something clever to say, but my mind was too consumed and distracted to form words. So, I stared at my bowl of steaming soup.

He laughed, leaning back in his seat. "You seem nervous. Is it because of me, or are you always this way?"

Because of him, but I wasn't going to tell him that. The light dancing around in his eyes felt like a challenge, waiting for me to admit that he made me nervous. "I'm not nervous," I said as convincingly as I could.

He took a short drag, blowing out smoke. "Liar," he smirked.

We then sat in silence, staring at each other, like a game ignited between us, and neither of us wanted to back down. The view was too good to care about the dark places his mind had drifted to as he continued to smirk at me with every spoonful of soup that entered my mouth.

By the time James finished smoking his cigarette, I finished the soup, and we headed out into the night, walking the dark streets side by side.

"Thank you for that," I said, nervously fidgeting with the sleeves of his coat. I didn't expect him to pay either, but he insisted.

"It's all right," he said, tucking his hands in his pockets. "I liked watching you."

"Watching me eat?"

"You could put anything in your mouth, and I'd probably like it."

"Anything?" I challenged.

He grinned with approval.

"So, if I pick up that rock," I pointed to the ground, "would you like that?"

He stopped, standing a few inches in front of me. "I've got something harder for you," he smirked. "Harder than a rock, some might say," he teased.

By the time I registered what he meant, my face was red-hot. Heart pounding as a nervous snort-giggle escaped my mouth. Embarrassing myself even further. Was he serious?

"James... that is not polite conversation."

"I'm not polite."

But I disagreed with him. Buying me soup and lending me his coat was extremely polite. My mouth moved, but this conversation was drifting into uncomfortable territory, constricting my throat and making my hands sweat.

"I'm kidding," he laughed, noticing my unease. "Sort of," he added with a grin, pulling me along once again.

"So," I blew out a shaky breath, recomposing myself back to more suitable conversations.

"So," he repeated, smirking at me in the darkness.

My thoughts began to race, as well as my pulse. We walked past an alley, and I could not stop imagining him kissing me. Pulling me into the dark alley and wrapping his strong arms around me... what would that feel like? And why did I want him to kiss me so badly? I barely knew him. Did he smoke as intimately as he kissed? I was dying to know what his lips would feel like on mine.

We stopped in front of the entrance of The Gilded Glow, and I could not stop fiddling with my hands. Were we going back in? Was he going to pull me into the alley and fulfil my dark dreams?

"So, what do we do now?" I asked, meeting his green eyes. Half afraid of his answer.

He grabbed my hands, stopping my fidgeting with a brush of his thumb. My body melted with his touch. "What would you like to do? Because I've got plenty of ideas of what you can do with these busy hands." His grin turned into something darker.

My knees started to shake, and for a moment, I thought I might ask him to kiss me because it was all I could think about. His lips. His mouth. What exactly does he have in mind that involves my hands?

Something sinful, most likely.

But then Margaret swung open the door and staggered out. James dropped my hands, to my dismay.

"Lizzie! Christ, I have been so worried. I've been looking for you for over an hour. Where have you been?"

"I'm sorry I—" and then I glanced at James. I shouldn't have because Margaret was now grinning in his direction like a fiend. "We just went for soup," I clarified.

Did that sound as ridiculous in my head as it did out loud? I've already said too many things tonight that I regret.

"Soup. Right," she added with a wink.

"James," he extended his hand for hers.

"I'm Margaret, Lizzie's sister," she pursed her lips.

"Charmed," James said.

"Her very single sister," Margaret winked at him, not letting go of his hand. James smiled with the corner of his mouth, popping that cute dimple. The sight of their hands touching and her words sent blood rushing to my heart too quickly.

"Well then, I think it's time we went home, Margaret." I pushed her with force along towards the car, looking back at James to say goodbye.

"I'll walk you," he said to my surprise.

I walked close by his side, following behind a staggering Margaret as we crossed the street and headed towards our car. His hands were now out of his pockets and dreadfully close to brushing against mine.

I opened the car door to let Margaret in, turning around to see James smiling with his hands back in his pockets.

"I umm—" I glanced down at his coat, which I was still wearing. "Oh. Here." I stripped off its embracing warmth and handed it to him. "Thank you for letting me borrow it."

"Anytime," he hung it over his arm.

A breath of electricity passed between us as I stared into his eyes. I tried to say something, anything, but I could only breathe shallow breaths. A gust of wind blew hair in my eyes. He reached out his hand, pushing back the stray lock of hair behind my ear before bringing his hand to my jaw, caressing it once with the pad of his thumb. Smooth and calculating.

I stopped breathing.

"Maybe I'll see you around," his voice was low, almost scratchy.

And then, when I thought he might kiss me, he pulled back, as something twisted in his eyes. Like a flickering pain, as everything from his posture to his eyes changed. All the heat burning up inside of me suddenly died as another cold gust of wind blew through my red silk dress. He walked away without another word, crossing the street back to the bar as I stood there breathless, watching him fade into the frigid night.

That's it?

Maybe I was wrong. Maybe he didn't want to kiss me. Maybe he just realised that he didn't want me at all.

Maybe I'll see you around.

But I didn't think he wanted to see me again.

After such an amazing night, I did not expect to feel such disappointment. Apparently, this date, if I could even call it that, did not go well.

Chapter 8

ELISABETH

Fever

THE SUN CAST SOFT morning light in my lavatory as I soaked in the bath. Unable to stop thinking about the dance, the soup and his last words. Last night was the best night of my life, and also the biggest disappointment. For the first time, I felt something. Something real. An overwhelming feeling that infested itself deep into my bones. I'm not sure what I did wrong, but it was confusing as hell.

After I finished putting on my white dress for church, I entered Margaret's room to wake her. Except it wasn't just Margaret in her bed. Someone was on top of her, grunting. The door creaked, which caused them to stop. He tumbled naked out of the bed, cursing and grabbing his trousers. I covered my eyes, but only after I got a good look. Curiosity and all that.

"Christ, Margaret," I said her name like it was a curse.

"Learn to knock, Lizzie." Margaret scowled, frustration laced her tone.

"Believe me, if I'd known, I would have." Why did Margaret always get the men she wanted? It wasn't fair.

He kissed her once more, and I stamped my foot in response. So unfair.

"Sorry. Happy Sunday," he jittered, leaving the room in haste.

I removed my hand from my eyes, glaring at her. "How did he even get in?"

Margaret rose out of bed, not bothering to cover her naked figure, heading towards her wardrobe. "It's called a door, Lizzie. And don't even give me those judgy looks. I have needs. It's not my fault you ignore yours."

"Needs," I muttered under my breath, covering my eyes again as I padded to her lavatory, starting a bath. She was definitely going to need one. I was not going to smell their mixed and sweaty scent for the entire church service.

An hour later, I sat in St. Martin's Church, packed full of finely dressed people. Margaret was on my right, wearing sunglasses, barely able to keep her eyes open. Did she sleep at all last night? And Father was on my left, holding a bible in his hand, completely oblivious to the precarious situation I discovered this morning.

Bright colours cast around the decadent church from the stained-glass windows, as I lost myself in my melancholy thoughts during the silence for reflection and prayer. And there were a lot of prayers that I needed to make this morning.

For one, I couldn't stop picturing his face when I closed my eyes. For two, I couldn't stop thinking about him in general. His green eyes, his unkempt black hair, his sensual mouth, his Irish accent, his strong arms, his alluring scent, the tiny freckles on his cheeks when he smiled, the way he looked when he smoked... I bit my lip just thinking about all of the things about him that set me on fire. Fire that had nowhere to go as it pushed itself deeper inside me.

Last night I rolled around for hours feeling too warm, too distracted, and too upset by everything that happened. Like a raging fever was burning inside me, and I couldn't break it. Maybe my needs were finally coming to the surface.

I prayed for relief and strength to forget him altogether.

Because if he felt even a fraction of what I did for him, he would have kissed me.

When we returned home, I played chess with my father. One of our usual games and one of the only times that we spent time together, just the two of us. Margaret was currently taking a nap with Finton in her room. She usually slept all day on Sunday, and I bet that she would sleep for the majority of this one, considering her nightly activities.

A shudder rolled through me at the memory of Margaret with her midnight lover.

"Checkmate," Father smiled under his thick-rimmed glasses. His dense grey beard was slicked down, trim and neat. "Lizzie?"

"Yes?" I turned my head from the window, meeting his concerned blue eyes.

He smiled a warm and knowing father's smile. "What's wrong? You're practically letting me win. That's very unlike you."

"Nothing's wrong." I sighed, moving a pawn.

"Did something happen last night?" he questioned.

No, nothing happened, and that was the problem. I didn't know what I did wrong. James was teasing me the whole night, flirting with his wicked smirk and impolite conversations. But when it came down to it, he just didn't want to take that step. Or maybe he finally realised that he wasn't attracted to me. That the thought of kissing me was too unbearable.

It was one dance.

And one bowl of soup.

It wasn't even a real date.

It shouldn't have meant so much to me.

"It was a great night. Thank you for letting us take the car."

"Of course," he smiled. "I'm glad to see you two spending time together outside of this house. I think it's important for young ladies to go out and meet people." He moved his king to one of my last pawns. "Have you met anyone, Lizzie?"

Heat rushed to my cheeks. "No."

"What about that guy from the shop... oh, what is his name?" He tapped his wrinkled forehead to jog his memory.

"Freddie. And no. It's not like that." Though I think he wanted it to be. At least *he* kissed me. Not that I wanted to brag about it. I leaned back in my seat, staring at the chessboard. "You win," I laid down my king and rose from the floral-patterned chair.

He grabbed my arm before I could walk away. "I'd just like to see you happy."

I placed my hand on his. "I am happy."

"I mean, happy," he said again. "With someone. You're getting older and—"

"Margaret was *with* someone, and did it make her happy?" It drove her to complete despair and a drinking problem, not happiness. And Father... same thing.

"You are not your sister," he laughed, adjusting the bridge of his glasses.

I didn't even know what he meant by that. Of course, I wasn't Margaret. We were very different people. I paused and glanced at the window, feeling over this conversation. "I'm going for a walk." I patted his shoulder.

"Perhaps I could ask some of the men I know from work. I believe at least two of them have sons that are around your age."

I shook my head, as if I could erase his words and opened the front door. "Goodbye, Father."

"See you for supper," he said before I shut the door.

It was a long and brisk walk to the park. Dead leaves fell to the ground, taken by strong gusts of wind, while colourful leaves clung to the branches, curling with the breeze. A storm brewed on the horizon. I should have brought my coat, but Father's ramblings about introducing me to his work friend's sons set me on edge.

Why did he need to say those things?

Of course, I was happy. As happy as anyone could be, really. I was just frustrated about something that I wasn't about to explain to him. I wanted someone to wrap his arms around me and kiss me, but they didn't. Perhaps I even wanted *more*... was not the kind of conversation I wanted to have with my father. We were close, but not that close. And talking to Margaret about it would only make it worse. This was something I would have to figure out how to deal with on my own. Somehow.

I blew out a frustrated breath as I entered the gardens, finding my soft grassy spot. The clouds loomed over me, dark and grey, as if they were about to burst. If I were lucky, it would probably rain soon. Perhaps it could wash away all of these feelings I never asked for.

I closed my eyes, waiting for the rain to quell my heated skin. Thunder rumbled in the distance.

And I waited.

And waited for the rain to wash it all away.

Chapter 9

JAMES
Drenched

LAST NIGHT WAS SUPPOSED to be fun, and my date was supposed to be better. Or were there two dates? One planned and one... accidental. I had hoped for a different outcome of events, but instead, that was the most 'date-like' date I'd had since I was seventeen.

And I did not like it.

But I did like *her*, too much.

Enough that some part of me I thought had died decided to come back to life, before eventually being crushed after I realised that we didn't want the same things. And if I'd just kissed her, she would have gotten the wrong idea about my intentions.

When I finally awoke the next morning after a fitful night's sleep, Cam was saying his goodbyes to his blonde-haired date with their tongues.

"Morning," I said as I walked down the stairs and into the drawing room to pour a glass of whiskey. The last glass, by the looks of it.

Cam pulled away from her lips, still wearing last night's suit. "How was your night?"

I sighed and slumped into the velvet chair. "I've had better."

"Cameron," the blonde started to say. "I forgot something in your room," she grinned up at him and then left the room.

"I think she wants you to follow her." I tossed back the rest of the dark liquid in my glass. Wishing there was more. Wishing someone wanted me to follow them to my room and give me a distraction that I desperately needed.

"I know," he smiled. "She's crazy about me."

"Good," I stared at my empty glass.

Cam leaned against the archway to the room, crossing his arms over his chest. "Where were you last night?"

"Left early. Came back here." Words that surprised me as I said them out loud. I returned home and pleasured myself thinking about a particular red-headed beauty, but it only did so much. Awaking this morning still as hard as a fucking rock. Laughable really, and terribly confusing, considering my nightmares of murdering for The Knives. I haven't felt this level of disgust with myself in some time.

He paused, noticing my discontent. "I can ask her to leave."

"Don't bother," I rose from the chair. "You deserve it." I slapped him on the shoulder, making my way to the front door. Cameron deserved this bit of happiness, and I didn't want to ruin it for him.

"Where are you going?" he asked, following me into the hall.

"To get more whiskey. I don't particularly feel like watching. But thanks for asking," I grinned at him.

He flicked me off and ascended the stairs.

After throwing on my shoulder holster, black wool coat, and flat cap, I left the house, taking the car.

Of course, it was fucking Sunday, and the shop was closed. I rested my head against the seat and closed my eyes, listening to the sound of the breeze flowing around the car. When I opened them again, I caught a glimpse of a woman walking down the street.

Wait, was I hallucinating?

I blinked twice, and sure enough, it was *her*. Stomping down the street. Even from a distance, I could tell she was angry about something. I turned the car off, staring after her. I should just leave this girl alone. She was too good for me. Innocent, pure, uncorrupted... all of the things that I wasn't.

Enter James.

Desire and curiosity took over my better judgment as she turned the corner and entered the gardens, vanishing from view.

I pulled off my holster and coat and went after her.

When I found her, she was lying on the grass. Her eyes were closed, and even the rippling sound of thunder around us didn't wake her. This would be a perfect position under different circumstances. I wondered how long I could stand here staring at her in her very sheer white lace dress... Not that I was complaining, but it was going to pour at any minute, and that dress would not survive it.

Despite my lack of judgment and interest in how she looked in that dress soaked to her curves, I decided to make my presence known. "You do realise that it's about to rain?"

She jolted awake and sat up, meeting my eyes. "James," she exclaimed, breathlessly. A rush of heat filled her cheeks as she took in my presence.

"Hi," I smiled. I couldn't deny how much I loved hearing my name on her lips, nor the way I could start small fires inside of her.

She narrowed her eyes at me. "Hi? That's all you have to say?"

"Isn't that how people greet each other?" I teased. Was I supposed to say something else?

She glanced around. "Have you been following me?"

"No. Did you want me to?" I grinned.

I was quite good at following people. She wouldn't even know I was there if I truly decided to stalk her.

She shook her head as her eyes fell to my mouth. "Just... I'm not doing this today. I can't."

"What about tomorrow?" I smirked, playing with her.

"Stop confusing me," she snapped at me. A surge went straight to my cock at her tone. "I'd like to be alone," she lay back down. "Please, just go away and leave me in peace."

Well, fuck. That wasn't at all what I expected her to say. I kind of hoped she would have been at least a little bit excited to see me. At least in the way my pulse quickened when I saw her from across the street. I wasn't sure what she truly wanted at that moment, but I couldn't just walk away. It wasn't in my nature.

I sighed and sat next to her.

She opened her hazel eyes and turned to me. "You do understand the phrase 'go away,' don't you?" Her eyes flared.

She wasn't just having a bad day. I was the reason she was having a bad day. "You're mad at me," I guessed.

She let out a quick puff of air and rolled her eyes, muttering something under her breath.

"Why?" I asked a bit defensively. What did I possibly do to offend her?

She sat up from the ground. "Why? Really?" Something like hurt flashed in her eyes.

"I think it's a pretty fair question. I've done nothing." I could understand her anger with me if I'd fucked her in the alley like I'd wanted to, and she felt lingering feelings of regret. But I didn't do that. She had no reason to be mad at me. "Is it because I confuse you?" I curved my mouth into a smile, wetting my lips.

She let out a forced laugh and then shook her head, staring at her hands. "Nothing is exactly why I'm angry."

"What?" She was making no sense. I placed my hand in hers to stop her incessant fidgeting. "Lizzie." Her cute nickname slipped out before I realised what I said.

She met my eyes, and her breath hitched at my touch. "Why

didn't you kiss me?" Red crept into her cheeks, blooming down to her chest.

"What?"

She dropped my hand and stood up in a huff.

I followed her pace, adjusting my flat cap.

"I mean, did I do something wrong?" she asked.

Thunder roared in the distance as electricity buzzed in the air between us.

"That's why you're mad at me?" I almost laughed.

So, she was angry that nothing happened... well, that was a first. I can count on one hand the number of women who were unhappy that nothing happened. It was always the opposite. Happy in the moment, pissed off at me in the next.

She let out a rush of air, trying to storm off.

I grabbed her soft hand and pulled her to me, holding her there. "Look. I didn't." I clicked my tongue, trying not to be consumed by her scent and her warm body so close to mine. "Because I realised that we wanted different things."

Her eyes drifted to my mouth. "What *things* do you think I want?"

It was then that I understood her frustration. But she had no idea the amount of frustration I felt for her. Even my hand on my cock last night only did so much.

"Because it's not like you bothered to ask me before you made whatever assumptions you have," she went on.

This whole conversation was putting me on the edge of something I didn't like, and I was losing control.

"Do you want to fuck me?"

"What?" Her cheeks were red in an instant, and her eyes went wide.

I laughed, retreating a step. She heard what I said. It was exactly as I thought. "You see. We want different things, sweetheart."

Thunder rumbled around us, and the wind picked up speed.

"Well, what if—what if I did?" She raised a brow, her red hair blowing all around her.

My gaze snapped back to her. She looked nervous as hell, but she was trying to play my game. For that reason alone, I amusingly smiled as she took a step towards me.

"What if," she swallowed, her voice shaking as she took that last step. Close enough that I could feel the warmth radiating from her body. "What if you just kissed me, and we see where it goes?"

"That's not how this works," my voice dropped an octave. I had my rules. For good reasons. I wasn't about to start breaking them now, even for someone like her.

"Why not?" she frowned.

I sighed. "Because I'm not a good person, sweetheart."

Her eyes dropped to the ground. The flash of sadness across her face made me feel like I needed to say more, and why? It shouldn't matter to me.

"Then why would you lend me your coat? Why walk me down the street for soup? Why not let me get kidnapped in the street?"

I laughed through my nose. Some valid points. But still. "I'm not a monster, sweetheart." *Not anymore, anyway.* I had at least some basic decency, but my end goal remained the same.

She bit her lip. "Are you just—are you not attracted to me?"

My hand found her chin, placing my thumb on her bottom lip without even thinking about it. "I'm very attracted to you." Probably the most attracted I had ever been to someone, and I think that's what scared me the most. And the fact that I was fucking terrible for her.

"Then, why?" She swayed, and I felt myself drawn to her lips—her full mouth, such at odds with her delicate features. I stroked her bottom lip, dragging it down.

Maybe I could just kiss her? Did she taste as good as she smelled? I bet she tasted better.

And then I leaned in close enough to feel her breath on my

skin, and she closed her eyes, parting her lips. My heart raced in anticipation. I was going to kiss her, or I was going to go insane.

Fuck it.

My lips barely touched hers before thunder rumbled above us. The clouds popped, letting down cold, gushing rain. Stopping the kiss. She looked at me, soaking wet, not knowing what to do.

"Come on," I grabbed her hand, and we ran to my car.

She laughed after she closed the car door, meeting my eyes. And for a moment, things felt different... but the sight of her soaking wet did something to me.

"Are you—" I started to say, but then my eyes got stuck on the swell of her breasts and peaked nipples. There wasn't a curve I couldn't see through her soaked sheer white dress.

My mouth dropped open. I'd fuck her right here in this car if she'd let me. My cock strained against my trousers just thinking about it. I debated asking her if I could.

Here and now.

She glanced down, noticing my stare and gasped, pulling the dress away from her skin while her cheeks flushed bright red.

"James," she breathed, asking for help that I really didn't want to give.

"Fine," I groaned and reached behind me to grab my coat, tossing it to her as she covered herself immediately. "You see. I told you we wanted different things."

We pulled up to her house and sat in silence as the rain continued to pour. She hadn't glanced at me since we left the park. Her eyes focused on the rain-soaked windshield, lost in her thoughts.

"So, this is it," she murmured, still not meeting my eyes. "You and me."

"Unless you're going to invite me to your room. Yes. This is it. I have nothing else to offer you." The words felt harsh even as

I said them. But I meant it. We couldn't be a thing or whatever this was in dangerous territory of becoming. A part of me wished she would invite me to her room, if only to drag my tongue along every crevice of her body and break the tension. But then she'd hate me even more, which perhaps was a good thing.

She should hate me.

"And you can't just kiss me?" she asked.

I glanced at the back seat. "The backseat works well for me, too. It's all the same to me." And the sooner the better, so we could go our separate ways, and I could stop thinking about her.

I could practically see her heart pounding in her chest as she whirled at me. "Something is very wrong with you." I'd have to agree with her on that. "You say these cold things, but then your actions..." She drifted away in thought, then turned back to me with a thoughtful look on her face as her voice fell to a whisper. "Someone... broke your heart. Didn't they?"

And any kind of feeling I had for her turned to anger. "Excuse me?"

Her voice was soft as she held my gaze. "I'm not a fool, James. Someone made you this way. I've seen love destroy good people. What happened to you?"

My grip tightened on the steering wheel. I already knew too much about her family story to understand what she meant. And I fucking hated that.

"You should leave." I stared out the windshield as the rain poured down, unable to meet her eyes.

"James. I'm—" she started.

"Now. Lizzie." My nostrils flared.

She flinched at my tone and then nodded. "I'm sorry," she murmured, and I swear I saw a tear fall down her cheek.

She opened the door, leaving my coat on the seat.

As soon as she shut the door, I flinched, feeling a tug deep down inside of me. But before I could analyse it, I took off into the rain, only glancing back once to see her still standing there on the side of the street.

The tug pulled harder.

I clenched my teeth.

Why the hell did she have to say that? No one made me this way. This was who I was, and she obviously wasn't okay with that. Which, fine. She didn't need to be. She couldn't hate me any more than I already hated myself.

It's a good thing *this* was over.

Chapter 10

ELISABETH

His Cold Heart

STEAM ROSE FROM THE tub as I soaked, chasing away the chill from my bones. My gaze was transfixed on the grey and stormy skies as thunder and lightning filled the overwhelming silence around me. Flashes of light illuminated the swaying trees, bending at the force of the wind. Raindrops glided down the cold glass, reminding me of teardrops as I sank deeper into the tub.

I knew I shouldn't have said those words.

I'd seen hurt, perhaps even too much of it. Enough to be able to see that same pain in someone else. Like a flash of light in the sky that suddenly revealed something in the darkness, everything snapped into place after he admitted that he had nothing to offer.

Because that was the first and possibly biggest lie that he told himself. Maybe I saw things in him that he could no longer see in himself, but I knew that he did have things to offer.

He wanted to kiss me, but he wanted more than just a kiss. The more he deflected, saying we wanted different things, the more I understood him. He admitted to only wanting sex, but I think that was also a lie. And for a moment, I thought maybe that's all I wanted too. That I was happy doing things *his* way.

But he was right.

We wanted different things.

I'm still not entirely sure of what I wanted. But watching him drive away in anger wasn't one of them.

A knock at the door, and Pearl entered. "Lizzie, it's time for supper. Shall I pick out a dress?" Her gaze snapped to mine. "Mistress, are you alright?"

"I'm fine," I sniffed, wiping away tears. "I'm not hungry. Please tell Father I'm sorry."

"Should I get Margaret?"

"No," I answered quickly. "No, thank you. I'm fine."

Pearl seemed hesitant but nodded and then left the room.

Once I rose out of the tub, Finton scratched on the door, as if he knew I needed him. I let him in, snuggling him in my bed while I sobbed into his soft fur. Whatever was happening between us was surely gone now. He couldn't even look at me before he left, and I think that hurt the most. I didn't realise how just one moment could hurt so badly. How just one moment could make you feel so much regret...

I realised how unhappy I was about him, about everything in my life, and I didn't know how to fix it.

The sun peeked through the large glass window as I sat at the piano bright and early the next morning, casting long shadows on the floor. My hands glided along the keys while everything else faded away.

The wooden floor creaked, and I paused.

"I missed you at supper last night," my father said, placing his brown bowler cap on his head as he approached me.

"I'm sorry. I wasn't feeling well."

He placed a comforting hand on my shoulder. "Is there something wrong, Lizzie?"

I shook my head. "I'm fine."

"Your mother used to say those words to me, and she was never just fine. In fact, she explained to me several times that being fine was not good," he smiled.

A laugh reverberated in my chest as some of my tension eased. "I am my mother's daughter." Mother was also very good at pretending she was fine, and she was never *just fine*. Terrible pretenders we were. Must be genetic.

He laughed at that. "I used to bring your mother pink tulips when she felt this way."

"I don't think tulips are going to fix this," I murmured. He stood in silence, hesitant to leave me alone. "You should go. Before you're late for work," I assured him.

"Perhaps a box of chocolates?" he smiled, knowing exactly how to make me feel better.

"I wouldn't say no," I smiled with the corner of my mouth.

"Keep your chin up, darling. Things will turn out. They always do," he smiled.

And then he left, grabbing his coat on the way out as I resumed playing.

The bass of the piano reverberated around the room, pulsating in my chest. High, sweet notes echoed off the walls as a tear slid down my cheek. I thought of him and his cold and broken heart, losing myself in the song.

A few minutes later, Margaret sauntered into the drawing room. Slumping down on the couch as she glared at me. I must have woken her, but I took a breath and continued playing, losing myself once again. Ignoring her presence as I gave everything to the song as it flowed out of me. A melody both haunting and full of conflicting emotions.

The longer she sat listening, the less she started to glare. Perhaps she was enjoying it?

I played the final chord, letting it reverberate around the room as my hands lightly rested on the keys. Moments later, Pearl came into the drawing room with a tray of coffee and biscuits.

"That was... very pretty, Elisabeth," Pearl said, setting down the tray.

Margaret began pouring herself a cup. "I liked it too."

"Let me know if you need anything else," Pearl smiled and then left the room as quickly as she came in.

Did she really? "You liked it?"

"Mhmm," Margaret sipped from her cup. "For a moment, I thought you were going to bring me to tears."

I snorted, thinking she was making a joke, but she didn't smile.

Margaret's face was suddenly serious, and perhaps a bit sombre. "Was that song for him?"

My heart dropped. "It was for me," I snapped, rising from the piano bench. Pouring myself a cup of coffee and shoving biscuits into my mouth as I sat next to her.

"So..." she started.

But I knew that, *so.* "Don't even start," crumbs fell from my lips as I spoke.

"He was very handsome," she curved her lips into a smile.

I let out a breath and rose from the couch, grabbing a few more biscuits to eat on the way back to my room. This conversation was not one I was willing to have.

"Like heart-stopping handsome," she continued, like I wasn't trying to run away. "When are you seeing him again?" She stroked the back of the couch in thought.

"I'm not," I bit out.

"Why?" She whirled around, staring at me as I stood under the archway where I briefly paused.

"He doesn't want to see me," I murmured.

And then I shoved another biscuit in my mouth and left the room, heading upstairs to wallow alone.

I lay down on my bed, staring at the ceiling. Admiring the intricate architecture as I finished off the biscuits in my hand. Trying to distract myself from crying. A few minutes later, Margaret opened the door and leaned against the doorframe.

"Why?" she probed.

"Why, what?" Frustration laced my tone.

"Why doesn't he want to see you? Because from what I saw, I think he really liked you," she grinned, admiring her nails.

"He doesn't," I murmured, feeling like someone had punched me in the chest. "We want different things."

"How so?" she asked.

I raised my hands in exasperation. "I don't know." There was something deeper about him pushing me away, some kind of hurt that I didn't know if he was aware of himself.

She crossed her arms over her large chest. "What does he want that you won't give him?"

Ugh. I sat up and faced her. "More like what *he* won't give *me*." Thank you very much. I was allowed to want things, too.

She cocked a brow and stared at me, waiting for me to say more.

I sighed, letting out a long breath. "The thing is... I wanted him to kiss me." She pursed her lips and started to laugh, but I continued, narrowing my eyes at her. "But he won't, because he wants more than just kissing."

She stopped laughing. Paused. And then her mouth curved into a slow smile. "Then go for it. You have my blessing if it's something you want to do."

Like it's that simple.

I scoffed and quickly rose from the bed, crossing my arms over my chest in frustration. "It's not about that. It's about the principle."

"Sex being the principle?" She looked even more confused.

I pressed a palm to my forehead, quelling the migraine beginning to form. "The kiss. I want him to kiss me first, Margaret. Then. We'll see," I shrugged, playing it off. As if this conversation wasn't one of the hardest I'd ever had. Or that the idea of kissing James was simple.

The smile she gave me then was one I'd never seen before, like she was genuinely happy and smirking at the same time. "Good for you." Her eyes then drifted to the wooden floors. "Heaven knows, I've never been one for restraint."

And that was an understatement. I nearly snorted.

"I always wondered if someday you'd turn out just like me," she continued. "Feared it even." I hadn't seen my sister worry since Mother died, and at this moment, she looked distraught.

"You and I are very different, Margaret," I assured her.

She snorted. "And thank goodness, for that."

A moment of silence passed.

"Do you think, you know, someday... maybe you'd want something more than a midnight lover?" I asked in a serious, but slightly teasing manner.

She stood for a moment in silence, thinking it through. But then she smiled and shrugged. "Maybe. But I do quite enjoy the thrill of midnight lovers." I let out an exasperated sigh at her response. "I don't plan on settling down anytime soon, if that's what you're asking," she playfully shoved my shoulder, heading towards the door with a grin on her face. Then she stopped at the door once more. "Make your handsome Irishman work for it," she winked and left the room.

Except I'd never get the chance to make him work for it.

My heart sank at the thought.

"He's not—" The door closed, cutting off my words. "Mine," I finished with a sigh. Even though a part of me wished that he was. For reasons I didn't understand. Why did everything about him have to be so confusing?

The days then passed as usual.

Father went to work each morning, I helped Pearl with the chores, played the piano, finished another one of my romance books, and then I devoured the entire box of chocolate Father left for me, and Margaret drank. Every night I dreamed about him. Whether or not I wanted to. And they were good dreams. Dreams

I didn't know I was capable of having. Which made not thinking about him even harder.

To my surprise, Margaret stopped asking questions. Even when she joined me for walks to the city gardens, she didn't push it. I needed to forget about him or find some way to replace those feelings. It wasn't healthy to have such an obsession with someone I barely knew. Perhaps a new hobby. Except the only thing I had been thinking about lately was that maybe kissing someone else might give me the release I was looking for.

"I think I'm going to ask Freddie for another date," I said, one afternoon as we walked around in the city admiring the pink and blue hydrangeas.

"Really?" I didn't miss the surprise in her tone.

"I think I'd like to give him another chance." I desperately needed a distraction, and I knew that Freddie would probably be okay with that. And he was handsome, or handsome enough. I could probably make it work for the sake of breaking this fever.

Perhaps the next kiss would be satisfying?

Either way, happiness wasn't just going to find me. I had to at least try. And I could no longer just ignore the needs welling up inside of me.

"When are you going to ask him?" she asked.

"Let's go now," I said, steering us in the direction of Cobb's. Might as well be now. It would save me a trip out here again, and the next time I might lose my nerve.

The bell chimed as we entered.

As soon as he saw me, he started straightening his tie, smiling like I was the prettiest thing he had seen today. My chest felt tight.

"Elisabeth," he said.

I smiled. "You can call me Lizzie." I'd actually prefer it if he did, so I could stop hearing the way that James said it.

Margaret headed towards the selection of wines.

"Lizzie," he corrected. Not quite the same, it needed more darkness and desire laced with a throaty rasp, but I appreciated his effort. "How have you—it's been a while," he nervously scratched his neck.

I walked closer to the counter, heart racing, checking for any last-minute regrets. But I couldn't think of one. "Freddie. Would you go on a date with me?"

He blushed. "I'd—yes. Yes, I would love that." He cleared his throat. "When would you like to go?"

"Tonight." Christ, did that sound as desperate as I meant it to be? "Pick us up at seven," I smiled, trying to convey confidence.

Margaret placed a few bottles on the counter, and I handed Freddie the amount.

"I can't wait," he brushed my hand, smiling as he lingered.

"See you later," I replied before walking out of the shop.

Yes, this was perfectly fine. This was good. This would be good. Now I just needed to find the perfect dress, and this dress definitely had intentions.

Chapter 11

JAMES

Possession

I SAT ON THE edge of a four-poster bed, pulling on my black trousers. Blankets were strewn about, candles were lit, and the walls were covered in strange art with streetlights shining through the one window on a moonless night. Her arms wrapped around me, pulsating warm breath in my ear. I didn't even remember her name.

"You don't have to leave so fast," she breathed, stroking my chest. Preventing me from rising from the bed.

"I have things to do." With that, I sat up, looking around for my shirt. Taking in the disorder and clutter of the room.

"My husband won't be home for a few more days." She stroked the bed, still lying fully exposed.

Husband? I froze.

Fuck. Well, now I felt even worse.

After picking up my shirt and vest off the floor, I threw on my shoulder holster and flat cap. My wool coat was still in the same place *she* left it, in the passenger's seat of my car. And it would stay there until her scent stopped driving me fucking crazy.

"Give him my regards," I replied while sheathing my revolver, leaving the room as quickly as I could, heading out into the night.

The Gilded Glow was busy tonight, over-crowded and loud. I pushed past drunken people, heading straight to the bar for a drink.

Of course, she was married.

Things were not going my way the last few days, besides last night's fight in the pit, which was too easy. Or perhaps I had too much pent-up anger and frustration.

First, Cam's stupid girlfriend who was at the house at all hours of the day, and the walls were way too thin. We were definitely having that conversation tonight. She needed to go. I needed some goddamn sleep.

And second, all of the things about *her* that put me on the edge of pure frustration and just plain fucking need. All I wanted was a release tonight, not something else to feel bad about. And it wasn't even that good or remotely satisfying.

Things were not going my way.

I slammed the glass on the bar, searching the room for Cam. Finding his face engrossed in his blonde date, noses touching. Most likely, he didn't even notice that I left, which was for the best. Explaining that questionable situation to him was not at the top of my list. I was about to leave and go snort some snow in the alley, but the rush of something else filled me with feelings I hadn't felt in a long time.

She was on the dance floor.

Dancing with someone else.

The light from the crystal chandeliers hanging above made the lustre of her red hair glow with colours I could only describe as a burning flame. Like firelight in the golden haze. She was wearing a long, black velvet dress with a considerable plunge in the front. Her hands were wrapped around his neck, while his were on the curve of her hips, and she was smiling at him.

I stared, unblinking.

Everything around me felt so quiet. So still. As if time suddenly stopped, and she was the only thing that existed. I couldn't make sense of what was happening. It all felt like a bad dream, like perhaps I was still in a nightmare of my own design.

And then she kissed him.

And I snapped.

Who the fuck was this guy?

My fists white-knuckled, and I clenched my jaw to the point of pain. The last of the whiskey in my glass burned on the way down as I tried to reason with myself, but it was too late. I was already heading towards her, shoving him away.

"Hey!" he yelled.

"James," she exclaimed breathlessly as her eyes went wide.

"What's your problem?" he said.

A laugh reverberated in my throat, ignoring him as I held out my hand for hers, meeting her golden eyes. "My turn."

She looked at me and then back at him, unsure of what to do.

My patience was reaching its limit.

"Do you know this guy?" He levelled his eyes at me, narrowing them to slits.

She placed her hand on his arm for comfort, or maybe they were actually a thing? When? And how? I was much better looking than this guy.

"Just give me a moment, Freddie. I'll find you after the dance," she smiled at him.

Freddie glared at me and then walked away.

When she finally took my hand, I pulled her in nice and close, splaying my hands on her waist. Feeling a deep satisfaction as I reclaimed her curves.

"What's wrong with you?" she asked, narrowing her eyes.

I laughed. "I think we've established I have many things wrong with me, sweetheart." That list was too long. I wouldn't even know where to start.

"You can't just—" her breath hitched as I squeezed her waist. "Do things like that."

"Well, I just did." Fuck, the feeling of this velvet dress against her curves... I felt myself being driven to madness by the second. My hand moved to the centre of her bare back, slow and meticulously. Aching to go lower and grab her ass.

She let out a shallow breath. "James. Look. Like you said. We want different things."

"Do we? I'm starting to think maybe we don't."

"I thought you were angry with me," she muttered.

"I am angry with you. But that doesn't mean I want to see you with anyone else." Was this jealousy? I didn't like the feeling.

"That is not your choice to make," she snapped. "At least *he* wants to kiss me," she muttered in barely a whisper.

Fuck, not this again.

I rolled my eyes, grabbing her hand. Pushing through people on the dance floor. Leading her out into the dark alley to finish this.

If she wanted to be kissed, I would kiss her.

I led her far enough away from the entrance that we were cloaked in shadows. My hands went to either side of her, bracing her against the brick wall. Her breath pulsated on my lips as my gaze drifted to her mouth. My other hand was firm on her waist, waiting to slide down to her ass and pull her up to me. She was going to like this.

"James," she put her hand on my chest, and I couldn't deny how good it felt. Every nerve in my body came alive at the sound of my name and the feel of her hand on my chest. "You can't kiss me."

"Isn't that what you want me to do?" I placed my thumb on her bottom lip, dragging it down. Fuck I wanted to kiss her so bad, and after kissing me, she'd never want anyone else again.

She grabbed my hand, pulling it away. "I'm on a date with someone else. This isn't right."

My gaze flicked to hers. "What?" She didn't miss the annoyance in my tone. "You can't be serious."

"I am," she shoved me back. "If you want to kiss me. You're going to have to ask me."

"Ask you what?" Now look who was playing games. My mouth curved into a smirk as I continued to stare at her full, red lips.

"Ask me on a date, James. And maybe, I'll let you kiss me." And then she took off down the alley back towards the bar, swaying her hips.

Was she doing that on purpose? Or am I just *that* distracted?

She turned back before opening the door. "Maybe, I'll see you around," she smirked.

And then she was gone.

Using my own fucking words against me.

I stood in the alley alone, watching her as she walked away. And all I could do was curse under my breath.

She was going to drive me to madness.

Chapter 12

ELISABETH
Trust Me

THAT WAS NOT EASY, but I was practically brimming with pride when I walked away. That I did not let him kiss me. I'd been replaying Margaret's words in my head for days.

Make him work for it.

I never thought I'd get the chance again, but then there he was. Jealous that I was kissing someone else, and I wanted to see him work for it. He would have to earn that kiss. And with that look I left on his face, and that glimmer in his eyes, I knew that what I said got under his skin.

I smiled at my thoughts and found Freddie sitting patiently in our booth.

"Are you alright?" He asked immediately, looking genuinely concerned as I sat next to him.

"Yes," I smiled. "I'm sorry about that."

"Is he an old boyfriend or something?" Freddie asked.

I chuckled. "No, he..." but I had no words to finish that sentence. What was he? "He just wanted a dance," I managed. "I think he was drunk." Drunk on his own ego. If he thought I was just going to let him kiss me after our last conversation, he was very wrong and very drunk.

Freddie nodded. "Well, as long as you're alright."

"I'm just fine." I started to sip from my drink when James approached the table, making me choke at the sight of him.

"Tomorrow night," his voice shook in his chest. "I'll pick you up at six. And after, we're going on a date," he smirked.

The way his tone commanded that we were going on a date made my body writhe. I didn't know how to refuse him.

"And what's... before?" I asked.

And a, *please go on a date with me, Lizzie or I shall never stop thinking about you* would have been nice. But I think it might have been the first time he's ever asked someone. I'd never seen him look so flustered. So out of his element.

He grinned with fire in his eyes, sending a flood of warmth through me. "You'll find out." He paused, pointing at my dress. "And wear this." He then looked at Freddie, cold and calculating. "Enjoy your last night with her." And then he walked away, and I swear I saw the flash of a gun bolstered to his side.

I blinked, shaking my head. Not knowing what to say as my thoughts began to whirl. Where were we going for this date? What was he planning? Was he planning on... *that* before our date? That would be pretty presumptuous of him, but it wouldn't be the first time. I couldn't stop thinking about it, nor fantasising about it.

He was going to kiss me tomorrow.

I just knew it.

For the time being, all I could do was apologise to Freddie, who was in a staring competition with the table.

My black velvet dress reflected in the mirror as I generously applied red lipstick. Margaret sat on my bed, stroking Finton as she watched me.

"You sure you want to wear the same dress?" she asked.

"Yes," I sighed. "He asked me to."

She grinned. "I like a man who knows what he wants. Are you sure you don't want to go alone tonight? Perhaps you would like some alone time with Freddie," she quirked her eyebrows.

I still hadn't told her I was going on a date with James, but he would arrive at any minute. And then she would know.

"I need you to come."

I had no idea what James was planning, and after stressing about it all day and making sure every inch of me was clean, I realised that she needed to come. Otherwise, I might end up in his bed. And I didn't think I was ready for that.

But perhaps he wouldn't even show up tonight.

Perhaps it would be better if he didn't.

"Oh. Is that what you *need*?" she teased.

I scowled at her and then heard a knock at the door, making my heart jump in my chest. It was exactly six o'clock.

James was at my front door.

"I'll get it," Margaret said, rolling off the bed.

Why did this suddenly feel like a bad decision? My hands began to sweat. With one last look in the mirror and one last calming breath, I descended the stairs.

When I laid eyes on him, I had to remind myself to breathe. He wasn't wearing his usual black vest. Instead, he was wearing only a white shirt half-buttoned up, with his sleeves rolled up to his elbows, and his thick black hair waving in his face. Leaning casually in the door frame. I'd never seen so many muscles, and I could not stop staring at his exposed skin.

He caught my stare, with a smile on his face that made my knees weak. "Is it alright if I say hi this time?"

"Yes."

"Hi," he smiled.

"Hi," I blushed, feeling heat everywhere.

"Oh," Margaret said. And I just remembered that she was here. She leaned closer to me, jabbing me in the elbow. "Are you sure you want me to come?"

"Yes," I murmured to her. "James. I'd like to bring Margaret."

He scrunched his dark brows, taking a moment. And then he softly laughed, wetting his lips. "You don't trust me."

I didn't trust myself, but I wasn't going to tell him that. "No. I just—"

"No, you don't trust me?" He stepped towards me.

I flustered, saying my words too fast. "I just think it would be best if she came. For safety."

And for my own sanity.

He could probably convince me of anything, and that scared me the most.

"So, you want her to watch?" He grinned, perhaps the most wicked grin I had ever seen.

Heat burned in my cheeks, burning like red-hot fire.

Margaret laughed through her nose. "He's good. I like him already." Then she took a step towards him. "But, if anything bad happens to her, I'll take these nails and gouge out your pretty eyes," she flashed her long nails at him.

My mouth dropped open. I'd never heard such violent things come out of my sister's mouth.

He smiled. "I like you too, Margaret."

Margaret walked off towards the drawing room, grinning at me as she went. I tried to call after her, but James took a step towards me, putting his hand on my arm and trailing down with his finger. I swallowed hard. How could one touch from him control me so completely? All my senses abandoned me, and I craved more.

This was definitely a bad idea.

"I promise to bring you back here in one piece." He brushed hair away from my face, caressing my jaw. "Besides, it's been a while since I've killed anyone. You're probably safe," he flashed a grin, but something dark lurked underneath his captivating smile.

I laughed nervously. "That doesn't comfort me."

"I'm quite fond of my pretty eyes. I won't do anything to risk them," he smiled. "Come on, we're going to be late," he grabbed my hand, pulling me out the door.

"Don't do anything I wouldn't do!" I heard Margaret yell before he closed the door. But that really didn't narrow it down.

Chapter 13

ELISABETH

A Man Untamed

ALL I COULD SMELL for the past twenty minutes was his scent, and he smelled like leather and bad decisions. My heart pounded in my chest as I fidgeted nervously with my fingers while sweat pooled between my thighs. It was probably going to leave a mark on his black leather seats. I glanced at him several times, but he only smiled at me in a way that made me writhe in my seat.

"Where are we going?" I said after some time. Perhaps he was really kidnapping me. I should stop enjoying it so much, just in case he actually was.

"We're almost there," he smiled.

Minutes later, he parked the car at a place that looked like an abandoned factory. Lit up in the darkness as crowds of people milled about. He hopped out to open my door, taking my hand as I stepped out like we were on a proper date. I didn't know what I was expecting for this date, but it wasn't chivalry. It felt like I was living in a scene from one of my storybooks. Except he resembled the villain more than the hero. The dark hair, the smirk, the greedy way his hands always seemed to grab me—and let's not forget the way he toyed with my emotions like it was his favourite game.

Margaret must have scared him because everything he did kept playing out like a dream.

He led me by the hand as we followed behind a massive crowd, entering the building. It was noisy and dark inside, with two levels stacked full of people. All of the lights seemed to be aimed at a ring in the centre of the room, like some prized possession.

"Are we here for a boxing match?" I asked. I'd never been, but my father used to go all the time before my mother... I stopped myself before the grief could settle in.

"Oh, I think you'll find this much more violent," he grinned, drawing attention to the dimples that perfectly formed in the corner of his mouth.

We moved through the crowd and into a lavatory where he closed the door, leaving us practically in the darkness with a single blue light on the wall and the smell of dank water. And that's where my date fantasy went to a very dark place. My chest constricted as I took shallow breaths in the small space. I opened my mouth to protest, but then he removed his shirt, and my jaw dropped open.

How was that even possible? All of *that*. Or fair. I was completely out of my element, and a little bit frightened to be honest. His strong body was clearly capable of breaking me in half.

"Relax," he smiled, like he could sense my fear. "I'm not going to kiss you in here."

Well, that was good to know. Having our first kiss in the lavatory was not at the top of my list.

"Or?" I blinked, clicking my heel on the cement floor. He needed to say a bit more, considering what I knew about him.

He smirked, seeming pleased with my question. "Or fuck you in here."

I let out a breath. At least that was clear now, though I couldn't help but flinch at his curse. Surely, he could find a better way to say that. The vulgarity of his language still caught me off guard.

"Unless you want me to," he added with a grin.

Heat filled my cheeks. "Not. Happening." He laughed, nodding at my reply. "What are we doing in here?" And most importantly, why was he still shirtless?

"I just need to do something quick." He turned to the mirror, retrieving something small from his pants pocket.

What was he doing?

Then he poured something that looked like powder on his hand, inhaling it up his nose—and his entire posture changed. He jumped around, cracked his neck, and turned to me, looking at me with razor-sharp eyes.

Fear coursed through me.

"It's alright," he said, brushing his hand on my arm.

"What was that?" I asked.

Something that looked a lot like regret flashed across his face. "It helps me."

A loud knock at the door made me jump, stopping my next question. James opened the door to a man who looked to be about the same age as him. With light brown hair and a trim reddish-brown moustache.

"It's time," he said. Then he turned to me, noticing my small presence next to James. His eyebrows rose in surprise, and... was that happiness?

I smiled at his authentic smile.

"Lizzie, this is my friend Cameron," James said, a little bit annoyed.

Cameron extended his hand for mine, smiling from ear to ear. "Pleasure to meet you, Lizzie."

I took his hand, staring into his kind brown eyes.

James stepped closer, and Cameron dropped my hand, laughing as he walked away.

"Come on," James muttered, grabbing my hand.

I was very happy we were leaving the lavatory.

We drifted through the animated crowd, but my focus was on

his hand in mine and his bare back, with so many rippling, perfected muscles that I lost sense of where I was.

Has he always been this fit?

He turned around once we were at the edge of the ring and took both of my arms, drifting his gaze briefly to my breasts before he met my eyes. I noticed a long, thick scar on his left shoulder.

"Now, you stand here."

"And where are you going?" Was he just planning on leaving me here? Because that was not acceptable.

He nodded to the ring. "I'm going in there."

"What?" In the ring?

He smiled, and then he was gone.

I called after him, but he had already stepped into the ring.

A tall man wearing a pin-striped suit stepped up to a micro-phone, and the volume of the room grew even more resounding. "This is Roy Roberts, and welcome to the pit!"

The crowd erupted.

My eyes stayed on James as if I could look anywhere else, knowing he was on display.

"How is everyone feeling tonight?" Roy asked the crowd. They answered with joyous screams and whistles, raising their fists and clapping their hands. He hastened to James's side, gesturing to him. "And look who's back again, our champion James fucking MacGuire! What do we think, Brummies?"

Champion? My mind roared with so many questions.

The crowd went crazy. Cheering, yelling, and a few people started to scream. I laughed, covering my ears before their screams shattered my eardrums.

Roy briskly moved over to the other side of the ring towards a large man with a thick brown moustache. "And what about our other contestant?"

The crowd continued yelling and cheering, but I booed along with some of the others around me. Unable to contain myself.

"We've got about thirty seconds left on the clock. Place your bets!" Roy shouted.

It was as if the lights suddenly dimmed because all I could see was *him*—and he looked strong. Formidable. As if something else was possessing his body.

A bell rang loud and clear.

James's opponent barrelled towards him, trying to take the first hit. But James dodged and swung at the last second, hitting him in the gut and the ribs. His burly opponent rushed in again, punching and throwing his large fists, landing some hard hits to James's back. Proceeding to strike him in the side until he pinned James to the edge of the ring.

My hands were clenched so tightly, shaking with a rush of adrenaline and fear. My eyes couldn't look away from the violence, from his muscled body on perfect display.

The burly man struck James in the face, and I winced.

But then James broke free and punched him in the ribs— striking him hard four, five, six times in a row. Digging his fists in so hard that the burly man staggered to the side. James brought him to the floor with one swift hit to his chin. Blood splattered on the floor.

I had never seen anything so violent, but I liked it. I liked the feeling, the rush that overcame all of my senses as I watched his muscles rippling with each swing. A sight that felt forbidden, and I was allowed to watch.

No, he wanted me to watch him.

The bell chimed again, and the man in the pinstripe suit held up James's hands as he spat out blood, and the crowd cheered. I couldn't help but clap my hands and join in. It was infectious. I felt just as much excitement, if not more, for the man who won.

A man untamed.

Dark and wild, with his midnight hair falling in his face as sweat glistened on his chest and down his forearms to his tattoo. All things that should not be exciting me.

But when I thought that was it, men and women around me began placing another bet. And James was not leaving the ring.

"Is there another fight?" I asked a random man wearing a black hat standing close to me.

"There are five tonight," he answered, keeping his eyes on the ring.

Five?

James's friend Cameron approached me. "How are you doing?" He shouted to me over the noise of the room.

"There are five matches?" I asked, whirling to him.

Cameron laughed. "He'll be alright. These are just the preliminaries for Friday night's fight. Whoever performs the best gets a chance at the big fight." James glanced over and nodded at Cameron. "He wanted me to make sure you're alright."

"I'm good." I was, but nervous as hell.

"Good," he smiled.

The bell chimed, and James started his next fight.

"So, where did you guys meet?" Cameron continued, shouting over the crowd.

I guess he hadn't mentioned me. "We met at the bar." My eyes stayed on James in the ring. I still couldn't believe he could move that fast or hit that hard. "Do you know The Gilded Glow?" My voice rang out as loud as I could manage, scraping my vocal cords. I'd never had to talk this loudly in my life.

"No shit," he brought his hand to his mouth as if to take back his words. "Sorry. I meant—"

"Fucking kill him! Knock out his mother fucking teeth!" A man next to us shouted as spit flew from his teeth.

Cameron gave me an apologetic look, turning back to the fight. It's not like I hadn't heard those words before. Maybe not in that exact order, but there was nothing gentle about these fights. I laughed with adrenaline flowing through my veins, and Cameron smiled, cheering on James.

By the time James was readying for his fifth fight, his face and body were covered in bruises, and blood was streaming down from his eyebrow to his chiselled torso. I wasn't even sure what blood was his or someone else's. But he was still going, smiling at the next contestant with his fists up and blood in his teeth, like pain didn't exist for him.

The final bell chimed, and the pinstriped-suited man held up James's bloody hands one last time in victory as the crowd roared. Cameron entered the ring, joyously slapping him on the back. James then turned his gaze to me, and my knees shook as I smiled at him. Even with the blood and the bruises, he was still the most handsome man I had ever seen.

All I could think was that he'd better kiss me tonight.

Chapter 14

JAMES
Velvet

THE FIGHT TONIGHT WAS a complete rush and everything I needed, considering the past few torturous days. Knowing she was watching me fuelled some part of me to punch harder and move faster. My heart rate was still working its way back to a normal level.

After washing myself off in the lavatory and throwing on my shirt, I walked her to the Rolls-Royce Phantom. Most of the crowd had filtered out, but a few people were walking around to their cars or mingling outside the warehouse in the crisp night air. The moon was full and bright, drifting behind the clouds.

"What did you think?" I asked, opening the door for her.

She turned around to face me. "I think I'll never try my luck at a fistfight with you."

A low laugh rumbled in my chest.

She turned to get in but then turned back around. "Was this all to impress me? Or scare me, James MacGuire?"

I laughed through my nose at the use of my last name. "How long have you been waiting to say that?"

She shrugged, trying to be breezy, but her blush gave her away.

"Well, were you impressed?" I licked my lips, smiling. "Or scared?"

She nervously bit her bottom lip. "Both," she answered quickly, hopping into the car.

Perhaps that was exactly what I wanted her to feel.

Impressed, and slightly terrified.

A satisfied chill ran down my spine as I laughed under my breath, closing her door and then taking off into the night.

"Where did you learn to fight like that?" She asked after about a minute. I guess she wasn't a 'sit in silence' type of person.

"When I was very young." I flexed my hands on the steering wheel, not wanting to say more.

Her eyes drifted to my hands, covered in cuts and dried blood. "Do they hurt?" she asked.

"Not anymore." After fighting for as long as I have, the pain was pretty minimal. Bloody fists were nothing new and a welcome release.

"And your friend, Cameron. Where did you meet him?"

I sighed. "You're just full of questions, aren't you?"

"Is it a secret?" she pushed.

"No. It's not."

She crossed her arms over her generous chest and continued staring at me.

"Fine. I also met him when I was young," I gave her a sly smile.

She let out a frustrated sigh. "You're aggravating."

I smiled. "I've been called worse." And aggravating her was fun, the highlight of my night besides my win in the ring.

She bit her lip as if to stop from asking more questions, fidgeting in her seat as she turned back to look out the window.

Five minutes later, I pulled up to a spot that overlooked the city. A place that I used to visit quite often for a different view. From up here, you couldn't see the poverty-stricken neighbourhoods or the danger lurking around every corner in the filthy streets. But everything always looked better from a distance.

"Impressive," she breathed, leaning forward in her seat. "The city. It's absolutely beautiful from up here."

Not nearly as beautiful as her, but I wasn't ready to admit that. I think she would have gotten the wrong impression, not that I had any idea of what impression I wanted to give her tonight. I was stuck between wanting her now and keeping her around just a bit longer... which was confusing as hell.

She bit her lip, turning towards me.

"You need to stop doing that," I warned.

"Doing what?" She scrunched her brows.

"Biting that goddamn lip." I was two seconds from biting it for her. And I would bite harder.

She laughed nervously. "Why? Does it bother you?"

"Everything you do bothers me."

She swallowed and parted her lips, taking a shallow breath.

A soft curse rolled out of me as I hopped out of the car. Needing some space before I decided to run my hands up her velvet dress. Normally, it was darker out here, but the light of the full moon lit up the colourful greenery around us. Seconds later, her door opened and slowly closed. But I kept my gaze on the horizon, taking a deep breath to steady myself as she came up behind me, stopping maybe an inch from where I was standing.

"James? Are you alright?"

I turned around, wanting to tell her that this was a bad idea. That I should've never asked her on a date. That she should stay far away from me before I decided to fuck her into next week. But I settled on. "I shouldn't have asked you on this date."

"Why?" she spoke softly, confused.

"I think you're getting the wrong ideas about me."

Her eyes drifted to the ground before bringing them back to me. "Why did you ask me?"

Well, that was simple. "I wanted to kiss you," I admitted. Her eyes lit up, and she started to sway. "But Lizzie, I want to do much more than that, and I'm—" I swallowed. "I'm no good for you."

She should turn around and run. If she knew about my past, she would. If she knew about everything that I had done and the man that I truly was, she would never look at me in the same way.

I was no good for her.

"Then don't be good for me." There was no hesitation in her words. My mouth opened and shut as she took another step towards me, placing her hand on my chest. Everything I was about to say floated away as the flecks of gold in her eyes consumed me.

"You shouldn't say things like that," I found my fractured resolve.

And she definitely shouldn't touch me and say things like that. Those were words that would make me show her all of the reasons I wasn't good for her.

"If you want to kiss me. Then, kiss me," she challenged, wetting her lips with her tongue.

Before I could speak or think, my lips were on hers as I pulled her in with one arm, lifting her body into mine, setting myself deeper into the kiss. Enjoying every second as she lost control and wrapped her arms around my neck. I groaned in her mouth, interlacing my tongue with hers. Never wanting to stop kissing her or feeling her warm body against mine.

The world around us faded, and I couldn't even remember why we shouldn't be doing this. It was just her and me. And my hands on her lower back as my mouth claimed hers.

When she pulled away, I felt her absence. It took everything in me not to pull her back in. She swallowed, breathing heavily as her eyes stared into mine, and then she focused on my mouth.

Like she needed to see what she did to me.

I licked my lips, smiling, and reached in to kiss her again. Softer, much more delicate kisses that drove me insane, until I was caressing my tongue with hers, pulling her closer to me. Harder, deeper, feeling every curve of her mouth as my hands finally reached to grab her ass. A sweet release that instantly hardened my cock against her.

I didn't know if she knew what that felt like, but I'm pretty sure I was the first man to lose myself with her. And then she bit my bottom lip, sucking it into her mouth, and I didn't know how to stop.

I was prepared to throw her to the ground.

"Fuck," I groaned into her mouth.

She pulled back. "Did I hurt you?"

I chuckled. "You're going to have to bite me a lot harder." I kissed her again, pulling her deeper into my erection. Hoping she *would* bite me harder.

"James," she laughed, pushing against my chest.

And then I picked her up.

"James, what are you do—"

"You asked for this, sweetheart."

Then don't be good for me.

A challenge I was going to make good on.

She was laughing as I opened the car door and laid her down gently on the front seat, hovering just inches above her with her hands still around my neck. Her legs were wrapped around me while her fingers played mindlessly with my shirt. I brushed her reddened cheek with my hand, and her smile turned into something more, something darker.

Blood rushed straight to my cock.

I expected to hear her say no or tell me to stop. But all she did was say my name with pleasure, and I felt myself coming undone. My hand slowly and gently dragged down from her face to her full breasts, tracing the curve of her.

She took a sharp breath, digging her nails into my shoulder, so I kept going. Trailing down to her thighs and lifting her black velvet dress as I splayed my hands on her warm upper thigh. Goddamn, her skin felt too good.

"Can I touch you?" I rasped. I needed to touch her more than I needed to breathe.

"You are touching me," she replied.

I smiled, pushing my hand up further. "I'd like to touch you there," My eyes connected down to my intended destination.

"Oh," a tremble rolled through her. She was slightly uneasy, but something in her eyes told me she was intrigued by the idea. "Okay," she replied.

My hand returned to her face, tracing a line with my thumb as her lips parted. "It has to be a yes."

I wasn't going to go further without it. I knew what it was like not to have a choice, to be forced into pain and pleasure. I didn't want to be that person for someone else. Even though a dark part of me fiercely craved being in control.

"Yes," she answered within her next breath.

"Maybe a yes, please?" I grinned, playing with her just a bit more.

She narrowed her eyes. "Don't push it, James."

I laughed. "If you decide you want me to stop, you just say the word."

She nodded, biting her lip.

Then I brought my hand back down, moving it slowly. Down, down, down. Until I realised, she wasn't wearing anything under this dress. When I connected with her warm, slick centre, I groaned, a deep vibrating noise that filled my chest. Her head rolled back, and she let out a rush of air as my fingers stroked her soaking-wet slit.

"Fuck. I think maybe you want me just as much as I want you," I said, slowly pushing two fingers inside of her as my palm pressed against her clit. Fuck she was so tight. All of the expletives and dirty words filled my mind as she moaned, arching her back in pleasure, clamping around my fingers.

I met her lips, hot and insistent as my fingers pulsed inside her. Filling her mouth with my tongue before taking her bottom lip in my teeth, biting her softly as I pulled back to see her face.

Damn, she was so beautiful.

"James," she breathed, scrunching her brows as my lips left

hers. "I... this... it's..." A look that closely resembled fear crossed her face.

"It's too much." I already knew what she was going to say, with her body tensing beneath me.

She nodded. "Yes."

I removed my hand, slowly dragging it back up her thigh. "I'm sorry. I didn't..." But I couldn't think of the words to say. I could only think about the wet liquid on my fingers that I desperately wanted to lick off. To taste her cum. How would she react if I did that?

She'd think you're disgusting, James.

My mind roared at me. Which I was.

"I just... I—" she started.

I smiled, running a finger on her chin. "That's alright, you don't need to explain it to me." I was already surprised she let me get that far. I never expected her to let me touch her. "Let's get you home."

I sat up and re-shifted myself in my trousers, sliding my hand down my length before starting the car. It took the entire drive back to her house for him to go down, and even then, I'd probably need to go do something about that after she left, or I'd go fucking insane.

It was about a thirty-minute drive back to her house, but neither of us said anything. Only heated silence as the moon shone above. For once, I would've loved it if she made conversation, if only to stop myself from thinking about touching her... about wanting to do so much more. But I kept my eyes on the road, not even daring a glance. Gripping the steering wheel firmly, like it was tethered to my wavering self-control.

We pulled up to her house, sitting there in the darkness. The stagger of her breathing was the only sound I could hear as my mind raced in a thousand different directions.

"Lizzie... I'm—" I started to apologise.

"Can you walk me to my door?" Her voice slightly shook as she desperately met my eyes.

"Of course," I smiled, feeling a bit relieved that she'd asked.

I stayed a step behind her with my hands in my pockets as we approached her door, unsure of what to say or do. And I always knew what to say, and definitely what to do.

She turned around a second later, with crimson in her cheeks. "I enjoyed watching you fight," she smiled.

I'm sure she did. I smiled with the corners of my mouth.

She started fiddling with her hands, biting her lip. "And I—I enjoyed everything else." And then she rose to her toes and kissed me before I could respond, lingering on my lips as the energy charged between us.

I grabbed her waist, pulling her to me once more, kissing her softly at first, then deeper as my hands trailed lower, intending to pull her to me as my tongue entered her mouth.

Everything inside me wanted more.

She laughed against my mouth and pulled away, looking at me with glassy eyes. "Goodnight, James," she smiled. "Thanks for the date."

"Anytime," I smiled back.

She walked inside, and I stood staring at the door as she closed it. Stuck in a daze.

Moments later, my gaze turned to the sky, taking in the stars and the full moon as I let out a breath in the cool night air. It was freezing out, but I only felt a radiating warmth as I touched my still-sensitive lips and smiled.

What the fuck was happening to me? And why was I already thinking about seeing her tomorrow? I was everything that was about to go wrong in her life, but I couldn't stop myself.

Chapter 15

ELISABETH

The Surprise

AFTER CLOSING THE DOOR behind me, I entered the drawing room where Margaret was still waiting. A glass of red wine in her hand, and surprisingly, a book in the other. I can't remember the last time I saw her read. Finton ran up to me, spreading wet kisses to my ankles. I pet him between his big ears, greeting him with soft words of endearment.

"How was it?" She smirked, sipping her wine.

"Did you wait up for me? And is that a book?"

She lowered her eyes. "I do know how to read."

I giggled and then slumped down on the couch beside her, unable to stop smiling. Feeling like a fever was burning inside of me, and it wasn't from the fireplace that was currently crackling with blooming orange flames. Kissing him was so much better than I could have ever imagined.

"Lizzie?" She tapped my leg, trying to get my attention.

"Hmm?" My eyes glazed up at hers.

She laughed. "So, he finally kissed you then," she said as more of a statement than a question.

"Yes," I bit my lip. *And much, much more.*

The best kiss of my life. And the best... well, I didn't really know the name for it. But that was also the best. I didn't know his hands could do such pleasurable things, but now I wouldn't be able to look at his strong hands and not think of them sliding underneath my dress.

She asked another question, realising I once again drifted away in my thoughts. "Where did he take you?"

I leaned forward and faced her. "Have you ever been to the pit?" I asked, saying it like it was the coolest thing I'd ever done. Which it probably was.

"What is that?" she asked.

Did I finally do something that Margaret hasn't? I felt pretty proud of myself at that moment. "It's a fighting pit. Like boxing. But no gloves."

Her eyes widened, seemingly surprised. I drifted in thought for a moment, feeling heat build in my core.

"James is involved in it. He's quite incredible in the ring," I managed after a few moments. Very, very good with his hands. I would never be able to stop picturing the sight of him in that ring, or the sight of him on top of me as he pinned me to the seat of his car. Another rush of heat filled my cheeks at the memory.

She laughed. "Sounds like you had a good time."

I leaned back, settling into the couch. "I did." I paused. "Margaret? Can I ask you about something?"

She leaned closer, smiling with pure delight. "I have been waiting so long for this conversation. Tell me every dirty detail."

"What?" Did she think... "Oh no. Not *that*. It was technically our first date, Margaret," I slapped her arm.

"Wouldn't have stopped me," she muttered and then slumped her shoulders, looking displeased. "Fine. What boring conversation would you like to have?"

Christ, why was I even trying?

I sighed, taking a breath. "James... did something in the lavatory."

"You were in the lavatory with him?" she asked, perking up a bit.

"Only for a moment," I defended before she could get any ideas. "He... inhaled something and he... *changed*." I didn't even know how to explain what I witnessed.

Margaret, to my surprise, started laughing.

"How do you find this funny right now?" I narrowed my eyes at her.

"That is not surprising given what you've told me about him. Men in fighting pits, boxing or otherwise, tend to have similar addictions to cocaine," she admitted.

Cocaine? "Drugs?" I stared at her blankly, letting her words sink in.

Margaret smiled. "There are worse ones. It probably just gives him a boost for his fights," she waved her hand.

I nodded, trying to make it seem like I was fine with the whole thing, but I wasn't.

James was doing... cocaine?

"If you're that worried about it, you should ask him. It's not like he's hiding it from you," she added.

Well, that was true. He did admit to me that it helps him, whatever that means. But I wondered how Margaret knew so much about it. "Have you ever... done that kind of thing before?"

"I'm not one for restraint," she grinned.

And that was when I decided that I didn't want to know anymore. I rose from the couch. "I'm going to bed. Has Father come home yet?"

"Yes. I tucked him in and everything. With Pearl's help, of course," she smiled, taking another sip from her glass.

A wall of warmth filled me, even more than what was already swirling around inside of me. "You did?"

"I am capable of such things," she glowered at me like she'd been doing it for the past few years. I can count on one hand the number of times that she has been involved in taking care of our father or anyone besides herself. And even then.

"Margaret, that's—I'm..." There were so many things I wanted to say, but none of those words came to the surface.

"Stop now, before you rupture something."

"Thank you," I managed with a smile.

She turned her gaze back to the fireplace, sipping her wine. "But tomorrow I plan on going back to my usual self," she grinned with the corner of her mouth.

I snorted. "I wouldn't expect anything else."

When I returned to my room, I ran myself a cold bath. Almost wishing I had never asked about what I witnessed in the lavatory. But at least this was something he wasn't hiding from me, although maybe he should have because now all I could do was worry about it and worry about him.

It was a chilly morning on the first day of October. The cold air was refreshing as I drifted off in thought on the back patio with a cup of tea in my hand, wafting steam in my face. Last night's dreams were so good that I had completely forgotten about last night's worries. The only worry that consumed me was that I had no idea when I was seeing him again, which I realised before I fell asleep last night that I should have asked. And then I spent the entire night stressing out about it, practically driving myself crazy because I needed to see him again.

Today. This morning. Now.

It was all I could think about.

His lips on mine.

And his hands...

"Good morning, darling. I have some friends here that I'd like you to meet," my father said, suddenly beside me with a wide grin on his face.

"Father," I brushed a lock of hair behind my ear, shuffling in my seat. "Aren't you supposed to be at work?" Did he forget? Did Pearl forget to wake him? Was he having another episode?

He chuckled softly. "I took the day off. Come to the drawing room with me," he held out his arm.

"You, what?" Father didn't just take days off. Not that he couldn't, but working gave him something to do. And from our past conversations, he told me that he quite enjoyed his job as a factory manager.

"It'll all make sense in a moment," he gestured to his arm again, and this time I took it.

But when we approached the drawing room, three men about my age were standing there. Finton was at Margaret's feet while she was on the couch, smiling so deviously that it suddenly connected to me why they were here.

Father was setting me up on a date.

I started to protest, but then he began introducing me. The tall one with brown hair was Andrew, wearing a tweed navy blue suit and matching trousers. John wore leather suspenders and a black bow tie, and the last one wearing a simple brown vest and suspenders was Henry. They all bowed and greeted me.

"Hi," I said shyly, feeling all sorts of embarrassment. "Father," I whispered. "What's all this about?" I was really hoping I was wrong about why they were here.

"These are all of the men from work I was telling you about." —*oh, no*—"They are very eager to get to know you. Well, I'll leave you to get acquainted." He stood there for a moment, looking like he felt just as awkward as me. "Perhaps some tea?"

And then he was gone.

I could hear Margaret's faint chuckle from where I was standing under the archway. Still uncommitted to entering the room.

"Thank you for coming," I clasped my hands in front of me,

holding in my nerves. "I uhh—I'm not quite sure what my father has said, but this is very unexpected."

"It's a pleasure to meet you," Andrew smiled, taking a step towards me. "I've heard so much about you."

"I have too," said John, straightening his bow tie.

"Me also. He loves talking about you," Henry said, then he glanced at Margaret. "And you, too."

My eyes darted at all three of them, deciding where to start, deciding the politest way to ask them to leave. Except I think it would hurt my father's feelings.

"Perhaps you should talk to them one at a time," Margaret suggested softly, picking at her nails like she had nowhere else to be.

"Yes, that's—that would be great." I smiled.

"I'll go first," Andrew said, standing forward.

"Right," Henry said. "We'll go see if your father needs any help." I wasn't sure where his accent was from, but he sounded different from the rest.

They left the room, leaving just me, Andrew, and Margaret. I wish she would leave, too. But she looked like she was having the time of her life as she picked up her book and pretended to read.

"Would you like to sit down?" Andrew offered.

"Yes. That would be good." I sat on the purple couch next to Margaret, crossing a leg over my knee, fixing my lavender dress with a beaded top and short, sheer sleeves to flow around me. He sat across from me in a matching chair. Finton plopped on my foot, providing comfort in this awkward situation. I patted him on the head.

"You seem like you had no idea this was happening this morning?" Andrew said with a grin. His voice was musical, proper, and very English. Did he grow up here, or somewhere more refined?

"It was a complete surprise." An unwanted surprise, but I would tell my father later about how much I did not want this, in the most polite way possible. They were all fairly attractive, which was nice of him, but I already had my mind on someone else.

He smiled. "Excuse me to be so blunt, but you are much prettier than he described." His eyes seemed to glisten in the soft morning light streaming through the windows as he flicked his gaze up and down.

"Oh?" I blushed. I did not expect that. "How did he describe me?"

"Well, of course, he said you are beautiful. He showed me a picture of your mother. Told me that you looked just like her, which you do." My heart felt warm. "But I'm afraid you're much more. In a way, I can't describe it with so few words."

"Thank you." Alright, he was charming and handsome in a way that I might have fallen for him had I met him first, if not for the man currently wedging himself into my foolish heart.

"I have been looking forward to meeting you since then," he smiled.

Margaret chuckled, turning a page in her book.

I rolled my shoulders, ignoring her. "What do you do at the factory?" I asked him.

He leaned back in the chair, grinning widely. "I've actually just got a new job at the bank. I start next week. Your father helped get my foot in the door. I owe him a great deal for his kindness."

"That sounds—" And then a knock at the door startled me as Finton barked. The high pitch of his voice echoed down the halls, followed by another knock.

"Would you like me to get that for you?" Andrew asked.

"That's fine. It's probably just the postman." I stood up, swatting Finton away, but he insisted on following me. "I'll be right back." I glanced a look at Margaret. "Unless you want to make yourself useful?"

She waved her hand, not looking up from her book. "Been there. Done that. Besides, I'm quite entertained at the moment," she curved her rouged lips in Andrew's direction.

Great. "Please, behave yourself."

She laughed, snorting a bit through her nose.

But when I opened the door, it wasn't the postman, but James. Staring back at me with bright green eyes and a wicked grin. Wearing his tight-fitted black vest with his white sleeves rolled up and shiny gold bands around his elbows. Looking better than I remembered him. It felt like my knees were going to collapse.

Chapter 16

ELISABETH
Tea & Jealousy

"J AMES," I BREATHED. "WHAT are you—" But before I could finish, his lips were crushing mine as the door swung wide and my back met the wall. One hand wrapped around my waist, and the other went to my face as he devoured me right there in the hallway.

I lost myself in his all-consuming kiss, feeling heat all the way to my core, but then I remembered we were not alone.

"James—" I pulled back, meeting his hungry eyes with my hands still on his chest. "I have company."

"Is there anyone in your room?" he asked.

"No. They're—"

"Then let's go there," he grinned, as something sparkled behind his green eyes.

He was absolutely predictable and infuriating, and I should have known he would say something like that. But then I was pulled under his spell by the softness of his lips, perfectly entranced by him and his arms around me.

James suddenly broke the kiss, bending down to Finton, who was sniffing his leg. "Who's this?" I had never heard his voice so soft and so sweet.

"That's Finton Montgomery."

He began speaking inaudible words of affection as he massaged his big ears and kissed him on the nose. It felt like I slipped into an alternate reality because this was not the 'James' I had come to know. "He's cute," he said, standing up to face me. "Elisabeth Montgomery," he added with a grin. And that soft side of him was gone, replaced by the one that set me on fire.

It was strange for him not to call me Lizzie or the god-awful *sweetheart*, but something tingled along my spine when he said my full name.

I crossed my arms over my chest, pursing my lips. "How long have you been waiting to say that?"

He laughed and pulled me back into him, trailing kisses from my lips to my neck. For a moment, it was him and I. Nothing else mattered. Just his soft lips on my neck and his hands on my lower back, while his tongue did things that drove me crazy.

"Elisabeth, are you alright?" Andrew stepped into the hallway. His face contorted to something frigid when he saw James's hold on me. "Is that man hurting you?"

"Who the fuck is this guy?" James spat.

"James," I scolded, gently tapping his chest and stepping out of his embrace. "This is Andrew. Andrew, this is my—" Boyfriend, lover, infuriating crush? I had no idea what he was or wanted to be. "Friend. James," I decided on.

James darkly laughed and turned to me, seeming displeased. "Friend?" He raised a dark brow.

"This is not the time," I whispered to him.

And of course, then John and Henry walked down the hall carrying a tray of tea and biscuits. Smiling and waving at me as they disappeared back into the drawing room.

"How many men do you have here right now?" James scowled at me with an edge to his voice. Was he jealous?

I cleared my throat, staring at the floor. "Three. Four, including you." This conversation did not make me come off well.

"Four?" His eyes narrowed to slits.

"Andrew, can you give me a moment? I'll meet you in the drawing room," I smiled politely in his direction.

"Are you sure you don't want me to remove him?" Andrew asked.

"Just fucking try," James scoffed, clenching his fists as he took a step towards him.

"Language," I scolded as I placed my hand on his chest and pushed him back, stepping in between them. "I'll be right there, Andrew." I faked another smile at Andrew, begging him with my eyes to walk away. I didn't know how much more James was going to take before his fist connected with Andrew's face.

Andrew nodded. "Just call out to me if you need me." He glared at James, straightening his waistcoat as he stormed off.

James snorted, saying something in a language I didn't understand. Possibly Gaelic. "If he thinks he can challenge me, he's sorely mistaken."

"My father wants me to date," I said simply, pulling back his focus, but his stare told me that I needed to say more. "He invited all of these men here. For me. I didn't even know they were coming until—well, like five minutes ago."

He annoyingly looked at me. "Friends?"

I crossed my arms over my chest. "Well, how would you describe us?" Because clearly, I couldn't.

"Do your friends usually stick their tongues in your mouth? Because if so, I have the wrong 'friends' in my life."

Heat crept up my neck, burning my cheeks. "Well, no but—"

He took a step towards me, causing me to drop my arms as he pushed me against the floral-patterned wall. "Do you need me to tell all of those guys that you're mine?" His voice fell deep into his chest as his warm breath pulsated between us. "Because all you have to do is ask."

Radiating warmth filled everywhere at his words, at the

thought of being *his*. But all I could do was let the rush fill my cheeks as I stared at his mouth, dazed by everything that was him.

"In fact, I think I fucking need to." And then he grabbed my hand and pulled me into the drawing room. But before we reached the archway, we ran into my father. Because of course.

"Lizzie, who's—" He adjusted his glasses on the bridge of his nose and cocked his head to the side. "Sorry, I don't remember you."

"I'm James," he extended his hand. "I'm dating your daughter."

My heart collapsed on itself at his words, while I choked on my own saliva.

"Oh?" My father's eyes flew wide, and then he smiled. "Well, James. You can call me Frank. It's a pleasure to meet you." Then he turned to me, eyeing me underneath his thick-rimmed glasses.

"I umm—just haven't had a chance to tell you," I mumbled. I did have the time. I just didn't want to ruin Father's tea party after all the trouble he went through in planning it.

"I see," Father replied. "Well, come join us for tea. This should be an interesting story, I'm sure." And then he walked into the drawing room.

But I did not want James to join us for tea.

"James, perhaps you shouldn't—" And then he pulled me into the drawing room with a devilish grin on his face.

Damn him.

James sat next to me on the couch with his arm around me and a firm grip on my left hip. Margaret put her book down and was now brimming like a schoolgirl on the other side of the couch. Andrew and Henry sat in the matching chairs. Beside it, John stood by the fireplace next to my father. And Finton was, of course, currently propped on James's foot, already betraying his family.

I couldn't blame him.

It was the most awkward and uncomfortable afternoon tea that I'd ever had.

James kept his gaze on Andrew, looking at him with a rigid expression and Andrew stared right back, not giving an inch. He was brave, I'd give him that. Winning a fight with James was futile. I'd seen how hard he could hit a man. If James wanted to, Andrew would be on the floor in two seconds, and then he'd think twice before staring him down. But the last thing we needed was an unnecessary brawl to break out in our drawing room.

My legs started to shake, feeling more nervous as each second passed. James placed his hand on my knee, squeezing it. I know he was trying to comfort me, but he needed to stop putting his hands on me in front of the entire room. Thankfully, Pearl came in a moment later and placed an antique silver box full of cigars on the wooden coffee table, breaking our awkward silence.

"Please, help yourselves," Father smiled, grabbing a cigar and placing it in his mouth before he sat on the piano bench.

All of the men took one, thanked him and lit up. I almost debated on taking one myself, just to calm my nerves.

"Sláinte," James said.

While James released his hold, I took this moment to pour myself a drink from the bar cart across the room. Desperately filling the glass and drinking it down before pouring another.

Thank goodness for alcohol.

"That's Gaelic for health, yes?" Father asked.

"Yes, sir," James said, lighting his cigar with an ornate silver lighter he pulled out of his vest pocket.

"Fascinating language," my father puffed out smoke.

"Lizzie, be a dear and pour me one," Margaret spoke in a saccharine tone.

I glared at her and then poured her a glass, shaking my head.

After handing Margaret a glass of wine, I returned to James and sat, and his hands went right back to my hip. I'd never seen him act so possessive. Well, since he pulled me away from Freddie at the bar. Come to think of it, perhaps this was just a part of his personality. Woven into the very fabric of him. I couldn't deny the thrill it sent through me, but perhaps it should have been a warning sign of some other deeper issue.

"So, James. Where'd you two meet?" Father asked.

It felt like cotton was lodged in my throat.

"Wait a minute, are you James MacGuire?" Henry asked.

James puffed out smoke, smiling.

How did he make smoking look so good?

"Christ. You're a legend in the pit," Henry said.

John's eyes lit up, seeming to know who he was, too. Andrew was still staring at him through narrowed eyes.

"I've seen him knock someone out in a single hit in less than ten seconds," Henry mused.

Andrew stopped staring at him as his gaze drifted to the wooden floor. It seemed that common sense finally hit him before James could.

"I saw you fight years ago before the war. It's good to have you back in Birmingham," Henry finished with a wide grin.

James nodded, saying nothing in reply.

I wondered if this was normal for him, for people to recognise him and stare at him with stars in their eyes. He didn't seem bothered or that he particularly cared about it all. Was he trying to be humble? It seemed so unlike the man who decided that a first date in the pit was a good idea. All so he could show off his talent and his impressive form... a sight I would never be able to forget.

For the next hour, Henry and John rattled off questions for James and educated my father in the sport of bare-knuckle fighting. By the end, my father was on the edge of his seat and excited to attend tonight's fight. The Friday night fights were bigger and better. James would have to survive seven rounds. I didn't like the use of the word *survive* but when I flinched, James squeezed my hip and smiled at me under his long eyelashes, comforting my nerves.

His hand stayed steady on my hip for the rest of the morning, tracing circles with his forefinger. Did he realise he was doing that?

Their conversations then shifted to the war. The regiments they served in, and how long they served, but I had stopped listening after my fourth glass of wine. All I could hear was buzzing in my ears, and my focus was on his hand—his very capable hand on me as warmth rushed to my cheeks. My breath staggered, and my pulse began to quicken faster and faster with each minute.

Pretty sure the wine was finally hitting me. I had never drunk so much in my life.

Henry wanted his autograph before they left. Father handed him a fountain pen, and James signed the top side of his hand. Henry was most likely going to get it tattooed on his skin later. John opted for a signed piece of paper, and Andrew left with a sheepish smile on his face.

"Well, that was interesting," Margaret murmured beside me while Father and James were at the door saying their goodbyes.

How they all walked away as friends is beyond me. Perhaps besides Andrew. I still think James was considering punching him in the face.

"I'll say," I finished my last sip of wine and set the glass on the wooden coffee table. "I'm surprised you didn't try to flirt with any of them. That's the longest I've ever seen you be quiet."

And thank Christ she was quiet. If Margaret had spoken her mind in her usual manner, things would have gone differently, as she loved to push the boundaries.

"I think they would rather date your boyfriend," she teased.

I blushed at the word *boyfriend*.

James stepped into the drawing room. "Lizzie." I jumped up at the sound of my name. "Come for a walk with me," he smiled.

Margaret scoffed. "Are you commanding, or asking her?"

I shot her a look.

"Whichever she prefers," he smirked.

Sadly, I preferred the command. I took one last breath and one last calming moment before I followed him out the door. Full of questions and burning desire.

I should not have drunk so much wine.

Chapter 17

JAMES

Friends

MANY TIMES, I THOUGHT about running. Punching that bastard Andrew for his lingering 'fuck me' eyes and then running away because that was too much. I didn't even know how I ended up at her door this morning. I woke up before the sun and decided to drive around. But the only thing I could think about was kissing her again and doing far, far more than that.

I planned to ask her on another date, but then she answered the door, and my need to kiss her won over my better intentions.

"I didn't know you were so popular," she said after some time as we walked down the street towards the city.

The afternoon sun was warm, glistening off her delicate lavender dress and rouged, heated skin. She'd drunk a lot of wine this afternoon, and I was very aware of her staggered breathing when I caressed my fingers on her hip. She needed this walk if only to clear her mind and ease the flow of alcohol in her veins.

I lit up a cigarette and kept walking. "None of those men were there for me," I blew out smoke.

"Well, you handled yourself better than I expected. And I think they would have come. Just for you," she teased, bumping her shoulder into mine.

I stopped, pulling the cigarette out of my mouth. "Let's make one thing clear, sweetheart. I am not your friend. Nor do I ever want to be." I put my hand on her chin, angling her face so her eyes met mine. "And those other guys. They also did not want to be your *friend*."

She took a sharp breath. "Sweetheart. Lizzie. What do you really want to be?" she challenged. "Because I don't think you know yourself."

Maybe not, but one thing I knew for sure. I pulled her closer. "I don't want to be your friend, Lizzie." My eyes drifted to her mouth. "And the only man I want in your house besides your father is me."

A smile curved on her pink lips. "You were jealous."

I pulled back, put the cigarette back in my mouth and continued walking down the street. But she wasn't following. I turned around, finding her in the same spot with her arms across her chest and a grin on her face.

"You know," she toyed with a strand of her red hair, wrapping it around her finger. "Andrew said some really nice things."

"Excuse me?" Was she trying to get a rise out of me?

"He told me that I was beautiful in a way that he couldn't describe with words." She was definitely toying with me. I was the hair wrapped around her finger, and she fucking knew it.

I laughed. "I think that wine has gone to your head." And that tweed-suit cunt probably didn't know many words.

She continued to stare at me with crossed arms. "Are you saying you disagree?" Her eyebrows furrowed with worry, as her chest heaved.

"I don't need words to make you feel beautiful, sweetheart. You already know you are."

"But. Do *you* think so?" she pushed.

I think she genuinely thought that I didn't, which was fucking crazy. So, I decided to cave and answer honestly. "Yes, I do," I said with a sigh.

Her posture changed as she relaxed a bit, dropping the hair from her fingers. "Well, it wouldn't hurt to say that every now and then," she shrugged a shoulder.

Words were pointless. I was going to show her.

I threw my cigarette on the ground and closed the distance between us, placing my hand firmly on her hip, while the other drew a line down her arm. Her breathing slowed to ragged breaths as her cheeks flushed crimson.

"Now, how does this make you feel?" I moved my hand slowly from her hip to her back, crushing her to me. My other hand dragged along her body to the curve of her breasts. "Or this?" I squeezed. "Surely this tells you how beautiful I find you."

"You do realise we are on the sidewalk," her chest heaved as she glanced around. "And people are watching us."

I grinned. "Good." I didn't mind an audience.

"James," she placed her hand on my chest and licked her lips. "We can't do this here." I went to tell her where we could do this as a smirk formed, but she put a finger to my mouth, stopping me. "And no. My father and sister are home." She already knew what I was going to say. "What about yours?"

I wasn't sure if I was breathing. "Mine?" Did I hear her correctly?

She nodded.

"You want to go... to my house?" A slow smile crept on my face as she nodded once more. There was no going back now. I hoped she realised that.

"To talk," she reiterated. "Since clearly you can't do that without causing some kind of scandal in the street."

I took that as a yes and grabbed her hand, walking her back to my car as a rush of adrenaline sent my heart racing.

Twenty-five minutes later, she sat on the plush green velvet couch in my drawing room, running her hand along the fabric. The light in the room was dim, faintly lit by a few lamps. The thick velvet drapes were closed, just the way I liked it—dark and moody. And the fireplace was unlit, but there were other fires that I intended to light.

I walked over to the drink cart and poured myself a glass of whiskey. The thought of offering her a glass crossed my mind, but I think she had enough alcohol flowing through her body as it was.

"This place is... not what I expected." She pulled her legs onto the couch, looking more comfortable than I would've thought.

I expected her to change her mind about halfway here, but now here she was. And I was happily surprised.

"Oh?" I sat next to her, holding my glass.

"I didn't expect it to be so lavish and... decorative." She glanced around the room, taking in the paintings on the walls and the bookshelves that towered in the corner.

Cameron did a great job of making this place look like we were normal people with good taste. You wouldn't even know that we had lived a life of crime, which was exactly the point. A fresh start.

"This is the first home I've ever had." I poured back the whiskey and set it on the glass table. The burn in my throat was exactly what I needed after that stressful morning. I was used to being put on display, but that sort of *display* was different.

Uncharted territory that I never wanted to do again.

She sat silently for a moment. "Where did you sleep before?"

"In pubs or Inns. Sometimes the car." And other women's beds, but I didn't think she'd want to hear that. Or the fact that I slept on the streets when I was nine years old.

"Why?" she asked.

"I didn't know any different, and buying a house meant I had to stay still." I paused, glancing at the window across the room, before turning my gaze to my hands. "After the war, that was the last thing I wanted to do."

"The war," she breathed. "I'm sorry... I sort of drifted off at that particular conversation this morning..." her voice trailed off.

Yes, she did. I knowingly smiled that it was because of me and the effect I had on her. And perhaps the wine, but mostly me.

"How old were you?" she asked.

I leaned back, resting my back against a pillow. "Eighteen at the start."

"So that makes you twenty-six or twenty-seven—"

"Twenty-seven next month."

She put her soft hand in mine, and her face contorted into something grief-stricken.

"Let's not talk about our sad stories, Lizzie," I brushed her hand. Talking about my past was not why she was here, and I think we both knew it. Besides, I was not ready to continue this conversation. Nor did I ever want to talk about my past with her. My hand drifted slowly to the warmth between her thighs.

But then she rose from the couch, heading to the fireplace.

"Wait, is that you?" She grabbed a framed photo from the mantle.

I sighed and made my way towards her. "Yes," I murmured, glancing at the picture of a younger version of me in a military uniform.

"You look so..." Her voice trailed off.

"Young?"

"Handsome in a uniform," she smiled, setting the picture back on the mantle. I smiled at her response. "Is that Cameron?" she pointed at the picture beside mine.

"Yes. But if you're about to say that he looks handsome too, we're about to have our first real fight," I said in a teasing manner, but I was more than serious. In all honesty, Cameron was a better match for her, though I'd never admit it out loud.

She laughed. "James... about last night. I can't stop thinking about it and—"

A surge went straight to my cock. "Then let's do something

about it," I taunted, interrupting her as I placed my hands on her waist.

She blushed and grabbed my hand, stopping my move as she retreated a step. "No. Not that. I mean, yes, that too." She flushed a brighter shade of red as she moved back to the couch. "I can't stop thinking about the cocaine. The drugs that you did in the lavatory."

Oh fuck. "What about it?" I sat next to her.

I didn't even know that she knew the name for it.

"My sister made it seem like it was a normal thing for you to do, but I just... is it safe?" Was she worried about me?

I didn't feel like going into a long discussion about cocaine with her, so I smiled and took her hand. "It's safe. And it's like I said before. It helps me." Thank fuck Margaret was on my side.

"Right," she murmured. "I'm sorry," she shook her head.

"Why are you apologising to me?"

"For being so naive," she admitted, as heat began to permanently set in her cheeks. "For asking."

Her naivety was new and exciting for me, and I was very happy to be the one to corrupt her. "That's probably what I like most about you." That and all of her physical attributes that I wanted to explore and claim as mine.

"That's probably the nicest thing you've ever said to me," she smiled, placing her hand on my forearm, slowly drifting her fingers along my skin. "What else do you like about me?"

"I like it when you touch me," my voice reverberated in my chest.

She bit her bottom lip at my response, staring at her hand on my forearm. "And... do you live alone?"

My heart started to race as blood rushed to my cock. "Cameron is out at the moment. And our maid is good at staying out of the way."

"Good," she swallowed. I leaned in closer to kiss her, like I'd been dying to do since we sat on this couch, but she placed her hand on my chest. "Because there are many things I need to know. And many more things I'd still like to discuss, James."

I sighed and paused, running a frustrated hand through my hair. But when she curved her lips into a wicked smile and bit her bottom lip once more, I cut the last tether to my self-control.

"We're done talking."

And then I met her mouth. My tongue collided with hers as I leaned her back on the couch, positioning myself on top of her. My hand glided down her body from her breasts to her perfect ass as I lifted her into my throbbing cock, awakening the devil inside of me. I didn't think it was possible to want someone so much.

Chapter 18

ELISABETH

Taste

THERE WAS NOTHING I wished to discuss. At least not at this particular moment in time. I just wanted to see what he'd do if I pushed him a little bit more. All I had been thinking about for the past two hours was this exact position and how I could get him somewhere alone. He was the only cure for this fever inside of me, and I felt as if I might incinerate if he didn't finish what he started. Or I'd burn from the inside out.

It was good that he liked it when I touched him because that's all I wanted to do.

I opened my legs wider, letting him push into me, and he groaned from the back of his throat as he kissed me harder. His hand was firm on my rear, but I ached for him to go lower. I ground my hips into him, and he laughed, soft laughter against my mouth.

"You don't seem like you want to talk, Lizzie." His mouth trailed down my jaw to my throat where he started to suck as his hand tightened on my hip holding me down.

And then he bit me.

Not hard in a painful way—it was soft and claiming.

The sensation sent something hot to my core as he bit once more, harder this time.

"James," I moaned as if in question, feeling his laughter reverberate in my throat as I gripped his shoulders.

"What do you want, sweetheart?" He said sweetly as he pulled back to meet my eyes.

I bit my lip. "I want you to touch me." Saying it out loud was so new and so exciting. A thrill rushed through my veins.

He smiled. "I'd like to use my tongue."

"What?" I breathed.

"My tongue," he smiled. "Will you let me?"

His tongue? Well, it didn't sound awful, just surprising and very intriguing. Words I didn't expect him to say.

I nodded, and he rose from the couch.

I couldn't help but stare at the generous bulge in his pants as he extended his hand for mine, and then lifted me off the ground, carrying me across the room. The strength of him continued to impress and excite me.

He set me down on a dresser or a desk. I wasn't even sure, nor did I care, as my heart raced in my chest.

"Spread your legs apart." I did as he said. "Wider," he smiled.

I spread them wider as his hands went to my thighs, taking his time before he went to his knees. And damn, I almost preferred him on his knees in front of me over being in the ring. Shirtless and sweaty on his knees, a vision I would love to see.

His hands slid under my hips, pulling me towards him and pulling me out of my fantasies. A small whimper escaped my mouth as I gripped his shoulders.

"Good girl." He watched his hand as it slid up my thigh and under my lavender dress. "Am I the first guy to do this to you?" He asked, his eyes a deeper shade of green, as he knelt before me.

I wasn't even quite sure what this was yet, but everything about this and us was new. "Yes," I said in barely a whisper.

"Good," he smiled, seeming very pleased with my response. He moved his hand closer, and a rush of adrenaline flowed through me. "And you want me to put my mouth on you?"

A shattered breath rolled through me. "Yes," I managed as I gripped him harder. "Yes," I said again as his hand rested between my thighs, moving in slow circles at the edge of where I needed him to touch. "Please, James," I breathed, feeling like I was going to fall apart if he didn't keep going.

"Are you sure this isn't the wine talking?"

Only slightly. "James," I groaned his name in anticipation, feeling slick between my thighs. "Please."

"I like you begging," he grinned, slowing his touch just enough to push me off the edge.

"James." I was going to slap him. I was going to physically slap him if he continued to tease me.

But then he laughed and lifted my lavender dress, wrapping his hands around my rear as he pulled me to his mouth.

All my anger and frustration dissipated as a screaming gasp escaped my mouth, and his tongue licked up my centre. The flat of his tongue dragged from the bottom to the top, and then it dipped inside of me. I ran my hands through his hair as he pulled my legs over his shoulders, giving him deeper access.

I felt myself coming undone already.

He was all I could see and all I could feel as his tongue moved in a slow and circular rhythm. But I needed him deeper. My legs squeezed him harder as I gripped the corner of the furniture that I was propped up on.

"Fuck, Lizzie," he groaned into my centre, and I felt myself leaking into his mouth. "You taste so fucking good." His words vibrated against me, and then his hand moved to my bundle of nerves. I bit my lip so hard I thought it might bleed.

This was like nothing I had ever felt before.

This hot and achy feeling only seemed to burn hotter with each lap and stroke of his tongue and every praise he managed to get out. But when he started to suck, I felt myself going over the edge.

I dug my nails into his shoulders and cried out his name, feeling like I was about to combust as his tongue dipped even deeper and his hand massaged my centre in sweet, relentless strokes. Every filthy thing he'd ever said roared in my mind.

"Not yet," he groaned into me. "Give me more."

But I didn't know how to give him more.

My back arched, and I felt my vision going dark.

I started to buck, grinding my hips into his mouth. Again, and again and again. This. Us. I was going to combust with one more stroke of his tongue.

"Such a good fucking, girl," he growled, which sent me soaring.

And that was the moment I felt myself shatter, and everything went dark as my head fell back against the wall. All I could hear was his cries of *you taste so fucking good* as he kept sucking and swallowing all that I gave him.

After coming down from ecstasy, the growing need in me started to rise again. A whole new world of pleasure opened up, and I wanted more.

But then I heard the door open and close.

James stopped, wiped his face and stood, blocking me as Cameron walked into the room. I pulled my dress down, trying to catch my breath.

"Fuck, I'm sorry," Cameron covered his eyes and turned around. "I didn't realise—"

"Cameron. Come back later," James barked.

"I wish I could, brother. We have a meeting."

"It can wait ten minutes. Or twenty." James smiled at me.

I stifled a giggle, biting my bottom lip.

"No, it can't." Cameron turned around to face us. "We have to go now." A hint of red tinged his cheeks as he noticed my presence.

"Oh. Nice to see you again, Lizzie." He awkwardly forced a wave that was almost like a salute.

I half-smiled at him. Mortified at the whole situation.

"I'll meet you in the car," Cameron said, and then he left.

James cursed under his breath. "I'm so sorry."

"What's the meeting for?" I stood from the dresser/desk, my heart still pounding.

"Probably for the fight tonight." He ran a hand through his hair, fixing what I did just moments ago.

I didn't even realise, but somehow my hand found his strong forearm. "So, I'll see you then?" I stroked his arm, peering up at him under hooded eyes.

"Fucking better," he snorted.

I leaned up to kiss him, and he pulled me in as the car horn sounded. Stopping the kiss.

He sighed, taking my hand as we headed out the door. I insisted on walking home, but James simply wouldn't allow it. So, I settled for the most awkward car ride of my life as Cameron sat quietly in the back seat.

Chapter 19

JAMES
The Deal

THE SUN WAS LOW in the grey sky, drifting in and out behind the brick buildings as I drove us to the warehouse with a cigarette in my mouth. A storm was brewing from the west, forming dark clouds behind us.

Cameron cleared his throat, finally deciding to speak.

"Don't. Fucking. Say. Anything." I emphasised every word, pulling my flat cap lower.

He laughed, stretching out his arms. "Just seems like you really like this girl. I mean, that's the second time I've seen you with her. That must be some kind of record for you," he smirked.

I rolled my eyes, blowing out smoke as I kept my eyes on the road. "What's this meeting for?"

"You like her. More than the others," he pushed, ignoring my change in conversation.

"Of course I like her," I muttered. I was not about to confess the real feelings I had for Lizzie to Cameron. Feelings that I was happy to keep buried inside me for as long as I lived. So, I played the card of deflection. "And I've been with plenty of girls more than once. I like her as much as them."

"Sure," he laughed. "Keep telling yourself that."

I sure fucking would keep telling myself that. I couldn't even think of the alternative. It was too terrifying. "What's the meeting for?" I asked again, layering my vexation on thick.

He scratched his moustache. "I ran into one of Aidan's boys in the street. They wanted to chat."

"About?"

"I don't fucking know. They didn't give me a list." He paused, glancing out the window. "I think something big is happening tonight. An investor, perhaps. Unless he's unhappy about something."

Aidan was always unhappy about something.

Black clouds ebbed and flowed around us as I blew out another cloud of thick smoke. Centring my thoughts.

"Do you have your gun?" I asked.

He pulled back his coat, revealing his holster.

I nodded.

"Is she coming to the fight tonight?"

I paused, popping my jaw. "Yes."

"Commitment," he teased. "She's a good look for you, James."

"Fuck off," I flicked him off.

Cam laughed.

When we pulled up to the warehouse, four shiny black cars were sitting outside, with seven men wearing flat caps standing nearby. I slung on my shoulder holster, covering it with my coat before I stepped out. Thunder rumbled in the distance as I tapped the knife that I always carried in my pocket, readying myself for anything.

Aidan's men guided us into a back room full of metal cabinets and boxes, sitting us down in wooden chairs behind a desk. Leaving us alone.

We sat there for a moment with only the sound of rain pouring outside, and Cameron's knee shaking on the concrete. I'd been in similar situations.

Intimidation. Isolation. Induced anxiety.

Gang tactics that worked on most, but not on me. I pulled out my knife and stabbed the table, making a statement. A custom-designed knife that was made for members of the gang with a black handle and a razor-sharp edge.

"James. That's not going to help us," Cam muttered. "You're just going to piss them off."

"Good." I was pissed off.

A minute later, Harry walked in with two heavyweight guys on either side, and I sighed in relief. It was just fucking Red Harry. He sat at the desk, placed his revolver on the edge and clasped his tattooed hands, staring at us intently under his flat cap. His shirt was open at the top, revealing the swirling black ink of his knife tattoo over his heart.

"Was that really necessary?" Harry gestured to my knife.

"Just sending a message," I smiled. I could tell by his frown that he understood my sarcasm. "Where's Aidan?" I asked.

His gaze stayed on my knife. The silver glistened in the warm light of the room. "He's busy. Out of town. Official gang business," he gruffed. "He thought you'd be more inclined to talk to someone you knew."

I let out a mirthless laugh, reaching into my pocket. Harry tensed, as did the boys behind him, reaching for their guns. "Fucking relax." I pulled out a cigarette, placing it in the corner of my mouth as I glanced at the men standing at the doorway. "Are these men here to scare us?" I lit it up. "Because I'm terrified," I grinned, blowing out a cloud of smoke.

Harry nodded to the men in the room, and they left. "It's honestly just for show."

That did not surprise me.

Harry leaned back and placed his long legs on the desk, making himself comfortable. His eyes were mostly hidden under his flat cap. "They're probably more afraid of you than you are of them."

They fucking should be. I took a drag. "So, what's this about? I've got better things to do." There were much better things I'd rather be doing than *talking*. His timing could not have been more inconvenient.

"Cameron, perhaps you could take a walk," Harry gestured for the door. "I need a moment with the boss." His eyes narrowed on me.

"Technically, I'm the boss—" Cam started.

"Cam," I muttered, keeping my eyes on Harry as I lowered my voice. "It's alright. Go and wait for me by the ring."

Cameron huffed and then stood, scraping his chair on the ground. Cursing and muttering under his breath as he left the room. Lightning struck outside, followed by gushing rain hitting the metal roof.

A few moments later, Harry relaxed and continued. "You've been fighting well. Better than Aidan thought you would," his voice was low and gruff.

"Aidan was never good at odds," I leaned back. "Now, like I said, I've got better things to do." Lizzie-things.

Harry leaned forward, resting his weathered, tattooed hands on the wooden desk. "There's an investor coming tonight. A very important one. He's—well, he's been a bit difficult to deal with," Harry scratched at his bristly scruff.

"Problems in paradise?" I teased.

"Aidan needs you to lose."

"What?" I snapped.

Harry leaned back and sighed. "You can win the first few rounds—"

"If he just wants me to get my ass kicked, surely there's a better way than losing the fucking fight?" *Fucking Aidan.*

"This investor," Harry continued. "This Mr. Coldwell has been accusing us of rigging the fights." I shook my head. I really didn't fucking care about their problems. "If you lose tonight, well, it will prove our innocence. And good faith will be restored. Everybody wins," he made a gesture with his hands.

Everybody wins except me.

And I did not like to lose.

His eyes fell to the desk. "I wish there was another way, kid."

"Don't call me that," I bit out. I was not about to take a walk down memory lane.

"Old habits," he shrugged.

I sat there for a moment, listening to the pouring rain outside as cars pulled up to the warehouse. Car lights flashed around the room as the ambience got darker and darker with the setting sun. Muffled voices of excited men and women grew more reverberant.

"If I do this. If I—" I gritted my teeth. "Lose. I earn nothing tonight, and a lot of people will lose their bets." Not to mention, I might walk away with a broken jaw. I leaned forward. "If I do this. Aidan's tax goes away, and all my earnings from the pit will belong to me."

Harry laughed. "He thought you'd say that." Then he sighed. "He's willing to go to thirty per cent."

"Then he can fucking deal with his own problems then." I stood up, pulling out my knife from the table.

I honestly did not care what Aidan wanted anymore. He could rot in hell. I wasn't going to be 'owned' by him anymore.

Harry stood up, following my pace, crossing his thick arms over his broad chest. "Alright. Twenty," he bargained.

I stopped and smiled, tucking my knife away. "Not this time, Harry." I moved around the chair and stepped forward, meeting his eyes under his flat cap. "Because you see, after tonight, I don't plan on losing. That's pretty good odds. Don't you think?"

Harry took a long breath. "He's not going to like hearing this, James."

"Good," I muttered, heading for the door. "I've got a fight to prepare for."

He put a hand up. "Wait." He glanced at the door and then back at me. "Your opponent tonight has a weak right shoulder. A few jabs there and—well, perhaps the damage in the end won't be so bad."

I scoffed. "Did Aidan tell you this?" Surely it was some kind of trick.

"No. I did." Something warm shone from behind his eyes. The friend I used to know was in there somewhere, a man just as lost as I was. He slapped my shoulder, "Good luck." And then he headed for the door.

"Why are you working for him?" I asked, staring at the crowd forming outside through the one window. Soaking wet from the storm as they bustled into the warehouse.

His eyes lowered to the floor. "The Black Knives are my home. Regardless of who's in charge," a muscle flickered in his jaw and then he left.

Harry's answer didn't surprise me. The Knives were the only home he'd ever known, but still, there was no way in hell I'd ever work for Aidan Murphy.

I headed for my usual lavatory and took out a vial of cocaine. Staring at it for the longest time before finally deciding to put it back in my pocket. If I had to lose this fight convincingly, not having any stimulants would make me look slow. Off my game. Which was how I was going to play this when angry crowds rushed me when I fell to the ground, feigning defeat.

Men and women patted me on the back as I ambled towards the ring with clenched teeth, cheering me on. Going absolutely wild.

It made my stomach sick.

"I'm betting it all on you tonight!"

"Knock him out, MacGuire!"

"Show this Londoner how we do things in Birmingham!"

Cameron made his way towards me, pushing through the crowd. "How'd the meeting go?" His brows rose in concern.

Before I could respond, I glimpsed *her*, waving at me from across the room. My heart stuttered in response, like the goddamn traitor it was with her. She wore a pink silk dress that clung to every delicious curve of her body with a fur shawl draped around her slender porcelain shoulders. Her sister and father were standing next to her, eyes glowing with excitement.

This was going to fucking suck.

"Well?" Cam said, bringing back my focus to him.

"He wants me to lose," I muttered under my breath.

"What?" Cam's dark brows formed a tight line. "What do you mean?"

But I already hopped in the ring.

With one last look at her, the bell chimed, sealing my fate. I was going to lose tonight, and it was going to hurt.

I fucking hated Birmingham.

Chapter 20

ELISABETH
Bruised

I HADN'T SEEN MY father or sister this happy in well—possibly ever. They cheered and hollered, immersing themselves in the atmosphere. Father even placed a considerable bet on James. But James didn't look like his usual self. He wasn't smiling and jumping around or looking like his muscles were going to jump out of his skin. He looked infuriated, like he was thinking of setting everyone on fire.

The first few fights were amazing. I thought maybe I'd just perceived him wrong. But before the bell chimed on his fourth fight, he looked straight at me with a tight smile and shook his head.

"Something's wrong," I grabbed Margaret's arm.

"What are you talking about?" she laughed. "He's astounding."

"Yes, obviously. But no. No, something's wrong." I didn't know how to explain what I felt. But something was terribly wrong.

And then he took a hard hit to his face.

Once. Twice. Three times.

Then James punched him back, nailing him hard in the shoulder. For a moment, I thought he would keep going, but he just stopped. Like he just decided to give up on the fight.

The next hit connected with James's spine, sending him thudding to the ground as he spat out blood. I expected him to rise and fight back, but he didn't get up. The room was ear-splitting, filled with screams and the voices of angry people. My heart thundered in my chest.

When the round ended, I darted for the ring, finding him sitting on the floor with a black eye and a cut across his eyebrow. Cameron stood beside him with a wet rag pressed against his head.

"James," I exclaimed before I dropped down in front of him, wiping blood off his lip.

He grabbed my hand, holding it firm. "It's alright. It's just a little blood," he smiled with blood in his teeth. Cameron muttered under his breath and handed James the rag. James held it to the right side of his face, placing his other hand on my chin. "You should go," he said.

"When is the next round?" Surely, I had more time with him before he needed to jump back into the ring.

"I mean, leave the pit. You should go home."

"What? No—" Why would he say that?

"He's right," Cameron interjected. "It's not going to be pretty." He let out a frustrated sigh and then sauntered away.

"What's he talking about?" I asked.

James rolled his tongue, which drove me insane. "Please, Lizzie. Just go home. This is not something I want you to see."

I stared into his tired eyes, admiring the flecks of brown in the green. "You're losing on purpose."

He smiled, dragging a finger down my jaw. "You're such a smart girl."

"But that doesn't make sense..." I couldn't even focus on the slow drag of his finger. I needed to know why he was losing.

He rose to his feet, placing his hand on my arm. "I'll be alright."

And then I kissed him, tasting the coppery tang of his blood, which only made me kiss him harder. My tongue entered his mouth as if I needed to taste every part of him before I pulled away.

"I'm not going anywhere," I told him.

"Thirty seconds before the next fight!" The announcer called, filling the room with his musical voice.

"Just do as I say, alright?" James nodded to me curtly, then jumped back into the ring.

But I wasn't going to leave.

I walked back to my family and told them to stop placing bets. Both of them looked at me, confused. And then I braced myself for the next four matches. The whole demeanour of the crowd changed as he kept losing, shouting insults and baring their teeth. I clenched my teeth so hard that my jaw was sore by the end of the fight.

I found him as he was leaving the lavatory, wearing his white shirt with his vest undone and black leather strapped around his shoulders. His coat hung over his arm, and he was wearing his flat cap. The bruise on his eye was darker with dried blood stuck to his left eyebrow. His lip was even more swollen, and there was a gash in his left cheekbone. Thankfully, most of the blood that had accumulated over his body during the fight was gone. Only faint traces remained.

"Lizzie," he looked around, confused. "I thought you left."

"How are you?" I didn't quite know what to say. What I witnessed was brutal and would probably haunt my nightmares for the rest of my life.

"Looks worse than it feels." He glanced behind me. "Is your family still here?"

"I sent them home."

"And they just—left you here? Alone?"

"I told them to." I stared at him with innocent eyes, fiddling with my hands behind my back. "Told them I knew a guy with a car," I curved my mouth into a smile.

He laughed, dark laughter. "I've had seven matches tonight, Lizzie. And most of them ended with me getting my ass kicked."

I flinched. "Yes, I'm aware. I watched." A shudder rolled through me. "There was no way I was just going home after that. I'd like to look after you." *Among other things.*

He let out a frustrated sigh that told me he was not happy about that. "Lizzie..." he protested.

I started walking back down the hall towards the exit.

I wasn't taking no for an answer.

And damn, did I love the sound of my name on his lips. It was much better than the *sweetheart* that always felt like an insult.

"And if you haven't noticed, I'm wearing a silk dress." I turned back, but he hadn't moved a single inch. His eyes trailed down my body, sending a rush of heat through me.

"I noticed," he murmured with a faint smile on his lips.

"And I can probably count better than you," I said over my shoulder as I kept walking. Those seven matches would never leave my mind.

He laughed, and I continued heading outside into the night. Hoping that he would give in and follow me.

I stepped outside of the warehouse, making my way towards his car, when I finally heard his footsteps approaching me. The rain finally stopped, and the air was full of a thick fog that swelled all around us. Drooping pools of ethereal mist formed at our feet.

When I reached his car, I turned around, smiling. Waiting for him to open the door for me.

"I'm fully aware of what you're trying to do." He took a few more steps towards me, closing the distance as his voice dropped deeper into his chest. "As much as I'd love to finish what I started with your intentional dress, this is not a good night for me."

I put my hand on his chest, playing with his undone vest. "I thought you said that it looks worse than it feels?"

He grumbled, wrapping his strong arms around me. His hands began bunching up the fabric on my hips as he pulled me to him, crushing me against him. And then he kissed me, deepening the kiss as his hand moved to my rear, pulling me closer still. His groan vibrated in my mouth as I met his tongue with mine, biting his bottom lip softly.

There were probably people watching us.

Plenty of people were still roaming about, making their way to their cars. But at that moment, I didn't particularly care. I was winning, and I wanted this, wanted him more than anything.

He pulled back, releasing his grip. "Let me take you home, Lizzie."

"I don't want to go—"

He placed his hand on my face, stopping my words. "I'll pick you up tomorrow. Alright?"

I stepped back from him into the fog, creating some space. "Do you have a date with someone else or something?" Why he wasn't taking me up on my very clear offer was getting under my skin.

He snorted. "I have a date with a bathtub and a bottle of whiskey."

"Great. That sounds fun." I opened the door myself and hopped into his car, leaving it at that. He let out a frustrated sigh before he closed the door.

I was going home with him tonight, whether he wanted me to or not. I had already made up my mind.

Chapter 21

JAMES

Bitter Bath

FOR THE FIRST FIVE minutes of the drive, I tried to reason with her. But she was so goddamn insistent on going to my house that by the end of it, I started questioning my own worries.

The rain started to pour down, and we sat in silence for the rest of the ride. Appreciated silence, as I no longer had the energy to fight with her. I was absolutely knackered, and my pride was pretty fucking bruised after all the insults I received before I locked myself in the lavatory.

And I get it. I was a safe bet—a trusted bet.

But I'd pissed off a lot of people tonight. People who didn't have two shillings to rub together. They thought they'd walk away with more coins in their pockets, and I left them feeling very disappointed.

At least every fight after this, Cameron and I wouldn't have to give half of our earnings to Aidan and his Knives. For that reason alone, I took every hit and every insult with a fucking badge of honour. Harry's information about a weak shoulder possibly saved my life tonight. Any harder of a hit to my spine and I'd probably be paralysed right now.

She was supposed to go home after the fight.

I honestly wished she would have left when I asked her to, but Lizzie was so fucking stubborn. And smart. I'd have to find some kind of excuse to get her home without her questioning it. I was not about to let her sleep in my bed tonight.

I had already broken enough rules for her.

The fireplace crackled with flame as we entered my room. Rain continued to fill the silence as it clashed against the glass windows. As unhappy as I was, I did have to admit how great she looked in this room. Her red hair and fair skin practically blended into the room like it was made for her, like she belonged here.

Too heavy of an emotion, I didn't want to feel tonight.

Or ever.

"This definitely feels like your room," she said, taking off her fur shawl and placing it on a chair as she took in the room.

I removed my holster and set it on the dresser, hanging my coat on the charcoal-coloured wall. Then I briskly walked into my lavatory that connected with my room, and sure enough, the maid left a cold bath waiting for me. I grabbed a bottle of whiskey and two glasses on my way back, finding her sitting too comfortably on my bed. The irony wasn't lost on me about how many times I'd dreamed of having her here. This was just not the night I had in mind.

All I wanted to do was soak in that tub and drink myself into oblivion—alone.

"This bed's softer than mine," she ran her hand down the black fabric.

"Whiskey?" I asked.

"Sure," she shrugged, grabbing one of the black satin pillows, fiddling with it. I poured two glasses. "How many girls have you had in this room, James?"

I paused, then walked over to her, handing her a glass. "You're the first." Which surprised me when I said it out loud. She was the first to be in this room... my thoughts began to consider that I wanted her to be the last.

Now I had a fucking traitorous mind as well.

I slumped down in a red velvet chair, placed the bottle next to me and took a generous sip. Washing my thoughts away.

"You're such a liar," she laughed through her nose, thinking I was making a joke.

"I'm serious." I took another drink, finished it and poured another. "I haven't lived here that long." A better man would say something comforting right now, but I wasn't the 'better man.' And I had nothing comforting to say.

Her eyes turned into something sad as she rose from the bed, setting the glass on the nightstand. "And how many women have you been with, James?"

Fuck. I choked on my whiskey and ran a hand through my hair. "You're going to like me a lot less if I tell you that." A lot, lot less.

Thunder rumbled in the distance, followed by a flash of light.

"Right," she nodded, staring at the rug for a moment before grabbing her glass of whiskey and tossing it back before I could tell her to take it slow. "Christ, that burns!" She wiped her mouth and started coughing.

"Sorry, I didn't get a chance to warn you," I laughed.

"How do you drink that so fast?" she asked.

"Practice," I shrugged. The burning and fuzzy feeling over-flowing my senses was a welcome release as I finished my glass, rising from the chair. "I'm going to take a bath. Can you behave yourself for five minutes?" I was hesitant to leave her alone in my room.

She shrugged her shoulders, pouring herself another glass of whiskey. Something felt a bit off about her, but I decided to leave her be.

I hopped in the frigid bath, soaking and washing off the sweat and blood as the rain poured down. Relief washed over me like a wave as the cold water began numbing the pain. The tension in my shoulders and neck released, allowing a moment of relaxation. My heart rate began to slow, but my mind was racing. The storm outside grew louder as lightning struck and the wind began to howl, colliding against the side of the brick. Almost like it was mimicking the storm inside of me.

I should have just taken her home.

She'd wanted to take care of me. A sentiment that made me want to punch a hole through the wall. Younger me would've loved that, killed for it... but the man I was now didn't deserve that. Why did I let her talk me into bringing her here?

"More?" The door creaked open, and she was holding a bottle of whiskey and two glasses.

I sighed, as my heart throbbed in my chest. *That's why.* "Sure."

She set it down on the counter and filled one glass, approaching me slowly before she handed it to me.

"Did you just come in here to see me naked?" I mused. Honestly, I wouldn't even be mad if she did. I would have done the same.

Heat filled her pale cheeks, and then something in her snapped as a blurred image of her rushed towards me. "Christ!" She exclaimed as she dropped to her knees, placing her hands on the bruises and cuts on my chest and torso.

"It's alright," I laughed in my chest. I'd almost forgotten that I had my ass kicked tonight. "They don't hurt," I assured her. I mean, they did a little, but the whiskey, cold water and her hands were minimising the pain.

Her hand slowed, moving to my shoulder. "And this?" She dragged her finger down my thick scar as if she were memorising it.

I could feel myself hardening with her touch. At least there were some parts of me I could still trust. "Old injury," I murmured.

"From the war?"

"Yes."

Her hands went to the middle of my chest. "Why'd you lose tonight?" she asked.

I took a breath, trying to slow down my erection. There was no way I could properly fuck her right now, though my cock wasn't listening to reason. "I had to. Some of the investors thought I was rigging the fights. I had to prove that I wasn't." Amongst other things that she didn't need to know.

Her hand traced patterns on my chest. If she didn't stop doing that, I was going to give her hands something much better to stroke.

I grabbed her hand. "Lizzie—"

"I was worried about you tonight," she cut me off. "I could tell from the start that something wasn't right."

"You shouldn't worry about me. And you're getting to know me too well," I playfully tapped her chin.

"And yet I don't know you at all," she quipped.

A sharp pain radiated in my chest at her words. I'd like to keep it that way, but I didn't think she was happy with that. This was exactly why she should have gone home.

"The James I met would've died at the opportunity to have me in his room," she continued after a moment. "And now... well, it doesn't seem like you wanted me here at all. Or even expected to see me after your fight."

Well, I didn't. But at that moment, I had forgotten why. My bitterness aside, I didn't want her to feel that way. Like I didn't want her, because I fucking did.

I placed my hand on her jaw, bringing her golden eyes to mine. "Any other night, and that James would have tied you to the bed, Lizzie. I promise you that."

"You would've tied me to the bed?" She flushed a shade of crimson, biting her bottom lip.

Yes, I fucking would.

And I couldn't take it for one more second. I drank the rest of the whiskey in my glass and rose from the bathtub as water dripped onto the floor.

"James!" She covered her eyes, but not before she looked.

And I definitely noticed.

"Hand me that towel," I gestured towards the wall.

She grabbed it and tossed it to me, peeking through her fingers. Once she satisfied her curiosity about how I looked, I expected her to leave. But when I finished drying my body, she was still there with open eyes. Staring at how hard I was for her with parted lips, chest heaving. Her crimson cheeks were the most beautiful shade of red that I had ever seen.

Who was I kidding?

My heart fucking fell a long time ago.

I no longer had the energy to fight it. Nor did I want to keep fighting it at this moment. The only thing I wanted to do was let go and lose myself with her. And by the look on her face, I think she felt the same.

I was glad I didn't take her home.

Chapter 22

ELISABETH
Rules

HEAT. BLAZING HOT HEAT, and it wasn't from the fireplace that roared to life with flame. I felt like I was on the verge of a fever that took over every thought and every need as I stared at him. His indescribable beauty and strength that damn near stopped my heart. He was sculpted all the way down his body, from his chest to his hips, where they formed a deep "v," leading to his sizable length.

I didn't even realise he was watching me until I heard him laugh, soft laughter that made me feel slick between my thighs.

"Come here," his voice was as soft as a midnight breeze.

My hands found his arms, and he redirected them to his torso, slowly sliding them down to his hard length. He groaned as I squeezed, stroking his smooth skin. How could he feel so soft, yet so hard and demanding? The small shattering noises that escaped his lips only made me want him even more.

I met his lips within the next breath, claiming and warm as his tongue entered my mouth. My arms went around his neck as he pulled up my dress, hiking it up to my waist before he lifted me off the ground. My legs wrapped around him and then fell open as my back hit the bed.

His body crushing mine consumed every thought as his hand brushed my thighs, moving under my pink silk dress.

"Do you want this?" he asked.

"More than anything." Why did he feel the need to ask? Surely, he knew how much I wanted him.

He smiled and moved his hand up further.

I lost control as he stroked that wet spot between my thighs, moving in patterns that drove me insane. My back arched, and my head fell back as he dipped his fingers inside of me. His mouth moved to my throat, and he swore soft curses, but I could barely hear him over the sound of my pounding heart.

"And what exactly do you want?" he murmured into my neck.

"I want you, James. I want you," I whimpered.

He softly bit that spot between my throat and collarbone and met my eyes with a voice that felt like velvet on my heated skin. "Do you want me to fuck you, Lizzie?"

His words didn't faze me this time. They excited me, and I desperately needed him to do that. "Yes," I writhed beneath him.

"Say it."

"I want you," I cried, reaching my hand to his strong chest.

"Word for word," he growled, putting a finger to my lips.

This man was going to destroy me. "I want—" Christ, I can't believe I was going to say this. "I want you to fuck me, James."

He curved his mouth to the side, revealing his dimple. "I like hearing those words from your mouth."

Saying those words to him made me feel a rush of heat straight to my core, as well as his praises, which made me feel like his.

"I want you too," he smiled, carefully sliding my dress off me and throwing it on the floor. "Damn," he breathed, hovering over me as he ran his hand from my breasts to my torso, like he was memorising the curves of my body.

And then his mouth was on my peaked nipple, tracing circles with his tongue. I dug my nails into his shoulder as his mouth moved from my breasts to my stomach, trailing suckling kisses as he went. Working his way down until he bit the inside of my thigh hard, and I writhed as his mouth moved to my warm centre.

That would surely bruise tomorrow, but it felt too damn good to start complaining. His mouth, his teeth... everything he did kept building my want for him to new heights.

Desperate for every part of him.

The flat of his tongue slid torturously slow, and I moaned, feeling the noise break from my throat as he slid his tongue inside me.

"James," I cried after a few skilful lashes of his tongue.

"Are you ready for my cock, Lizzie?" His voice vibrated between my thighs.

"Yes." I couldn't think about anything but that.

A midnight laugh and he licked once more before he moved the tip of his cock at my entrance. Then he kissed me softly, cupping my face as he pulled back.

"Please tell me to stop if I'm hurting you." His green eyes were so bright—the brightest, purest shade of green that I had ever seen.

I placed my hand on his jaw. "Don't stop."

And I meant it.

He smiled, moving his cock slowly inside of me.

Inching his way in.

I was not prepared for how good it felt when I felt *him*. I bit my lip, and he pushed deeper. A loud cry escaped my lips when he reached a spot that felt like a wall, and everything in my body tensed.

His hand rushed back to my face. "Are you alright?"

"Yes," I grabbed his hand.

"It should only hurt for a second," his eyes searched my face. "Lizzie, I can stop—"

"No. Keep going." I breathed. It was too much, waiting for him, wanting him so badly, wanting to know how this felt.

His lips crushed mine, sucking in my bottom lip and then he slid the rest of the way in. My teeth bit into his shoulder hard as I cried out. But the pain was nowhere near the same as the pleasure that began to consume me. Each thrust felt better and better. Warming me deep into my core, sending tingling sensations everywhere. I could feel him in my throat, and yet he kept pushing himself deeper.

Right where I needed him.

"You're so fucking tight, Lizzie," he moaned, thrusting harder.

His black hair rose and fell with each stroke, slashing over his eyes. I dug my nails into his back, appreciating how strong he felt above me, as he bit his lip, watching me intensely. I wanted him more and more with every beautiful noise he made and every dirty thing that escaped his perfect lips. His hand moved to my hip, adjusting his angle, and I cried out his name. My head tilted back as his hand firmly gripped my rear, anchoring me to his driving thrusts.

"I'll never be able to get enough of you," he groaned.

Everything blurred, and my body became his. Intense and hot for every minute that passed as I got lost in watching him thrust into me.

The silk friction was too damn good.

I couldn't get enough.

I never wanted him to stop.

"More," I breathed when I felt him beginning to slow.

"Fuck. You're going to destroy me, Lizzie."

I felt the same.

Sweat glistened on his chest as he thrust harder, giving me what I asked for. Then he grabbed my hands and placed them over my head, holding me down. Driving himself into me again and again and again. The curve of his hips grounded into me, and I moaned at the sensation.

"You're so fucking beautiful," he rasped, as his mouth moved to my nipple. Tracing circles that made me shiver.

His words made me want to put my hands on him, but I

couldn't move. "James," I cried as my back arched. "James, I want to touch you."

I needed to touch him. Needed to feel his skin.

"Just a little more," he smiled, with a wicked look on his face, tightening his hold on my hands.

With one hand still bracing me, the other moved down to my bundle of nerves, and I felt myself going over the edge with each stroke of his finger and each thrust that hit all of the right places inside me. Breathless moans escaped my lips as I bucked beneath him, feeling my core tighten and clamp around him. I cried out his name once more, and he finally released my hands. I threw my arms around him, pulling him closer.

"Come for me, baby." His voice was velvet soft against my lips.

And I did just that.

In a giant wave of release, I shattered and burned beneath him. Releasing all of the tension in my body. He said my name in pleasure, and then his eyes rolled back as I writhed with him until he found his release.

Moments later, he slowly moved over, lying next to me, entangled in the red satin sheets as he caught his breath. I felt so full and relaxed in ways that I never felt before, staring at him with new eyes.

"Fuck," he rasped. I felt the same. "That was so—"

"Amazing," I finished as my heart rate continued to burn in my chest. Better than I imagined it could be.

"Fucking amazing," he added with a smile and we both laughed, coming down from our high. "Imagine if I didn't have that fight tonight. I'd still be fucking you right now." His hand found mine as he intertwined our fingers, fiddling with them for a moment.

And then he took a deep breath and closed his eyes. Looking more exhausted than I'd ever seen him.

I arched my brow. "You mean, you could've given me more?" I was definitely playing with him.

He opened his eyes, and I could see a small fire still burning there. "So, you are trying to destroy me," he murmured.

I laughed, playing with the silver Celtic ring on his hand. The one he told me his mother gave him before she died. This moment of intimacy, just touching and quiet breaths, felt like the most natural thing in the world. I could lie here for hours and just fiddle with his hand in mine and never tire of it. His tired gaze drifted to our hands. Pausing there for a long while as the circles under his eyes grew darker and darker.

"I'm supposed to be taking you home." His breathing slowed as he turned towards the ceiling, closing his eyes. "I have rules, you know," he murmured.

"Rules about sleep?" An ache in my heart began to grow. I tried to pretend that his words didn't hurt me... but had he always intended to take me home? Even after *this*?

"Mhm," his voice rumbled in his chest.

I watched him for a moment as his eyes stayed shut. Thinking over his words, drowning in what he just said. Why did he have rules? First, his rules about kissing, and now his rules about sleeping?

A thought began to fester inside my mind.

A cruel and defining thought.

"You seem to break a lot of rules for me," I said softly.

But he didn't respond. He had already fallen into a deep sleep with his hand still clutched to mine. His chest gently rose and fell with each breath.

"Why is that, James?" He was fast asleep, but I continued, unable to stop my racing thoughts or my emotions from getting the best of me. I trailed my finger to the tattoo of the black knife on his forearm, tracing the line of thorns. Remembering that night when I first noticed it and how he immediately hid it from me. "What are you hiding?" My voice fell to a whisper.

I began to picture him in every moment that made me question him. Seeing flashes of his cold face and his empty eyes.

I think you're getting the wrong ideas about me.
I told you we wanted different things.
I have nothing else to offer you.
Because I'm not a good person, sweetheart.
You should leave.

And then I saw him very clearly. While I'd wanted him with everything that I had... he never wanted me in the same way. And this... this is exactly what he wanted all along. When we woke up tomorrow, I already knew he was going to tell me to leave. Push me away, as he always did. I didn't know why it took so long for me to see it.

I had been so consumed by him, and all the while I was slowly falling in love with him... but he would never do the same. For reasons I knew that he'd never share with me.

He would keep his safe distance.

His rules.

And maybe I had no idea what love was, but this... *this* wasn't it. This was lust.

My father had chosen my mother again and again—through her sickness and even in her death, he loved her still. A kind of love that I truly wanted... a kind of love that I needed.

And so, I felt no reason to stay.

When I rose from the bed, I noticed a spot of blood, and my stomach churned. Wracked with guilt and shame for wanting him so much that I refused to see how this would end. After slipping on my dress and shoes, I grabbed his black wool coat from the wall, taking one last look at him with tears in my eyes.

Unmoving. Peaceful. Still. With walls around his heart, as they always would be.

"Take care of yourself, James," I murmured.

And then I left, deciding to walk home in the rain alone.

Perhaps a broken heart was the only thing we had in common after all.

When I opened the front door and headed out into the night, I burrowed myself into his coat, protecting my face from the frigid rain. Swearing that a shadow was following me. And then I heard a man laugh, and my heart stopped.

Someone was following me.

Watching me from the darkness.

I bolted.

Chapter 23

JAMES

The Edge

SUNLIGHT STREAMED IN THROUGH the window, drifting slowly across my broad chest. I reached over expecting to find her there, but to my surprise, I woke up alone. She must have already woken up. A lingering soreness radiated everywhere as my eyes caught a stain almost blending in on my red satin sheets. I'm not sure why, but it made me smile to know I was her first, that she had picked me. I smiled like the goddamn fiend that I was, and then I changed into my usual attire, not bothering to grab my gun.

"Lizzie?" I called out, noticing her fur shawl still hanging on the chair.

No answer.

Perhaps Cameron drove her home already.

I made my way to the drawing room and began pouring myself a glass of whiskey when Cam entered the room.

"Morning," I murmured.

He plopped down on the sofa, saying nothing.

"Thanks for taking Lizzie home," I said, sitting in a chair across from him. He started to laugh, catching me off guard. "What's funny about that?" I asked him.

He twitched in his seat, glowering at me. "Oh. I don't know. Maybe it's because... you fucking left me at the warehouse!" he bellowed.

Oh. "Oh." I had completely forgotten about Cam.

He leaned forward, gritting his teeth. "Do you know how long of a walk it is from there?" I went to speak, but he interrupted. "Three fucking hours! I walked home in the pouring fucking rain, for three fucking hours, James!"

I put my hands up in surrender. "Alright. I'm sorry."

He leaned back, muttering and cursing under his breath.

"I was distracted. It wasn't intentional, alright?" I stifled a laugh. Cam would not appreciate that I found this humorous. "Why didn't you hitch a ride with someone?"

"Everyone was fucking gone, James," he blew out a breath and crossed his arms over his chest, glaring at me.

"It wasn't intentional," I repeated. "Now." I leaned forward. "How was Lizzie when you saw her?" I needed to know.

He scoffed, rolling his eyes. "You're such a prick."

"I know. Now, how was she?"

He threw his arms in the air. "I don't know. I didn't see her."

"What?"

"I didn't fucking see her," he repeated louder.

I blinked. "You... didn't take her home?"

"No!" He yelled.

I froze as a million possibilities formed in my mind, and all of them ended badly. Then I jumped off the couch, calling out her name. Perhaps she was somewhere in the house. She had to be. She wouldn't just leave.

Right?

Cameron followed me down the halls, calling out her name when he realised my distress. A moment later, Althea, our old grey-haired maid, came out of the kitchen, wearing an apron over her black dress.

"Have you seen her?" I asked, short of breath.

"The lady left. Sometime after midnight," Althea replied.

"Fuck!" I gripped the bridge of my nose and then rushed for the car. Cameron tried to ask me what happened, but I was already gone.

That was the longest twenty-minute car ride of my life as my mind went to all the dark places of what could have happened to her. Walking alone. At night. In fucking Birmingham. It's bad enough that Cam did, but *her?* At least Cam was fucking armed.

My tyres screeched on the pavement as I pulled up to her house. I rushed to her door, banging on it repeatedly, bracing the doorway for balance before I collapsed. If anything happened to her, I would never forgive myself.

Fuck, Lizzie answer the goddamn door.

And then the door opened.

"Liz—" I started. But to my dissatisfaction, Margaret was there with Finton at her heels.

"What do you want?" She glowered at me.

"Lizzie is—is she here?" *Please let her be here.*

Margaret crossed her arms. "I'm not happy she walked home in the middle of the night, but—"

"Thank fucking, Christ." I blew out a breath, letting my heart rate catch up to my breath.

"You seem... relieved to hear that," her eyes meshed together in a hard line. "Did you not tell her to walk home?"

"No! I would never fucking do that." I took another breath, calming the nerves in my stomach. "Please. I need to see her."

Her face softened. "She doesn't want to see you, James."

"Well, that's too fucking bad." I didn't mean to snarl at her, but I was way past pleasantries. First, she decided to leave in the middle of the night, and now she doesn't want to see me?

I'll break through her goddamn window.

Margaret paused as a smile crept on her face, tapping her fingernails on the door. "Fine," she caved. I sighed in relief, passing the threshold. "She's upstairs. Last door on your right."

"Thank you."

"Oh, and James..." I stopped and turned around. "If she ever comes home like that again, I'll break your neck," she smiled a devil's smile.

"She won't," I assured her. I'd make damn sure of it.

And then I rushed up the stairs. Finton tried to follow me, but he couldn't keep up with his short little legs.

When I found her room and opened the door, it felt like my knees were going to buckle at the sound of her voice. After locking the door behind me—because we were about to have a very heated discussion—I followed the sweet treble of her voice to the lavatory. Her hair was tied up with a few strands hanging loose as she soaked in a steaming bath smelling of lavender and something citrusy. Her face was red and blotchy, like she had been crying all night long. Rage burned inside of me, taking in her distressed state because this was *her* doing. I was the one who woke up alone because she decided to leave.

"Margaret, is that—James!" She gasped, covering her breasts with her arm. As if I hadn't had them in my mouth last night. "What are you do—"

"Do you have any idea how worried I've been about you?" My voice shook as I approached her. I wanted to yell, to scream, to tell her just how fucking angry I was at her. But I needed to know why she left.

"James, please—"

"Why would you do that?"

"Do what?" she snapped.

"Do you have any idea how dangerous this city is?" My hands started to shake. "How many things could have happened to you?"

"James I—"

"Are you that fucking stupid?" I practically shouted at her.

"You wanted me to leave!" She shouted back.

"What?"

"Oh, for Christ's sake," she rose from the bath, reaching for a towel and draping it around her. "I left because you wanted me to, and you know it."

She tried to move around me, but I stopped her, bracing my hand on the wall. "No. No, I don't fucking know it. I never told you to leave in the middle of goddamn night, Lizzie."

Her chest heaved. "Let me pass."

"Tell me why." I refused to move.

"Let me pass," she tried again.

"Tell me why, Lizzie."

Her eyes flared, highlighting the flecks of gold that mixed with the green. "So, it's Lizzie now, is it? How convenient."

I sighed, dropping my eyes to the floor, knowing exactly what she meant.

"Let. Me. Pass," she spat.

I fumed for a breath and then dropped my arm, letting her pass.

She walked into her room, turning around to face me a second later. "Great. Now, you can leave," she gestured towards the door.

Scraping laughter escaped my throat. I couldn't understand her and why she was so angry. Why suddenly, she was acting like she hated me. "Do you—" I swallowed. This was harder to say than I thought. "Do you regret sleeping with me?"

Her eyes dropped to the floor. "No. Because that requires you to break one of your rules." Tears started to form as she flicked her eyes back to mine. "And I'm done with that."

"Rules," I murmured, needing to say it out loud.

"Yes. Now, please go," she held back tears.

"What rules?" I couldn't remember talking about rules last night.

She fired off, like rounds in a gun. "That you were supposed to take me home. That I wasn't allowed to sleep in your bed. The fact that you didn't even want me there in the first place!"

Sounded like me, but I didn't remember having that conversation.

I took slow steps towards her, needing to close this distance between us. "Whatever I said last night, I didn't mean it. I don't even remember saying that."

She shook her head, pulling away from me. "You know you meant it. This entire time... you've been pushing me away. Avoiding my questions with short answers. Calling me sweetheart. Telling me you have these stupid rules. You didn't even want to kiss me, and for what?" Tears fell, staining her pale cheeks. Breaking my goddamn heart. "You got what you wanted, James. You can go now."

I closed the distance, wrapping my arms around her. "You think me fucking you once was enough for me?" I put my hand on her chin, lifting it towards me. "Lizzie." Her golden eyes met mine, and she dropped her arms to her sides. "Didn't I say I would never be able to get enough of you?"

She sighed. "You say a lot of things, James." The harsh expression on her face began to soften as pink brushed her cheeks.

"Well, I meant that. More than anything else that I said." I brushed the fresh pink of her cheeks with my thumb. "Sex can be very confusing. Emotional. I'm sorry I fell asleep... and I'm just sorry." And I was. About all of it.

Her gaze drifted to my mouth, parting her lips. "Why do you have rules, James?"

I brushed the hair from her face, tucking it behind her ear. Taking a moment to find the resolve to answer her. "I have rules so that I don't fall apart. Because I... I can't fall apart again." She took a moment, longer than I thought she would have, as thoughts passed behind her eyes. I brushed her jaw, bringing her back to me. "Never. Ever. Leave like that again. Alright?"

"Alright," she murmured.

Then I crushed her to my chest, wrapping my arms around her as I breathed in her scent. Like sweetness and warm afternoons after a long and harsh winter. Her heartbeat raced in her chest as she wrapped her arms around my neck, pulling me closer. A comfort I didn't know I needed.

"And for the record. I did want to kiss you. I would've taken you in the alley on that first night we met, but I don't think you would've let me," I murmured into her hair.

She laughed. "You should've started with this," her voice muffled against my shoulder. "I don't feel so angry now."

I laughed and then brought her lips to mine, kissing her softly. Wanting more time, but there were things I needed to take care of first. "I need to go home," I pulled back. "Find some way to make things up with Cam."

"Why? What happened?" she asked.

"We left him at the pit." It was amusing, flattering even, that she also forgot about him because she was so focused on going home with me. Cam wouldn't find it so amusing, or even remotely flattering. He was most likely already planning his revenge for me. That three-hour walk home was going to be my payback soon. I just knew it.

Shock crossed her face. "Oh."

"Yeah," I couldn't stop the small smile on my lips.

"I didn't even think... wait. I might have something," she grabbed my hand, pulling me towards the door. "Oh. Also, I borrowed this." She grabbed my wool coat off the wall and handed it to me.

I didn't even realise she took it, but I was glad she did. If she had just walked home in that pink silk dress last night... I didn't even want to imagine it. We'd still be having a fight.

She pulled me into the hall.

"Lizzie," I stopped her. "You're still wearing a towel."

She glanced down, turning red. "Right." Then she went back into her room.

I debated on following her, on punishing her for what she put me through this morning. But I needed more time for that.

She stepped out about two minutes later wearing a dark green silk dress and a beaded headband while her red hair cascaded down so beautifully to her porcelain skin.

"What?" She asked, noticing the amused expression on my face.

"I'll tell you later," I smiled, grabbing her hand.

I didn't know if she was ready. Hell, she probably wasn't. But if my past had taught me anything, it was how to inflict certain types of torture. Torture that I knew she'd enjoy if she would allow me. Not that I planned on giving her much of a choice.

She needed to know how much she meant to me, and I only knew one way to prove it.

Chapter 24

ELISABETH

Fear

FEAR AND PAIN SHONE behind his eyes when he told me that he couldn't fall apart, and I understood it. Grief and I were very familiar with one another. Whatever had happened in his past to instil these rules for his heart was solely his grief... a pain that had forced the walls around his heart. His anger stemmed from the fear that something could have happened to me, because he cared for me—a truth I didn't fully realise until that moment.

James was afraid of falling apart, but so was I. My increasing feelings for him were new, confusing, and equally terrifying. But perhaps not as terrifying as leaving in the middle of the night. An absolutely foolish and terrifying mistake, which I realised shortly after walking a few blocks down the street. Shadows of men seemed to follow me, peeking out behind brick buildings and trees. I burrowed deeper into James's coat, hoping to blend myself into the darkness, but then a man laughed. And I ran, as one voice turned into many.

It was one of the scariest moments of my life.

After I returned home safely last night, Margaret noticed my distress and followed me to my room. Despite how afraid I was to tell her what I'd done, she was supportive... understanding. Her teasing manner was gone, replaced by the protective and wise older sister. I'd missed that soft version of her, and although it was an embarrassing conversation, I was glad that we had it. That I didn't have to go through my feelings alone.

Margaret made me realise that while I was filled with instant shame and guilt, I didn't have any lingering regrets. And regardless of how things turned out, I still would've done it. He asked me at every step if I was okay, if I wanted it... and I did. With all the things he made me feel, I didn't know how to fathom regret.

I only regretted leaving in the first place.

James opened the front door to his house, gesturing for me to walk in first. Cameron appeared from around the corner a second later, looking stressed and dishevelled.

"Did you find her?" He stopped, registering my presence. Then his focus shifted to the pineapple upside-down cake in my hands, staring at it like it was the most beautiful thing he'd ever seen.

"It was my fault," I pushed the cake towards him.

"It's not your fault," James mumbled behind me.

"Quiet," I murmured to him. It absolutely was my fault. Had I not been so insistent on going home with James, poor Cameron would not have been left behind.

"Lizzie, that's—" Cameron took it in his hands. Emotional over the gesture. "Thank you. Come in." I smiled and moved past him, crossing the threshold. "And it was definitely *his* fault," he said over his shoulder, sparing a glare at James as he walked past.

James sighed, and we followed Cameron to the drawing room. Each of us reached for a piece of cake and let the explosion of flavour fill our mouths, while the fireplace crackled softly in the background. Buttery, sweet and tangy pineapple with notes of cherries melted on my tongue.

"Damn, did you make this?" Cameron asked as he took another bite.

I laughed. "I wish. My maid Pearl has tried to teach me over the years, but I can't quite make it the same as her."

"Well, I'm glad he found you this morning. I've never seen him so worried." Cam glanced at James, who was shaking his head for him to stop talking about sentiment. I quirked my mouth to the side, warmed by his friend's words. "I would have offered you a ride home, but I would've still been walking home myself at that hour," he levelled another icy glare at James.

"Yeah. Yeah. Won't happen again," James murmured.

"Better not," Cam replied.

James muttered something in Gaelic to Cameron as I popped the last bit of cake in my mouth, licking my fingers clean. Cameron replied in the same language, and James laughed. Then I felt his gaze on me. Staring at me, with something dancing around in his eyes.

He pushed the rest of his cake in his mouth and rose off the couch, offering his hand. "Let's go," he said as he chewed.

"Go where?" I stared at him with a puzzled look on my face. I didn't know there was somewhere else we needed to be.

"Are you going to make me say it in front of Cam?" he taunted.

"Say what?" Did I miss something?

He grinned, practically asking me to do just that in true James fashion. And then I made the connection, sending a rush of warmth to my cheeks. We were going to his room.

"Oh," I bit my lip. "Right now?" I asked with reddened cheeks.

"Yes, fucking now. We have things we need to talk about," he smirked.

"You can tell him to fuck off. I do it all the time," Cameron murmured to me.

James frowned at him.

I mean, yes, I could. But I also wanted to go to his room. I laughed at Cameron's words and grabbed James's hand, taking a few steps towards the stairs when he stopped me.

"I'll meet you up there," he whispered in my ear, kissing my cheek softly before he pushed me towards the stairs.

As I ascended, I overheard a few bits and pieces of their conversation.

"Where's what's her name?" James asked him. "That blonde you were always with."

"Turns out, I wasn't the only one she was seeing," he replied.

"I see. I'm sorry to hear that." I could hear the sorrow in his voice. He truly cared about his friend.

"Lizzie is a very nice girl, James. Too nice for the likes of you. Are you sure you know what you're doing?"

And then I could no longer hear them as I reached the top of the stairs.

I sure hoped he did.

After opening his door, I found that the bed had been freshly made. But before I could fantasise about rearranging the sheets, he briskly entered the room, closing the door behind him. Sparing me a glance before he poured himself a glass of whiskey.

"Now, take off your dress," he ordered.

My toes curled at his tone. "Excuse me?"

He took a sip from his glass. "Your dress. Take it off."

"What about Cameron?"

"This is not the time to say my best friend's name," he growled.

"I mean, isn't he downstairs?" And in earshot of what was about to happen.

"I told him to take a walk. Now, take off your dress."

I put my hands on my hips, holding my ground. "You could ask me nicely."

He laughed, shooting back his drink. "Normally, I would. But after the hell you put me through this morning, Lizzie. I am not in the mood to play *nice*."

My pulse skittered, and my breathing accelerated as something dark reverberated from him. I thought we'd moved past this morning, but the tension in his body told me otherwise.

"Or am I going to rip it off you?" he levelled his voice at me.

"Alright!" I began removing the sleeves. "This is one of my favourite dresses." He was not about to rip it off me. I removed the beaded headband and pulled my dark green silk dress to my ankles, sliding it away. "Happy?" I gestured to my pale and freckled body. I honestly didn't understand the appeal of me, but the way he worked his jaw and smiled told me that he found it very appealing.

"I'm getting there," he smirked. Then he reached into the top drawer of his dresser, pulling out a rope.

My heart jumped out of my chest. "James... what the hell is that?" I stepped back, chest pounding to the point of pain.

He pulled the rope taut, grinning like the devil himself, and I felt my soul leave my body. "This is your punishment, Lizzie."

"What?"—*what the hell was he saying?*—"For what?" I stepped back again as he moved closer. I couldn't breathe. The roaring in my ears had become so loud that I couldn't think straight.

He continued to smile. "For leaving my bed. For making me fear for you."

I put a hand up to stop him from coming closer. Scared to death of this version of James standing in front of me.

He stopped, and my breathing slowed.

"Give me your hands." The sweet thickness of his voice was confusing. All charm, and not a hint of the sick torture he was offering.

"No, are you crazy?"

"Debatable," he smiled. "Your hands," he repeated.

I shook my head, not giving an inch.

"You're going to like this, Lizzie," he added with a smile—a 'James' smile that sent heat rushing between my legs.

"Th-then why are you calling it a p-punishment?" Was I stammering right now? I haven't stammered since I was a child.

"Not all punishment is bad," he grinned.

"Pfft." The noise rose out of my throat, followed by a gust of air.

I didn't believe him one bit.

This was bad. This was all bad.

He smiled, stepping closer. "You don't need to be afraid, Lizzie. You're always safe with me."

"This doesn't feel safe." No, this felt very, very unsafe, and it needed to stop turning me on. This body of mine was a treasonous thing.

He smirked. "How do you know if you've never tried it?"

I let out a nervous laugh. Chest heaving. Debating on Cameron's words to tell him to fuck off.

His eyes grazed my body, and heat washed over me. "Aren't you even a little bit curious about what I want to do to you?"

No.

Maybe.

But I was too scared to admit that.

My back hit the wall, and he placed a gentle hand on my face. "I need you to trust me." His thumb trailed down my chin in the way I always loved, and my body swayed, shivering at his touch. *Treasonous body.* "You're safe with me, Lizzie," he repeated.

"This is a very odd way to earn my trust."

He chuckled under his breath. "You won't think so in a minute."

Sometimes I hated how confident he was. "You're crazy."

"Most definitely." The smile he gave me then sent a pulse straight to that spot between my thighs. "This is important to me, Lizzie," he gestured to the rope once more.

My curiosity started to win. "Why?"

His gaze drifted to my mouth, and I felt myself cave. "To show you how much you mean to me."

Warmth circulated in my chest as I stared at his lips. "And you can't just tell me with words?"

"No," he smirked. "Trust me, Lizzie," he said once more with his velvet voice.

Against my better judgment, I held out my hands. I couldn't deny I was at least a little bit curious. And I did trust him. For the life of me, I couldn't figure out why at this particular moment. Maybe I was just as crazy as he was, and perhaps even crazier for feeling the thrill for whatever he was planning to do to me.

He started wrapping the rope around my wrists. "I need you to pick a safe word."

"A what?" I breathed, insides roaring.

"A word that tells me if it's too much, or if it hurts." He paused, thinking for a moment. "Like... pineapple," he grinned.

"Pineapple?" I repeated, narrowing my eyes at him.

"That's right." He tightened the rope. *That was a lot tighter than it needed to be.* "You say that word, and I'll stop."

"Does it need to be this tight?"

"Yes," he grinned, tugging it tighter. Trapping my breasts between my arms as he pulled me towards him.

I whimpered, unable to stop the noise breaking from me as his lips met mine in a tender kiss, swallowing my cry.

He pulled back, meeting my eyes. "I want you to understand that you're safe with me," he brushed my jaw. "But you are not safe out in the night alone."

His hands began grazing my body, like it was his. Squeezing. Pinching. Sending waves of pleasure to my core at his heated touch.

"Nor are you safe with anyone but me," he growled.

He truly was going to destroy me. Ruin me.

And I wanted it more than anything.

His tongue entered my mouth, kissing me fervently before tugging me towards the bed. I expected him to throw me down, but instead, he turned me around. Bending me over at the edge of his bed with my forearms out in front of me on the clean red satin sheets. Leaving me fully exposed.

"James," I breathed. A wave of fear rushed through me as I was now fully in his mercy.

"This ass has been driving me fucking crazy for too long, Lizzie." His hands slowly slid down my back to my rear as he put a hand on each cheek and squeezed.

Then his hand moved to my slick centre, sending a shiver up my spine. Releasing each vertebra into a bliss of sensation and need.

"I knew you would like this." His voice was like leather and velvet. So soft and yet filled with so much texture.

He slapped a cheek, and I yelped as his fingers kept doing things that sent me over the edge.

Was he spanking me?

He slapped again, harder this time. I felt pressure as two fingers dipped inside me, filling me with need.

Yes. Yes, he was. Did I like it? Yes, I did. Though I would never admit that to him.

His wet tongue trailed down my spine, all the way down until he stopped and bit a spot on my rear. My body filled with something I'd never felt before as I gripped the sheets with the tips of my fingers. Trying to loosen the rope so I could wrap my arms around him and bite him back. Except I would bite him harder.

"So, fucking wet, Lizzie," he groaned, biting me again.

"James," I cried. "I want—I want to see you." All I could feel was two fingers inside me as the other hand moved to my hip. The sting of his slaps and his bites started doing something crazy to my insides. I desperately wanted to feel his lips.

"I'm going to take you like this, and then I'm going to turn you around and take you again. And I'm not going to release you until you understand what you did to me."

He fiddled with his pants, sending a shocking sensation to my core as I readied myself. Fear and excitement coursed through me. A sharp breath escaped my lips when I felt the tip of him at my entrance.

"Are you ready?" he asked.

"Yes," I bit my lip.

And then he slid all the way in, and I whimpered at how good he felt at that angle. Each slow thrust hit somewhere deep in me that I didn't know would feel so good. His hips ground into the swell of my rear again and again, deeper and deeper with each stroke. Harder and harder as his hands gripped firmly on my hips. Guiding me and holding me in a way that made me feel weightless while he pounded me from behind. I bit my lip, moaning from the friction.

I didn't know being punished by him could feel so good.

"I could do this all fucking day, Lizzie."

So. Could. I.

"You're so fucking beautiful," he exclaimed in a ragged breath. And I felt it. I felt like everything and nothing at once. "Tell me. Tell me you'll never leave like that again."

"I won't," I rasped, feeling myself going over the edge from his thrusts and his velvet, breathless voice.

"Promise me," he growled.

"I promise. James. Please," I cried, gripping the sheets harder.

"Beg me to release you."

I felt a small wave of orgasm at his words, arching my back. "I beg you. Please. Please let me touch you, James."

And then he slowly pulled out and turned me around. Tugging on the rope to release my hands in a quick motion. In the next second, I threw my arms around him, kissing him hard as I ran my fingers through his hair. He guided me back to the bed, pulling me on top of him as he brought his hands to my hips, rocking me back. Keeping his fingers on my centre as he guided himself inside me, and I whimpered at how full he felt while I straddled him.

My eyelashes fluttered, and he groaned as he cupped my breasts. Sweet pleasure took control of me at the sight of him beneath me, leaving me in full control.

I think I understood the appeal of the rope.

Control. And it *did* feel good.

I'd never felt more powerful in my life as I rolled my hips, rocking into him in a slow and steady rhythm. Then I moved faster, feeling pressure building in my core. Breathless curses escaped his perfect mouth, and my thoughts turned so filthy that all I wanted to do was ride him harder and harder into oblivion. To ride him until he exploded inside of me, screaming my name.

"Fuck, Lizzie," he cried out.

My hands went to his chest, steadying myself as I glided on him until my legs started to burn. Never wanting to stop. He was at the edge with me, but I wanted more. So, I pushed him further, increasing the tension until he desperately cried out my name once more, and then he and I shattered.

Both of our bodies were covered in sweat as we came back down in sweet, recovering breaths. The bedding was strewn about, in a mixture of red and black. I'm not sure where the satin pillows ended up. He ran a hand through his dark hair, steadying his breath as I propped myself up on my elbows, trailing my gaze along his perfectly toned body.

"How long have you had that rope in your drawer?" And what else did he have in there?

He laughed in his chest. "You never know when you're going to need it. Have I scared you away yet?" He grinned like he was trying to be playful, but I could tell a part of him was afraid that he might have.

"Surprisingly, no," I laughed through my nose. "But I stand by what I've said before. Something is very wrong with you, James."

He braced his arms over his head, drawing attention to his muscled chest. "You liked it, and I let you off easy. Next time, I'll force you to your knees. You just remember that if you ever try to endanger yourself," he tapped my chin.

Force me to my knees?

My chest felt warm at the reminder of how much he cared, at how much I meant to him.

"You let me off easy?" I tapped his chest, biting my lip. "And was letting me ride you a part of your punishment?" Because that felt like a bonus.

His eyes turned into something feral. "Are you challenging me?"

I smiled and rose from the bed, walking around the room until I found my green dress on the floor.

He propped himself up. "Did we not just discuss this? Or are you curious about my offer?"

I laughed. "I need to go home, James. Have a bath—"

"Believe it or not, but I have one right through that door," he pointed. "I'd think you'd remember that."

I shot him a look of annoyance. "Of course, I remember. But I also need to check on my sister and help Pearl with the chores," I said, slipping on my dress. It was still the morning after all. There were plenty of things that needed to be done today.

"Isn't Pearl your maid?" he asked.

"Yes."

"Then I should think she's quite capable."

He really wanted me to stay, didn't he?

"She appreciates the help, and it's a lot for her. She's used to running a house full of maids, and now there's just her." His gaze drifted to the bed in thought. I found my shoes and slipped them on. "Besides, I'm sure you have important things to do today as well."

"Besides you, not really," he muttered, rising out of bed. Placing his hands around me in a few strides.

As if doing me was something of importance. Warmth shot straight to my core at the gesture.

His lips drifted from my neck to my collarbone. "Then tonight," his voice reverberated into my skin.

"What do you want to do?" I asked.

"What do you think I want to do?" He nipped my collarbone.

Goosebumps trailed along my skin at the feel of his breath on my neck. I laughed and turned around, wrapping my arms around him. "How about a date then?" I asked.

He frowned. "I'm not a date-type guy."

"You so are." He seemed unhappy with my acknowledgement, looking even more annoyed. "Perhaps you could even give me flowers this time. Like a proper gentleman," I added with a playful smile.

"Flowers?" He arched his brow, looking even more vexed as his voice dropped into a growl.

"Yes," I smiled.

"I'm no gentleman, Lizzie," he clicked his tongue. "And I'm definitely not proper. I think all of this improper sex has gone to your head," he teased with a tight expression.

It probably had, but I laughed, knowing that if I died tomorrow, my gravestone would read:

Beloved Daughter and Sister.
She enjoyed playing the piano and annoying James.

"Now get dressed. I need you to drive me home," I threw his pants at him, hitting him in the face.

Chapter 25

ELISABETH

Confession

I SPENT THE AFTERNOON washing dishes, folding laundry, and listening to Margaret complain. It seemed she had been very bored the past few days, and she was not happy that I wasn't inviting her out for my date with James.

"You cannot take my cake and then leave me here to rot, Lizzie. Do you really hate me that much?" She said to me as I was fixing my hair in the mirror, trying to get ready for my date.

The pineapple upside-down cake was her favourite dessert, and although I felt bad for taking it, giving it to Cameron was for a good cause. I had definitely benefited from it anyway.

I placed a pearl crown with a white feather sticking out of it around my head. "Of course, I don't hate you, but—"

"No buts. Besides, I need to meet this... Cameron that you told me about," she fluffed up her short brown hair.

"He's off limits." I would not have her meddling with James's best friend, and I'm sure James would agree with me.

"That only makes me want him more," Margaret grinned.

Before I could protest, she was gone.

After hearing a knock at the door, I descended the stairs to find James leaning against the door frame, holding a bouquet of red tulips. My heart dropped at the sight of him, and my mother's favourite flowers in his hand. He wore black trousers, with a white shirt rolled up to his elbows, with gold elbow bands and black leather suspenders paired with his leather wristband. His hair was slicked back with a few strands waving in his face, and the top three buttons of his shirt were undone.

"I knew you were capable of such things," I smiled, taking the red tulips.

"Capable, sure. Willing? Not likely."

"These are beautiful. Thank you," I smiled, taking in the vibrant red of the fresh flowers before me. Mother preferred pink tulips, but these were perhaps the prettiest ones I had ever seen and my new favourite.

"I've seen prettier things," he murmured.

Red crept into my cheeks, and his mouth curved into a smile. Cameron waved at me from behind James, leaning against the car. Would it ever stop being weird seeing Cameron after what he witnessed? Probably not.

"My sister is coming," I murmured to James.

"Good, she can keep him busy," he nodded over his shoulder, seeming happy about the whole thing.

Which was not the reaction I expected from him.

"James, my sister is..." How to find the words for such a person as Margaret? "Well, she'll try anything."

"He's not a virgin, Lizzie. He'll be alright."

Then Margaret pushed past me, heading towards Cameron to introduce herself.

Typical.

To my surprise, things worked out better than expected. The chemistry between Margaret and Cameron, thank goodness, wasn't sexual. After a few flirtations, they just... stopped trying.

Then they danced and laughed, continuing the night as friends. Honestly, having a friend is what I think Margaret had been desperately needing in her life, someone to talk to other than her distracted sister. And lately, I have been very distracted.

James held me close as we swayed side to side to the soft jazz music playing in the background. The golden ambience of the room reflected around us as my thoughts began to wander, and his hands pulled me closer. I realised how much I loved dancing with James. The way his hand cradled my lower back in a way that said that I was safe, that I was his. The way he smiled at me, watched me constantly and how his hands always seemed to find mine. Would the butterflies he gave me ever disappear?

I hoped not, because I never wanted them to.

But most of all, I loved the way that he made me feel, the way everything seemed to disappear when he was around. All my grief, sadness and worries were distant memories in his captivating presence. Being *his* was the best feeling in the world.

"Is this what you had in mind?" he asked, caressing my fingers while we danced.

"Better than I could have imagined." I would honestly stay in this moment forever if it were possible. Just him and I... dancing while his gentle touch drove me mad.

"Well, just so you know. I don't put out on the second date," he teased.

I laughed, playfully slapping his shoulder. "You're a terrible liar," I smiled. "And it's our third."

"It's our second proper date, but I'm glad you count me tying you up as a date," he grinned, sending my blood racing.

Crimson filled my pale cheeks. "I was counting the first time I watched you fight in the pit, and then the walk after that terrible tea situation when I first came to your house."

"Sure, you were," he smirked.

"Why are you so aggravating?"

His fingers started to trace patterns on my back. "If you'd like to punish me, feel free to tie me up anytime."

A shiver rolled through me at the thought. "Perhaps I will," I smirked, playing his game. A wicked grin crossed his face as he tried to pull me off the dance floor, but I pulled him back. "I'm still dancing, James," I laughed, wrapping my arms tighter around his neck.

He sighed. "Fine," he rolled his eyes, but then he smiled at me in a way that I felt warmth everywhere.

And this was just another thing about him that I couldn't get enough of—his constant playful side that caught me off guard and made my pulse quicken. I realised that I loved all of James, and I couldn't think of a single thing I didn't like about him.

We returned to my house a few hours later.

Cameron was drunk, beyond drunk and no matter how many times James told him to slow down over the evening, he just kept going. I wondered if it had anything to do with that girl I'd overheard about. The one who wasn't loyal.

We let Cameron sleep on our couch for the night, and Margaret even brought him a glass of water. Then she stayed in the drawing room, waiting for Father to come home as James and I went upstairs, smirking at me as we left the room.

Of course, I let him ravage me, but I also ravaged him.

I dragged my tongue on new areas of his body that I hadn't yet explored and found there wasn't a single inch of him that I didn't enjoy. Learning the curves of his body was a new experience, and I loved every minute of it. The taste, the feel... it was like all of him was designed just for me.

"What's your middle name?" I said after some time, as we lay there catching our breaths, entangled in each other in my pink sheets.

"My middle name is unnecessary," he grumbled.

I propped myself on his chest to look at his face. "Well, I don't think so."

"Of course, you don't," he mumbled, not meeting my eyes.

"Mine is Rose."

He paused for a moment. "Elisabeth Rose Montgomery." His smile turned into something affectionate, and for James, that was a big deal. He seemed to like the way it sounded. "What?" He asked after noticing my smile.

"Nothing. Now, what's yours?" I dragged a line across his chest, tapping my fingers impatiently.

"I didn't say I was going to give it to you."

"James," my eyes glazed over, and I thought about slapping him. "Is it something embarrassing or something? Is your middle name Francine?" I gave him a sly smile.

He scowled, looking at me like *how dare you*. "It's a very masculine name."

"Then, tell me." He stayed silent, and I swear it was just to get under my skin. I knew things like this scared him. Every intimate moment that got a little too personal for him, he shut down like clockwork. Except I knew more about him now, and I knew what I needed to say to pry it from him. "Tell me, so I can scream it out the next time you're on top of me."

And that got his attention, as I knew it would.

"You play a dirty game, Lizzie." He sighed, taking his time. "Fine. It's Flynn."

"James Flynn MacGuire," I repeated.

He rolled over, pinning me to the bed. "Are you going to scream out my full name when I come inside you?"

And then I could only think of one response. One that he said to me the day that we met. A conversation and a place in time that I could never forget. "Wouldn't you like to know."

His lips met mine in a deep and heated kiss.

Then he pulled back. "Actually, I need to stop doing that." I stared at him blankly, still breathless from his kiss. "Unless you want a bastard version of me crawling around on your floor," he smirked.

Warmth filled my cheeks as I smiled, picturing it. I think some deep part of me yearned for that, for that version of happiness. "Would that be so bad? I mean, someday." Not that I was ready at this moment in time, but I would like to think that someday he would want that, too. That a future like that could exist in the years to come.

His throat bobbed as pain flashed across his face.

I placed my hand on his jaw, bringing him back to me before he strayed too far in his thoughts. "Where is your mind going, James?"

"I have three alternatives," he smiled, coming back. "Here," he tapped my belly. "Or here," he drifted his finger to my breasts. "Or here," his gaze darkened as he tapped my mouth. "Which one do you prefer, Lizzie? Or shall I experiment?"

Every nerve in my body came alive as I brought his mouth to mine. I didn't know when this part of me would stop wanting him, or if it ever could.

I expected him to leave sometime afterwards, but he stayed. He pulled my back to his chest and held me all night long as if it was something we'd done for years, as if I were something precious to him. It was so familiar and comfortable. I wondered why we hadn't done this before. It seemed so... natural.

Sometime in the middle of the night, I was wide awake, watching the blue moonlight drift in through the window as it softly caressed James's strong chest as he slept.

For the first time in so long, my heart felt full and happy.

Everything hit me all at once.

I wanted to tell him that I loved him—even *needed* to. I had been in love with him for quite some time, and I was ready to admit it, to let myself fall. But James was... complicated. While I know he cared about me, I wasn't sure what he felt beyond that.

Would he run if I said those three words?

I debated on waking him and telling him here and now, but fear took over. Crippling looming fear and anxiety that this man, this sweet and vexing man lying next to me, might never feel or allow himself to feel the same things. And so, I lay awake watching him sleep, burning up inside with all the things I desperately wanted him to know.

It was my fourth attempt to get out of bed the next morning, but James was too damn strong, refusing to let me out of his arms.

"James, I have church. I have to go."

He flashed me a wicked grin. "Or you could stay and let me worship you. I'll even go to my knees for you. Trust me, Lizzie, you'll feel good and cleansed once I'm done with you." His finger trailed down my abdomen, past my belly button, then stopped as it reached my hip, tapping there, and I shivered.

This man.

If I weren't already running late this morning, I would be more than happy to take him up on his offer.

Except I wanted to be the one to worship him.

"James," I tried again. This time, he removed his arm with a sad sigh. "You know, you could come with me if you wanted to," I said over my shoulder. He laughed as I made my way to the closet across the room, tripping over something cold and hard. "Ow!" I yelped.

"You alright?" he laughed.

Steel. Cold hard. *Steel*.

My world suddenly shifted.

I couldn't breathe.

I couldn't move.

Flashes of horror consumed me at the sight of a gun lying on my bedroom floor. The dark silver glinted in the morning light, bringing attention to a name etched into the steel. The black leather straps I had seen him wear on his shoulders lay next to it—a holster. Had it been a holster this entire time?

I dropped to my knees, picking up the gun off the floor, staring at the name MacGuire etched into the barrel.

The sounds of ricochets echoed in my mind.

James was there a second later, snatching it from me. "Never touch a man's gun, Lizzie. For fuck's sake. You could've hurt yourself." The gun made a clicking sound as he tucked it into his wool coat that hung on the wall.

I rose from the floor. My body shook involuntarily beneath me, remembering the last time I saw a gun in this house.

"Why do you have a gun?"

He grabbed my hand, looking concerned. "Lizzie, you're shaking."

I pulled my hand away from him. "Why do you have that?" My voice rose an octave higher.

"It's fine. I'm sorry, I didn't realise I brought it with me."

"Why do you have it, James?" My voice shook as tears stained my cheeks.

He had a gun. Why in the hell would he have a gun?

"I would never hurt you, Lizzie." He placed a gentle hand on my arm.

"Why do you have it?" I screamed.

"Because I need it!" he yelled right back.

I blinked. "What?"

"I need it," he repeated.

"Why?" It made no sense. Why would he *need* it?

"Because there are many men out there who would try to kill me, and without it..." A muscle rippled in his jaw as his voice trailed off.

"Why?" I repeated louder.

"Lizzie, please—"

"Why!" I yelled.

He shoved his tattooed forearm in front of me, voice shaking. "Because of this! Because of this goddamn fucking tattoo! Because of the man that I used to be. I need it. Alright?"

I stayed quiet, watching him as he ran a shaky hand through his hair and paced around the room. The tremors in my body had stopped, but breathing in and out felt heavy. Like someone was sitting on top of my chest.

He walked over to the fireplace and braced his hand on the mantle, staring into the flames. "I was a gangster, Lizzie. Before the war." I watched as the flames flickered orange, warming light over his features, highlighting the strength of his jaw. "I was in a gang called The Black Knives for nearly a decade. Since I walked off that ship from Dublin—" He stopped, as if saying more was too painful. "And even though I never returned, what I did, the people I hurt... I can never truly walk away from it." He dropped his hand from the mantle, turning to me with a hard expression on his face. "I carry it to protect me. Nothing more."

I should've been scared, and maybe I was a little, but mostly I was thankful he was being honest. I remember when I first saw his tattoo on the night I met him... how he rolled his arm over, hiding it. And now that I knew what it stood for, I should tell him to run in the other direction. He just admitted that he had hurt people and most likely killed people.

He was a gangster, and I should've known.

I had read about gangs in the newspapers, and particularly this one, many years ago. Just as he mentioned, before the war—and well, after the war, I stopped reading them. Things were bleak enough as it was to read about any more sad stories in The Times. Stories that I would never forget about robbery, stabbings, and cold-blooded murder...

"And you—" my voice caught in my throat. "You've..." I couldn't find the words to ask about the people he had hurt, but perhaps a part of me never wanted to know.

He crossed the room and placed his hand on my arm, caressing my skin with his fingers. "I'm not that man anymore, Lizzie. I haven't been that man in seven years, and I would never hurt you."

I should tell him to leave and never return. To stay far away from me and my family.

But I couldn't.

Maybe I could have, days ago, if he had told me... if I had known the truth before I let myself fall for him. And maybe I was lying to myself that this information would ever have swayed me at all. Because who he was in the past was not the man standing in front of me—a man I didn't know how to let go. And I knew that he would never hurt me.

"My mother she... she took her own life with—" I inhaled sharply. "If you hurt yourself with that... I—I couldn't bear it." I couldn't lose someone I loved like that again.

He shook his head. "No. I would never." He ran his hand down my arm, soothing my thoughts.

"Promise me, James." I met his green eyes.

He smiled, placing his hand on my chin. "I have survived for so long, Lizzie. I will not go gently, and definitely not by my own hand." He brushed his thumb on the groove of my chin, looking at me with confoundment in his eyes. "I just admitted that I was a gangster. You should be running."

I'd thought about it. "I'm not fond of running." And I didn't think that I ever could. Not from him.

"And if I asked you to?" I could see the pain in his eyes.

"No." I placed my hand on his face, willing his dark thoughts to leave his mind. "I'm not running. I can't."

A muscle flickered in his jaw, and then he kissed me.

After I put on a simple red gown for Church, he decided that he wanted to join, holding my hand throughout the entire service, as if he thought that maybe I'd run from him. But I couldn't do that. I trusted him. He'd already proven that I could. I was in too deep to let James's past confuse the future I saw with him.

The only future that mattered or made any sense at all was the one that he was in.

When he drove me home afterwards, he stayed, watching me as

I played chess with my father during our usual Sunday routine. Finton plopped down on James's lap, but he didn't seem to mind. He stroked his fur and played with his ears, making me jealous that his hands weren't doing that to me.

I was indeed distracted, so I let my father win, although he didn't seem concerned this time. In fact, I think my father was seeing too much with that grin on his face. Then James left, needing to check on Cam and "deal with some things," or so he said. But he seemed distant... different from the man I woke up with this morning. I hoped he wasn't considering running away from me. He was so concerned about *me* running that I forgot that *he* could be the one who ran.

I spent the rest of the afternoon at the piano, distracting myself from my apprehensive thoughts. Hoping he'd show up at my door in a few hours, but he never did.

Chapter 26

JAMES

Boundaries

I SHOULD HAVE PUNISHED her harder. I should have put the fear of God in her so that when my truth came out, she'd tell me to fuck off. Not that I'd want her to go, but if she chose to, I wouldn't stop her. I was the worst thing for her, but no matter how many times I told her that she just refused to see it, or she just didn't fucking care.

And now I felt like a complete mess.

Sleeping in her bed while I held her close, the date, the gun, the confession and then the fucking Sunday family ritual? I was tiptoeing on a very slim edge that plummeted to my death. This line I'd chosen to walk with her felt like it was going to snap.

I was going to snap.

I just needed a day or two of just space. Which was fucking hard because, of course, I wanted to be next to her. I wanted to hear her laugh, see her smile, watch her fiddle with her hands when she became nervous, listen to her while she frustrated the shit out of me and watch her bite that bottom lip because I said something that made her squirm.

She was an addiction that I never wanted to quit—the only addiction that stopped the nightmares from coming to the surface.

But I needed her more than she needed me, and there was still so much that she didn't know.

Five glasses of whiskey, and still all my thoughts were just... her. Goddamnit.

"I'm surprised to see you here," Cam said as he walked into the drawing room, finding me sprawled on the couch.

"I live here," I muttered, keeping my eyes on my gun resting on the glass table in front of me, freshly polished and cleaned.

"Do you?" His brown eyes flickered with amusement. "Because I think you're over there more than you are here these days." He sat in a vintage green chair across from me.

I met his eyes, and I was not amused. "You should get yourself a girlfriend, and then you won't care about where I am."

"So, you admit that she's your girlfriend," he smiled.

"I don't know what she is." She was more and yet... I wasn't sure if I wanted her to be. When did things move past being simple?

"Don't do that. Pretend you don't care."

I sighed, pulling out a cigarette. "The problem is that I care too much." I lit up, taking a long drag and blowing out smoke into the air. Listening to the crackle of the fireplace. "I told her, Cam." I paused, turning the cigarette in my fingers as I watched the smoke roll off the tip. "I told her about the past."

His eyes lit up. "You told her about Mads?"

"Don't—fucking say her name!" I couldn't stand hearing her name. Every time I heard it, my heart broke a little more. That name was nightmares and endless torture, reminding me of all of my failures and regrets. A constant reminder of what happened when you cared too much about someone.

He put his hands up, "I'm sorry, I just thought—"

"You fucking thought wrong." I pinched the bridge of my nose, trying to keep the fractures of the past at bay. "I told her about The Knives, alright? And she should've ran. That's what normal people do." And Lizzie was the most normal girl I'd ever been with. Why didn't she run? Why wasn't she afraid of me?

He leaned back in the chair, assessing me. "Do you want her to?"

No. Of course, I fucking didn't want her to. "She should."

He stood up and poured himself a glass of whiskey. "Well, I've never seen you happier. And now that we can make all of our earnings in the pit, we—"

"I'm still leaving Cam."

He was about to take a sip, but he stopped. "What?"

"Two more weeks and I'm leaving Birmingham. As I always planned to." Living here was temporary, and I'd never planned on staying. This distance from her was necessary if I was ever hoping to leave this godforsaken place.

"Then, what about Lizzie?"

I inhaled the fumes. "I don't know." I really didn't. She'd never leave her family, and I couldn't stay here. There were too many bad memories and ghosts around every corner waiting to end me. "She's safer without me in her life."

And deep down, I knew that she would be happier with someone else. Someone who wasn't so broken and wrong for her in all of the ways that I was. I could never truly give her what she wanted. There were too many reasons why we didn't work.

He laughed mockingly. "She's not going to feel that way."

"I know," I murmured.

He sat for a moment and then stood, shaking his head. "This is probably the biggest mistake you'll ever make, James." I felt a brush of wind as he rushed past me, pausing at the threshold. "Madeline Grey was cruel"—*I flinched*—"She abused you, tortured and played you. She never fucking deserved you."

"Don't," I snapped at him. Yes, she had done all of those things, but I didn't want to hear it. None of that mattered anymore. She was gone, and it was all my fault.

He pulled something out of his pocket. A vial of cocaine. "I found this in your room. You told me you stopped?"

I took another drag, not wanting to answer him as my eyes fell to the floor.

"You finally have good things in your life and all you want to do is fuck it up. I'll never understand you," he spat and stormed out, slamming the door behind him.

I lay back down on the couch, staring at the ceiling while blowing out smoke. Trying to refocus my mind and not think about Cam's words. Trying not to think about her.

Two days passed, and I didn't leave the house. I didn't even leave the drawing room. I slept on the couch and only returned to my room to bathe. Cameron had barely spoken to me either. He grumbled a few words here and there, stomped about and then spent his days out somewhere, doing what I wasn't sure.

I hated this space, but I needed it. If only to remind myself of where the boundary between us stood. Of where I needed those boundaries to be. Boundaries that Cameron never understood. He might have witnessed the worst moment of my life, but he didn't experience it. That kind of heartbreak changes you... but fuck I missed her.

The clock struck four, and my legs started to shake.

I couldn't stand it for a minute longer.

Fuck the boundary.

About twenty-five minutes later, I was knocking on her door, waiting for her to answer. She had probably written me off by now, but there was no way I could go another day without seeing her. A truth that terrified me, yet here I stood, outside her door in the brisk air. Waiting. Hoping.

The door opened, but it wasn't Lizzie standing in front of me.

"James," her father smiled, wearing silver-rimmed glasses, a green tweed vest and a brown bowler cap. "Please, come in."

I followed him to the drawing room. Seeing Frank was not what I had in mind, but at least he wasn't angry with me. Which was a good sign that perhaps Lizzie wasn't either.

"I've been wanting to talk to you." He gestured to the couch. "Please, sit."

I sat. Maybe I was wrong. Maybe he was just preparing to tell me to stay the fuck away from his daughter. In all honesty, that's exactly what he should do.

He opened a small drawer from a wooden desk in the room and pulled out something small. "I know it's soon, but—" he sat next to me, and my eyes widened at the sight of an engagement ring in his hand. "I've seen the way you look at her and the way she looks at you. And well, I'm getting old. She needs someone to care for her."

Blood rushed too quickly to my heart.

"Sir, I can't—"

"I want my daughter's happiness more than anything." He placed the ring in the palm of my hand. The engagement ring featured a marquise-shaped setting from the Victorian era, crafted from both silver and gold. A vibrant green emerald sat in the centre, surrounded by a dazzling cluster of diamonds. "This was her mother's. Victoria's ring," he said softly.

Fuck. "I can't accept this."

"You can." He placed his hand on mine, curling my fingers around the ring. "I'm sure you'll find the right time to give it to her," he smiled.

My throat felt dry, like I hadn't had a sip of water in days, which was probably true. I had drunk far too much whiskey in the past couple of days while wallowing in my thoughts.

Why was he trusting me with something so special? It didn't make any sense to me. Why was he smiling at me instead of looking at me with disdain or fear? I'd never had a father, but the way he was looking at me now was the way I used to dream about as a boy. The sort of kindness in a man that was soft and rare in the world I knew.

Just as I was about to give the ring back to him with a well-thought-out rejection, she walked into the room.

"Father... Oh—" she started.

I stood at the sight of her, tucking the ring in my pocket.

"James," she smiled, and I felt my heart skip a beat at her genuine smile. But then she frowned, crossing her arms. "Where the hell have you been?"

My mouth couldn't form words.

"I'm famished," Frank said, rising from the couch. Sensing the tension between us. "I think I'll go see what Pearl has prepared for afternoon tea," and then he left the room.

As soon as he was gone, a flurry of red hair whirled towards me. I expected her to slap me, but instead she embraced me in a tight squeeze, enveloping me in her delicious scent of fresh strawberries and slow, drifting fog in the early morning. I wrapped my arms around her, burying myself in her hair. Taking whatever she would give me.

"Aren't you angry with me?"

"Yes." Her voice vibrated against my neck, then she pulled back. "But I'm also just happy that you're here," she smiled, and I felt a wave of relief. "What were you and my father talking about?"

A jolt of fear rushed back into my veins. "Nothing."

"And where were you, James?" She lifted a brow.

Before I could answer, Margaret bustled into the room with Finton at her heels. Finton ran to me when he saw me, asking for attention. Which I gladly gave him. Thankful for the distraction.

"Oh. You're back." Her eyes narrowed on me. "Even bloody Cameron came to visit in the past few days. Did you forget how to find the house?"

"Cameron, came here?" I was filled with plain green jealousy.

"We played chess and had a few drinks. Nothing else," Lizzie said, making eyes at her sister.

Margaret scoffed. "At least make him sweat it a little bit. He deserves it."

I agreed with her, but making me think Cam was making moves on her was not good for my blood pressure.

Lizzie rolled her eyes, mouthing the words *I'm sorry*.

Margaret walked over to a tray of teacakes and took a bite, plopping herself down on the couch. "So, are you losing the fight again tonight? Or winning? Because if it's the first, I have better things to do with my time."

I bit my tongue. "Winning."

"Alright, that's enough, Margaret," she scolded her sister.

Then she grabbed my hand and pulled me out of the drawing room, while Margaret muttered under her breath.

When we entered her room, books were lying everywhere, along with various pieces of paper, a half-eaten box of chocolate and an empty bottle of wine. The tidiest thing in her room was her bed with the red tulips I had given her in a vase on her antique wooden nightstand. Still as fresh as the day I gave them to her. But everything else was a chaotic mess. And Lizzie was not a messy person, or so I'd thought.

"What happened in here?" I asked.

She picked pieces of paper off the floor, gathering them into a pile. "I was writing something. I didn't expect to see you today, or I would've—" she stopped, taking in the disarray. "Cleaned up a bit."

"I'm sorry."

"Why? You didn't do this," she plucked a few more papers, stacking them on her desk.

"I feel like I sort of did."

She stacked books in her hands and neatly placed them on her dresser. "I was just... bored. And angry at you. But I kept myself busy."

"With that?" I pointed to the wine and chocolates, trying not to laugh as a smile spread across my face.

"So, I drank wine and ate chocolate," she rolled her eyes. "*You* just... disappeared," she put her hands on her hips, overcome with frustration. "I needed something to keep myself busy, so I didn't bother you when you clearly didn't want to see me."

I flinched. "I'm sorry," I said again. She was trying to respect my space, seemingly going just as crazy as me. "I did want to see you, Lizzie," I admitted.

Her facial expression softened. "Are you going to tell me where you were? Or should I just assume you were in a bathtub drinking whiskey?"

I chuckled. "I was home. Not in any bathtubs, but there was lots of whiskey." She waited for me to say more, demanding it with her pretty eyes. "I just needed... space," I sighed.

And although I was sick of the space, the engagement ring in my pocket felt like it was burning a hole through the fabric of my trousers.

"Space from me?" Her voice came out in barely a whisper.

My chest tightened. "From everything."

Hurt flashed across her face. "And now?" Her hazel eyes met mine. "Do you still need space?"

There were so many things I needed to tell her, but I didn't want to think any more about it. I'd spent too much time in my mind over the past few days. The only thing I wanted was to feel her skin on mine and place my mouth all over her body.

"Fuck the space."

I lunged for her, and we became a mesh of teeth and tongues. Her hands went to my shirt, untucking it until she caressed my skin. Running her hands along my abs before drifting them lower into the waistband of my trousers. I smiled against her mouth, picking her up with one arm. Then I threw her on the bed, bringing my hand to her wet slit. Stroking her until she trembled, crying out my name.

"James," she cried. "My father is downstairs," her voice was breathless, writhing beneath me.

I put a finger to her mouth. "Then try to be quiet," I smirked.

From what Lizzie has confessed to me, we couldn't be any louder than Margaret was with her partners, and I did not want to stop. I needed her at this moment, and from what I could feel between her thighs, she needed me too. I would apologise to Frank later if I had to.

She laughed, and then I took her hard and fast, removing minimal pieces of clothing. Relishing in the sounds of the noises she made as I thrust inside her, filling her with every inch of me. Enjoying the curves of her mouth and the sensation of her skin.

She was the sweetest drug that I'd ever known. All my fears floated away in a moment, burying themselves deeper as she consumed me.

Chapter 27

JAMES

Run

THREE ROUNDS LATER, MY opponent fell flat. It felt so fucking good to hit something. To hear the crowd cheering and overcome by my performance as blood dripped from my fists. Everything in the world felt right as she smiled at me, standing next to the ring with Frank and Margaret.

I kept having a suspicious feeling that something was wrong all night. A spine-tingling sensation that I let distract me a few times, but I still fought like hell, never missing a window to throw a devastating blow. It had to have been the past two days I spent in dark places and the overconsumption of whiskey. I glanced at her when I could, feeling my trepidation ease with every sweet smile I received.

I planned on having a conversation about my plans after the match. Whatever that looked like for us. Maybe I could visit, or maybe she could? But the more I thought about it, the harder it became. Spending weeks or even months apart would not be ideal.

I needed her more than I needed the drugs.

I was inevitably fucked with my feelings for her. Some time ago, she forced her way in through the defences of my heart, and I wasn't sure how to let her go or if I ever could.

The bell chimed, starting the final match.

I swung left, he swung right and after about a minute I knocked his ass to the ground in one final hard punch to his jaw. Grinning widely at my captivated audience. The announcer, Roy Roberts, wearing his iconic black pin-striped suit and leather gloves, lifted my fists in the air.

"Winner!" He cried out to the roaring crowd.

But when I turned back towards her, my heart stopped. Time stood still as the crowd continued to cheer, and Aidan Murphy was standing next to her. Standing too fucking close with a smile on his greedy face.

Everything in my world went dark.

I gripped the edge of the ring, trying to get Cameron's attention to distract Aidan, but it was too late. Lizzie was already pointing at me with a big smile on her face, not realising the threat. He took her hand, and I hurtled towards her a heartbeat later, putting myself between him and her.

"I was just getting to know your girl," Aidan smiled.

"Stay the fuck away from her," I growled, clenching my fists.

"James, it's fine. We were just talking," she murmured behind me, placing her hand on my arm.

Just talking? There was never *just talking*. He approached her for a reason.

His eyes, mostly concealed under his flat cap, flashed to me for a moment with a look of pure malevolence. Then he turned to her with a grin. "It was lovely to meet you, darling," he said with a tip of his flat cap, and then he slithered away.

I braced her arms. "What the fuck did you say to him?"

"James, he was just—"

"What did you say!" I shook her, tightening my grip.

I didn't mean to, but I couldn't control it. The cocaine, the fight and then fucking Aidan Murphy? My heart rate was never coming down to a reasonable level.

"James, you're hurting me."

"James, stop," Margaret approached me, firmly grabbing my arm as her nails dug in deep. "Let her go," she growled at me.

"I'm sorry," I loosened my grip, realising how hard I was holding her.

Frank stepped up, staring me down as if he was debating on hitting me. "Lizzie, are you alright?" he asked her.

"Yes, I'm fine," she replied, keeping her eyes on mine.

Frank turned to me, placing a firm hand on my shoulder, a death grip. "What's the matter, son?"

"I didn't—I just need a moment with her," I said.

There was no time to explain things to them, so I grabbed Lizzie's hand and tugged her with me. Her sister tried to follow, but I pulled her away too fast, locking us in the lavatory.

Light from the moon drifted in through the small window as she stared at me with frightened eyes. "James, you're scaring me," she breathed, chest heaving. "Who was he?"

My chest felt tight. I could barely breathe as I braced my hand on the wall. "What. Did. You. Say?"

"I didn't say anything!" she yelled with a shaking voice. "He just asked why I was here, and then I said that I was with you and—"

"Fuck!" I slammed my hand on the wall, causing her to flinch. How long had he known about her? There was no way in hell this was a coincidence. He was too cunning for that. "Have you seen him before?"

"No. No, I—I don't think so," she replied.

Someone pounded on the door. I opened it a crack, but when I recognised Cam's familiar face, I let it fly all the way open.

"Margaret's really worried, what's—" Cam started.

"Get them out of here," I grabbed her hand once again and moved past him, heading towards the ring.

As I walked back into the crowd, at least a dozen other Knives were roaming about in black wool coats, flat caps, and black ties.

Slinking in the shadows like finely dressed snakes, waiting for a moment to strike.

"What?" Cam questioned, keeping up his pace with mine. Still not noticing the danger closing in around us.

I whirled back. "I said, take them home, Cam!"

He put his hands up. "Fuck, alright."

He double-backed to collect Margaret and Frank while I briskly walked Lizzie to her car, pushing past people on the way out. The cold air did nothing for the inferno burning inside of me.

I never should have brought her here.

"James, stop! What's happening? I don't want to leave—" She tried to free her grip from mine, but I was stronger.

I opened her car door. "Get in the car, Lizzie."

"No," she mumbled, looking paler than I had ever seen her.

Cameron was approaching in the distance with Margaret and Frank in tow. I could feel *his* shadow, watching us, closing in.

"Please, get in the car," I repeated more gently, or as much as I could manage given my accelerated heart rate.

"No, just tell—"

I slammed my hand on the hood of the car, jolting her attention. "If you fucking care about me at all, you will get in the goddamn car, Lizzie!" I roared with shaking hands.

Her lip quivered, and she got in.

I shut the door, taking a glance around at his men appearing out of the darkness. Cam noticed my gaze, cursing under his breath, and hurried them along.

Margaret glared at me as I opened her door, but thankfully, she hopped in next to Lizzie without a fuss.

I turned to Frank. "Please, go home. Lock your door." He tried to respond, but I interrupted him. "Cam, drive them home."

"What? No, you need—" he started.

"Stop questioning me and go with them," I bellowed.

He cursed and blew out a breath, hopping in the driver's seat.

"Please," I begged Frank, who was hesitant to leave.

"Are you in some kind of trouble?" he asked, as worry crossed his face.

"I don't have time to explain. Please, just get in the car." I glanced at the danger, and that's when Frank saw the men—twelve of them walking out of the darkness towards the car. "I'm sorry," I murmured as he made the connection. "But please, you need to leave right now," I gestured to the car once more, and he finally got in.

I sighed with relief, watching them drive away fast into the night. A chill rolled down my spine as his footsteps sounded behind me, crunching in the gravel. He slowly clapped his hands, and I cracked my neck, turning to face him.

Aidan stopped mere inches in front of me, grinning from the corner of his mouth. "Well, well. That was quite a performance. You know, there's nowhere they could go that I wouldn't find them."

His men formed a wall behind him, circling me.

I reached my hand closer to my knife.

"Was that really necessary?" He gestured to their car before it faded into the distance. "I was only talking to her," he smirked.

"You have no reason to talk to her," I barked.

He rubbed his chin. "She's quite bonnie. You and I always had the same taste in women."

"I will fucking kill you," I stepped towards him, seconds from stabbing him in the chest.

He laughed and clasped his hands in front of him.

His men pulled out their guns, aiming at my head.

My hands rose in surrender, catching Harry's worried eyes trained on me. His left eye was black, and his lip was split open. I'm guessing Aidan did that after he found out about my new deal. I recognised John and Mack standing next to him. Both were around my age, and both must have decided to stay in the gang when they returned from the war. Their harsh expressions softened when they recognised who I was.

"I'm getting quite sick of that mouth of yours," Aidan frowned. "First, you try to rob me of my half."

Harry's eyes fell to the ground.

"And then you try to tell me what women I can and can't talk to? Do you realise who I fucking am?" Aidan held out his hands, gesturing to the small militia behind him. "I didn't realise the rumours of you and this girl were true. But you played a very convincing hand tonight. Throwing yourself in front of her. Sending her home at the mere whiff of danger," his smile grew into something cruel. "I think you're in love with her, James."

I dropped my eyes to the ground, realising how much I fucked up for reacting so quickly. For letting fear control me.

"Yes, love makes us do stupid things. I thought you would've remembered that," Aidan continued. "Tell you what. I'm feeling generous despite your fucking lack of respect. After all, I've made quite a bit of scratch from your fights. I'll give you a choice." He pulled out a cigarette and lit it up. Blowing out smoke into the frigid air. "You leave and promise to never return, and I'll promise not to slice her pretty throat."

My hands started to shake, wanting to scream at him to never fucking threaten her, but it would only encourage him.

"It's a good deal. You should take it," he crooned. "I'll know you'll be miserable for the rest of your pathetic life, and she lives," he smiled. "It's a fair trade, don't you think?"

But nothing about this was fucking fair.

"Or I could just fucking kill you now," he reached impatiently for his gun.

My nostrils flared. "Fine. I'll leave tomorrow," I turned to walk away.

"No. You'll leave tonight." He took out a shiny gold pocket watch from his dark grey vest, glancing at the time. "You have one hour, James. And I'd better not fucking see you again."

⬦

I raced to my house, grabbing a few of my things from my room, plus the scratch I had hidden under my bed. Then I drove as fast as I could to her house.

I knocked a few times on her door, greeted by Cam holding his gun. He smiled in relief, and I smiled back.

"Thank fucking Christ," he murmured.

I stepped inside, closing the door behind me.

"What did he want?" Cam asked.

"I need to leave." I shoved the money in a bag towards him with shaking hands. "Give this to Frank, and... take some for you."

"James, there has to be—" he started to protest, shaking his head as a wrinkle formed in his brow.

"Take care of them, Cameron."

His head hung low, and his mouth formed a tight line as he nodded. "Yeah, alright."

"Leave where?" Her voice flooded through me.

I caught her reddened eyes staring at me as she stood in the hall with her arms tight across her chest. She looked so small and so scared. I wanted to wrap my arms around her and never let her go, but I stopped myself from rushing towards her.

If I left, he wouldn't harm her.

He was a snake, but his deals were stone. It was the only thing I could trust at this moment.

"I'll go entertain Frank and Margaret in the kitchen," Cameron said, placing a firm but shaky hand on my shoulder. "Stay out of the trenches," he murmured with worried eyes. Words we'd often said to each other when the nightmares of our pasts would win.

I pulled him in for a quick hug. "You, too."

He gave me one last look and then walked away, rounding up Finton, who went trotting along with him down the hall. I gestured for Lizzie to enter the drawing room. She followed silently, sitting on the couch as the fireplace bloomed in vibrant colours. I glanced at the clock on the wall.

I only had five minutes.

And I needed to make them count.

"Lizzie—" I dropped to my knees in front of her.

She pulled away, tears falling. "Why?"

"I have no choice." My eyes burned.

"Does it have to do with that man from the pit?"

Shit. "Lizzie—" I grabbed her hand.

"Take me with you," she said, squeezing my hand.

My chest felt tight. *Fuck I wished I could.* "I can't." I placed my hand on her chin. "And you can't leave your family."

She placed her delicate hands on my face, brushing the hair from my eyes. "Please. Please, don't leave. If I've done something wrong—"

My mouth formed a smile, as much as I could manage. "You've done nothing." The last thing I wanted her to feel was that this was her fault. It was mine.

"Then why, James? What has you so scared?"

The less she knew, the better. I didn't want her to worry or fear for anything after I'd gone.

"Look, I don't have a lot of time," I reached for her face, but she pulled away, rising from the couch.

I followed her pace, watching her chest heave as tears stained her face. "Do you need more space? I can—you can have more—"

Then I wrapped my arms around her, stopping her words that were tearing me apart. Needing to hold her, but she pushed me away again. I wasn't going to accept that, so I pulled her tighter, crushing her to me, and she finally gave in, snuggling her head against my chest.

I almost fell apart at that moment alone.

"You're going to be fine," I stroked her silky hair as she sobbed. "And you're going to be happy." The words scraped in my throat at the thought that I would no longer be the one who made her happy. I swallowed, willing myself to tell her to move on.

To do the right thing for once in my damn life.

"And you'll meet someone new and—"

She pulled away. "Just stop! Stop. I don't want someone new, I want you!"

I wanted her too, so goddamn much, but I couldn't have her. And to be honest, I never deserved her in the first place.

She placed her hands on my chest, fidgeting with the collar of my shirt. "I want you. I love you, James. I love you so much," she cried as tears rolled down her cheeks. "So please, please just stay. Whatever it is, we can—"

"We can't." I opened my eyes and pulled her hands from my chest. "I have to go," I said, moving briskly to the front door.

I needed to get out of here. And the faster the better, before my heart collapsed.

"No, no, please. Don't do this. Please! Please just tell me why?" She followed me to the door, grabbing my arms.

All I could hear was the sounds of her falling apart as I stood at the threshold. Sounds that would haunt my dreams for the rest of my life.

But at least she would live.

"James, please! P-please, please just tell me why!" She cried, begging and trying to pull me back. Unwanted tears fell from my eyes. "If you love me at all, you'll stay. Please, please just stay!" Her voice broke.

But I couldn't stay, even if I wanted to. I needed to know she would continue to breathe. That her heart would continue to beat even if I were no longer around to feel it. There was nothing more important than that.

I turned around, facing her one last time at the doorway. Staring into her hazel eyes, taking in the swirls of gold and green, the freckles across her face, the fullness of her pink lips, and the shine of her vibrant red hair for one last time. Committing it all to memory.

I shut my eyes and then opened them, willing my heart to turn to stone. "I don't."

She stood frozen.

And then I left.

The only sound I could hear was the clock ticking and my breaking heart as I drove off into the starry night. I didn't even glance back as my car was engulfed in the fog.

Chapter 28

ELISABETH

Collapse

I COLLAPSED IN THE doorway as he left. Unable to breathe. Unable to think as my body trembled beneath me.

He didn't love me.

He didn't love me...

Margaret and my father were there a moment later as I fell apart in their embrace. Repeating the words over and over until my voice was lost to the sound of my sobs. This pain was devastating, and I was drowning in it.

He didn't love me.

And I guess some part of me knew it all along.

I shoved both of them away and dashed upstairs to my room, locking the door behind me. I threw the bouquet of red tulips into the fireplace and watched them burn as I fell to the floor and cried.

Chapter 29

ELISABETH

Honesty

THERE WAS SOMETHING SLOW about heartbreak. It didn't happen all at once, but in stages. Shock. Numbness. Denial. Anger. Fear. Loneliness. Depression. I wasn't sure what stage I was in anymore, or how to stop the depression from eating me alive.

It was now November.

It had been a month since he left.

Some days I felt nothing at all, others I woke up feeling the need to break something, like my mirror that was now shattered into pieces on my bedroom floor. I still hadn't cleaned it up, nor did I let Pearl. The glass was a reminder that he wasn't coming back, and I needed it when denial crept into my thoughts that he'd show up. That it was all just a bad dream.

Because he was never coming back.

He never loved me.

I cut my long red hair to my shoulders one evening, needing a change. Margaret had to fix it afterwards, shortening it a bit more to make it even at the ends. I should not have tried to cut it when I was crying on the floor in my lavatory. I burned the red dress and the black velvet dress. Then I set fire to anything that reminded me of the past. Everything that he touched... everything that he claimed. If only I could set fire to myself, seeing as he tried to claim that, too. And then other days, I struggled to get out of bed.

Today was a numb day as I sat at my mother's grave. I couldn't even force myself to cry, not for her or him... Maybe the chill in the wind made it harder for tears to form, or maybe I didn't have any tears left to give.

I was so sick of crying.

I pulled the black fur of my coat closer to my face as another gust of wind blew through me. "I wish you were here, Mother," I placed white snowdrops on her stone. Tulips triggered too many emotions. "We all do."

The wind blew through the dead trees, reminding me of the fear I had felt the last time I was here. But I felt nothing besides the chill in the air. I rose from the ground and headed towards the car —the only car parked in the Warstone Lane Cemetery. I hopped in, blowing out a breath of water vapour as I tried to start the car.

Grinding noises responded and then silence.

"Damnit!" I slammed my hands on the steering wheel and jumped out of the car.

Great. It was freezing and the damn car wouldn't start.

I leaned back against the side of the car and closed my eyes, cursing at whatever God above that hated me so goddamn much.

"Car trouble?"

That *voice*. I snapped my head up, making contact with dark brown eyes. Familiar, yet strange. He wore a black wool coat, a matching flat cap and black leather gloves. And there was a scar on his right cheekbone... a scar that I feel I'd seen before.

He pointed at the car. "I can take a look if you like?" His accent was Irish. Too Irish. I didn't like it. "I'm quite good with cars," he added, curling his mouth to the side.

"Fine," I muttered, stepping back from the car. What other option did I have?

He opened the car door, turning the key. "You don't remember me, do you?"

"No," I crossed my arms. "Are you important or something?"

He chuckled, listening to the noises the car made. "I think I know the issue." He shut the door. "I know a guy not far from here." He pulled out a shiny gold pocket watch, glancing at the time. "I can get it fixed in about an hour."

"Great," I blew out air.

He shoved the watch back in his pocket and extended his gloved hand. "Aidan." And just like that. I knew exactly who he was. I didn't take his hand. "You've remembered," he smiled.

He was the man I met in the pit. The man that J—... I couldn't even think of his name. All I knew was that *he* didn't like him. My heart pounded. "Actually, I think I'll figure something else out."

"It's already taken care of."

"What?" Was the car going to magically fix itself? There was no one else around us, but he seemed confident that it was *taken care of.*

"Come have a drink with me," he offered.

This guy had some nerve. "No thanks," I scoffed.

"In an hour, you'll be on your way," he said casually as his smile grew bigger. "Come on, you'll freeze to death standing out here. Let me buy you a drink."

Well, if he was buying. "Lead the way," I gestured. "But if you decide to screw me over and steal my car things are going to end badly for you."

He laughed. "I wouldn't dare."

I followed him to an old pub around the corner.

It was the middle of the day, so it was quiet as we sat at a small, rickety table. The dust-covered walls were covered in crooked photos, and the lights in the room were dim. A pub that I would never visit after the sun went down.

Aidan ordered a whiskey, and I did the same, which shocked him.

"I would have assumed wine or some bubbly thing," he said, pulling off his leather gloves.

"You assumed wrong." Wine no longer helped me. Perhaps I had drunk too much of it. Whiskey was the only thing that numbed the pain these days. Lots and lots of whiskey.

He pulled out a cigarette and lit it up, wafting smoke around his rigid features. Thank Christ the whiskey was there a second later to drown out the memories coming to the surface. The warming sensation was euphoric. I grabbed the bottle sitting on the table and poured another glass, needing more.

"You seem different," he said after some time. "Not the same girl I met that night at the pit."

The worst night of my life.

I slammed my glass down. "One. You don't know me. Two. Why am I here?" I had zero patience these days and zero tolerance for games.

He smiled. "I'm helping you with your car."

"And you're randomly at the cemetery in the middle of the day?"

"I have family there."

Oh. I leaned back, taking another sip. "I'm sorry." I guess that checked out.

"Actually, I wasn't one hundred per cent sure it was you, so I let my curiosity get the better of me. Your new haircut almost fooled me. But when I saw your face, well, I couldn't resist asking you out," his eyes darted from my eyes to my breasts.

Old Lizzie would have blushed, but all I could do was laugh in his face. "I'm flattered. But it's never going to happen," I laced my words with venom.

He was handsome, sure, and in a weird way, probably my type with his choice of fashion. But I had no interest in getting to know him or anyone else ever again.

"I bet I could change your mind," he grinned, as light danced around in his brown eyes, barely visible under his black flat cap.

"You seem too confident about that, considering I have no interest in you," I stared back at him, not giving an inch.

He leaned forward and dropped his voice an octave. "Let's not start lying here, Lizzie. You've been honest so far. Let's keep it that way. You know that you find me attractive," he smiled, curling his lip.

I dropped my gaze to the table and back again. "Fine." I leaned forward, pinning my gaze to his. Holding his challenging stare. "I'm honestly not interested in you. How's that for honesty?"

His eyes drifted to my mouth and back again. "I honestly like you a lot more than I thought I would."

I pulled open the front door and was greeted by Cameron with Finton at his heels. My weird day just took a turn for the worse.

"I've told you to never come back here," I said through clenched teeth. I thought I had made that clear to him the last time he was here, "checking in" as he called it.

"We're still stuck on that?" he questioned, with a vexing tone. His reddish-brown facial hair was longer. In the past he donned a trim moustache, but now his face was scruffy, like he hadn't shaved in weeks.

I pushed past him, running into Margaret.

"You were gone later than I expected," she put her hands on her hips.

"Car trouble. I fixed it." I took off my coat and hung it on the wall. "Why is *he* here?" I pointed with my thumb.

"Lizzie—" she started.

"No! Don't *Lizzie* me! I've told you I don't want him here. I don't want to see his face. I never want to see him again!" His face was a reminder of a past I wanted to forget.

And ever since Cameron said that what *he* did was the *right* thing, I couldn't stand the sight of him. What he did was selfish and cruel—and I would never forgive him for it.

Cameron raised his hands in defeat, shaking his head as he left without another word.

Margaret crossed her arms, glaring at me. "That was very rude. He's only trying to help," she snapped.

"I don't want him here." I ground out each word, and then I sauntered up the stairs to my room, hearing the clicking of Finton's nails on the wood floors as he followed me.

A few minutes later, Margaret pushed open the door, leaning against the doorframe. "Perhaps we should go out tonight. Have some fun. Let out some of your rage."

I shot her a glare as I finished tying around my pink silk bathrobe. "You go. I have plans." I gestured towards my lavatory, where a hot bath with lavender salts waited for me.

"Right, because drinking whiskey in the bathtub is *so* much better," she rolled her eyes.

"You've spent many nights in the bathtub, Margaret. Don't even judge me." I grabbed the bottle of whiskey from the nightstand and headed for the bath.

Thudding footsteps echoed in the hall, drawing our attention to my bedroom door. Pearl rushed in a moment later. Her grey hair was plastered to her sweaty forehead. "It's Frank," she spoke breathlessly.

Margaret and I looked at each other, and then we were running down the hall, down the stairs and into his study.

Father was coughing up a fit.

We ran to his side. Pearl wrapped her arm around him, steadying him. His face was turning blue, and there was blood on his handkerchief and around his mouth.

My hands started to shake.

"I've called the doctor, but I couldn't get through." Pearl's voice shook. "He needs to go to hospital."

Margaret and I lifted Father off the ground and helped him into the car. Taking off fast into the frosted night.

We sat at the hospital for hours, waiting to hear if he was going to be alright. Thankfully, I grabbed my brown coat before we left so I wasn't walking around in public in my pink bathrobe. Not that I cared about what anyone thought anymore. I was becoming more and more like Margaret than I cared to admit.

"Montgomery?" A nurse called.

We both stood up and followed her to the room.

The sight of my father in a hospital bed nearly made my knees buckle. A mask covered his face as I held his weathered and wrinkled hand while he slept, inoculated with pain-relieving drugs. Margaret held back tears as she took his other hand.

He looked so peaceful in this moment, in the moment before everything changed. The doctor came in moments later, well and truly shattering my heart completely. Our father had an incurable disease known as tuberculosis.

He would die, and there was nothing we could do about it.

I ran outside, needing air, needing something I would never find because he decided to abandon me. I threw up in the bushes. Retching and retching until my sobs swallowed me whole.

Chapter 30

JAMES

Burn in Hell

BARE-KNUCKLE FIGHTING PITS in London were bigger than I last remembered. Over the past month, I found an underground ring that paid me pretty well. I sent money whenever I could to Cameron, knowing he would know what to do with it. Last week I even wrote a letter to Lizzie.

Of course, it came back with 'burn in hell' written on the sealed envelope. I'm not sure why I expected something different, and I didn't blame her. I kept it, though, if only to look at her handwriting. Maybe someday I'd try again, although I didn't expect a different outcome.

When I last spoke with Cam, he told me that she was doing well, or well enough considering. It was all I could ask for, and I didn't ask for much these days.

"James," Riley Hennessy murmured as he approached me. He was a man in his early twenties with dirty blonde hair and a devil with a gun. A nickname well-known in the darkest corners of London.

"Riley," I murmured back, sipping my whiskey as I kept my eyes on the bar.

Riley ordered a glass of gin and took off his black fedora, setting it on the bar. Then he slumped down in the seat next to me, lighting up a cigarette. Warm morning light bounced around the room as I played with my Celtic ring on my finger.

"How are things?" he asked, blowing out smoke.

I didn't answer him.

"That bad..." he murmured. "Well, maybe this will cheer you up." He set down a stack of notes on the bar. "I need help with something, and before you say no, just hear me out."

Riley was in a gang in London known as The Dice, and I wanted no part. Something I'd made clear weeks ago.

"No. I don't associate with gangs, I don't know why you keep talking to me." I glanced at the tattoo of a skull in flames with an ace of hearts and dice on his hand. Something I wish I'd noticed sooner before I started hanging out with him.

Of course, he was in a fucking gang.

It was the only kind of friend I knew how to make.

He reminded me of a younger version of myself. Except I didn't think that Riley was ever looking for redemption. He was still living in a violent darkness that I didn't want to get swallowed back up into.

He sighed. "Stop being a dick. I'm the only fucking friend you have here. You should treat me better."

I laughed. "I wouldn't say we're friends, Riley."

"Frenemies, then," he smiled, shuffling closer to me. The smell of his strong cologne wafted in my face. "Now, it's a simple job. An easy game of cards—"

"I suck at cards." We frequently played cards together, and let's just say I was unlucky. Or rather, I just didn't give a shit enough to pay attention at the table.

"I know. That's why you're not playing," he grinned, taking a long drag from his cigarette.

I set down my whiskey. "I'm not following."

"I need another gun. Oh, and look," he gestured to my gun resting on the bar. "You have one," he grinned.

"I think you have me confused with someone else." I was not going to work for Riley Hennessy. No fucking way.

He pushed the stack closer to me. "All you need to do is stand there and look intimidating. Should be easy enough for you, and that permanent frown on your face. You shouldn't even need to use those prized fists."

I slid the notes back. "I don't want your money, Riley. And I sure as hell don't want to work for you." I was already walking a thin line with his 'friendship,' and I didn't need any more targets on my back. "You should get out while you still can," I took another sip, hoping he'd just walk away.

"Get out?" He laughed. "My family will always come first."

"Your family is going to get you killed."

He smiled. "They'll have to catch me first. Besides, I like the darkness, James, and you know you do too," he slid it back with a crooked smile on his face. "You're fucking bored as hell, and I know you need the money. Money for that girl you have back in Birmingham."

"Excuse me?" I looked at him, for the first time since he sat next to me, clenching my fists. It took everything in me not to wipe that devilish grin off his young face.

"Are you really surprised that I found out? You've been sending money to Birmingham for weeks. Only a man with a girl does that," he grinned.

"Wrong." I would deny that until the day I died if only to keep her safe.

He glanced at my clenched fists. "So fucking tense," he blew out a cloud of thick smoke still smiling. "You should fuck something, preferably a woman but I'm not one to judge. And watching doesn't count," he snapped at me.

"How do you even—" How did he even know that?

"Girls talk," he leaned in, putting out his cigarette in the glass ashtray on the bar. "I need another gun at the tables. I'm not one to beg, but I'm pretty fucking desperate," he glanced at the money, begging me to take it. "If you make me say please, I'm going to have to shoot something. And my eyes are set on a stubborn Irishman."

"You pull out that gun and I'll remove your face," I warned.

Riley smiled with a wicked gleam shining in his steel grey eyes. "I dare you. It would be the most interesting thing to happen to me all day."

He was fucking crazy.

"Fine." I sighed and grabbed the money off the bar, sliding it into the pocket of my coat. Hoping he would shut up and leave me alone before I decided to break his jaw.

I knew hanging around him was going to end badly, but I just couldn't get myself to care. Today or tomorrow. I already knew where I was going to end up if I died, words she'd written so beautifully on the envelope of my letter.

"Just this once, Riley. But never fucking mention I have a girl in Birmingham. Not to a single goddamn soul. Got it?" I didn't want to have to kill him, but I would if he didn't keep his mouth shut—and a part of me might even enjoy that, just so I could feel something other than heartbreak.

"Deal," Riley smiled, grabbing his fedora and rising from the bar stool. "And please, for everyone's sake just fuck something, James. Killing me is not going to make you happy."

But it might

It's like he could read my thoughts.

I darkly laughed and waved him off as he left, pulling out a letter from Cameron that I received this morning, ripping it open as I read his neat scrawl. He wished me a happy birthday and told me he had purchased a new car. A red one in my honour, as red was always my favourite colour. Then he told me that he needed to give Lizzie space... perhaps for a month or so, because she hated him and didn't want him around anymore.

The only thing I could do for her was send her money, and she wouldn't even take it. And now I'd have to go a whole month without hearing how she was. I crumpled Cameron's letter and stuffed it in my pocket, grabbing my gun and flat cap before I set off, making my way back to my room at the Inn across the street.

The room began to spin as I lay down for a nap, feeling the whiskey hitting me hard. I'd barely slept in weeks, and I needed all my strength for the fight tonight.

But as sleep came, so did the nightmares.

Except everything felt so real... like I'd slipped back in time.

I was working for The Knives, doing one of my usual haunts, prying information from a man by cutting off his fingers.

One by one.

Blood spattered on the sleeves of my long, crisp white shirt. He started to pray, begging for me to stop. Four fingers later, he finally told me what I needed to know, and then I killed him. As I was told to do. I exited the room afterwards as four others stayed behind to clean up the mess. I didn't feel guilt or even a hint of repulsion. I'd seen so much dismemberment and death from a young age that it didn't faze me.

Violence and I were old friends.

I cleaned my knife on my wool coat and turned the corner, seeing a flash of red hair standing in the fog. Her cries filled me with such desperation that I ran to her. But every time I got closer, she was farther and farther away.

I couldn't reach her. I couldn't see her face.

Fuck, if only I could just see her... hold her, but my dreams were never that kind.

When I finally awoke, I was covered in sweat.

The fight that night was the only thing that brought me peace, but something in me had decided to snap. I'd already taken my opponent down, and yet I couldn't stop hitting him.

I hit him again, and again, and again.

I didn't feel a thing.

Three men had to pry me off him, but I wanted more. I wanted the pain, the blood, and the fear in his eyes. I wanted the violence because it was the only thing that made me feel release.

Chapter 31

ELISABETH

In the Snow

EVERY WEEK, FATHER GREW sicker and sicker. But some days, like today, he acted like everything was fine. Walking around the house with a smile on his face, whistling a carefree tune I could never figure out.

"Where are you going?" I crossed my arms, watching him put on his coat and hat like he thought he was leaving.

"I just need to stop by the factory to—"

"Oh no," I grabbed his arm, pulling him back. "I don't think so."

"Lizzie, I'll only be gone for a few hours."

I frowned, opening the door as a flurry of snow blew in. "You, see? You're staying right here."

It was the first week in December, and the snow had already covered Birmingham with a thick white sheet.

He placed his hand on my arm. "You and your sister have taken such good care of me these past few weeks. I just need to sort some things out. It's very important, Lizzie."

"A few hours?" I arched my brow.

He smiled. "I'll be back soon." He reached down to scratch Finton between the ears. "Perhaps a game of chess when I return?"

I sighed. "Fine. But please take the car."

He nodded, leaning in to kiss me on the cheek. I threw my arms around him, hugging him tightly. "If you're not back in three hours, so help me—"

He pulled back and patted my arm. "I'll be here, don't you worry." He went to step out the door but then stopped. "Lizzie... are you... Well, I've been so worried lately. We haven't talked much about him and—"

"I don't want to talk about him," I snapped, but then immediately regretted it as hurt flashed across my father's face. "I'm sorry. I didn't mean—"

"It's alright. I understand," he smiled and placed a comforting hand on my shoulder. "I should have listened to your sister when she told me not to ask." I snorted at that. "But... I just need to know if you're going to be alright." His deep blue eyes searched my face. "You are going to be alright?"

He was worried about me? He was the one who was dying, not me. "Yes, I'm going to be fine." At least I had hoped that someday I would be. Surely, one day the anger in my heart would just die. "You don't need to worry about me, Father."

He smiled, bringing attention to his white whiskers. "Keep your chin up, darling. Things will turn out. The—"

"They always do," I muttered before he could finish.

He laughed. "You are so much like your mother," he smiled. Tears began to form in his eyes. "Beautiful. Strong. And fiercely stubborn just as she was."

I stifled a laugh. "I'm going to take that as a compliment."

He smiled. "I'll see you soon." And then he walked out the door and into the snowy night.

I watched him as he waved and hopped into the car, driving away, as he left tracks in the snow. Then I tugged on my brown boots and brown wool coat with a fluffy black fur collar.

"Pearl?" I called to her as she approached me down the hall with clean linens in her hand.

"Yes, Elisabeth?"

"I'm going for a walk. I'll be back in an hour," I pulled on my matching wool gloves.

"Please be safe. I'll put on some tea for your return," then she turned the corner, vanishing from view.

I placed my hat on my head, peering down at Finton, who looked up at me with sad eyes. "I'll be back soon, Fin." I patted him on the head and then headed out into the snowy, dark streets of Birmingham.

I walked a few blocks with my hands in my warm pockets as thick snowflakes fell from the sky, tingling my freckled nose. I loved the city at night. The serenity. The stillness. And with the city cloaked in snow, old things looked new and different—with the possibility of making new memories as the snow covered everything recognisable. Walking alone at night in the city gave me a thrill that I couldn't find anywhere else, and there was no one who could tell me otherwise. Not anymore.

I approached a pub sitting on the corner of a street and glanced in the windows, finding people laughing and dancing in front of a roaring fire. My stomach clenched as old memories tried to rise to the surface. I pushed the black fur higher around my face and headed towards the frozen canal. The frigid, icy water ebbed and flowed beneath a thin sheet of ice while I stared at my reflection, lost in my melancholic thoughts.

I couldn't believe that he tried to send me a letter, as if I would even consider or want to read about more of his lies... that I even cared. I debated on burning it, but I found it more spiteful to send it back with a warm gesture. I could only imagine how that sentiment found him.

I'm not sure how long I was standing there until footsteps in the snow snapped my attention.

"Of course," I groaned, narrowing my eyes at a man walking out from the darkness. "Do you not understand the meaning of the word 'no'?"

Aidan laughed. "I've never been one to take no for an answer. You'll learn that about me." Heavy snowflakes clung to his black coat and flat cap as he approached me.

"You say that like I want to learn." Which I didn't. I thought I'd made that clear during our last conversation.

I wanted nothing to do with him.

He stood next to me, staring at the canal. "You will."

I glanced around at the empty streets. Not a single car passed by. "Are you following me?"

"Not today," he smiled. "But it would be easy if I wanted to. I know these streets like the back of my hand."

I let out a long, frustrated breath, watching as it dissipated.

Why won't he just go away?

"Have you thought any more about my offer?" he asked.

"Which one? To date you? I'd rather eat snow. To work for you? I'd rather jump in the frozen canal."

At the end of our last conversation at the pub, Aidan asked me out and then offered me a job. What that was, I didn't care, nor did I ever want to work for him. And dating him? He was dreaming if he thought that would ever happen. I didn't want to date anyone.

"You don't even know what I'm offering," he grinned.

"Don't need to because I don't want it." He could never offer me something that I would want.

"Well, I do not suggest jumping into the frozen canal." He laughed and reached into his pocket. "But, here." He pushed a card in front of my face that was stuck between the fingers of his black leather gloves. "My card should you ever need it."

"I don't." I glared at him, refusing to take it.

"Are you always this stubborn?" he asked.

"Yes."

"Take it and I'll stop following you," he insisted.

So, he *was* following me... why was I not surprised? I glanced at him and the card. Then I snatched it from his gloved hand and tucked it into my pocket. "There. Now leave me alone." I turned and walked away, heading towards home.

"Goodnight, Lizzie." I didn't even have to see him to know that he was smiling.

It took around an hour to walk back home. I didn't realise how far I'd walked until I reached my street. My feet and nose felt frozen as I approached my house.

But the front door was wide open, blasting yellow light from the house into the dark and snowy night. Two police cars were parked in front, and our car was parked behind them. The blue lights reflected off the snow, drawing my attention to Margaret. She was standing out in the snow wearing nothing but her night-gown. Barefoot, as makeup streamed down her face, looking as pale as the snow. Pearl stood next to her with tears in her eyes.

"Where have you been?" Margaret cried as five policemen stood solemnly behind her.

"I was—" And then I noticed the blood-stained hat in her shaking hands.

Our father's brown bowler cap.

"What is—" I couldn't form words.

I couldn't breathe.

I couldn't even think about what was happening.

My voice didn't feel like my own. "Is that... is he home? Tell me he came home, Margaret. Tell me—"

Tears filled Margaret's eyes. Her voice was lost to her cries as Pearl embraced her.

My body shook beneath me as a policemen explained that Frank Montgomery had been found frozen in the snow, suffering from a heart attack. I collapsed into the snow as my entire world ripped apart.

My father was dead.

I'd never felt more alone.

Chapter 32

JAMES

The Dice

THREE WEEKS LATER, I was still working for Riley as a hired gun for his underground card games. I stood at the back watching the corners and shadows while he played. When I wasn't in the ring, I was following him around simply because it was something to do instead of spending my days at the rundown Inn inhaling opium until I blacked out. I desperately needed the distraction, and the money was pretty good, too.

Not that anything mattered anymore.

But tonight was different. I assumed it was Riley's boss who walked in an hour ago and sat at the table. The three men he brought in with him all had traces of dice and cards tattooed into their skin, matching black fedoras and serious expressions on their faces. They nodded to me, but only one of them introduced himself. A man named Perry, who was a few years younger than me, with short hair that was buzzed on the sides and a tattoo on his neck.

"I saw your fight last night. I shouldn't have bet against you," Perry smiled with his arms crossed in front of him. His features were blended into the dark corner in which we stood, keeping our eyes on the game table.

My eyes were trained on the window behind the boss, swearing that I kept seeing someone outside. "Well, you'll never make that mistake again," I murmured.

And there it was again. A shadow.

There was someone outside.

"What?" Perry whispered.

"Don't move. Don't look around. Keep your eyes on the table. I'm going to sneak around the back," I murmured to Perry, and then I stepped back into the wall, cloaking myself in shadow. Making my way out the back door into the snow.

I pulled out my revolver as I neared the corner. Slowly and carefully, so I didn't make too much noise in the crunching snow beneath me. Heavy snow fell from the grey skies above as I made out a shape in the flurry.

"Turn around slowly," I growled to the man peeking through the window. He whipped towards me, throwing his hands in the air when he saw my gun pointed at his head.

Fuck he was young. He had to be ten or eleven with a frightened look on his dirty face.

"Please, I had no choice!" he cried.

I lifted my gaze, scanning from right to left until I found a shooter placed on a rooftop across the street. His aim was targeted at the one window moulded into the dark brick of the game table.

"Run," I whispered to the boy.

I fired three times in the air, watching as the boy jolted, disappearing into the powder. The gunmen on the roof fled. I lowered my gun, relaxing it at my side.

But when I turned around, Riley had his gun pointed straight between my eyes.

"Duck," he murmured with a faint smile, clicking it back.

I ducked, and in the next second, he fired, taking out a man across the street who was about to shoot me. The bullet went right between his eyes.

"Shit," I breathed, heart racing to the point of pain.

Riley smiled, spinning his gun in his hand before he sheathed it in his shoulder holster. "Good thing you move fast," he curved his mouth to the side and ran a hand through his blonde hair, pleased with himself.

"Fuck Riley," I huffed.

"You're welcome. This is going to make the boss happy," he slapped me on the shoulder and headed back inside.

I stood in the snow catching my breath, almost wishing I'd just let him shoot me. It would've been an easy way out, but I guess some part of me still wanted to live, and I'm not sure why. I had nothing to live for.

I did not want to meet with Riley's boss, but he found me anyway the next afternoon, sitting at a table in the back of the bar. He walked in like he owned the place, wearing a custom-tailored suit paired with a red tie, slicked-back dark hair, and a trimmed circle goatee. Two men followed him in, standing at the front door, guarding it.

"May I sit?" he asked.

I nodded, taking a puff of my cigarette as I placed my gun on the table as a reminder that I would use it if I had to.

He leaned back in his seat, staring at me under his black fedora. He appeared to be in his forties, with hard lines on his cheeks. "You must be James," he glanced at the gun sitting on the table. "Riley has told me a lot about you."

"I'm sure he has." I blew out smoke, filling the air around us.

He eyed me for a moment and then extended his gloved hand. "I'm Jay Green."

I didn't take it.

He laughed, dropping his hand. "I wanted to give my thanks in person. What you did last night, well, it would've gone very differently if you hadn't been there."

I flicked my cigarette in the glass ashtray. "I'm sure your other men are quite capable. Riley especially." If the shot he made last night to save my life was any proof of his capability, which it fucking was.

Jay chuckled as the bartender delivered him a glass of scotch. "Riley said you'd be... difficult." He pulled out a cigar and a silver lighter.

As he lit up, I noticed a large tattoo on his neck. Dice and an ace of spades, similar to Perry's tattoo. Perhaps they were related, or this gang just really liked neck tattoos.

"I could use a man like you," he blew out smoke. "Someone older. Wiser. More experienced. I'm prepared to offer you a job, a high rank in The Dice."

I laughed under my breath and leaned forward. "I don't know what Riley's told you about me, but I have no fucking interest. I'm not planning on staying here. I've spent enough of my life serving in a fucking gang." And serving someone else's agenda. "Or did Riley skip that part?"

"He said you'd say that." The corners of Jay's mouth turned up. "I'm well aware of your loyalties to The Knives."

"I have no fucking loyalty," I laughed. "This has been interesting, but I have plans." Plans to drown myself in a void of pain-free nothingness. I rose from the table, grabbing my coat with a cigarette still burning in the corner of my mouth.

"So, where will you go? Back to Birmingham?" Jay mused.

I stood still as thick smoke clung to the air.

I was going to kill Riley after this. I clenched my teeth and sat, meeting his icy blue eyes. "What do you want?"

Jay smiled, forming wrinkles around his mouth. "I can understand your hesitation, James. But I am not Murphy. I'm an honourable man."

As honourable as a con man with a gun, but sure.

"I play by the rules of the game. You saved my life last night. The rules of the game are that I owe you. Now, you don't want a job, fine. But there must be something that you want. I don't like to leave loose ends."

I shifted in my seat and dropped my eyes to the table, thinking for a moment. Of course, there was something I wanted, but I couldn't have it. And *she* wasn't a thing to be had. She was the air I breathed, and the only thing that I'd ever want. "There's nothing that you could give me," I murmured.

"I see." He pondered for a moment as white smoke swirled around his cigar. "Well, you think about it. It seems you've found your calling anyway, James MacGuire. Despite how you may feel," he smiled and rose from the table. "I'm betting on you tonight in the ring." He tipped his fedora to me and left.

As much as I hated it, he was right. I had come so far to try to change, and look where I ended up. Back where I fucking started. But there was nowhere else that I belonged. I was done with that part of my life, but that part of my life wasn't done with me.

I didn't know what I was supposed to do.

A few moments later, I pulled out her engagement ring that I still kept safe in my pocket, watching the emerald and diamonds sparkle in the dim lights of the bar. I thought about sending it back to her, but since my last letter was unsuccessful, I doubted the next one would be. Knowing my luck, she'd burn the next one with it wrapped inside, and then she'd hate me even more.

It was the only proof I had that she existed at all, and every time I stared at it, I felt closer to her—a light in my darkness. I'd send it back someday, but for now, it was all that I had left. And I didn't have much.

Chapter 33

ELISABETH

The Card

THREE WEEKS AFTER MY father's funeral, things started to crumble. The healthcare costs from the past month, the funeral costs, and our sole income from our father's money from the factory was gone. On top of that, as if things weren't bad enough, Father had racked up quite a bit of gambling debt that Margaret and I knew nothing about.

Sometimes I wondered if we knew our father at all. I knew he was hurting over the loss of our mother. But this was so unlike him... perhaps he was worse off than we thought. He had tried to settle our finances at the factory the day he went out into the snow. Trying to pay off debts with what little we had, asking for an advance, which now they wouldn't give.

And I absolutely refused to accept *his* money.

I even threatened to burn it, so Cameron stopped sending it. In fact, I hadn't seen him in over a month. Lucky for him, because hitting something sounded so good, and his face was the perfect target for my rage.

This morning, I sent Pearl home, back to the Cotswolds. She cried and refused, but we could barely afford to eat, and I wasn't going to let her suffer any more years with this cursed family. I also debated on finding a new home for Finton, but I just... couldn't. And neither could Margaret. In some small way, his unconditional love and affection had helped us both during the last few weeks.

Margaret worked at two different jobs and failed both times, for reasons she wouldn't disclose to me. After she came home the second time in tears, I decided that it didn't matter why it didn't work out. Nothing was worth more resounding grief.

I held a job at my father's factory for about a week, but I ended up losing it because they didn't want me sobbing all over the machinery. But I couldn't stop crying even if I wanted to. I also showed up drunk most days, causing a scene, and they did not appreciate that. On my way home after they fired me, I frustratedly kicked a brick wall, breaking my middle toe. Never before had I publicly yelled obscenities, but there was a first time for everything.

Things were looking bleak.

Nothing was going right in my life. Only a dark cloud that seemed to cover us constantly. The loneliness was becoming unbearable, and desperation was starting to settle in... and desperate times call for desperate actions.

I stared at the card lying next to the telephone, tapping my fingers on my crossed arms—the card that Aidan had given me weeks ago. At first, I thought it was some kind of sick joke. The front of the card said *The Black Knives*, and the back was one name.

Aidan Murphy.

I shook my head and grabbed the handle of the phone, dialling the number as I transferred my weight to my unbroken toe. I knew it was him by the sound of his husky voice.

"Hello?" Aidan answered.

"It's Lizzie."

"I was wondering when you'd call."

He sounded so smug. What a prick.

"Is the job you offered me still available?" I asked, laying my impatience on thick.

"Of course it is," Aidan said.

"When can I meet you?"

"Tomorrow morning work for you?" he asked.

"Fine."

"Fine. Happy Christmas, Lizzie."

And then I hung up.

I needed the job. But mostly I needed to know about The Knives. My thoughts had been driving me crazy, and honestly, I probably had gone crazy. I'm sure that none of this was a coincidence, and he was going to tell me everything that he knew. Everything that I should've known a long time ago.

The next morning, I stood outside our home with Margaret, insisting that she come. I didn't trust Aidan for a damn second to meet with him alone.

"Are you sure about this?" Margaret asked, playing with a ring on her gloved finger. Snowflakes clung to her soft brown curls.

"No. But it's worth seeing what his offer is." It's not like we had many other options.

"And he's just going to show—Oh," her gaze snapped to a fancy car pulling up to the house.

I adjusted my black silk gloves as we approached the shiny car. I expected him to be in it, but a man whom I'd never seen before stepped out wearing a grey flat cap. His high cheekbones complemented his bristly red and grey facial hair.

"Never mind," Margaret whispered to me. "He's very handsome."

"Good morning, ladies," he greeted Margaret and me. "I'm Harry."

"Margaret," she smiled, pursing her red lips as she extended her hand. "Pleasure to meet you, Harry."

"Where's Aidan?" I asked, breaking up whatever weird connection that was happening between them.

Harry gestured towards the car. "He's waiting for you."

"And he couldn't come get me himself?"

Harry chuckled. "That's not how he operates."

Something about this did not seem right.

"I call the front seat. Next to handsome Harry," Margaret winked at him.

Perfect. I sighed.

Margaret talked to Harry for the entire forty minutes it took to get to his house... or should I say gothic Manor. When we pulled up in front of a large two-story brick mansion on the outskirts of town, my mouth dropped.

This was where Aidan lived? I didn't know what I was expecting, perhaps a dingy pub on some random corner in town, but it wasn't grandeur.

The chill in the air pricked my nose as I stepped out of the car onto the gravel, taking in the frozen water fountain, the trimmed dead gardens, and the various men walking around in flat caps. I'll bet in the springtime this place looked magical, but right now it looked eerie and haunted... like a place I would avoid at all costs if I wasn't so desperate. Everything inside of me wanted to turn around. To tell Harry to take us back. But I had come too far to turn around now, and I had questions that needed answering.

The men smiled and nodded at me as I entered through the large front doors, trying to hide my limp from my broken toe. I didn't want to appear weak just in case Aidan, or his small army of flat caps, had other ideas. Art Deco lights clung to the dark mahogany walls as we followed Harry through the decorated halls until we reached closed double doors.

"Margaret," Harry's eyes lit up as he met hers. "You can wait out here with me." He turned to me. "He wants to see you alone." He gestured towards the door.

"Of course he does," I muttered.

"Good luck," Margaret said.

I grabbed her arm. "Keep your wits about you."

She patted my hand. "Believe me, if I need to use my nails," her slow gaze trailed Harry's form up and down. "I will." Then she took off, following Harry down the hall, holding his arm.

Unbelievable.

I took a breath, rounding up my courage, and knocked on the door.

After hearing his voice, I entered, finding him sitting behind a large desk with tidy stacks of paper. He stood and offered for me to take a seat in a brown leather chair opposite the desk. A large window let in a stream of soft, hazy light as the snow outside continued to fall.

"Whiskey?" He offered.

"Sure." I nodded and sat.

He poured me a glass, sliding it towards me, and sat behind his desk. "I'm sorry to hear about your father."

"How did you—never mind. Of course, you know. You know where I live. I should just assume you know everything." I took a sip, and damn, this brand of whiskey was so smooth—better than what I could afford to drink at home.

He smiled and ran a hand through his brown, slicked-back hair. "I don't claim to know everything, but knowing you is something I'm interested in." I rolled my eyes at his clever response before I could stop myself. "And I'm truly sorry. I can't imagine what you must be going through."

His brown eyes looked genuine, but I didn't want to talk about that particular subject.

I took another sip of the smooth liquid. "So, you're a member of The Black Knives?"

"Darling, I am The Knives," he grinned. "Everything you see here is mine. I would've thought James would—"

I flinched. "Don't. Say that name." I closed my eyes, trying to centre myself, as I drank the rest of what was in my glass. Desperately needing more. Half-tempted to take the bottle with me before I left. I mean, he could obviously afford more, and I needed it more than he did.

"I'll never say it again," he vowed.

I took a few moments, preparing myself as Aidan refilled the glass. "So, you knew him," I said flatly.

"Yes," his eyes fell to the desk. "For many years. We grew up together. We worked together."

I had so many other questions, but this was too hard—more so than I thought it would be. I didn't want to think about him. It hurt too damn much. And in the end, I guess it didn't matter. He was gone, and he wasn't coming back, and even if he did, I'd tell him the same thing I wrote on that godforsaken letter.

Burn in hell.

"What's the job?" I took another sip.

He grinned, leaning back in his chair. "It's simple. Paperwork mostly, but I'll pay you well for it."

I rested my arms on the edge of his desk, holding the glass in my hands. "And you're just going to give me this job?"

"That's the plan."

"No conditions?"

He smiled. "Just one."

I stared straight into the depths of his brown eyes, setting the glass down on the desk. "I am not going to fuck you, Aidan Murphy." If he even thought for a moment that I'd consider it, then this whole meeting was pointless.

He laughed and rose from his chair, making his way towards me in a dark grey suit. "Well, then it's a good thing I'm not asking you to." He sat on the edge of the desk closest to me and put his hands in his pockets. He was so close that I could smell the faint musk of his cologne. "All I ask in return is that you live here."

I laughed, rolling my eyes. "Right. I think I've heard enough," I rose from the leather chair.

Aidan sat perfectly still and calm as he spoke. "If you work for me, you're going to need protection. I can't protect you when you live so far away. I've told you who I am. What would make more sense?"

"I'm not living with you," I spat, heading for the door.

"A lot of my men live here. Women too. You'd have your own room, and you can leave whenever you want. I'm not holding you prisoner."

I debated, hovering my hand over the golden door handle. I'd been wanting a way out of that house of cursed memories for months. I even considered burning it to the ground, starting with my bed. But logically, I didn't think we could afford the house too much longer, even with this new job, but still... living in *his* house?

I turned around, facing him. Taking in the well-dressed man, still casually leaning against his desk. "What about my sister, Margaret?"

He smiled. "I thought that would come up. She's welcome here, too."

"Do you have a job for her? Margaret will need something to keep her busy." Christ knows the trouble she would get up to in a place like this. Full of handsome men in well-dressed suits and seemingly bad intentions. In all of the five minutes we've been here, I'm pretty sure she was already causing trouble with Harry.

"She can do whatever she wants. There's plenty of work here."

"And my dog?" I asked.

"He can come, too." So, he knew that he was a *he*. I should stop being surprised about how much he knew about me. "As long as he's not barking at all hours of the night, I'm fine with it," he continued.

Finton would never do that, but still... this seemed too easy.

I glanced at the window behind him, watching snowflakes twirl and fall to the ground. "Why me? I'm sure there are plenty of other girls who'd love to work for you." He seemed to be a man who had everything, and there were plenty of desperate women in Birmingham.

He rose from where he was perched on the desk, striding towards me until he stood mere inches in front of me. "Well, regardless of how you feel at the moment, I plan on asking you out again. And one of these days, Lizzie. You'll say yes," he curled his lip into a smile.

I scoffed. "Really?" Was he that damn confident?

He glanced at my mouth. "I'm really good at getting what I want," he grinned. "Welcome to The Black Knives, Miss Montgomery."

Chapter 34

JAMES

All the Dark Places

HIDDEN UNDERNEATH THE CITY, in the brick tunnels of the underground fighting ring, a dark-skinned man slammed his fist into my jaw. Blood spewed from my mouth as I fell to the ground, losing my balance. He was easily twice my size, but that wasn't the problem. The tremors of the past had found me, seizing control of my mind and body. All I could do was lie there as he punched me, cursing and kicking me as I refused to rise.

Stay out of the trenches.

But Cameron wasn't here to save me this time, and I couldn't think of one reason to fight back. Let him take me into that deep, dark quietness...

One second, the crowd was cheering, and the next, they were screaming words of violence as a man stood next to me in shiny black shoes.

"Fight's over," Riley barked at my opponent.

The crowd booed at him, and then Riley pulled out his gun and fired it into the air. Sending the crowd screaming and running in a panic. Dispersing in a matter of minutes. Riley chuckled, sheathing his gun in one swift movement.

"Time to get the fuck up, James," he barked at me, holding out his hand, but I shoved it away, struggling to rise to my feet. He sighed and reached for me, grabbing my arm.

"Don't fucking touch me," I snapped at him, steadying myself upright.

He laughed under his breath, stepping back while I grabbed my things, throwing on my clothes quickly.

Then he followed silently behind me as we walked the long tunnels towards the exit near the Old London Bridge. Light snow fell from the grey sky while the cold air filled up my lungs. Patches of ice formed on the water as I stared at the streetlights lining the bridge, reaching into my pocket for my cigarettes.

"Here," Riley shoved a fancy Italian-made cigar in front of me.

"Where did you get that?"

"Stole it off some Italian guy," he smiled.

I took it and lit up, blowing out smoke into the frozen air. The strong and bitter taste was a welcome release. But I needed more. "Do you have anything else on you?"

Riley sighed, shaking his head as he reached into his coat pocket, holding out four white pills. I shoved all of them into my mouth, swallowing them down.

"Are you going to tell me what happened tonight?"

"There are dark places a man's mind goes that you'd never understand." I paused, blowing out smoke. "I'm assuming you were what... eighteen when the war ended?"

"Just," Riley murmured. "But I think there's more than war haunting you, James."

"Well, there's nothing I wish to share with you. So, you can fuck off."

"Fine. Have it your way," he started walking away, but then he quickly turned around. "I'll give you tomorrow. Odds are you're going to wake up with bruised ribs anyway. But the day after, I need you at the table. So, whatever the fuck this is. Figure out your shit."

But I didn't know how to do that. All I wanted was something to take away the pain, and so far, nothing was working.

He stepped closer. "Is this about that fucking girl? She's not worth it, James."

"Watch your fucking mouth." She was everything, and he would never understand that.

He clenched his jaw, shaking his head. "Have it your way, then." And then he walked away, leaving footprints in the snow.

I stayed out in the cold until my body felt numb, staring at the stars hovering above the bridge. Wondering if she still thought about me as much as I thought about her.

Chapter 35

ELISABETH

Falling In

LIVING IN AIDAN'S MANOR was surprisingly a good distraction. I had spent the last month learning the ropes and filing paperwork. Which varied from lists of racehorses, winners and losers, news clippings, and gambling and fighting rings around Birmingham. Information I didn't really know what to do with, so mostly I just sat there doodling fancy images on the side to pass the time.

I shared an office space with a woman named Isabella, but everyone called her Izzy. She was a frightening woman with high cheekbones, short black crimped hair, and fair skin. Every day, she showed up in the office wearing the most gorgeous glittering gowns, like every day was a party, and she was the main event. I liked her, though, and I dare say we were becoming friends. Her frigid glares and ill-tempered frowns have started turning into mirthless smiles. So that was something.

I sat at my desk, twirling a pen in my hand with Finton at my feet. Glancing at Izzy, then back at the stack of files. Margaret's voice captured my attention as she greeted Harry and then kissed him right there in front of the glass doors of the office.

She'd also found a good distraction.

I couldn't believe they were still seeing each other, or that Margaret suddenly decided to be loyal. Her entire wardrobe changed over the past few weeks. Glamour and lace with black gloves and feathered hats seemed to be her new style. I think she was really trying to fit in with The Knives...

Or fit in with Harry.

I rolled my eyes, trying to focus on the papers in front of me.

"Jealousy doesn't look good on you, Montgomery." Izzy didn't even glance at me as she spoke. The stacks of paper on her desk were neat compared to the disaster that was my desk.

"You can call me Lizzie. And I'm not jealous. I'm annoyed. There's a difference," I snapped at her.

Her cold blue eyes met mine. "There are plenty of men around here you can play with," she said with a devious smile.

Yes, I knew the men around this manor quite well now.

In the past month, every man had introduced himself once, if not twice. Then proceeded to tell me that they knew *him*. Which did nothing but anger me. I didn't know why everyone knew more about me than I did about them. I hated it.

I dropped my pen. "I'm annoyed that I'm in here working and she's—" I pointed at her, still latched onto Harry's lips.

That was it.

I stormed towards the glass doors, opening them with force. "Get a room, Margaret!"

Margaret pulled away, giving me a sheepish smile. "Sorry, Lizzie."

I slammed the doors shut and plopped down at my desk. Collapsing my face in my hands.

"Like I said. There's plenty of men for you to play with," Izzy mused. Then she paused, setting down the stack of papers in her hand as she admired her long nails. "Or you could take Aidan up on his offer? Christ knows he's asked like a dozen times."

I glared at her. "I'd rather kiss a goat."

"I'm sure we could find one for you," she smiled, the first real smile she'd ever given me. Then she stood, cracking her long fingers. "Come," she said, heading for the doors.

"I wasn't being serious, Izzy."

"I'm actually relieved to hear that," she replied. "But no, I mean let's go get drunk."

Oh. Well, in that case, I was definitely going to follow her.

"So, why do you work for Aidan?" I asked her.

We were an hour into drinking in one of the drawing rooms, each of us sprawled out on a couch with a glass in our hands. The drawing room we decided to occupy was filled with velvet furniture and plush geometric rugs. A blazing fireplace sat in the corner, keeping the room warm and comfortable despite the cold chill in the rest of the gothic manor. Finton was curled up in front of the fire with his legs in the air, sleeping soundly.

She laughed. "That's not the question you really want to ask, is it?"

"Alright. Why aren't *you* dating Aidan? You seem to get along well, and... I've seen him look at you."

She was possibly the most beautiful woman I'd ever seen. Why wasn't he trying to sleep with her? And why wasn't she trying to sleep with him? I couldn't deny that Aidan was good-looking, and he probably knew his way around the bedroom—I choked that thought down as fast as it came to me.

She laughed, but it sounded more like a whoosh of hair. "Aidan doesn't look at me like that anymore. I've known him for years, that's not to say he hasn't tried, but... we work better as friends than lovers."

That was more honest than I thought she'd be with me.

"And you?"

I took a breath and then a long sip of my whiskey. *Here we go.* "My father died and—"

"Not that. I want to know why you won't go on a date with Aidan," her red lips curved into a smile.

Of course, that was what she wanted to know. "I just don't think it's appropriate. He's my boss and—"

She sat up, crossing one long leg over the other. "It's because of James, isn't it?"

I coughed up my drink. "Excuse me? How did—"

"Oh, I know a lot more than you think I do," she smiled, playing with a short strand of her crimped black hair. "I've known James since I was fifteen."

"Please stop saying that name," I begged, pinching the bridge of my nose.

"Fine," she rolled her eyes. "Anyway, I don't see what the fuss is about." She grabbed a cigarette off a nearby side table and lit it up, blowing out smoke. "I mean, sure, he has a great body, but I've had much better lays."

Something inside me snapped. "What did you just say to me?" Did she... with *him*?

Perhaps I'd misheard her.

She laughed, but I didn't find it funny. "We fucked once, no wait twice. But I really don't see why he's preventing you from better options."

Better options? I jumped off the couch, staggering to my feet. Finton flipped over and was now on his feet, mirroring me.

"Lizzie—" she started.

"You what?" I couldn't breathe or even take in that she'd said my name for the first time. "When?" I asked.

She rose to her feet in one graceful movement, not even the slightest bit affected by the drink. "I was seventeen. Relax. Don't have a panic attack. It was over a decade ago," she rolled her eyes, taking another puff.

I sat, my heart pounding in my chest as I poured more whiskey. Did they date? Why only twice? I couldn't stop my racing thoughts, nor could I stop picturing them together. The whiskey was hitting me all at once.

She sat, eyeing me carefully, pouring herself another drink with a cigarette still in her hand. "I'm sorry, I didn't realise you still cared, or I wouldn't have said anything."

"I don't," I barked. "I just—you caught me off guard." And maybe I did care, but admitting that hurt too damn much. "Let's just talk about something else."

A migraine started to form, pounding in my skull. I knew this was *his* gang, and the possibility was always there, but... that was more than I ever wanted to know. I didn't want to imagine him with anyone else. Of course, I knew that he had a past, but it was too much. Just thinking about it made me sick.

She sipped her drink. "Maybe you could let go if you moved on with someone else."

And that was it.

I rose from the couch again, grabbing the bottle with Finton at my heels. "I *have* moved on, and I don't want to talk about it. Not now. Not ever."

And then I left, staggering upstairs to my room where I finished the bottle and cried until I passed out.

Bright morning light flashed in my eyes as Margaret, who was dressed to impress, pulled open the velvet drapes to my windows. I put my hands over my eyes, cursing at her under my breath as Finton jumped off the bed.

"Margaret, it's too early." And I had a splitting headache. "Go bother Harry," I grumbled.

"It's the middle of the day, Lizzie," she said flatly.

Alright, so it was *afternoon* light that burned my corneas.

"Your point? I didn't sleep well." At least my nightmares had changed. I no longer dreamt about the day *he* left me, crying until I couldn't breathe. Or the day my father died alone in the snow from a heart attack. Last night I dreamt about Izzy fucking the man who broke my heart right in front of me.

I'd say that's progress.

She plucked an empty bottle off the floor and placed it on the nightstand. "Yeah, I wonder why." She shook her head. "You're supposed to be downstairs working."

"Oh, well, I'm sorry I'm the only one working while you play kissing Harry all damned day!"

She crossed her arms. "Well, I would work. Except he wants you. And you know, I don't even know why. You're a mess."

"You're just full of compliments, aren't you?" I narrowed my eyes at her.

She sighed. "When am I going to get my sister back? I can't believe I'm saying this, but I miss her."

I ignored the tug in my heart. "Well, I'm right here. Partially blind thanks to you." I pulled the covers over my face, refusing to get up.

She pulled them right back. "He's been calling for you for hours."

"What?"

"Aidan's been calling for you for hours," she repeated louder.

Damnit. My eyes widened.

"Well, get dressed and go figure it out! Before we're both in trouble." She stamped her heel on the wooden floor.

"Fine," I rolled out of bed, plucking a simple black chiffon dress from my closet and then slipping it on.

"And I'm taking Finton today. You've hogged him enough lately," Margaret muttered.

"Fine," I rolled my eyes.

She stopped me as I tried to walk past her. "Black again? Surely you have something a bit more vibrant in your closet. You look like death."

I narrowed my eyes at her. "This dress is fine," I pushed past her, making my way downstairs to Aidan's office. Filled with anxiety. I'd skipped yesterday and was basically skipping today. He was probably furious with me.

I entered the office, finding Izzy at her desk with a stack of paper in her hand and a cigarette in the other. After that confession last night, and my disgustingly vivid dreams, I didn't know how to look at her the same, or without thinking of him. I never should have agreed to get drunk with her.

"He's in his office," her eyes gestured to his door.

I nodded, taking a steadying breath before I entered. Readying myself to make one hell of an apology, but he smiled when he saw me. Which was strangely confusing.

"There you are," he said, leaning against his desk. Wearing his usual grey suit and black tie.

"I'm so sorry," I said, making my way towards him.

"For what?"

Did he truly not know? "I got drunk yesterday, and well... I just rolled out of bed moments ago." It sounded less embarrassing in my head. I really was a mess.

He chuckled. "I don't care what you do, Lizzie. Drink. Work. I've told you before, you're not a prisoner."

"You pay me to work for you," I levelled my eyes at him.

"Yes, I do. And while we're on the topic, I have a job for you today." He stood from the desk, closing the distance between us. "I'd like you to accompany me to the racetracks this afternoon."

"What? That doesn't sound like a job," I laughed. "And the horses don't race in January as far as I'm aware." Was he being serious? I knew nothing about horses, only that I enjoyed reading their silly names in the papers.

Why would he want me to accompany him?

"I've asked you to come, so it is a job. I need your opinion on a horse," he smiled, brushing my arm, and for some reason, I let him. The physical contact felt comforting, warming something that had been frozen in my core for a long time. "My car leaves in twenty minutes."

Over the next few weeks, I felt myself change.

Despising him less and less. His smile became something I looked forward to. Of course, I denied it over and over again, but then he'd ask me to have dinner with him or go for a walk around the grounds of the Manor. And something in me slowly started to sway to his charms.

Last night he took me to the cinema in Small Heath, and on the way home I let him hold my hand. Feeling that hole in my chest starting to lessen with every touch he offered me. He'd even started buying me gifts. His first gift was a dark red fur coat, made of the softest fur, and the second was a short pearl necklace that I wore often. Perks of working for the company, he called it. But I'd never been given such beautiful and expensive things.

And I was so lonely. More than lonely. I could barely stand the feelings building inside me, the aching need for something the drink and the work couldn't provide.

The next afternoon in March, I asked him to go for a walk. He was surrounded by men and stacks of paper in front of him, but he smiled and accepted, placing his hand on my lower back as we exited the Manor.

A feeling that I didn't realise I had missed.

"I'm sorry, I'm sure you have lots of things to—"

"It's alright," he smiled, lighting up a cigarette. "The work can wait."

We walked around the grounds of the manor with nothing but the sound of the chill in the air and my fingers fiddling inside my leather gloves.

"What's on your mind?" He asked after a while.

I stopped and turned towards him, pulling my red fur coat tighter around my face. "I think I should quit."

He blew out a stream of smoke. "Really? Why?"

"I'm terrible at my job."

And I was. I shuffled papers around, mostly to make it look like I was busy. And since that day I got drunk with Izzy, I stopped talking to her. So, asking her for help or training was out of the question.

I couldn't stand the sight of her.

His brown eyes sparkled in the morning light as he blew out another cloud of smoke. "This may come as a surprise, but I know you are. I'm well aware of all that goes on in my house."

"So, why aren't you firing me?"

"I like having you here." He pushed a lock of my hair behind my ear, lingering as he glanced at my mouth.

In the next moment, I brought my hand to his face and kissed him, a quick kiss before I pulled back. But when he smiled, I found myself kissing him again, ignoring the memories coming to the surface as I lost myself in his kiss and his hands pulling me closer. I didn't realise how much I missed being kissed until his mouth consumed me.

I'd been denying myself this for so long, denying that I felt something for him. But in all of the small moments when he chose me over the work or pulled me out of the office just to talk to me, I began to feel less broken inside. And this kiss was all of the things I had been missing. Touch. Intimacy.

A week later, I knocked on his bedroom door, unable to fall asleep. Unwilling to sleep, so I could relive old nightmares. When I entered his room, he was sitting in a black leather chair, cleaning his gun. Guns were a huge part of living with this gang. Every man in the Manor carried one, but I barely noticed them anymore as I'd grown accustomed to them. The fear I once felt had long since disappeared.

"Can't sleep?" he asked, setting his gun on the glass table in front of him.

I shook my head.

He rose from the chair and strode towards his golden drink cart. This was probably the most underdressed I'd ever seen him. His suspenders were hanging loose, and his white shirt was unbuttoned at the top. "Whiskey?" he offered.

"No," I murmured.

He set down the bottle and smiled at me. "Is there something else I can offer you, Lizzie?"

I approached him, wrapping my arms around his neck, and kissed him. I wasn't even sure if I could do this, but I wanted to try. I needed to erase him, to erase the pain in my heart. And perhaps Izzy was right. I was never going to let him go if I didn't move on.

Chapter 36

JAMES

In the Opioid

I SLIPPED INTO A haze-induced coma. I wasn't even sure where I was anymore or what day it was. All I could see was smoke and darkness in a room I didn't recognise. Occasionally, Riley appeared in and out of the room.

Or at least I think it was him.

The walls were made of stone, and the room was small. A bed, a dresser, and a fireplace. I watched the flames twist and flare as I lay in a white bed, slowly losing my mind.

I was desperate to stay in this constant dreamland. For it was the only way I could see her anymore. Weeks ago, my dreams stopped, and when I did dream, they were nightmares. I used to say that one day she'd drive me to madness, but I did that all by myself.

I tried to open my eyes when I heard footsteps, but I couldn't feel my body.

"Give him this instead." I heard a man's gruff voice, but he was a blur. "I'll be back in a couple of days. Make sure you keep him hydrated."

The door opened and closed.

A man sighed. "What have you done to yourself, James?"

Sounded like Riley's British accent, but I wasn't sure.

"I already saved your ass once, no fucking twice. But you just had to be all dramatic, didn't you?"

Yes, definitely that bastard Riley.

"When will he recover?"

I recognised this voice too... Cameron?

And then I slipped back into the dark void.

A month passed, and it was March, or so the doctor told me one morning as I slowly recovered from overdosing. Riley had found me lying on the floor in my room at the Inn, bringing me to a small cottage home on the outskirts of London. A small and private place where I could heal, whatever that meant. I preferred the dreamland.

The Doctor begged me to come see him to talk or whatever, I told him to go fuck himself. There was nothing I wanted to talk about. To anyone. And now here I was with my revolver in my hand, shooting at glass bottles I had collected and placed on a cobble-stoned wall.

Recovering, as they say.

"So, he is alive," I said to Cam as he approached me, firing a round into a bottle, shattering it from where it stood. Keeping my eyes on my target as I heard footsteps in the wet morning grass.

"That's real fucking rich coming from you, seeing as you tried to kill yourself," he muttered.

I darkly laughed. "I wasn't trying to kill myself." That was merely an accident. A moment of selfishness, and it was almost my last.

"We need to talk," he muttered.

"So, talk." I fired again, taking off the top of a glass bottle.

"Put the gun down first."

"I'm angry you couldn't do the one thing I asked you to do, but I'm not going to shoot you, Cam."

"And the one thing I asked you to do was to stay out of the fucking trenches!" he yelled.

I closed my eyes, blowing out a breath. "I'm sorry." He had every right to be angry at me. "I really am."

He sighed. "Put the fucking gun down, James."

I put down the gun, facing him with my arms across my chest. I hadn't seen Cam in months, but he didn't look like the clean-cut man I remembered. His reddish-brown facial hair was longer, and dark circles clung to his brown and hollow eyes.

"So, how is she?" My voice cracked, searching his face.

He flinched.

My pulse started to accelerate. "Tell me she's alright, Cam."

"Sh–she's fine. I mean, I think she is," he mumbled.

Was he nervous? He blew out a breath and shifted his weight from one leg to the other, cursing under his breath.

"You think? Or you know?"

"I don't—" he let out a breath. "James, this is not easy—"

"Fucking spit it out." My heart couldn't take much more of this waiting game.

"She's with Aidan," he yelled.

My vision narrowed, and I felt like I was going to black out. But then I started to laugh. "Aidan? That's really fucking funny, Cam. You almost had me," I reached for my bottle of whiskey and took a drink.

He stared at the ground. "It's not a joke," he murmured.

I slammed the bottle down, clenching my fists. "Stop it."

"I wish I could, but she's with *him*," his voice sounded hoarse. "I—" his throat bobbed. "I saw them together." I felt myself coming undone as rage consumed every vein in my body. "She—"

I grabbed him by the collar, cutting off his words. "Don't fucking say it. Don't you fucking say it!" My hands started to shake.

"I'm so sorry," tears formed in his lifeless eyes.

"Fuck." I released him and paced around, running a shaky hand through my hair. "What do you mean she's *with* him?" I could barely see past the tears in my eyes.

"I—" His eyebrows meshed together, and he looked like he was going to vomit. "She kissed him."

"Willingly?"

He nodded, staring at the grass.

I grabbed the bottle of whiskey and chucked it as far as I could, cursing as loud as I could manage before falling to my knees in the grass. Birds flew out of the trees at the sound of my voice as I sat in the deafening silence.

The world around me went pitch black.

All I could hear was a faint buzzing sound as the trees around me blurred in strange patterns. Cameron was saying something, but I couldn't even register his words as I started to laugh hysterically.

It all made sense.

He wanted me to leave, to run.

You don't have anything I want.

He'd said once.

But he wasn't fucking taking *her*. I'd burn the world to the ground before I ever let that happen.

Madness slowly consumed everything that I was and everything that I would become. I tipped my chin to the sky, taking in the dark and heavy clouds looming above. Sending a promise up above as my soul turned fucking black.

"He's dead. I'm going to fucking kill him," I vowed.

Chapter 37

ELISABETH

Masquerade

A FEW DAYS LATER, I found myself in a silver sparkling gown that came to a silver fringe at my thighs—another gift from Aidan, along with matching diamond earrings, silver sparkling shoes, and a matching jewelled mask.

I wasn't sure what to call Aidan after our midnight encounter, but he insisted that I attend a masquerade party this evening as his date. I'd been avoiding him for three days since I found myself in his bed. But I was suddenly persuaded when my gifts were delivered to my room this morning. They were the most expensive things I'd ever worn, and I felt good wearing them. It made me feel like the grief and brokenness that always seemed to follow me were finally in the past.

That I was finally starting to live again.

An hour later, we pulled up to a grand estate on the edge of town. I took Aidan's hand as he led me into a shimmering scene of black and gold.

Champagne towers sat on round tables, and the corners of the room were filled with golden trays of all different kinds of food and liquor. Golden chandeliers hung above polished stone floors, and dark and vibrant music filled the ballroom. Swelling and flowing through me as I walked around the room on his arm. The women wore sparkling gowns with intricately designed masks, and the men wore fancy suits with matching masks. Some of the masks had feathers, and others had sequins or beads hanging from them like fringes. Feathers, masks, and *look how much money we have* seemed to be the theme of this party.

It was the most glamorous party I'd ever been to. Although I wasn't sure who owned this mansion or how we'd been invited to such an exquisite place. But it felt like I was momentarily living in a fantasy as golden light cascaded around the decadent room, shimmering off my silver dress.

"You look stunning this evening," Aidan smiled, pulling me from my thoughts. He wore a silver mask and a grey suit with silk on the collar, an intentional outfit so we could match.

I was fully aware of how good I looked. And after months of looking like a mourning peasant, this was a welcome change. "Thank you," I glanced at Margaret, who was already slow dancing with Harry, wearing matching blue masks. "I didn't expect them to last this long," I muttered.

"I don't think any of us could have predicted that," Aidan laughed.

We stopped near a table full of food, and Aidan pulled out a cigarette.

I grabbed his arm. "Dance with me first," I smiled, nervously.

"Alright," he put the cigarette back in his pocket, taking my silver silk-gloved hand.

He led me onto the dance floor, pulling me in close. Gently resting his hand on my hip as we swayed side to side.

"You've been avoiding me," he said after some time. "I wasn't sure if you'd even come tonight."

"Your gifts definitely helped."

He laughed. "Did they?"

I glanced at a few others dancing around us. "I'm surprised you secured an invite to such a grand party."

"I'll try not to take offence to that," he said flatly.

I laughed. "I mean, I don't see how you fit in a place like this." Did gangsters really enjoy lavish parties? It just seemed so out of place for the normalcy of what I witnessed at the Manor. Liquor, cigarettes, business, horses, guns... that was what Aidan enjoyed.

"I think I fit in quite well here. And so do you, by the way," he glanced down at my silver sparkling dress.

"I'm a girl from the country. I probably fit in the least out of all of us. Margaret, too. Although she could fit in anywhere." I'd always been jealous of her ability to blend. From the Cotswolds to Birmingham to this damn palace, you'd never know where she came from.

He chuckled under his breath. "Just take the compliment, darling."

"Fine." A few moments passed, and my thoughts kept spinning. "We showed up here with nine cars following us. Something tells me this party is something else for you, isn't it?"

His eyes lowered to meet mine. "You can't just enjoy a moment, can you?" he sighed. "No, I'm not just here for the party."

"So, why did you need me?"

"I don't." I was just going to pretend that his words didn't hurt. "I wanted to see you in this dress, and now that I have, I think it was worth it."

A small smile formed in the corner of my mouth.

"I have business." He stopped the dance.

"Of course you do," I murmured.

He placed a hand on my face, angling it towards him. "But then, I'd like another dance, and maybe later you can stop avoiding me at the Manor," a teasing smile formed at the corner of his mouth as he once again pulled out a cigarette.

"I can try," I smiled.

He pulled me closer. "I'm going to knock on your door tonight, Lizzie. Are you going to answer?"

Heat crept up my neck. "Maybe." I'd felt so dirty after our first time... wracked with guilt and unwanted memories. He knew what he was doing in the bedroom, but it just felt... wrong. Bad. Maybe I could slow him down next time and find a way to bring some type of passion into it. But I wasn't entirely sure that I wanted to. "I'll think about it."

"Good," he smiled.

One of his men walked up and whispered in his ear as sparks lit up his cigarette. Aidan nodded and turned to me, blowing out a cloud of smoke. "You behave yourself," he smiled, brushing my arm before he disappeared into the crowd.

An exasperated breath escaped my lips before heading to the champagne table as the music vibrated around the room, humming deep into my bones. Getting drunk by myself would have to be my entertainment tonight, seeing as Aidan was busy and Margaret was still in dreamland with Harry. And it's not like I had any other friends. A depressing thought that made me take a generous sip from my glass of champagne.

But then I felt a hand slowly sliding on my hip from behind me—a bigger hand than I remembered from previous nights.

My breath hitched at the sensation.

I didn't realise Aidan knew how to touch me like that... was he capable of this kind of passion and tenderness all along? I wondered if he'd read my thoughts just before.

"Did you change your mind?" I smiled, still facing the tower of champagne.

His hand trailed down my bare back, giving me goosebumps as he caressed the skin around my lower back. "About what?" His voice dropped deep in his chest, sounding huskier than usual. The uneven rhythm of his breathing quickened my pulse.

"Me. Business." Where was this months ago when I desperately needed a distraction?

"Never." His hands drifted to my neck as his fingers slid gently along my collarbone.

"Then," I swallowed. "What are you doing?"

Whatever he was doing was better than I thought he was capable of. It was as if touching me gave him pleasure, the way he caressed every curve with the tips of his fingers. My skin felt feverish, and all I could focus on was his hands roaming my body like it was *his*.

Damn, I missed this feeling.

Admitting it to myself made me recognise the brokenness, but I didn't care. I was two seconds from asking him to take me back to the Manor and finish this. To rip me apart and put me back together with those sensual hands.

"What I should've done months ago, Lizzie."

I stopped fantasising.

His voice.

That *voice*.

It... no, it couldn't be. Was I hallucinating? Did someone spike the champagne? I turned around slowly, catching striking green eyes under a shiny golden mask. My heart stopped, squeezing the air from my lungs.

Tears welled in my eyes at the flash of his familiar grin, a smile that could stop time. "Ja—"

He put his finger to my lip. "Don't." He glanced behind him, doing a quick scan of the crowd as his body crowded mine. "Don't say my name."

My chest heaved. I wanted to scream, to slap him, and kiss him all at the same time. No. No. I would *not* do that. Slapping him, punching him, inflicting pain, that's what I would do. I wasn't going to kiss him. Screw him!

"What the hell are you doing here?" I snapped.

He wet his lips, and I felt my body begin to burn. "Dance with me," he smiled.

I scoffed and tried to push past him, but he was a wall of muscle. Damn him.

"You never learn, do you?" He held out his hand once more.

"Fuck. You." I burned my eyes into his.

He flinched. "I can't say that I don't deserve that and worse," he frowned as his mouth formed a tight line. "But right now, I need you to dance with me, Lizzie." He grabbed my hand, pulling me onto the dance floor by force.

"I don't want to dance with you."

What was he thinking? He could just show up after all this time and pretend that nothing happened? And I don't know who gave him the right to look that good wearing a black suit and bow tie, but screw him!

He glanced behind me, and his grip tightened. "Then fake it. Or do you want me to get shot? Because that's what will happen if you keep causing a scene, Lizzie. Do you really hate me that much?"

I did hate him, but never that much. "What are you talking about? No one is going to—"

He pulled me in closer, and I felt my body coming alive at the feel of his body against mine. It took everything in me not to inhale his scent or wrap my arms around his neck and lick all the way down—*Stop it, Lizzie!*

"Aidan will kill me if he knows I'm here." I could feel his breath on my ear as he held me close. "Or worse. So please, please just dance with me."

I'd never heard James beg, and I quite liked the sound of it. "Fine," I huffed. But then my mind betrayed me as I began to wonder what else James would beg for... *nothing you're going to give him, Lizzie.*

I shook away my disastrous thoughts, focusing on my breathing as we swayed from side to side. Keeping my eyes away from his. For a moment, it felt like nothing had changed as the slow music reverberated around the room. We fit together so perfectly. The feeling of his familiar hands, his familiar exquisite body against mine... but then I remembered that this was the man who broke me and left me to rot.

The hole in my heart started to ache.

"Aidan wouldn't kill you for dancing with me," I muttered after a few moments.

He pulled back, meeting my eyes. "He'd kill me on sight, Lizzie. That's why I left." His eyes fell to the floor.

I could see the pain there, but it was too much.

Damn, the pain he felt.

I laughed. "Because of Aidan?" How many more lies was I going to tolerate?

"There are so many things I need to tell you about—"

"More lies?" I cut him off.

"The truth."

"Right. Because you're so capable." And that was all I could take.

I pulled back and shoved him as hard as I could, walking away to the nearest door that led to the outside.

A rush of cold air greeted me as I tried to catch my breath, losing myself in the surrounding gardens. I wasn't falling for him again. This wasn't happening.

My stomach felt sick.

I rested my hand on a nearby tree, steadying myself before I fell over or decided to retch on the flowers. The chill in the air was calming and numbing but satisfying.

Of course, James was there a second later. His hands were tucked into his pockets as he kept a distance, walking towards me slowly.

Why wouldn't he just leave me alone?

"Stay away from me," I cried with shaking hands. "I can't—" I couldn't do this. Not now. Not ever. I didn't want to hear one more lie from him. I couldn't.

"Lizzie, please—"

"No! No, you-you left me! You left me, James!" Christ, saying his name was like inflicting some kind of torture. Ripping my heart open while he watched me bleed. He should've just set me on fire all those months ago. It would've been less painful than losing him and everything else that followed.

A distraught look crossed his face. "I know, and I'll explain everything, please—"

"Explain, what? I practically threw myself at you and you—" I lost my voice from my uncontrollable shaking, sucking in a breath of cold air. Holding back tears. But if I started crying now, I'd never stop.

No. No, he wasn't worth it.

"You know what, you don't even deserve the air it takes to talk to you." I turned on my heel, heading back inside the grand manor.

I knew he was still following me, so I tried to lose him. I pushed through the crowd, making my way down the gilded halls, trying random doorknobs to find an open room.

There had to be somewhere I could hide.

Somewhere I could escape him.

After a few more tries, a door finally opened.

I slipped inside to what appeared to be some kind of study, a bookshelf sat in the corner next to a large desk, and a plush couch sat in front of a blazing, ornate fireplace.

Thank goodness this room had a drink cart. I threw my silver mask onto the cart and poured myself a glass of whiskey, feeling a moment of relief as the liquid burned in my throat. The faint hum and rumbling of the music from the ballroom filled the silence as I stared at the snow falling outside the large window.

The door opened a moment later.

"Christ, James! Just stop. Just—" He grabbed a chair and barricaded the door. "What the hell are you doing?"

"What does it look like I'm doing?" He snapped, catching me by surprise with the anger in his voice.

"So, what, you're just going to lock me in here with you?"

"Sure, fucking looks like it. You're not giving me any other choice," he said through clenched teeth.

I took angry steps towards him. "Perhaps it's a new concept for you, but when someone runs from you, stop following them!" I tried to move the chair braced against the door, but it was like trying to move steel.

"Since when do you drink whiskey?" His anger shifted to something softer and more reflective.

I glanced at the glass in my hand, less than half-full. "For months, what does it matter to you? Let me out of this goddamn room, James." Damn, how did he do this? I tugged harder at the chair, placing the glass on a nearby shelf so I could use both hands.

But it wouldn't budge.

He smiled, which pissed me off.

Then he leaned against the wall and crossed his arms like he didn't have a care in the world. And damn, he looked good doing it. "I think it matters," he mused. "Does it remind you of me?"

That goddamn smile! How dare him! "Burn in hell, James."

He smirked and laughed under his breath, bringing a hand to his lips. Watching me under his long eyelashes. My pulse ignited at his laugh, burning under my skin with the way he was looking at me. All I could feel was the aching desire to slap him. I tried to strike, but he caught my fist right before it landed.

So, I swung my other hand, but he caught that one too. I was a ball of rage with nowhere for it to go as he held me down. Holding me close enough to feel the intense heat radiating from his body.

"I'm tempted to let you hit me, but I don't think that's what you really want to do, is it?" He stared at my mouth and parted his lips, wetting them with his tongue.

"Burn. In—" And then my words were cut off by his mouth in a consuming kiss as his hands went to my face, guiding his mouth on mine.

My anger dissipated in a second from the warmth of his heated kiss. It was everything and better than I remembered. The softness. The taste. The curve of his mouth against mine. Yes, this was exactly what I wanted to do.

I pulled back briefly to remove his golden mask, taking in the face that haunted my daydreams and my nightmares. And his green, dark, and sultry eyes that I could never forget.

His mask fell to the floor with a thud, and I pulled him back in, needing to feel his soft lips on mine. His lips begged for my mouth to open, and then his tongue entered my mouth.

I lost all control.

I wanted to feel him everywhere.

My arms wrapped around his neck, and his hands slid to my thighs, hiking up my silver shimmering dress to my waist. He pulled me up, sliding me up his body as my back hit the wall. My fingers ran through his hair, and I moaned against his mouth when I felt the hardness of him pressing against me. I pulled him closer, craving the friction, and his hands slid up my back and into my hair, tilting my head for better access. Slowly turning my body into an inferno.

I hated him. I hated him so much.

And I hated that my body was so turned on in this moment. That, despite everything, I wanted him so badly. His scent alone... like leather and all of the dirty things I wanted to do to him controlled me. I wanted him to burn in hell, but I was already burning for him from the inside out with each deft stroke of his tongue.

His mouth drifted to my neck, biting and sucking there, and damn it felt so good... But then I started to cry. Breaking guttural cries rose from my throat, and I couldn't stop.

I couldn't control it.

"Lizzie," he pulled back to examine my face.

I couldn't respond. All I could do was cry, feeling the hole burning in my chest, threatening to tear me apart.

All of the places that he'd broken.

He dropped slowly to the floor, pulling me close to him. Cradling me as I cried in his arms.

Chapter 38

JAMES

The Past

"I'M SORRY. I'M SO sorry," I stroked her red hair, much shorter than when I last saw her and breathed in her scent. Fuck I missed that. It was so familiar, and the only way to describe it was that it was mine. Saying sorry would never be enough, but I couldn't stand seeing her cry, knowing she was falling apart because of me.

Because of everything I did to her.

But *I'm sorry* were the only words I could form, and I was so fucking sorry.

She suddenly shoved me away, rising from the floor. I followed her pace, wondering what the hell happened for her to look so angry at me again. Maybe I should've let her hit me. It seemed to help the women in my past.

"No, you don't get to say you're sorry! It's too goddamn late for that, James," she cried, wiping tears from her reddened face.

A muscle flickered in my jaw as I put my hands in my pockets to prevent myself from reaching for her. I stared at the floor. "I'm sorry."

"Why are you here?" she asked.

Well, if she wanted to play that game, I could play it too.

"Why are you with Aidan?" I tensed.

When I saw him dancing with her, I nearly slit his throat right then and there. But then I'd be dead right now, and I wanted to live. I needed to live for her. I knew it the moment I saw her from across the room tonight, shining brighter than the North Star, pointing me towards everything that I truly wanted.

I'd give up everything else but not her.

She blinked. "You don't get to ask that. You abandoned me. Who I'm with is none of your concern. Not anymore."

"Like hell, it isn't."

"I'm not yours, James," she spat, the gold in her eyes flaring.

I took steps towards her. "Yes, you are. You will *always* be mine, Elisabeth Rose Montgomery." She was delusional to even think otherwise.

She shook her head, blowing out a ragged breath. "You're impossible."

"No." I closed the distance, grabbing her hand. "I'm just a man who's impossibly in love with you. And you have no idea what it feels like being in love with you, Lizzie."

"Since when?" she snapped.

Fuck, she was so stubborn.

I brought my hand to her chin, placing my thumb under her bottom lip. "Since our first date. When you asked me to walk you to your door. I knew."

She laughed, rolling her eyes. "Right."

"Don't do that," I bit out. "Not when I'm being honest with you. Don't laugh it off like it means nothing to you." I'd break down and cry if she laughed at me again, and then I'd have to punch a hole through the goddamn wall.

She let out a shaky breath. "That was months ago, James. In September. You truly knew you loved me then?"

"Yes, I did." That's why it scared the shit out of me.

She stepped back. "Then... why did you continue to act the way you do? Do you really not know how to love someone?"

No, I didn't. All Mads ever wanted to do was fuck me, and Aidan, too. Convincing me often that she was going to leave him for me. But honestly, I didn't think she ever would have. She enjoyed the pain she gave me, and over time, I started to believe that I deserved it—that it was how love was supposed to be.

"Why did you—"

"Because the first person I ever loved, Lizzie, was murdered right in front of me," my hands started to shake.

Her eyebrows creased. "What?"

I blew out a breath and paced around the room, running a hand through my hair. I needed to tell her. I had needed to tell her for so long, no matter how hard it was. But... how?

"James," she spoke softly.

I rested my fist on the wall, facing away from her. A hard shadow fell on the left side of my face. "Her name was Madeline. Mads," my throat bobbed. "She was..."—*fuck*—"She was pregnant with my child." My fists were white-knuckled as my voice dropped to a murmur. "And Aidan fucking shot her right in front of me."

"What?" she gasped, taking a step back with a look of horror on her face. "When?"

"I was eighteen. It happened just before the war," I turned around to face her, coming back into the light.

"Why would he... d-do that?" she stumbled.

Because he was a fucking monster, is what I wanted to say. But I was trying to be honest with her. And I was equally a monster in this story.

"She was engaged to him. He had no idea we were... seeing each other. He thought the child was his, and when she admitted it wasn't after finding us... Look, it's not a pretty story." I pulled out the envelope containing my letter that I had tucked into my vest and handed it to her. "It's all in here. I wrote it all down for you. I've wanted to tell you for such a long time."

She ran a finger over her words.

"And you don't have to worry, I already know that's exactly where I'm going to end up."

"James..." she shook her head.

I paused, watching as her facial expression softened. "You need to stay away from Aidan," I said after a while, waiting for her to collect her thoughts. "He's dangerous."

"He's not going to hurt me," she laughed.

I clenched my teeth. "Did you fuck him or something?" There was only one reason she'd keep defending him, and I was tired of tiptoeing around it. I needed to know.

Her silence did not comfort me.

"Tell me you didn't fuck him, Lizzie?"

"You left me!" she seethed.

"That is not an answer." She let out a breath and tried to retreat a step, but I grabbed her. "Tell me you didn't—"

"Yes! Yes, alright. I did," she admitted with tears in her eyes.

And in that moment, I felt something inside of me break, shattering me until it burned and burned. Consuming me with violence and pain. Tears streamed down my face as I strode to the drink cart, filling up a glass of whiskey with shaking hands. Then I filled up another, tossing it back. It was everything that I feared, and it was happening all over again. My unending nightmare...

"James," she murmured.

I threw the glass across the room into the fire.

But it wasn't enough. I grabbed the entire cart, throwing it across the room as glass shattered on the floor.

"James, please," I heard her cry.

I took out my gun, spinning the chamber around as the steel glinted in the light. Fully loaded and ready for what I needed to do.

"What are you doing, James?"

Glass crunched under my boots as I picked up my mask from the floor and placed it on my head. I headed for the door, but Lizzie was there a second later, braced against it.

"Stop! Are you crazy?"

"Move." I reached for the chair, but she grabbed my arms.

"No."

"Fucking move." I was going to kill him, or I was going to break down here in this room, and I did not want to fucking wallow in this pain when he was just outside. I could end it, and I would end it right fucking now. That bastard was mine.

"No, James!" She dropped the letter and placed her hands on my face. "Look at me," she snapped, ripping off my golden mask and throwing it on the floor. My jaw clenched as I met her golden eyes. "If you go out there and kill Aidan, his men will kill you."

"Sounds like a kindness," I said mirthlessly.

She shook her head as a shudder rolled through her. "You don't mean that."

My eyes dropped to her mouth as a moment passed. "You need to move, Lizzie. Before I make you."

Tears welled in her eyes. "I'm not going to lose you this way!" she cried. "I can't—" her words were cut off by her sobs.

My forehead rested on hers as she held me closer. Her hands held my arms firm as warm air caressed the inch of space between us. "Did you fuck him to hurt me?"

She shoved me back with tears in her eyes. "I did it for me. Because I needed to move on, James. I mean, isn't that what you wanted? What you told me to do before you left?"

"And did you?"

"Did I what?" she snapped.

"Move on," I murmured.

She crossed her arms, holding herself in tight. "I don't know," her eyes fell to the floor, and a tear rolled down her cheek. "I never expected you to come back."

I couldn't blame her, but fuck it hurt so bad.

A swift *knock* at the door and she flinched. I didn't react. Everything inside of me felt like it died. "It's probably Cameron."

"Cameron's here?" she asked.

I glanced at the frosted window. "I need to leave."

"It's what you're good at," she wiped tears from her face.

I placed my hands on her arms, holding her, needing to make things clear for her before I left.

"Everything I've done, I did for you. To protect you and your family. And I'd do it all again, just to make sure that your heart continued to beat. Broken is better than gone, Lizzie. Now, you can hate me. Hurt me. Fuck, that's exactly what Aidan wanted you to do. But just read the goddamn letter. If you still decide you want nothing to do with me, then fine. But you are not staying with him." I removed the chair from the door and opened it, letting Cam in.

"There are too many men here, James," his voice jittered.

"I know." Aidan had brought a small army here tonight, foiling my plans to catch him alone and finish this once and for all. What I should have done years ago.

"He's looking for her," he said. "We need to leave while we still can."

"Start the car," I said to him as he ran off. Then I grabbed the letter and my mask off the floor and put it back on as I stood at the door, needing to leave but not wanting to leave her behind. "I saw Margaret here, too." Dancing with Harry of all people. "Does your Father know you two have decided to join a gang?" I handed her the letter.

"My father is dead," she snatched the letter from my hand.

"What?" Pain radiated in my chest.

"He died in December."

"December? How?"

She shook her head and closed the distance between us, stopping inches from me. "If you really loved me, James. You would have been here when I needed you the most."

I shut my eyes, feeling my heart crack for him and for her. "Lizzie, I'm... I'm so sorry."

"You truly didn't know?" She looked sad for a moment, but

then it faded too quickly back to bitter discontent. "I'm surprised your spy didn't tell you."

I clicked my jaw. "Cameron has spent months trying to find out where you are. And I do love you."—*more than anything*—"But right now I don't even know why. Because all you seem to want to do is break my goddamn heart and push me away."

"Now you know how it feels to love you," tears filled her eyes.

I rolled my tongue and let out a breath. "Read the letter." I paused. "And you'd better get out of this goddamn gang before I slit his fucking throat." Because all hell will break loose once I finished this, and the farther away she was, the better.

"You can't kill him, James."

She looked at me like I was joking, but I wasn't. His time on this Earth was coming to an end. I wouldn't rest until the light faded from his eyes.

"Watch me." I paused, realising I needed to rectify the lie I told her to keep her safe. Fuck, if she'd just read the letter, I wouldn't have to say it. "Don't tell anyone that you saw me. Promise me that."

"It's a little late to be asking for promises, don't you think?"

She was walking a very thin line. I didn't want to scare her, but she was making this difficult, and I was running out of time. "If he finds out I was here, he'll kill *you*."

"Me? I thought you said—"

"I lied earlier, Lizzie. I lied to protect you. He doesn't want to kill me. He wants you so that I'll suffer. That's been his game all along. I don't give a shit about what happens to me, but if anything happened to you..." I shook my head. My throat constricted. "Do not tell anyone that you saw me," I growled. "Alright?"

"Alright," she swallowed.

I headed towards the door, pausing at the threshold. "You have two days, or I'm going to burn his fucking house to the ground."

And then I was gone.

Chapter 39

ELISABETH

Sinking

THE PAIN IN HIS eyes was too much. I had been so angry with him but watching him cry nearly tore me apart. If I hadn't stopped him, he'd probably be dead right now. Something in him had snapped tonight, and now that he finally told me what happened in the past, I understood why. I'd never wanted to punch him and hold him as much as I did in that single moment.

I never expected him to come back.

Everything he did was to protect me... and I wanted to believe that it was true. But would Aidan really kill me?

I knew he was a man of business and preferred whiskey and gold over silver, but I didn't know much of anything else about him. Aidan offered me a job and a home... why would he do that if he wanted me dead?

He wants you so that I'll suffer.

After the story he told me, it made perfect sense. Madeline was Aidan's, and he lost her, so it would only be fair if... No. I was just scaring myself. It couldn't be true.

Aidan would never hurt me.

I didn't want to believe it.

I ran to the window, wiping away the fog from my breath,

catching a glimpse of him as he got in his car. I was so sick of watching him run. He admitted that he loved me multiple times. Words I'd wanted—no *needed* to hear him say for so damn long. But it felt like he was a lifetime too late. And here I was, once again falling apart as he left.

I don't give a shit about what happens to me.

Well, I did. And if anything happened to him... I felt a cold shiver roll through me as I shoved the letter into the top of my dress, cursing under my breath that I wouldn't just rip it apart piece by piece and let him go once and for all.

But I was so confused.

Seeing him, hearing about his past, then finding out that I was a pawn in this game... I didn't know what the hell I was supposed to do. Or how to stop caring so damn much about someone who didn't really care for me. When I lost my father, he should have been there.

I needed him months ago.

I grabbed my sparkling silver mask off the floor, careful not to cut myself on the broken glass, and put it on. Then I took a deep breath, centring myself before heading back into the loud and crowded ballroom.

"There you are," Aidan smiled as soon as I closed the door behind me. I tried to smile back, but I physically couldn't.

You need to stay away from Aidan.

His voice echoed in my mind.

"Where have you been?" he raised a brow.

"Why, did you miss me?" I did my best attempt at teasing him.

He grabbed a strand of my hair. "What happened to your hair?"

Damnit. "Oh. I wasn't feeling well, so I laid down for a bit." At least it was a half-truth. I did lay on a wall, and I did physically feel like I was going to be sick.

He stared at me for a moment. "Who were you dancing with?"

The blood rushed from my face, making it feel cold. "Am I not allowed to dance with other people?"

"Who?" he repeated with venom in his thick voice.

"I'm not sure. He wore a mask. I didn't see his face."

"What colour were his eyes?" His gaze tore into me like he was trying to look into the depths of my soul.

"Blue. I think." My hands started to sweat. He smiled, and for the first time in months, that smile scared me. "I don't know why you're asking so many questions. He was a lousy dancer," I shrugged, playing it off.

He laughed. "Good."

"I umm—I'm not feeling well. I think I'll ask if someone can take me home," I moved past him, but he stopped me, grabbing my arm.

"Nonsense. My business is done. I'll take you."

The car ride home was long and quiet. Aidan didn't say another word, but he kept his hand on my knee for the entire ride home. Normally, I would've found the gesture comforting, but tonight it made me feel all sorts of wrong things. I had so many questions, but I stayed quiet, realising that I still didn't trust him... and I wasn't quite sure why.

By the time we arrived back at the Manor, I had a splitting headache from my dark and overwhelming thoughts.

I needed to read that letter.

Aidan walked me upstairs to my room, stopping at my door. "How are you feeling now?" he asked.

"I'll feel better in the morning," I reached for the door handle.

He placed his hand on my face, stopping me. "I feel like you're hiding something from me."

"Well, I'm not. I must've drunk some bad champagne or something," I defended, feeling my pulse race.

"Or something." His eyes dropped to my mouth. "Or someone."

I took a sharp breath. "You're being paranoid." Does he know? I had to keep denying it until I figured out the truth.

He flashed a grin, the one he uses when he sees right through people. Perhaps I knew him better than I thought. "I've been in this game a long time, Lizzie. I can sniff out a liar miles away."

"I'm not lying." My voice started to shake. I took a breath, trying to calm my nerves and racing pulse.

"Prove it, then."

"Fine, I will." I pulled him in and kissed him.

And it felt so wrong. Every nerve in my body repulsed every second. This wasn't what this was supposed to feel like.

His hand moved to my rear, and I pulled back, pushing my hands against his chest. He stared at me for a moment as his brown eyes consumed all of the light in the hall. I didn't know what to do or what to say, but he was truly frightening at that moment.

He smiled. "Interesting. Are you sure you didn't see anyone?"

"Who would I see?"

He curled his lip into a smile and walked away, without another word.

I rushed into my room, locked the door, and pulled out the letter, needing to know what he said. My heart wouldn't stop pounding as I read pretty much the same story he told me earlier, with a few new additions.

It started with why he left, and what Aidan had threatened to do if he came back, all because of their history.

James and Aidan were close growing up, but when he started dating Madeline Grey, everything changed; *he* changed. A year later, she was engaged to Aidan, and when James turned seventeen, she turned her attention towards him.

But Madeline was awful to him.

She pursued him. Abused and trained him so she could have them both.

James tried to push her away, but he eventually fell for her. Admitting that it was the biggest mistake of his life.

Months later, she became pregnant with James's child. Aidan caught them together and started beating him, but James didn't fight back, feeling too consumed with guilt.

Madeline tried to stop him, but Aidan shoved her away.

Then Aidan pulled out his gun, aiming it at James, but Madeline jumped in front of the gun at the last second.

Taking the bullet that was meant for him.

James held her while she died, then beat Aidan within an inch of his life before running off with Cameron, who witnessed the entire thing. If Cameron hadn't torn him away, James would've killed him.

After I took a shaky breath, I got to the part about me.

I told you once that I was shipped off to war when I was eighteen. Well, when I returned home, everything was different.

I was different.

The nightmares threatened to destroy me, and I turned to drugs, sex and violence. Anything that could make me feel something other than grief.

But when I first saw you in that red dress, time stood still. I'd love to say that I fell for you then, but I think we both know I didn't have good intentions. Even back then, I tried to push you away so many times... but fuck, you are so stubborn, Lizzie.

And when I kissed you under the stars that night, I felt something. I was ready to run, too scared of the feeling, but then you asked me to walk you to your door.

And I fell.

Though I tried to deny it many times after that. Pushing people away is what I've done for so long, and I'm sorry I didn't know how to love you the way you deserved to be loved.

Because I do.

I do love you—and that's something I never thought I'd feel again. I thought I was in love all those years ago, and I couldn't have been more wrong.

There is nothing I wouldn't do for you, Lizzie. You're the only thing in my life that makes sense, the only thing that truly makes me smile or feel anything at all. I honestly don't know how to live without you, and I wouldn't want to, but I have to.

Leaving you was not my choice.

I had to leave to protect you from him. And honestly, you deserve someone better, someone who isn't so broken... This version of myself I'm becoming again scares me. I don't know how to keep going on day by day, but I promise I will.

Whatever it takes.

I miss you. I miss you so goddamn much.

And I'm sorry I asked you to dance all those months ago. I think we both would've been better off if I'd never met you at all.

I'll be looking for you in the next lifetime.

Yours,
James

Tears dripped on the paper as I folded the letter back into the envelope with shaking hands.

He was a fool.

A complete and utter fool.

Maybe he didn't deserve my love, but I didn't deserve his.

I slipped out of my room and knocked on Margaret's door.

Harry's brawny frame filled the doorway. "Hey, oh—are you alright?"

"Yes," I wiped away more tears. Harry opened the door wider, and I found Margaret sitting in bed reading a book. I handed her the letter. "Please don't say anything, just read it."

"Alright," she looked at me hesitantly, then unfolded the letter.

I turned to Harry. "Can you give us a minute?"

He nodded and left the room.

Margaret went through the same stages of shock and horror, and a few minutes later, she was sobbing, quickly returning to horror. "Christ, that's a lot to take in."

"We need to leave, Margaret." It was no longer safe here in Aidan's Manor, and we needed to leave now.

"Well, what about Harry?"

"Really? It's been three months."

"Yes, and I love him, Lizzie. I'm not just going to leave him—"

"Margaret Katherine Montgomery, don't be ridiculous!" I wasn't leaving here without her. That wasn't even a possibility. "I'm not leaving without you. Do you not understand the gravity of this situation?"

"Oh, I'm ridiculous? Really?" Margaret rose out of bed in her sheer nightgown, crossing her arms. "You were with James for what... a few weeks? I don't even know, yet you fell apart when he left you."

My nostrils flared. "This is hardly the time for this fight." And it wasn't the time at all for this conversation. We needed to leave this Manor as soon as possible. It was no longer safe here, not that it ever was. Goddamn Aidan and his games.

She pushed past me and headed for the door to get Harry before I could finish protesting.

Harry stepped into the room and placed a gentle hand on her arm, noticing the tension between us. "What's wrong, love?"

Love? Their relationship was so much more than I thought it was. I thought they were just fooling around, but I think perhaps he loved her in the same way that she loved him.

"Is it true? About Aidan," her bottom lip quivered as she held up the letter to him.

"Margaret!" I scolded. Great, she was going to get us killed.

"Is. It. True?" she repeated.

They locked eyes for a moment, like some unspoken language, as Harry glanced at the letter, making the connection. "Yes, love," he admitted.

Margaret started hitting him, punching him in the chest and the arm. "You played me, Harry Gardiner!" she cried.

He grabbed her arms, restraining her. "No, I didn't. I promise I didn't."

"Margaret, we need to leave," I grabbed her arm, pulling her away from Harry, but she wouldn't move.

Harry glanced at me, releasing her arms as he cupped her face. "Please, love. She's right. You should leave."

Margaret pulled away, holding back tears. Giving him a glaring look I was very familiar with. I felt my heart die a little for them, but I was thankful Harry agreed with me. I stepped up to Margaret's side, taking her trembling hand.

"Give me two hours," he started. "I'll prepare a car, and then we should be able to slip out unnoticed. Safely." He headed for the door, glancing back over his shoulder. "I will explain everything to you, Margaret. I promise," he hesitated for a moment, swaying in the doorway. "I'm sorry. To both of you," and then he left.

Chapter 40

ELISABETH

Fire & Whiskey

TWO AND A HALF hours later, I found him in his room, sitting in a red velvet chair by the fireplace with a glass of whiskey in his hand. It'd been ages since I'd been in his room, but it still looked and felt the same. Besides his gun resting on the table next to a golden candelabra burning with flame.

He didn't even realise I was there watching him as he stared into the fireplace, looking calm yet ready to burn the world to the ground. His black wool coat was hanging on the wall, and he wore only a white tank and suspenders, paired with black trousers and boots.

"I didn't like your letter." I crossed my arms over my chest.

"Lizzie." He jumped up in a fluid movement, setting his glass on the table next to him. Lethal vexation dispersed in a moment to startling relief. "How did—"

I put a finger up. "No, you've said your piece. Now it's my turn."

He put his hands in his pockets. "Alright."

"I didn't like your letter," I repeated, taking steps towards him. Feeling the heat from the blazing fireplace, but it was nothing compared to what was burning inside me.

"Of course, you didn't," he ran a hand through his black hair, longer than I remembered. "Can you at least tell me why?"

"It was the most selfish thing I've ever read."

He winced, dropping his eyes to the floor, looking pained like I'd physically struck him. "I'm sorry," he murmured.

Tears formed in my eyes, making it hard to see as I inched myself another step closer. "Because if you think for one moment that life would've been better if we had never met..."—his eyes snapped to mine—"Then you truly deserve to be miserable for the rest of your life." I stopped in front of him, heart pounding. "Because meeting you was the best damn thing that has ever happened to me, James."

He exhaled a breath, smiling with glassy eyes.

"And you're wrong. You do deserve to be loved. You are not broken, James. But if you don't choose to love me in this lifetime," my voice started to shake. "You will never find me in the next. I am not going to give you another chance because *I* am that selfish." It would be all lifetimes with him or none at all. I would not accept less.

"I can do that," he grinned, placing his thumb on my chin. "I will do that," he corrected.

"Good, because I love you." I wrapped my arms around his neck. "And I don't want to live without you either."

He smiled. "I love you."

And then we collided in a storm of tongues and teeth. I bit his bottom lip, and he caressed my mouth with a swirl of his tongue. This was everything that love was supposed to feel like. Passionate. Warm. Safe. Like everything that was missing, suddenly found its home.

He pulled back a second later. "Lizzie, how'd you get here?"

"Don't worry about it." I brought his mouth to mine, sucking on his bottom lip.

He pulled me back again with firm hands on my waist. "Lizzie," frustration laced his tone.

I swallowed, preparing myself. "Harry." His eyes flared as he tried to move past me, but I tightened my grip around his neck. "James, it can wait. It's safe. No one saw us leave," I placed my hands on his face, pushing the hair from his eyes. "Please just kiss me," I stared at his mouth.

I needed him to kiss me. My heart felt like it was going to burst out of my chest if he stopped kissing me. Everything would just have to wait because all I could think about was him. He paused for a moment, but then he gave in, interlacing his tongue with mine in a deep kiss.

My body flooded with warmth.

His arms wrapped around me, pulling me against him before his hands glided down my curves, reaching for the clasp on my silver dress. In a few seconds, it fell to my ankles, and I began removing his white tank, running my hands across his chiselled torso, enjoying the sensation of his skin. My impatient fingers drifted to the waistband of his trousers, and he smiled against my mouth.

"Give me a second," he said against my lips.

He stepped back and bent down to unlace his boots while I stood there, fully naked, watching him until he was naked before me. And damn, what a glorious sight. The body of my dreams, and I couldn't believe that it was mine.

My heart skipped a beat as he stepped back towards me, tugging at a strand of my shoulder-length hair as the other grabbed my waist. "I like this, by the way."

"I cut it out of spite."

"I wouldn't expect anything less."

I laughed, and he pulled me up into him as my arms wrapped around his neck.

My back hit the bed seconds later, met by his tongue and his teeth as he trailed along my body, as if he were claiming his territory. Licking and biting down, down, down until he got to that spot that I loved. My back arched, and I writhed under the pleasure of his tongue until he had me panting and shattering under his mercy. His lips met mine in a slow, deep kiss as I cried out his name, and his hands curved under me. Squeezing my rear until he thrusted slowly inside me.

Working his way in one inch at a time.

He groaned as he guided me with him, keeping one hand on my hip as we fell into a rhythm. Torturously slow, and then he picked up the pace as his hand went to that sensitive spot, building me to a breaking point, and I felt my vision blacking out.

I dug my nails into his strong shoulders and his lower back, pressing him deeper as I felt another wave of orgasm coming to the surface. He kissed me deeper, sucking in my bottom lip before biting it softly.

A few more thrusts and I was overcome, releasing the tension in a blissful wave of orgasm as my head fell back.

His hand went to my face, trailing down my jaw to my chin, and I got lost in the texture of his green eyes. "I love you, Lizzie. I love you with everything I have."

I wanted to start sobbing as I felt every emotion all at once. So, I brought my mouth to his, pulling him closer. I missed this. I missed him. I never wanted to part with him again. This passionate and consuming love was everything that I would ever want.

"Forever?" I breathed.

"In every lifetime, Lizzie. This one. The next one. My soul will always find yours."

Chapter 41

JAMES

A Reckoning

AFTER LIZZIE FELL ASLEEP, I softly kissed her freckled shoulder and carefully moved out of her embrace, trying not to wake her. Quietly putting on my trousers, shirt, vest, and boots before slipping on my shoulder holster. Then I sheathed my Webley Revolver, slicked back my hair, and pulled on my flat cap. Descending the stairs to finish the job I came here to do.

Muffled voices echoed through the hall, but there should only be one voice in this house right now—Cameron's. Two shadows flickered on the walls in the dim light, and one of them was wearing a flat cap. I pulled out my knife for a silent approach, readying to strike as I entered the drawing room.

"James! Stop." Cameron's eyes flew wide as he stood, placing a hand between Harry and me.

I kept my knife pointed at him. "What the hell is he still doing here?"

"Harry brought them here," Cam said. "We were just talk—"

"Them?" I arched a brow.

"Margaret's upstairs sleeping," Cam replied.

"And Finton," Harry husked, pulling his grey flat cap lower. "And we need to talk."

"So, you just decided to switch sides? How convenient." I did not believe in the 'goodness' of Harry's heart. Especially since he had The Black Knives tattooed across it.

"No," he replied. "You know I can't do that," he pulled up his collar, hiding his ink. "But I had to make sure Margaret was safe." Harry's eyes softened.

I laughed. The gleam in his blue eyes told me more than I wanted to know about their relationship. "No one's safe while Aidan is alive," I lowered my knife. Well, since he was here, he might as well be useful. "You're going to tell me how to break into his Manor." I sheathed my knife back in my pocket.

Harry huffed a laugh, crossing his burly arms in front of him. "Right. You do that, and you're fucking dead."

"As long as he dies first," I countered. I'd already made my peace with that. Lizzie knew how I felt, and she was safe. Nothing else mattered now except killing Aidan.

I walked over to the window, pulling back the thick curtains to observe the street. The streetlights flickered in the darkness, their warm glow barely piercing the heavy, swirling fog that enveloped the streets. Eerily quiet and calm. But things always appeared that way before something big was about to happen.

"You're not serious?" Cam questioned.

I closed the curtain and headed for the door. "I've never been more fucking serious."

"It's the middle of the night, James!" Cam roared at the same time Harry said, "Don't be fucking stupid."

I smiled. "The perfect time to slit his throat."

"And what about Lizzie?" Cameron pushed, his worried expression creasing the lines on his face.

"She's not safe until he's dead." There would be no happily ever after until he was frozen in the ground. I opened the door, greeted by a rush of cold air. Harry was there the next second, slamming it shut.

"There is no back entrance, James." Harry gruffed.

"Get the fuck out of my way," I glared at him.

"You go there, and you'll die in five seconds. He's got more men than you can imagine and fucking machine guns."

I shook my head, reaching for the door handle. "I'll take my chances." I would find a way even if I had to scale the goddamn walls. He needed to die. I wasn't going to waste any more time arguing about it.

Harry shoved against the door harder. "We need to talk."

"Move." I was two seconds from drawing out my gun.

He paused. "I may know a way."

"I didn't know you cared so much," I fired back.

"Just listen to me for fuck's sake!" Harry barked.

I stepped back and leaned against the wall, gesturing for him to continue.

"Now, I've known you since you were nine years old," Harry continued. "I taught you how to hold that bloody knife in your hands, how to shoot and—"

"Yeah, and a lot of good that did me," I scoffed. It got me into a world of trouble, is what it did.

"Well, you're still breathing, aren't you, kid?"

I let out an agitated breath. As much as I hated him right now, he was right. When I joined The Knives, Harry was the one who taught me how to stay alive. "Well, what's your way?" I asked him.

Harry stepped back from the door, relaxing his shoulders. "He'll be at the same place tomorrow morning that he's been going to for the last nine years. The Warstone Lane Cemetery. Marking the anniversary of Madeline Grey's death. He goes alone. One, maybe two cars at most."

He had her buried? I always assumed he let her rot in the street. Has he been visiting her all this time? Perhaps he loved her more than I ever thought was possible.

"Why would you tell me this? Do you really expect me to believe you'd betray him?" This could all just be a trap. A clever trap to lure me into my own grave, and how convenient, since I'd already be in the graveyard.

Harry tensed. "I'm loyal to The Knives. Not fucking Murphy." He paused with a sigh. "And if you die, Margaret will never forgive me."

"Aidan *is* The Knives, Harry." Or has he forgotten who was in charge these days?

"You'd be surprised how many of his men don't feel that way. The new guys, sure. They're young, dumb, and don't give a fuck as long as they get paid. But there are still many of us who remember what he did. And how he became the boss. And—" His eyes fell to the floor. His mouth moved, but words weren't coming out.

"And what?" I scoffed.

Harry's eyes then went bleak. "It's about Frank Montgomery."

I pushed myself off the wall. "What about Frank?" If he was about to say what I thought he was, I was going to lose my fucking mind.

Harry lowered his gaze towards the floor. "He murdered Frank Montgomery back in December."

"Fuck!" I didn't even let him finish before I cursed and started pacing around, feeling like my knees were going to buckle as tears burned in my eyes. I should've killed him months ago. I should've knocked him off when we were kids.

"How did he get away with it?" Cameron asked.

"Covered it up and paid off the coppers," Harry continued. "It was all a part of his plan. I only just heard about it from one of the other lads."

Fuck. This would destroy her.

I returned to the window, staring at the foggy streets, clenching my jaw. Planning my next move.

"What would he get out of cutting Frank?" Cameron continued. "It doesn't make sense."

"He wanted her to be vulnerable," Harry murmured.

Weaken her, then move in. Sounded like something the devil

would do. I ran a shaky hand through my hair. "Well, it's settled then. What time?"

"Sunrise," Harry murmured.

I nodded, glancing at the clock. "That gives us two hours."

The floor creaked, and she appeared out of the shadows. "Lizzie—" I crossed the room to get to her side, but she put a hand up.

Her face was red and blotchy with murder in her eyes. "Take me back to Aidan's." She said, looking at Harry.

All three of us in unison responded with, "What?"

She took a breath, steadying herself. "When he wakes up and realises, I'm not there, he might not go to the cemetery."

Fuck, I loved her.

She was too smart for her own damn good.

I shut my eyes, trying to figure out all the ways that she was wrong. But deep down, I knew she was right. "There's no way in hell I'm letting you go back there, Lizzie." I wasn't risking her.

She turned to me with that fire in her eyes. "Oh? And what were you just about to do, James?" She crossed her arms, looking very angry with me.

I lowered my gaze. "How much did you hear?"

"All of it. I can't believe you were just about to leave. After everything!" I stepped towards her, trying to grab her when I knew she was falling apart inside, but she pushed me away. "Don't. I'm going. And you don't get to tell me otherwise." She pointed at Harry. "He knows I'm right. Don't you?"

My gaze snapped to him. "It's not a bad idea," Harry shrugged.

Goddamn you, Harry.

"If he realises she's not there, he's going to suspect something. It would at least eliminate the possibility," he continued.

I shook my head. "No. Not a fucking option."

She put her hands on my face. "It's two hours, James."

I placed my hands on her hips, pulling her closer. "Two hours is a long time, Lizzie."

Her hands moved to my chest. "He kil—" she swallowed, unable to finish. "I'm doing this. Because, although you might not care about what happens to you, I do." Her golden eyes met mine, giving me a look that I was helpless against.

I looked at both Harry and Cameron, who seemed sold on the idea.

"I'm sorry, but she's right," Cam sighed, tucking his hands in his pockets as he stared at the wooden floor. "His game falls apart if she's gone."

"Fucking hell, fine. But I'm giving you something first." I grabbed her hand and walked her back to my room.

If she was insistent on going back into the snake's den, the least I could do was arm her.

Chapter 42

ELISABETH

Golden

JAMES THOUGHT THAT HE snuck out of bed, but I awoke the moment I felt him leave. At the top of the stairs, I overheard the whole conversation, almost running down to prevent him from being so stupid, but then Harry did that for me. And when Aidan's truth came out of Harry's mouth, I almost vomited right there at the top of the stairs.

He wanted me to be vulnerable, and he did exactly that.

He took away the only constant thing in our lives, the only parent we had left, and it destroyed us. But if Aidan discovered I had left, it could ruin everything. Perhaps the last chance to catch him off guard. And after all that he had done, he deserved to pay. I had no choice but to go back there, because I had to do something.

I wasn't just going to let James be a martyr.

Silently, I followed him upstairs to his room, unsure of what we were doing. But then, he reached into his top drawer, and my eyes flew wide as my heart stumbled.

"James, if you even think—" I expected him to have the rope in his hands, but instead it was a small golden gun that he placed in my pale hands.

"It's called a derringer." He grabbed it from me, showing me how to fire, and then placed it back in my hands. "Aim for the heart or the head."

The steel was chilling in my hands, but I couldn't deny how pretty it was. "Where did you get this?" I needed to inspect that drawer someday. Thoroughly.

"I stole it." My eyes flashed to his. "Years ago, before I met you. It was always too pretty for me," he smiled.

I smiled and ran my fingers along the intricate designs embossed into the gold. Months ago, this would have frightened me, but I felt no fear.

"Did you think I was going to tie you up?" he curved his mouth to the side. I glared at him, wishing I could burn him with my lethal stare. "I'm still debating on doing it," he smirked.

"Were you really just going to leave? Alone?" I snapped. He hung his head. Silent for once in his damn life. "When we get back, I'm going to be the one punishing you, James. For being so goddamn reckless."

He laughed, and I swear his green eyes sparkled. "Something to look forward to," he reached into his pocket and held up a shiny ring. "And this, too," he smiled.

I snatched it from him, recognising it immediately. "Where did you get this?" He grabbed the derringer, so I didn't drop it as I admired the ring glistening in the dim light. Tears formed in my eyes. "This... was my mother's."

I loved this ring since the first time I saw it glistening on my mother's finger. The vibrant green centre stone was her favourite colour, and mine too. I didn't realise my father had kept it. I always assumed that she was buried with it.

"I know. Frank gave it to me the day that I—" He stopped, lost for words. "I'm sorry you're only hearing about it now."

I couldn't believe my father gave it to him. If only he were here, so I could tell him how much it meant to me. This ring explained why James's mood was so heightened after I'd found him sitting on the couch with my father. And why he was on edge for the rest of that terrible day. It would have scared him to death. My heart warmed at the thought that James had kept it after all this time.

"No," I quickly placed it back in his hands.

"No?" Devastation crossed his face, and then something between fear and anger shone in his eyes. "Do you not want to marry me?"

"I mean... not now. Give it to me when this is all over," I clarified.

"And you'll say yes?" he grinned, tucking the ring back into his pocket.

"Right now, let's just focus on staying alive." There were too many other things to focus on, like the real danger that was still in front of us. Whatever was waiting for us in that graveyard, I needed him to be wholly focused on his plan.

His shoulders rose and fell as he let out a breath. "Are you sure I can't convince you to stay? I don't like this."

I brushed my fingers along his jaw. "I know, but this might be our only chance to catch him unaware. So no, you can't." Aidan was always surrounded by a small army of men. If Harry was right about tomorrow morning, it seemed like the only chance we were ever going to get.

"And if I tied you to the bed?"

My toes curled. "You won't. You won't because you love me, James. And you will let me make my own decisions."

A muscle ticked in his jaw as he squeezed my waist. "If anything happens to you—"

"It won't." I brought my hands to his chest, fiddling with his black vest. Pondering for a moment. I wasn't exactly a fan of this plan either, but what choice was there? "But what if we ran?" I asked, bringing my eyes to his. "I mean, just you and me. Somewhere far away from Birmingham. Somewhere, he can't find us."

He chuckled softly, tucking a lock of hair behind my ear. "I've thought about that at least a hundred times in the past few months." He paused. "But then he threatened to kill you. And then he had his fucking greedy hands all over you."

His jaw clenched, and I flinched at the memory of his hands roaming my body, at the memory of that night I found myself in his room... one of the worst mistakes of my life.

"And then your Father," he brushed my jaw with the pad of his thumb. "There is no going back, Lizzie. I can't just run. I won't. I have to end this."

I understood it all, but I didn't hate it any less.

"Then let's end it," I murmured.

He reached in and kissed me. Soft. Urgent. Whispering, "I love you," before we left the room.

"So, you knew James when he was just a boy?" Ten minutes had passed since I hopped into the car with Harry, but I couldn't sit in silence anymore, not with everything still running through my mind. He nodded in answer to my question, but that wasn't enough. "What was he like?"

"The same, mostly, though his hair was longer back then. Always had a habit of getting into trouble. But his heart was usually in the right place."

Or in the wrong place, considering what happened with Madeline. "And Aidan?" I asked, feeling my throat swell.

He deserved to die for what he did, but still, knowing his life was about to end gave me mixed feelings. I'd spent the last few months with him... shamelessly falling for him. But all the while, he was using me to hurt James.

"Aidan was never the strongest man, but the smartest. Had grand ideas of how he'd run a business, even at the age of eleven." He paused. "But cost never mattered to him, and it's hard to be loyal to a man who only cares about himself. It's taken me too long to figure that out."

I'd seen that side of him. The business side that made him hard, unrelenting, and cold. But I'd also seen the side of Aidan that I thought cared for me... The man who showered me with gifts and continually asked me to be a part of his world. Was any of it ever real?

There was still a part of me that didn't want to believe it, to accept just how cold he could be. But regardless of how he felt, or whether he'd felt anything at all for me, he still chose to murder my father. For *his* benefit. And so, I agreed with James. This game needed to end. Whatever goodness I thought he had left in his soul, it wasn't enough, and it never would be.

"Aidan said they grew up together. Do you think James will be able to... to do it?" I didn't know too much about their history, other than the bad parts. The parts that made them enemies. But I'm sure somewhere down the road, they were friends. Otherwise, he would've killed him long ago—for Madeline.

Harry stared out into the night, gripping the steering wheel tighter. "I don't know. Aidan is the one who found him when he docked in England. Invited him into The Knives."

"Aidan did?" Well, that was new information.

Then Harry laughed, catching me by surprise. "You know, I remember the first day Aidan brought him in. Scrawny, lanky little thing. I thought he would die in the first week. No one could've predicted his fists of steel. Talent that Aidan was always jealous of," he smiled as he recalled the memory. "Man, that kid could throw a punch."

I smiled, feeling at ease that Harry cared for James in a way I never would have imagined.

He glanced over at me. "But I think when it comes down to it, he'll do it for you."

I nodded, turning to the window, watching the moon drift behind the clouds. Sending a prayer for my soul, because if James didn't pull the trigger in a couple of hours, I would. For him and for me.

No one would hurt my family again.

"Are you going to marry my sister?" I asked after a few moments, pulling myself from my dark thoughts.

"Do you think she'd say yes?" He peered at me under his grey flat cap.

"I never thought she'd have a serious relationship ever again, but... yes. I think she would." As crazy as it was, I think she'd be happy if he asked her.

Harry smiled widely.

"But if you break her heart, or anything bad happens to her, I will—"

"I won't. You have my word," he smiled.

Chapter 43

JAMES

The Graveyard

THE ORANGE SUN PEEKED over the pines as I sat in the cemetery with Cameron, taking cover behind a large gravestone. It took me an hour to find Mads's grave. For a moment, I thought Harry was playing us, but then there it was. Madeline Grey's final resting place.

Not much was on the headstone besides her name, the date of her birth, and her death. Not even a mention of the child she carried—our child. But at least he was decent enough to bury her. I'd have to come back and leave her favourite flowers if I managed to pull this off.

Fog rolled over the headstones as I lit up a cigarette, inhaling it deep into my lungs. Cameron played with his M1922 in his hand, spinning it around. I told him to stay at the house with Margaret, but of course, he wouldn't listen to me either.

It seemed to be a common theme this morning.

"Do you remember when Aidan turned sixteen, and we threw him that birthday party?" Cam started. "You bought him that whore who turned out to be a con artist. Robbed him of everything he had the next morning."

I blew out smoke. "Yes, I remember. He was not too happy

with me." And he never wanted any more gifts from me after that. "Why are you bringing that up?"

"I just still find it funny."

"He dies today, Cam. I will not feel remorse for him." If he was trying to trigger an emotional response, he wasn't going to get it from me. I felt nothing for Aidan but rage.

He nodded, staring off into the distance. "Let's just hope Harry is still on our side."

"You think he lied?"

"Do you?" He turned to me.

I inhaled and blew out another cloud of smoke. "If he did. He's dead too."

Cameron shook his head. "Let's not kill all of our old friends in one day, hey?"

If it came to that, I would. I wouldn't even hesitate. I'd been waiting for vengeance for too goddamn long. Nothing was going to get in the way of my happy ending. Not this time.

"You miss it, don't you?" Cam asked. "The violence. Being a part of The Knives. That's why you joined The Dice."

I cracked my neck, relieving some tension. "I didn't join them. I was a hired gun." And he knew damn well I liked violence. I didn't just enjoy bare-knuckle fighting, I loved it. I had loved it ever since I threw my first punch and broke a man's nose. It was my gift. And for a boy who grew up starving in the cold and merciless streets of Birmingham, my gift was everything.

He huffed a laugh. "Right. Well, you seemed pretty cosy with them."

I glared at him with narrowed eyes. "Are you trying to piss me off?"

"Just making sure you're thinking about how this is going to play out. You kill Murphy and—"

"I am killing Murphy," I growled.

"Right, well, you kill him and then what? What does that make you?"

"Then I walk off into the sunset and marry the girl that I love. Making me the happiest fucking guy alive. Look, if this is too much for you, you can leave," I gestured towards the car hiding in the distance.

"Oh, here we go. Fucking push me away as always," he muttered.

I laughed and tossed my cigarette on the ground. "Everyone likes violence, Cam." I pointed to the gun in his hand. "That's why you kept that." A newer version of what he had, but he hadn't let go either.

Cam glanced at the gun in his hand, twirled it once more, before sheathing it at his side. Staring at the horizon as his legs started to shake.

"You're right." I stared at the trees in the distance as the morning light filtered through, taking a breath. "I haven't let go. But I want to, Cam. I really do."

I needed to let go of my vices. To let go of all of the things that have been wearing me down for so many years. For her, for me, and for Cam's sake. I wanted something better for all of us, and what that looked like, yet I wasn't sure. I'd figure it out after I bashed Aidan's fucking face in.

"Good." A small smile formed at the corner of his frown. "So do I," he kept his focus on the horizon.

I scratched at the stubble starting to grow on my face. "I know I don't seem like it, but I'm glad you're here."

And a part of me was. I would have preferred him safely at home, but it was comforting to know I could count on him. Just like I always could.

"Well, I couldn't just let you run off and get yourself killed, could I?"

I laughed.

"But this better be the last damn time, James."

"Deal," I extended my hand.

He stared at it, frowning even more intensely. "We haven't done the shake since we were fourteen," he deadpanned.

"Seems we're overdue, then."

He sighed and slapped his hand in mine, pulling back as we pretended to shoot each other. The corners of his mouth turned up into a smile, though he tried to hide it.

"Are you really going to marry her?" he asked.

"If she'll have me." I still wasn't sure if she was planning on saying yes, which was a new kind of fear.

"Good," he smiled, and some of my tension eased.

A cold breeze blew through the cemetery, snapping our gazes to the sounds of engines approaching. My heart rate thundered in my chest.

It was go time.

I grabbed Cam's arm, pulling him back to cover as we watched Aidan's silver ghost Rolls-Royce Tourer approach us. And only one car pulled up behind him.

Already, I liked our odds.

Aidan stepped out wearing his black wool coat, leather gloves, and a flat cap. He scanned the ground once before making his way towards Madeline's grave. One man stayed near his car, leaning on the side with his arms crossed.

In the car behind, no one got out.

Strange.

I pointed at the guy by the car, communicating to Cam to distract him. He took off quietly, making his way there as Aidan kneeled to her grave, brushing off the stone.

A minute later, I was behind him with my gun pointed at his head. I clicked it back, and then I heard him fucking laugh.

"Did you think you'd kill me today, James?" He slowly lifted his hands on either side of his head.

"Don't fucking move," I seethed.

"You pull that trigger and Lizzie's dead."

I laughed. "Not going to work this time, Aidan." I placed my finger on the trigger, hearing the hum of the vibration about to flow through me. Lizzie was at his Manor far away from this.

"You should see who I have in that car before you make your next move."

What? I turned to look at the car with my gun still pointed at his head. The car doors opened, and two men pulled her out in a red velvet dress, throwing her to the ground.

She yelled out my name in fear.

Lizzie. My pulse ignited. She was not supposed to be here. "Fuck." I stepped back, still aiming the gun towards him as he stood up to face me. "Let her go. This is between you and me."

"Give me your gun." He was so calm. Too calm.

I aimed higher, pointing it right between his soulless, dark brown eyes. "Not a chance." They were just restraining her. I could still do this.

I started to squeeze the trigger.

"Boys." He glanced over, and I heard a clicking noise as they put a gun to her head.

"Alright, alright!" I raised my gun over my head, surrendering in a heartbeat. "Just please fucking stop."

He wriggled his fingers, gesturing for the gun.

"Tell them to lower their guns." My voice shook as I held my gun firmly in my hand. I wasn't giving him my gun until they took away theirs. "Tell them to lower their fucking guns!" I yelled. My heart was going to explode with how fast it was pounding. How did this plan go so terribly wrong so fast?

I fucking had him.

Aidan nodded, and his men relaxed their guns at their sides. I clenched my teeth, blowing out a breath before handing him my revolver.

He smiled, opening the chamber to take out all the bullets. "You know, she begged me for your life the entire way here. Tried to convince me of my better self," he grinned, tucking the bullets into his pocket. "But we both know, this is the best version of myself I've ever been." He pulled out his gun from his holster and pointed it at my head. "On your knees. Take off your cap."

Lizzie started to scream, crying out for him to stop.

I fell to my knees, doing as he said. The cold, hard ground reverberated in my bones. "Let her go, Aidan." I did not want Lizzie to see one more tragedy, to witness my death. She'd been through enough darkness for a lifetime.

I never should have let her go back with Harry.

"Kill me, but please, please let her go."

"Where's the fun in that?" his lip curled. "I dressed her in red. You'll barely notice the blood."

"Please," I begged again. "For fuck's sake, Aidan, please," my body started to convulse. *Please let her go.*

The darkest laugh escaped his throat as his hands started to shake, holding the trigger firm. "It should have been you all those years ago, James. You. Not her. Mads was mine." He bent down to my level, hovering next to my ear. "So, tell me. Do you love this one more than you loved her?" He glanced at Lizzie.

"I said let her go!" I bellowed.

He looked around, laughing while tremors seized control of my body. "Was this really it? Just you and a gun against the world? I'm pretty fucking disappointed. I have to say, I expected a hell of a lot more, James."

Where the fuck were Cam and Harry?

"Let her go," shallow breaths escaped my lips as I struggled to breathe.

"Do you want to say a prayer or shall I?" He pushed the gun to my forehead. The steel was chilling against my feverish skin.

I stared up at him, trying to catch my breath. To beg him for her life. If I had to die, I needed her to live. But I couldn't breathe. I couldn't form the words.

Lizzie's screams filled the silence.

"Shoot her," Aidan drawled.

My heart stopped.

What? "NO!" My gaze snapped to hers.

She mouthed something as the gun went to her head.

"No! Please, please—"

BANG!

I shut my eyes at the shock of the sound. And when I opened them, she slumped to the ground with a thud.

She didn't move.

My mind went to all of the sweet moments that I'd never have again as my eyes burned. Her smile, her soft hand clutched in mine... her laugh. I didn't even get to tell her about the future I was planning with her. I barely had the chance to tell her just how much I fucking loved her.

And then I screamed.

Loud enough to fracture the heavens. Splitting my way to where I knew she'd be. As if I could break my way into heaven instead of the eternal hell I knew was waiting for me.

Gunfire exploded around us, but I could barely hear the noise as tears welled in my eyes.

The world went dark as I narrowed my eyes on Aidan.

He turned toward the fire, noticing the commotion. In that one split second that he lost control, I was grabbing his arm, pulling him to me. I punched him hard in the jaw, lunging at him to pry the gun from his hands.

He threw a few punches, hitting me in the gut.

I pulled out my knife.

He dodged my first strike, but when I struck again, I sliced his shoulder, narrowly missing his throat.

"I forgot how much fun you are, James." His eyes lit up in amusement as blood dripped down his chin.

"I'm going to fucking kill you!" I lunged at him again, crashing us into the ground as I drove the knife towards his heart.

Aidan fired off his gun, narrowly missing my head.

I grabbed his hand and slammed it into the ground, releasing his grip on the gun as I pinned him beneath me and punched him hard across the face, drawing blood.

Then I punched him again.

Again.

Again.

Again.

Again.

Again.

I hit him like hitting him hard enough would bring her back, tearing into his flesh. I was going to break his fucking jaw and then cut him up piece by fucking piece. And after I saw the light fade from his black and hollow eyes, I would take his gun and end it.

I made her a promise once, but I didn't want to live one more minute knowing I'd never see her again... that in every room I walked in, she'd never be there.

I couldn't.

I didn't want to live in a world like that.

My vision blurred as the sadness consumed me. This was not supposed to happen, and it was all my fault.

Aidan's knife pierced my thigh, and I cried out in pain.

I cursed as I rolled off him, examining his knife stuck in my upper right thigh. A blurry and bloodied image of him rose from the ground, towering over me.

"You should've just stayed away, James." Blood trickled down his face. His right eye was swollen shut. "From Birmingham. From Madeline." He wiped blood from his mouth, almost falling over in the process, as he reached for his gun on the ground. "Why couldn't you just fucking stay away?" he yelled.

"No," Lizzie said, pointing the golden derringer at him.

"Lizzie?" My entire world came alive at the sound of her voice, at her angelic presence before me.

Was I hallucinating? Did I already die? Tears welled in my eyes as a shiver rolled through me.

"You never should've killed my father."

Chapter 44

ELISABETH

No Regrets

WE NEEDED IT TO look real. We needed everyone to think that Aidan killed me, and then we planned to force the others to see how truly mad he was, to convince them to join our side.

It was the role of a lifetime, and I played it very convincingly.

After returning to Aidan's Manor last night, Harry stepped into my room with two other men. He'd got wind that Aidan knew that James was at the masquerade party, and he planned to bring me to the cemetery as bait. We worked out a plan for one of them to fire a blank round into my head when Aidan gave the order to kill me. Orders that snapped something inside me when I realised that Aidan never cared for me at all.

That he would kill me just to spite James.

I wasn't entirely in love with Harry's plan, and I knew James would lose his mind... but it did prove our point. And I would do anything to keep James alive. I tried to tell him it wasn't real before the gun fired, but the sound of his scream will haunt me forever. I almost ran to him at that moment, but I needed to keep playing the part to send a message.

When the gunfire finally erupted, I shot up from the ground

and ran, ducking behind the car. I caught a glimpse of Cameron and Harry working together, taking down a few men who, I guess, couldn't be persuaded to join our side. But many of them were already lowering their guns, looking at me like I was some kind of deity for taking a bullet to the head and living to tell the tale.

James tackled Aidan to the ground, and that's when I made my way towards them.

After Aidan stabbed him, I pulled out my gun, aiming at his heart, waiting for my moment.

"You should've just stayed away, James. From Birmingham. From Madeline," Aidan staggered to his feet, grabbing his gun as I snuck up behind him. Getting close enough so that I wouldn't miss. "Why couldn't you just fucking stay away?" he roared.

"No," I clicked it back. "You never should've killed my father."

And then I fired, as rage consumed me.

The vibration in my hand sank deep into my bones as blood splattered across my face and my red velvet dress. Aidan slumped to the ground with a deafening thud.

He would no longer be able to hurt anyone else.

He was dead.

I lowered the gun and dropped to my knees next to James, wrapping my arms around him. His body trembled beneath me as he squeezed me so tightly that I thought I might break in half.

"It's alright," I assured him.

Harry's voice rang loud and clear, calling the fight over and demanding everyone drop their weapons and leave.

The gunfire ceased.

James brought a shaky, bloodied hand to my face, caressing my cheek. "How? Or are we... are we—"

I grabbed his hand. "It wasn't real. It was a blank."

"What?" A crease wrinkled between his eyebrows.

"Harry's idea." His eyes shot to Harry, and I knew that look too well. "You can scold him later. Let me take this out," I reached for the knife sticking out of his thigh.

He stopped me. "No, no. Leave it in. It's safer."

I leaned back, grabbing his hand. "Alright."

His face was so pale with a sheen of sweat lining his forehead and cheeks. I pushed the hair out of his eyes, feeling the burn of his feverish skin.

Cameron rushed up to us. "You alright?"

"He needs to go to hospital," my voice shook in my throat.

"I'm fine," he said as he tried to lift himself off the ground.

Cameron and I jumped in, steadying him to his feet.

He was not fine.

I wrapped his arm around me, trying to hold him up as best I could, but damn, he was heavy.

"You?" he asked Cameron.

Cameron glanced at me. "I'll need therapy after that, but I'm good."

"Yeah. Me too," James agreed.

And then he took another step and collapsed.

I couldn't hold him.

I washed off the blood in the lavatory at the hospital with shaking hands. I couldn't stop hearing the gun. The loud clang of metal grinding in my ear, or the thud of Aidan slumping to the ground.

I killed him.

Perhaps the old me would've felt some type of remorse for him, but I didn't. Not even a little bit. The shock of the violence in my bones was all I felt, but I didn't feel even a hint of remorse. It was either him or James.

And I would always choose James.

I sat in the waiting room with Cameron while James got stitched up. He asked if I was alright, and I nodded. Then he brought me a cup of hot tea as we sat in silence, both staring at the clock ticking on the wall. It was like time ceased to exist, and we were stuck here in this anxiety-inducing hell that never ended.

"He's going to be fine," Cameron assured me, glancing at my shaking knees.

But I wouldn't feel fine until I laid eyes on him.

He had collapsed, and nothing about that was fine.

About thirty minutes later, Harry walked in and sat. Saying nothing, only nodding to us both. I didn't expect to see him so soon after everything that passed, but here he was. Just as nervously, glancing at the clock.

Each second became worse as my thoughts grew darker and darker. The last time I was at this hospital, it was one of the worst moments of my life.

"He's going to be fine," Harry finally said.

I sipped the tea with shaking legs, trying to hold myself together.

An hour later, a nurse finally called us in to see him.

"Thank Christ," I jumped up from the chair and followed her, not bothering to wait for Cam or Harry.

When I entered the room and saw his smile and those perfect dimples, I ran to him, throwing my arms around him as I kissed him fervently. His hands cradled my lower back as I settled next to him on the small bed.

My body began relaxing at his soft and eager touch.

"How are you?" I pulled away from his lips to see his face, admiring the freckles on his cheekbones.

"Just another scar for my collection," he joked and grabbed my face, bringing his forehead to mine. "I thought I lost you today." He pulled back and brushed his finger along my jaw. "Are you alright?"

"I'm fine," I smiled, staring into his eyes.

"I'm so sorry," his voice lowered into his chest. "I never wanted—"

"I have no regrets, James." And I didn't, my hands were still shaking, but I didn't. If I had hesitated in that moment, I could've lost him. And in some small way, I felt like I honoured my father's death by ending the man who ended his. "I would do it all again," I brushed a strand of black hair from his face. "For you."

"I'd never have you do it again."

I smiled. "Then I won't."

He pulled me in for a kiss, slow at first, and then he kissed deeper, harder—stroking me with his tongue.

For a moment, I thought I was going to straddle him right here in the hospital as I felt my body begin to burn. But then Cameron and Harry entered the room, removing their flat caps.

Cameron grinned at the situation he walked in on.

Harry cleared his throat. "Good to see that you're alright, kid."

"We're going to have words later," James grunted, reaching for his cigarettes on the table next to him. He lit up, leaning back on the bed. "What happened out there?"

"Lizzie gave a very convincing performance," Harry started, glancing at me. "They couldn't believe he'd kill her in cold blood... After that, there were only a few who needed to be... persuaded to join the new team," he smiled.

"Who's going to take over, now?" James asked.

"Well, the boys thought that I should do it." Harry straightened his flat cap. "Seeing as how I've been around since pretty much its inception. But I think we'll hold a vote this time. Make it fair. New beginnings and all that."

James nodded, blowing out a cloud of smoke.

"And uhh... there's a place for you. If you want it," Harry added, scratching at his grey scruff.

"I'm not in that life anymore," James responded.

"Well, if you change your mind. You know where to find us." Harry glanced at Cam. "And one for you, too. You fought well out there."

Cam smiled, thanking him. "I think James and I are done with that life. New beginnings and all that."

James smiled with the corner of his mouth.

Harry huffed a laugh. "Well then, I should go see Margaret before she wakes up. Fill her in on everything. But perhaps, we never speak of 'the plan.' She'd kill me if she found out," he turned to leave.

"Harry," I murmured, and he paused. "Thank you. For everything." Things might have gone very differently if Harry hadn't been there and formulated that brutal but clever plan.

Harry nodded, tipping his flat cap to me.

"I'll go too. Give you two some space." Cam smiled, and he left the room, followed by Harry.

James began playing with my hand before running the palm of his hand flush with mine as he interlaced our fingers.

"You sure you don't want to take Harry up on his offer?" I asked. It was his home long ago, after all—a part of his past that would always exist.

He laughed. "I'm sure. I've lived that life, Lizzie." He paused. "Why? Do you want me to?"

"I just... well, I already know Margaret is going to marry Harry. So, either way, The Black Knives will be in our future."

Harry would ask her, and she would undoubtedly say yes. I wasn't quite sure how that was going to work, but something told me the gang would be in our lives for a long time.

One way or another.

He laughed, taking a drag from his cigarette. "Do you want me to be a gangster again, Lizzie?" he teased, twinkling his eyes in a way that tore apart my insides.

My cheeks started to burn. "I don't know. No... but where else would you see us?" Perhaps his vision of the future was clearer than mine.

He put out his cigarette in the ashtray next to the bed. "In a bed, naked with whiskey."

A much, much clearer vision.

Heat rushed to my chest. "Well, that sounds nice." I laughed and placed my hand on his chest, sliding my hand under his shirt to feel his bare skin.

"And maybe a house in the country," he continued softly. "Somewhere quiet where Finton can run free," his finger caressed my jaw. "And after some time... maybe a family. If that's what you want."

Was he serious? I placed my hand on his forehead.

"What are you doing?" he asked.

"I think you may have a fever," I teased.

He laughed, grabbing my hand. "I'm serious, Lizzie."

"So, you've really thought about this?" I smiled at him.

"I've had a lot of time to think of what I would do differently."

Warmth filled my chest. "And would *you* want that?" I asked, nervously biting my bottom lip. Hoping that he truly meant those words.

But he only grinned at me in a way that set me on fire. I had never wanted a future more than the one James described. My heart was nearly swelling with happiness.

"You're lucky you're injured," I traced patterns on his chest, enjoying the sensation of his smooth skin. "I believe I promised you a punishment for your reckless behaviour." The vibration of his groan thrummed under my hand. "But seeing that you got stabbed, I don't think it's necessary anymore."

He frowned. "And, do I get a say in this?"

I slowly smiled and then bit my bottom lip. His eyes glinted, tracking the movement.

"Right, let's get out of this fucking hospital before they kick us out."

Chapter 45

JAMES

Without Fear

BACK AT MY HOUSE, I spent the next week in my bed, and I didn't have a single complaint. We ate a lot of food, and sometimes we shared it with Finton. We talked and laughed for endless hours, drank a lot of whiskey, and because of my injury, Lizzie spent countless hours on top of me—a sight I'd never be able to get enough of.

I'd have to say it's the best week I'd ever had, with the most peace and love that I'd ever known. It would be a few months before we could move to the country, but I was so ready for that next chapter of our lives.

Cameron decided to stay in Birmingham, but he promised to visit us often. And Margaret decided to stay at the Manor with Harry. She called up every other day to talk to Lizzie and visited occasionally for dinner. I wasn't sure how all that was going to work out, considering Harry's line of work, but he promised us that she'd be safe. And perhaps one day Harry would walk away himself. I doubted that he ever would, especially as he took over as the new head of The Knives by popular vote, but for Lizzie's peace of mind, I'd remain optimistic.

I never planned on going back to that life. Fighting in the pit or even fighting again in the underground in London was all the violence I planned for the future. But for now, I was ready to put all of that behind me. All the violence, all the scars... there were just a couple more things I needed to make my peace with.

The sun was setting behind the gravestones through the pines in the Warstone Lane Cemetery, painting the sky with soft hues of pink, blue, and orange. I placed a rose on Madeline's grave, and another rose for our child.

"I'm sorry I failed you. Both of you." My chest felt tight as I spoke words I'd been wanting to say for so long. "You may have been my first love, but your love was wrong, Madeline. I've held this pain in my heart for so long. Wishing I could've taken your place." I shook my head, taking a breath. "I wish things had turned out differently for you, and for us, but... thank you for saving my life. I'm still not sure why you did, but thank you. I lost sight of what it meant to be alive, but I know now." I turned my gaze to Lizzie walking in the distance with Margaret, Harry, and Cameron. "And I promise, I won't waste another second of it."

Lizzie left a red tulip for Frank and Victoria. Then she made her way to Margaret, Harry, and Cameron standing by the pines. I walked a bit unsteadily to Frank's grave, bending down to touch the stone. The air around me suddenly felt warm as if perhaps someone was standing next to me.

"You deserved more, Frank. I wish I had the chance to tell you just how much she means to me. But I promise I'll always take care of her, no matter what." I glanced at Margaret, locking arms with Harry as Lizzie laughed about something. The most beautiful sound, until Margaret's cackle. "And I'll look after Margaret too." I sighed, then stood up, pulling the engagement ring out of my coat pocket, watching as the emerald and diamonds glinted in the evening light. "Wish me luck," I kissed the centre stone.

As I approached Lizzie, she broke off from the group, making her way towards me with her hands tucked into her coat. The sight of her and her golden eyes still made my heart soar—an overpowering feeling that would never change.

"So," she smiled, biting her lip.

"So," I smiled.

My mind wandered to the first night I met her. How badly I wanted to be close to her... to kiss her, to feel the rush of her skin. And now I was the luckiest guy alive to be the one who made her smile. Perhaps two people who had experienced such darkness could still find the light. Because every time I looked at her, I saw hope for a new and better tomorrow.

"What now?" she asked after a moment.

"Well," I got down on one knee, not as gracefully as I would've liked to, but hey. "Now, you marry me, Elisabeth Rose."

"Elisabeth Rose... MacGuire?" she pursed her lips, smiling.

"Is that a yes?" I curved my mouth.

She continued to smile, lighting up my entire existence.

Acknowledgments

I am so grateful that you are here. I started writing *Love & Knives* at the age of sixteen. But it was called *James & Elisabeth* back then, and it was a vastly different story, as a younger me could not have written a Peaky Blinders-esque smutty historical romance. Though she may have tried. I have had the idea of this love story for so long, and I can't believe it's finally finished. I am so thankful for everyone who encouraged me to keep writing when I wanted to give up. Writing has given me so much enjoyment and peace, and I encourage anyone who has a dream to keep fighting. Because it's never too late. There is always time. I believe in you.

A huge thank you to my amazing husband, Will, for your endless support and for the thousands of hours you have spent talking to me about my book or listening to me talk about my book. I could not have finished this without you. Last year was a blur as I spent every moment I could stuck in my story. Thank you for picking up my slack and for always loving me even when it wasn't easy.

To Sally, for your pages and pages of notes. Your feedback drastically shaped me as a writer. For your honesty, your time, and your love, I will always be thankful. You have truly gone above and beyond for me, time and time again. You are a bright light in my dull existence. You will now be selected to read all of my novels.

To Chanel for helping me shape my characters and educating me in military aspects. I could not have done this without you. And for your love of reading that is infectious—without your push towards romance books, I don't know where I'd be.

To my amazing friends Jasmine, Barb, Tammi, and Chey. This

story would not have been the same without each one of you. Thank you for your encouragement, your excitement, and your endless friendship. You have kept my dream alive. I cherish you all so much.

For my Corgi Gatsby, for your endless cuddles and emotional support while I spent hours and hours in front of a computer.

And finally, to my readers. I love every one of you. Your support means more to me than giggle juice.

About the Author

Born in Traverse City, Michigan, Whitney Walquist now lives in Townsville, Australia. She can often be found writing wherever she is—in the gym, in the car, at the office, tucked under blankets in her bed, or wherever she feels inspired. She loves travelling and draws inspiration from her surroundings, adventures, and experiences. She believes that a good cup of coffee and good company can fix any bad day.

Connect with Whitney:

Instagram: authorwhitneywalquist
Facebook: authorwhitneywalquist
YouTube: authorwhitneywalquist

Want more?

More is coming in the *LOVE & KNIVES* universe!

Devil with a Gun (coming soon)
— the Riley Hennessy story.

Connect with Whitney to stay updated.

* 9 7 8 1 7 6 4 2 6 7 0 6 9 *